DOG OF

Dean Kastle

Copyright © 2024 by Dean Kastle

All rights reserved.

No part of this publication may be reproduced, distributed, or transmitted in any form or by any means, including photocopying, recording, or other electronic or mechanical methods, without the prior written permission of the publisher, except as permitted by U.S. copyright law. For permission requests, contact dean@deankastle.com

The story, all names, characters, and incidents portrayed in this production are fictitious. No identification with actual persons (living or deceased), places, buildings, and products is intended or should be inferred.

Edits by Michael DeAngelo

1st edition 2024

Acknowledgements

Long is the list of friends and family who helped bring these stories to life, but I have to mention a few. Many thanks go to Mike Pontarelli, authors Steve Karas, Michael DeAngelo, and Lou Anders, and Dean B.—my number-one story consultant. Finally, my wife and motivator in chief, Marilyn, deserves a shout out. You have my love, appreciation, and deepest gratitude.

This book is dedicated to Dean B, my foremost confidant and source of inspiration.

Contents

1. Chapter 1
2. Chapter 2
3. Chapter 3
4. Chapter 4
5. Chapter 5
6. Chapter 6
7. Chapter 7
8. Chapter 8
9. Chapter 9
10. Chapter 10
11. Chapter 11
12. Chapter 12
13. Chapter 13
14. Chapter 14
15. Chapter 15
16. Chapter 16
17. Chapter 17
18. Chapter 18
19. Chapter 19
20. Chapter 20
21. Chapter 21

22. Chapter 22
23. Chapter 23
24. Chapter 24
25. Chapter 25
26. Chapter 26
27. Chapter 27
28. Chapter 28
29. Chapter 29
30. Chapter 30
31. Chapter 31
32. Chapter 32
33. Chapter 33
34. Chapter 34
35. Chapter 35
36. Chapter 36
37. Chapter 37
38. Chapter 38
39. Chapter 39
40. Chapter 40

A Message from the Author

An Excerpt from HAIR OF THE DOG

About the author

Chapter one

A low-burning campfire lit the circle of faces red, chased shadows across dirty white tabards and pitted iron blades. Geth sat shoulder to shoulder among the other so-called soldiers, but as the new man kept quiet, listening with hidden contempt to the tales being told.

"It's one thing to kill a man in a dust-up," their pock-faced sergeant was saying. "It's something else to look him in the eye and cut his throat. Traitors, wounded men, prisoners—" he flicked a significant glance at the greasy-haired captive in their charge. "The gods know I've bled my share."

The men to Geth's left and right hooted. It only took one glance at their shifty eyes and sunken knuckles to peg that lot. Conmen. Outlaws. Cut-throat murderers. The kind that would sell their own sister for a copper, their mother for two.

But in the wake of the Affliction, with more dead to be buried than living to swing the shovels, rats like these had all left their hiding-holes. Geth stole a glance at the prisoner they'd been scraped together to guard over, shackled beside the row of tethered horses. Now *there* was a true rogue. Blue eyes met his dark ones and the big warrior spit a curse.

"What are you looking at?" Quick as a whip, he hurled the rabbit thigh he'd been gnawing at to pelt the prisoner across the cheek. The little thief scrambled to retrieve it, devouring the morsel like an animal.

That brought the gaze of the sergeant swinging toward Geth. "How 'bout you, half-breed? Bet you've settled a score or two with a stab in someone's back."

Derisive laughter echoed around the fire. Geth did his best to look cowed.

For some reason, the sergeant hated him. Even more than he hated everyone else. Perhaps it was the patterns of swirling ink on each forearm, peeking out of Geth's cuffs, marking him at least part Mog and a foreigner. Perhaps, noting his height and broad shoulders, the sergeant feared him as a rival. Or perhaps the old bastard was just filled with more ire than blood and piss combined.

Whatever the reason, Geth ignored the jeers. He reached for the stewpot on its tripod for another pull off the carcass. Someone chucked a gnawed-on bone that struck him full in the face and tumbled down the front of his white tabard.

"That's right, hide under your collar!" someone sneered as he ducked, too late.

"Big dumb bastard!"

Geth blew out a long breath, reined in his temper.

"Well, if it's tales you want, I suppose I've killed a scratch or two."

"I'll bet he has," Pock-face cut in. "A woman once, while she was sleeping."

More laughter.

But Geth raised his voice over it. "I've never been in the army as we are now," he lied, "but I've bloodied a blade more than once over the years. Been to the east, where the wild men breathe fire and tattoo their skin with devilish patterns. And I did a stretch in Turia, where they make the finest blades and remember an insult for decades and more. I've sailed with an Iyrund slave-trader from Halicarn clear across Longsea, and yet I've sent just as many souls to Vorda's keeping in the alleyways and dark corners of our own Golden City."

"Golden *bloody* City," someone echoed and spat.

"Better for a tavern-tale than a tavern brawl I'd wager," Pock-face snorted.

But every eye had fixed on Geth. They wanted tales and he had plenty. He found himself warming to the task.

He spoke of blood-soaked battlefields and feuds ended with stealthy midnight murder. Of crushing a slave rebellion and being forced to wear the chains himself. Eyes widened around the fire at the most gruesome descriptions of war's true horrors and the matter-of-fact delivery of the butcher who gave the telling. Those were the first truths to be spoken that night, Geth was sure of it. He'd just started in on his days as a pit-fighter in Adamar when a voice from behind cut him off.

"That's enough."

The shaved white pate of Palladine, their captain, materialized out of the darkness beside the horses. Firelight gleamed red on a cuirass polished to perfection as the unblinking stare of a real soldier swept over them. Their greasy-haired prisoner shied away. Geth cursed himself for being so absorbed in his own voice he hadn't heard the captain arrive.

Pock-face sprang up to salute him, a gesture copied hastily by everyone else. "Just having a bit of a laugh, my lord." The sergeant jabbed a thumb in Geth's direction. "This big whoreson was telling us how many women he's killed."

Palladine's gaze fell on Geth, taking in every detail. Geth tugged down at his cuffs lest his tattoos make notice.

"I suggest you all take your rest," Palladine said. "We wake before dawn. It's twenty miles to Sorn. The Tower of the Moon awaits."

At mention of the Tower, their greasy-haired captive moaned. Reserved for only the worst offenders, that prison was kept pitch black during the day. Each night, however, the moonlight was let in through a hole in the roof. They said it could drive a man mad.

Palladine didn't mentioned it by accident either, he knew what sort of men he led. He wanted them to know he had the power to see that their road ended in the Tower as well.

Pock-face rounded on Geth. "You heard the captain, enough of your lies. You take first watch. To bed with the rest of you. Don't make me say it twice!"

"Yessir."

But Geth hid a smile as Palladine turned and the clop of horse's hooves faded into the distance. The captain had decided to ride on to the next town in search of lodgings befitting someone of his rank. And away from the carnage that was about to unfold.

How many tyrants had Geth called master over the thirty some years of his life? How many men had used him, mistreated him, haughty as Captain Palladine or hateful as old Pock-face? *Too many.* Geth slid the tripod and remains of their rabbit stew back over the fire, stoked the flames. He made no attempt to suppress such memories. He welcomed them.

"Bastards," he muttered. "Back-stabbing cowards. Lying thieves…"

He listened for the rhythmic breathing of Pock-face and the other four guards. The pot had begun to tremble, threatened to boil over. Rising with care not to make a sound, he drew his sword quietly from its sheath then took the end of his cloak in the other hand to lift the steaming pot from its hook and spill it full in the sergeant's face.

"*Ahhhhhh!*"

The agony of that scream startled the other four from their sleep. Geth turned from the writhing sergeant to run through the nearest of his bleary-eyed companions. His blade darted in and out, swept to one side to stab the back of a second as he rolled from his bedroll, struggled to rise. The third raised his hands in plea for mercy but Geth chopped through upraised forearm and skull alike. The last of his pathetic, would-be companions tried to run, got tangled in his blankets and was hacked down from behind. That left only Pock-face.

"Mongrel bastard!" he cursed. Even with half his head a burned, swollen mess, the sergeant had managed to gain his feet and draw his sword. Geth turned to face him across the fire.

But old Pock-face hadn't lived to sprout those gray hairs without a few tricks of his own. One foot kicked the flames, the burst of glowing embers blinding Geth so he barely caught the arc of the sergeant's left arm as he hurled a knife. Geth twisted, felt the blade brush past his shoulder.

He wasted no time with words. With a lightness of foot that always took his enemies by surprise, Geth circled toward Pock-face's maimed eye. A nimble pass of his sword from right hand to left allowed him to thrust past a desperate, blind parry, piercing tabard, mail, and flesh.

The sergeant grunted, tried to return a backhanded swing, but Geth caught his wrist with his free hand. He pulled him in close, rammed his sword blade deeper, twisted. That grunt turned to a squeal. Pock-face's one good eye met Geth's and his lips worked, tried but failed to utter one last curse.

Geth spit in his face. With a yank, his sword came free. Pock-face collapsed in a heap like a puppet with cut strings. Blood dripped from Geth's hand, and he wiped it on his white, army-issue tabard as he moved toward the wagon where the greasy-haired prisoner waited.

"You're not going to kill me too, are you?"

Geth smiled. Tossing his sword down, he stooped to pick up an axe that had belonged to one of the others. He could only imagine how he looked, blood splattered, still panting, axe in hand. The prisoner knelt, stretched his shackled hands out in front of his face. The thrown rabbit thigh had left a red welt on his cheek, but he smiled right back as Geth worked the axe-head to hack through the chains that bound him.

Chapter two

Sunlight warmed the back of Geth's hands, the familiar smells of horse and road dust in his nose as they wended through overgrown fields, past abandoned cottages on two packhorses stolen from Palladine's convoy. Pock-face was dead, and they'd put a dozen miles between themselves and the night's misdeeds. It was impossible to stay mad at Phelan for long.

"Well, what was it this time? They don't reserve lodgings in the Tower for just anyone."

Phelan rubbed his scraggly cheek. "I never thanked you for that rabbit."

"Fine. Keep it to yourself. I'll get it out of you next time you're drunk."

Geth eyed his friend out of the corner of his eye. Phelan was like an overgrown child, eyes big and blue with straw-yellow curls. And a penchant for mischief. He was the best friend Geth could ask for, even if the big warrior wanted to wring his neck half the time.

"Here's the problem," Geth told him. "We're outlaws now."

"Not the first time."

Geth ground his teeth. "Because of our absence, the lady's gonna figure us for deserters."

"Is that where you're leading us? Back to Lady Brega?"

"Where better to disappear until this all blows over?"

"Golden-*bloody*-City." Phelan yanked on the tether that led a third mount behind them, piled high with boots, coin-purses, and everything else he'd stripped from Pock-face and his crew.

"Other than your escape," Geth said, "Palladine will be more disappointed by the loss of these horses than the bastards he rounded up as guards. As soon as he realizes I'm not among the dead, he'll figure out my part in this. He'll be hunting for the both of us."

"He won't bother chasing for long. They'll probably strip his captaincy and put him out on his ass. First inn we find, I'm drinking to that."

"Drink all you want; it won't right things with the lady."

Phelan reached over to take Geth's reins, pulling them to a halt. "You do what you want, but I'm not going back to work for the Queen of Shit."

"Now you've got standards?"

"She's a crook, Geth. It's not exactly a secret she's no actual lady."

Geth shook his head. "She's always been fair. May have a bit of dirt under her nails, but I reckon a woman like that understands us better than most."

"And why are you so afraid to go into business for ourselves?"

"Business for ourselves? What are we, turnip farmers?"

"Let me give you something fat to chew on: you don't need that bitch—or anyone else—to call master."

"It's not about calling some highbrow sonofabitch master, Phelan. A man with a sword needs someone—some*thing*—to fight for, otherwise he's nothing. What am I without that?"

"Free?"

"A strong-arm cutthroat, that's what. Robbing and killing for my silver. That's why no one wants a masterless man. But the lady took a chance on us. And with Brega, there's promise of bigger things too."

"Is there?"

"There was. All I had to do was wait for Clydon to slip up and the top job would've been mine."

"Clydon. Another piece of shit. Are you forgetting you broke his nose?"

"He had it coming. Brega knows that."

"Listen, Geth, from here on out, you just let me handle the money. I'll see to it we never work for anyone again."

Geth peeled Phelan's hand from the reins. "Says the man who booked himself at the Tower of the Moon. No, I'm going back to Brega. You can sell all this shit and gamble yourself broke if that's what you want."

It was midmorning before they dared stop to water the horses. Geth led his mount along the course of a tree-lined creek until he found a shallow pool at a bend. Phelan stripped all the way down and jumped in to rinse off the filth of a week's captivity.

Geth knelt on the banks to examine the state of his own reflection. Dark eyes peeked out from under heavy brows, sun-streaked tangles fell in a mass to his shoulders. The rough beard he'd grown did nothing to help. He drew Pock-face's knife and scraped until it was gone. All but the mustache.

"Why stop there?" Phelan asked.

"You think it makes me look too much like a Turian?"

"It's like a muskrat's latched onto your face."

Geth stroked the hair on his upper lip. "Well, I like it. Makes my nose look smaller."

Phelan burst out laughing. Geth grumbled a curse and splashed him. His friend ducked under the surface and came up on the other side.

Phelan started in on one of his backwater songs, something about a hayward and a dairymaid. He really was a country boy at heart. Geth sat back on the grassy bank, watched him search the creek bed for slingstones. The sun was high, but the flies weren't biting. Geth could've stayed there a while under better circumstances.

But they had to make Paellia before news of Phelan's escape reached the gatemen.

"Let's get moving," Geth said. The promise of ale and a room at an inn at day's end finally got Phelan back on his horse.

They made good time. It was dusk when they passed the crumbling arch of Paellus' Gate, marker of the Golden City's former bounds. Stout walls and tiled rooftops beyond caught the late day sun, shimmered yellow and orange in the distance.

Golden Bloody City. Geth had mixed feelings about the place. Still, if the ruins of the city's old walls stood as a reminder of how far she'd fallen, no other city in all the Sworn Realms could compare to her in sheer size and wealth. With so much bread, there were plenty of crumbs, even for a gutter-born sellsword, if he was willing to scrap for them.

"I still can't believe you mean to go back to her exalted ladyship," Phelan said. They slowed their mounts as they reached the end of a line of carts entering the city. "What if we left Pellon altogether?"

Geth was hardly listening. The line trying to enter the city had come to a standstill. Rag-clad beggars weaved among the throng, pleading for a crust, an apple core, anything. A steady stream passed in the opposite direction, unimpeded. Geth felt his hackles rise.

"You there," he asked the nearest beggar. "What's the hold up ahead? Wagon broke an axle?"

The man held out a hand.

Geth gestured to Phelan. He cursed but produced a copper round. The beggar snatched it, slid it into a pocket.

"Lily whites are all stirred up," he said. "Pair of outlaws killed some of their lot up north."

Phelan waited for the man to duck off. "How the hell?" He ran a hand through his hair.

"Must've sent word by pigeon," Geth said. "Damn! They'll see us if we turn back now."

"They're looking for a pair. Let's split up."

"You're right." Geth cast a glance to either side. "Hey there, my lady. Want to make a few rounds?"

A blurry-eyed beggar-woman with wine stains on her blouse staggered over.

"You're his wife, alright? Just for an hour. No need to consummate the marriage either."

"Make it a silver," she said. "You in some kinda trouble? Gimme a silver. I can keep a secret."

Phelan grumbled but dug deeper into his pouch.

"Half of that now," Geth said, "half once we get a ways inside the city."

"I got no love for the lilies, not after what they done to me."

Geth nodded. "Up on his horse then, missus."

Once they'd moved Phelan's spoils and got the woman up in the saddle, Geth leaned in close to his friend.

"I'll hang back a few paces, pretend to be from Turia."

Phelan nodded. "Meet you on the other side."

Geth dropped back further in the line. The gatemen were out in numbers, but they waved Phelan and his new bride through when he finally made it up front.

Geth came a few paces after. A balding sergeant halted him with a raised hand.

"Steady there. What's your business?"

Geth squared his shoulder, put on some Turian pride. "Just come down from the mountains. Been hired to mend armor for your betters."

"My betters?"

"That's how things run in these parts, no? Men with skinny necks and fat purses make the calls."

"You got that right," a soldier chuckled from over the sergeant's shoulder.

The sergeant stared his guardsman down. He turned back to Geth. "Alright, in with you. But mind your manners with that skinny-necked lot. They'll land you in hot water if you don't."

Geth forced a laugh, knuckled his brow, and passed inside the city.

The Lady Brega's mansions stood in the wealthy quarter, far from the Netmender's Daughter where Geth booked them for a night of much needed rest. Phelan was still snoring the next morning when the big warrior left the fishmonger's stalls of the wharves for streets lined with moneychangers and clothier's boutiques.

He didn't spare a thought for Palladine. The captain could have walked right past him on those crowded streets and not seen him. All thoughts were on the lady.

Brega, of course, was no actual lady, even if she was wealthier than many titled folk. From a mere spice merchant's widow, she'd grown rich enough to demand the respect of Pellon's highborn familae, thus naming herself 'lady.' She was a woman of power, pedigree or no. Everyone in the city owed her money, and Geth was just one man in the small army she employed to make sure the debts got paid.

"What the hell am I walking into?" he asked himself as he made the final turn down her street. She wasn't going to be thrilled to see him after a week's absence, no matter how well he'd served her up 'til now. Neither was her master-at-arms, Clydon.

Geth snorted a laugh. *Little wonder about that.* The man was nothing more than an aging mercenary, with bad eyes and creaky joints, propped up by the likes of Geth and the others. With every job it became more clear he'd need replacing.

Geth hadn't exactly endeared himself to the old scratch when he broke his nose either. Clydon wouldn't forget that. If the master-at-arms had his way, Geth reckoned Brega would be the least of his worries.

Straight to the lady then. Beat him to the punch.

Geth focused on what he'd tell Brega: the truth. Most of it anyway. The sun was still low in the east as he arrived. He reached for the knocker, a heavy thing of iron, the ring forced into the grimacing mouth of a man with splayed hair.

"Who's there?" came the challenge.

"It's me."

Cracking it a fraction, a bodyguard inside smirked when he recognized Geth. "Where you been? Decided to crawl back?"

Geth bit down a nasty reply. Smashing a few teeth out of this bastard's face wasn't going to win him his job back. He crossed the anteroom and continued through another set of doors into a courtyard warmed by smoking braziers. Lady Brega sat at a table spread with a plate of figs and various cheeses. She cupped a steaming mug in her hands, hair up in a simple bun as always.

"My lady."

Brega's mouth tightened but she held her tongue, watching him with bird-like eyes.

Geth fell to one knee. "I'm sorry for my absence. I've returned."

Brega tapped the side of her cup. "What was it? Had to help your sick mother? Got nabbed by the lilies or some such?"

"No, my lady. My friend landed himself in a jam. It's been handled, but he won't be back."

"That squirrelly child with the yellow hair? You're better off without him."

Geth kept his eyes down and his mouth shut.

"But here you are now, on your knees wanting nothing more than to serve. Isn't that what you were about to say?"

Geth looked up. "I served you well up to now."

The noise of footfalls turned them both as Clydon stamped in, the bridge of his nose still red where Geth had hit him. His eyes found the big warrior and he ground to a halt. His mouth opened but the lady spoke before he had a chance.

"And here is our master-at-arms. I have a dilemma, Master Clydon. My hardest hardman disappears for a week, only to reappear just as suddenly. What to do?"

"Whip him bloody, quarter what's left."

"He's worth five men in a fight. You said so yourself."

Clydon spit. "Feed the remains to the beggars at the Greater Gate. That's what I'd do."

Brega's bird-like eyes turned back toward Geth, weighing the possibilities. She was a shrewd one. The silence stretched on. Geth's knee began to ache where it rested on the cold flagstones.

"I could demand you buy your way back into my service. Silver up front." She raised an eyebrow.

"I haven't got anything but my sword, Lady. I could pay it over time."

Brega turned a significant look toward Clydon. He didn't look pleased.

"No coin." She leaned back, took a sip from the mug in her hands. "I told you he was no turncoat."

Geth's eyes narrowed. "Never, my lady."

"See, if you came back with silver in your pockets it could only mean my enemies had bought you."

Clydon stamped up alongside Brega. "So, he's loyal. A dog is loyal. If you're asking me, I say put him down and take no chances."

"You make a good point. He's loyal, yes. Loyal to his friend. I need him to be loyal to me."

"My lady," Geth said. "I never left you. I told the master-at-arms I needed to take leave to help my friend."

Brega sniffed. "That's not the way he told it."

I'll bet. "We may have disagreed, the master and I. I'm back now though, just as I promised."

Clydon's color was up, but Geth had always reckoned an angry man less dangerous than a man with a cool head. "You need a right whipping. I need discipline among my men. You think you can wander in and out of town like some fortune-teller from the Dominion?"

Geth ignored him, turned to Brega. "Let me prove my worth to you, earn my way back."

"And how would you do that?"

"Who owes, who needs a visit? Say the word and it's done."

A look passed between the lady and her master-at-arms. "I can think of someone."

Geth smiled. He was in.

Chapter three

Geth didn't like the shifty look on Clydon's face as he ushered him out, but there was nothing for it. They left out the back. The master-at-arms even volunteered to usher Geth to the mark.

"The job's in River Streets," Clydon said. "This bastard's been a stone in the lady's shoe for far too long."

Geth bit down a curse. River Streets. He didn't like the sound of that. The lady's clients consisted mostly of foolish lordlings squandering their wealth, merchants in need of emergency coin. The odd gambler or widow. A mark from River Streets would be a whole different sort. "What's the name?"

"Fion."

Geth nodded. They set out on horseback, balconied mansions and awning-covered boutiques giving way to earthy taverns and crowded bazaars. Slouchy characters leaned up in doorways, street urchins darted among the walking traffic. Geth flicked a sideways glance at the master-at-arms. He didn't miss the curl at the end of his lips as they reached the crammed tenements and reeking whorehouses of Paellia's underbelly. Gods but he hated the bastard.

"There it is." Clydon nodded toward a dingy inn halfway down the street. Weeds grew out of cracks in the walls and a broken chain dangled over the door. The placard must have been stolen. A boy of about twelve sat on the curb whittling wood as watercarriers and laborers wended past. That would be Fion's lookout.

"He own the place?" Geth turned his back on the inn, pretended to peruse the trinkets of a front-door vendor.

"No, but this is where he does business. He keeps a few toughs on the payroll. He won't be alone."

"That boy there, he's keeping an eye on this stretch. I don't like the idea of coming in the front."

"What are you telling me for? I'm not going in."

Geth muttered a curse. "Well how much does he owe? At least tell me that."

"The lady wants it all."

Clydon's grim tone said as much as the words themselves.

Not likely to be any negotiating on those terms. Geth pulled at his mustache. It was gonna have to be a bust up: in through the back, hit hard and fast, come out with the shine.

But Fion would be well guarded. Of course he would, Brega wasn't stupid. Why else give the task to a man like himself? He searched Clydon's face. The evil bastard didn't even try to hide the smirk anymore.

"Gimme your blade," Geth said.

"My sword? Not a chance."

"I need a shortsword. I'm not gonna have room to swing mine in there."

"That's your problem."

"I got the impression Brega wanted this scratch handled. You gonna stand between the lady and her pay?"

Clydon scowled. He reached to the small of his back, drew out a dagger. "Use this."

Geth resisted the urge to shove the weapon straight up Clydon's ass. *A bloody dagger!* But it was something. Geth took the plain-handled weapon, thumbed the blade. Razor sharp.

"Remember," Clydon said. "Fion's the name. Make sure he knows it's the Lady Brega that sent you. Even if it's the last thing he hears."

Geth slid the dagger in his belt opposite his sword and strode right past the inn, turning at the next cross street and ducking down the first alley. At the end, he peered behind the buildings. It wasn't hard to pick out the rear of the inn with its small stable and large, cudgel-bearing doorman.

"Damn."

Built up against the neighboring buildings, there'd be no side entry either.

Think like a thief! Geth looked up. The inn stood taller than either of the tenements beside it. If he could get up on the rooftops, there was bound to be a window he could sneak through.

Fortunately, the stonework in this part of the city wasn't in good repair. Geth studied the walls of the alley for handholds and plotted a way up. Scaling buildings and crawling through windows had been one of the only ways to eat as a street child in Sorn. If he'd waited for his mother to remember to feed him, he'd have starved.

Geth put those memories aside, set his mind back on Fion. This was a chance to show his worth, earn some respect. One handhold at a time, he climbed. Within minutes, he was two stories up, on the dusty red tiles. He stepped carefully from gently sloped rooftop to rooftop until he was looking through a cracked shutter at a whore on all fours for her client. Creeping down a few paces, he found the next window shuttered tight.

A quick listen. The room was empty. Clydon's dagger lifted the latch easy enough and he was inside.

Crossing the room, Geth entered a dark hallway. He drew his sword, quiet as he could, and cocked an ear. Voices drifted up from a stairwell at the rear of the building. He followed the sound, tread slowly to avoid creaky steps, and descended toward them.

He paused halfway down. By the sound of things—the scuff of a chair, the scrap of cutlery on a tin plate— the stairwell opened at the rear of the inn's common room. Fion would be there. And once Geth made his entrance, there would be no time to think—just to kill or be killed.

Geth muttered a curse.

That's not how a warrior lived to his thirties, not even a warrior like him. Geth stared down the last few steps at the common room floor, forming a picture in his mind. From the noise to his right, he reckoned the stairwell let out beside the bar. A hallway led away to the left, presumably to the stable and back door. He could see an empty table straight ahead but everything else stretched further to the right, judging by the voices, toward the storefront.

He crept down another few steps, stopped cold, and smiled. The gods loved him that day. *Of course they do,* he thought, *they always love a bloodbath.* A gnarled, preserved appendage that had once been a man's arm had been encased and nailed up on the wall, the glass providing a decent reflection of the place, catching the light of two wide windows looking out on the street. He squinted, surveyed the battleground.

The angle wasn't right to make out the bar, but an armed foursome passed cards at a table about halfway down the room while a few singles stood scattered around the place. The lone barmaid leaned against a wall and fanned herself with one hand. By the sound of his voice, Geth reckoned the innkeep stood behind his counter.

He took another step down, peered into the reflection. *One past the bar, a second at the front door. Another by the…is that a pantler?*

Judging by the lumpy midsection and white apron, it was. He sat at the only other occupied table, opposite a second scratch wearing what appeared to be a thick silver chain clasped at the nape of his neck. That one had his back to the big warrior. Geth couldn't make out much more, but by the position of a bodyguard beside him, it had to be Fion.

Geth passed his sword to his left hand, wiped sweat on his pant leg. Excluding the innkeep, his barmaid, and the pantler, that still left seven toughs, not counting the mark himself. Seven against one. Plus the guard at the back door. He cursed Clydon's entire lineage. It wasn't too late—

A door creaked open somewhere upstairs and Geth almost cursed out loud.

"…soon, my sweet," a man's voice said.

The man he'd seen trading sweat upstairs, he reckoned. Had to be. The door clicked shut and footfalls scraped down the hall. Geth, flicked a glance at the glass ahead. There was nothing for it.

He closed his eyes, imagined his movements around the room, the reaction of each enemy. At least he'd catch them by surprise. The footfalls above reached the top of the stairs. "What the…?"

Geth sheathed his sword, drew Clydon's dagger, and leapt down the last few steps.

He turned right, went for the man at the man at the bar first. Clydon's dagger slid in and out of the side of his neck before he'd even looked up. Eyes were just turning toward him as he grabbed the lip of the nearest table, flipped and hurled it into the foursome and their card game.

"Shit!"

"Hey!"

The impact scattered cards and coin, tangled that lot among their chairs and among each other. The tough beside Fion drew, but it was a long-bladed weapon and in that low-ceilinged room, it nicked a header beam, allowing just enough time for Geth to cross the space and plant his dagger straight into the bastard's chest. Eyes went wide and the bodyguard staggered. The sound of heavy footfalls turned Geth in time to meet the rush of the tough at the door.

He came at the big warrior with the ferocious swing of his cudgel. Geth's sword scraped free to meet the blow, splitting the head right off it with the noise of splintering wood. His enemy stumbled sideways but caught himself against a table, looked down at the half a cudgel still in hand, and ran for it.

But the card-players had thrown Geth's table off by then. "Get the bastard!"

Instead of ushering their boss out the back, they reached for swords and came at Geth, one right after the other, almost in a straight line.

"Ha!" Geth couldn't help but laugh. The first of them went down after a parry from Geth's blade and a thrust into his stomach. Geth steered the skewered bastard between himself and the next onrushing foe, then slid his blade out and kicked the man into his fellow with a raised boot. He thrust over the shoulder of that first cardplayer, into the face of the second to send him reeling into the third as that one came up behind him. Geth closed the space to chop again and again at the mass of bleeding, shouting bodies until all three were down. The fourth card player fled out the back.

"Fion!" Geth turned on his mark. The pantler had wisely made a break for it, but Fion just stood there dumbly beside his table, tiny red dots splattered across one cheek. No doubt he'd expected *someone* to put the intruder down. His eyes widened as Geth started toward him. He turned to run.

Geth caught him by the back of the collar. "In a hurry, Fion? I'll need Brega's coin before—"

A bear-hug around Geth's middle cut him off, pinned his arms to his sides. "You bastard!"

"Shit!" Geth shifted to grappled with the man behind him and Fion lurched free.

But the cocksure sonofabitch didn't even run for it. He whirled to face the big warrior. "Ha!"

A whiff of stale liquor from over the shoulder told Geth it was the innkeep who'd popped out from behind the bar to grab him. He hadn't expected *that*. A great heave twirled the foolhardy bastard around until he crashed into Fion with a wail, knocking that smile right off the mark's face and sending them both to the wine-stained floor.

Geth raised his sword but let it fall as the innkeep curled up into a ball, wailing like a child. He turned back to Fion instead.

"Brega's coin. *Now!*"

"Brega?" Fion looked up, still on his knees. He spit at Geth's feet. "You mean to tell me after twenty years of fleecing the rich, the old whore's decided to scour the gutters as well? This is my patch! That bitch—"

Geth threw out a boot, kicked him straight back to the floor. Snatching him up by the tunic, he dragged Fion out the front before the remaining card-player or back-door tough could muster the courage to have another go.

Outside, he threw Fion down on the muck-littered street outside the inn. "Give up the coin." Shutters all around pulled shut from the inside. Passersby went wide-eyed, fell over themselves to turn back the way they'd come.

"Tell that bitch she can suck a pig's cock. She won't get a round out of me!"

Clydon appeared from the shadow of a doorway. He shook his head, whistled, flicking a glance at the entrance to the inn and back to Geth. The bastard hadn't expected him to pull it off.

"No shine, eh?" But for some reason, the master-at-arms smiled as he said it.

"You owe the lady and you're gonna pay," said Geth. "All of it. Everything down to the linen on your ass."

"I haven't got shit for that whore. You tell her—"

Geth stepped on one of Fion's hands, turned his words to a whimper. He looked to Clydon.

"You want me to put him upside down and shake him?"

The sound of horse hooves turned them both down the street. Geth wiped blood from his face with the back of his sleeve as the lady herself, flanked by a pair of toughs, arrived.

Clydon knuckled his brow. "You came, my lady."

"We don't share the same faith in our soldiers?" She turned a hard eye on Fion. "I would have warned you, but would it have made a difference?"

"Why?" Fion sat up on his knees. "You've already got all the gold of the Archon."

Brega nodded to Clydon. The master-at-arms set his mouth in a grim line.

Fion stammered a frantic protest. "Wait! Wait!"

That short sword came out and Clydon ran him through. Fion spit a mouthful of blood as the blade pulled free. Eyes full of accusation flicked from the lady to the master-at-arms and finally to Geth. Then he collapsed to one side.

Brega turned her mount, left the way she'd come. Geth looked back to the inn. "Well, if you want your dagger," he told the master-at-arms, "it's in there. Maybe you can find the shine while you're inside."

Clydon snorted a laugh. He stooped, took the silver chain from Fion's neck and tucked it into his belt. "Fool. It was never about the shine."

Chapter four

Phelan was waiting with an ale when Geth returned to the Netmender's Daughter.

"Nice trick turning your tunic inside out, but I can still see the splatter."

Geth pulled back the chair across from him and sat with a grunt.

"Didn't go so well?"

"She took me back."

"Doesn't mean it went well."

Geth downed half his ale in one long pull. "I need something to eat."

He flicked a glance around their inn, a ramshackle establishment little better than the one he'd just painted red. The entire district stank of fish guts and sweaty trawlers. An assortment of local drunks and shifty-eyed foreigners sat the mismatched tables in twos and threes. No doubt Phelan had used his talent with languages to eavesdrop on the lot. If he'd caught a whiff of anything amiss, they'd already be gone.

Phelan waved down the serving girl. "They fry the smelts here in pure olive oil. It's the one thing they get right in his place."

"We have enough for another round of ale?"

"I sold one of the horses. And most of the knives and boots."

"That should pay the rent for a while. What about the other two mounts?"

"Thought I'd hang on to them for a while."

"Huh."

"I got us each a new tunic and breeches. We could leave tonight. Ride out and never look back."

"And start over again?"

"Just think about it."

"You know I'm no good at making friends. I'm staying here."

Food arrived. Tiny, pan-fried fish and a day-old loaf, sprinkled with sesame seeds. Geth shoveled it in, tried to enjoy the meal. But Phelan's words hung in the air.

"Listen," Geth said, sopping up grease with his bread, "Clydon's not getting any younger. It's only a matter of time before I take his place. I'll get you back in with Brega."

"So I can make the old whore rich and live off whatever scraps she throws my way?"

"It's better than knifing travelers for silver, Phelan. Or creeping through windows until it's one of us that gets knifed."

"I'm not saying I have the answer yet. But don't pretend you love working for that bitch either."

"Well—"

"When we need those horses, we'll have them."

Geth had always liked high places. Perhaps it was his warrior instincts telling him to take the most defensible position. Or maybe it was simply the want of a breeze on his face. Whatever the reason, when he needed to think, he took the high ground.

That's why he'd broken into one of the lookout towers perched beside Paellia's habor that morning. He rubbed his forearm where a bruise purpled the skin under his tattoos. If that innkeep had been any kind of a warrior, Geth knew he would have been dead.

And for what? To kill a man that didn't owe Brega a bent copper round?

But to the lady, Fion's insult cut much deeper. Best Geth could figure, he'd opened up shop as a rival moneylender. Brega didn't care if he serviced only the poor. She had risen from the mean streets herself. Couldn't blame her for being ruthless.

Geth grimaced, spit out over the quays. She was a clever one, Brega. She'd used him, punished him and squashed a rival all at the same time. *With no risk to anyone but me.*

No, Phelan wasn't wrong to be wary of the lady.

Then again, wasn't it Geth himself that had run off? And wasn't it Phelan who'd landed himself afoul of a hand of justice in the first place? Brega hadn't been gentle upon Geth's return, true, but many a captain would've decreed the pillory, or even the noose, as penalty for desertion.

Geth squinted out over the water, east toward Rath where a rising sun lit the underside of the clouds pink. A string of rootless years had carried him and Phelan from port to port, across the Sworn Realms and the Outlands beyond. Not to mention the years before their reunion. Callous masters, brutal slave-handlers, conniving sergeants and captains. Phelan wasn't wrong about Brega, the woman was no shining paragon. But the gods knew he'd lived with worse.

Climbing down from the platform, Geth stepped over the moaning, white-clad guardsman he'd laid flat at his post. "Oh, quit crying for the sake of Thram. My mother gave worse lumps over spilt porridge."

Geth arrived early at Brega's manse. The lady hadn't yet emerged from her chambers, but the handful of bodyguards that slept under her roof milled about the courtyard. By the way they watched him, he knew they'd heard about Fion. Not a one offered so much as a nod. *Jealous bastards*. Clydon eyed his approach like something poisonous.

"Any action today?" Geth asked.

"Pick-ups. A few check-ins."

The lady arrived, gliding across the court in a fine stola, cinched at the waist with a gold studded belt. A half-dozen rings glittered on her thin fingers. She smiled at Geth as she passed, a small gesture but significant. Clydon didn't miss it. His expression went even more wary. Geth wore a smile of his own after that.

The master-at-arms split them into two groups, sending Geth and two others in one direction while he and a larger group escorted Brega on her errands. No accident there, but Geth didn't let it rankle. The lady seemed content to forget past transgressions. That's what mattered.

Geth knew just where to find the debtors on his list too. Brega never lent money to anyone that could skip out or hide. She knew where they lived, how to get to their children or lovers. She knew if they had horses, cattle, land. Sometimes she held collateral. The lady never discussed her methods, but Geth's years as a slave to the Mog had taught him to watch his masters closely, keep both eyes open. Brega's system was almost without flaw.

Things could only go wrong if the mark didn't have any means to pay.

"Here's the place," one of the toughs beside Geth said.

The big warrior nodded. "Haerco, the cloth-merchant."

They'd decided to split up, each tough "checking-in" on a separate mark. Brega knew the chattels her clients owned, but if they spied a debtor suddenly selling off assets, or if their business went dry, it was time to cut losses. Geth watched patrons file in and out of Haerco's storefront for a time before catching one of his apprentices lugging his product across the plaza.

"Almost too many orders to fill, eh boss?"

The apprentice turned with a start. "Why always me? I'm just an apprentice, I don't know anything about the master's business."

Geth smiled. "I'll kill you anyway if your man skips out."

The merchant's apprentice sagged under a long roll of flax slung over one shoulder. Geth took it off him, set it over his own. He motioned with the flick of his chin, and they started walking.

"See? I can be a good friend if you let me."

They wended through a steady stream of pedestrians, up the gentle rise that led to the great palace of Pellon's kings. The apprentice led Geth along at a nervous clip, but the burden didn't trouble Geth.

"So, no problem getting your wares, even after the Affliction?" he asked. "Business good?"

"The back of the store is full."

"And no lack of buyers?"

"Almost too many to handle. A lot of grandfathers died, leaving fortunes to be spent. I heard the master's hiring another boy."

"That can't be bad."

"Soon I won't have to make these deliveries anymore. And you'll have to pester the new guy."

Geth gave him back the roll of fabric. "Done with me already, eh? That hurts, friend. You were glad to sing for a few coppers the first time we met."

"That was before you threatened to cut off my balls."

Geth's companions waited with an ale in hand at the agreed upon inn. The big warrior downed one himself without sitting and waved them up. They muttered curses, kicked back their chairs.

Maybe Phelan was right. He might make a friend or two if he tried a little harder, let them sit, share a drink. Listen and smile.

But for Geth, it wasn't so easy to forget the calls of "whoreson" and "Mogi bastard" Brega's men had first welcomed him with. He'd rather punch in a few more noses. Besides, it was the lady he worked for, not these lying sonsabitches. And he wasn't about to shirk his job on their account.

At least the pick-ups went smooth. The way each mark rushed to make good, Geth wondered if the whole city had heard about the River Streets. By mid-afternoon the day's work was done. And a good thing too; a message-runner arrived soon after with a summons from the lady.

"To the wharves, twelfth pier." the boy said. He turned toward Geth. "She said you should bring your sword."

Geth never went anywhere without it. In a half hour his feet thumped down the planks. He caught sight of Clydon and a crowd of Brega's toughs. The lady stood at the center of the knot, frowning at a man in baggy sailor's britches as he blocked her path over the gunwale onto a ship.

"...and that's all fine," she was telling him. "But he's paying the new rate whether he wants to let me aboard or not."

"And what if the captain decides he's done doing business with the likes of you?"

"Then he can settle his debt here and now."

"And what if he decides not to pay?"

By the smirk he wore, the man thought he had her there. He had a ship full of sailors beside him on the deck, weapons near at hand. Clydon stood at the ready with a good dozen men of his own on the pier.

Brega raised her voice loud enough to carry. "I know you can hear me, Captain Rand. You've made a fortune, bringing your grain into this starving city. But who financed your first cartload of Lachian wool? Who helped you pay for those rarities from the Tiger Dominion? I've been more than generous with you, Captain. Now it's time to show some appreciation. If you don't want to be generous in turn, I have no choice but to cut your line, as of today. If you want gold, you can dig for it.

"And as for the outstanding debts—" she looked down the line at her men, past Clydon to meet Geth's eye.

He nodded.

"As for the outstanding debt," she repeated, "I'm prepared to take it."

Looks passed among the sailors. Geth studied the height of the gunwale, the sharps Rand's seamen carried, the numbers on each side of the fight. Mostly he studied the faces across from him—the faces of sailors, not killers.

The ship's cabin door burst open and a red-faced seaman in a fine Lachian tunic stamped down the deck toward them. "You're a greedy bitch, you know that Brega?"

"Don't you take that tone with me, you little eel. Without me you'd be trawling for tuna in a leaky rowboat. It was my coin that paid for this ship. I made you rich, rich beyond your wildest dreams. Now it's time you showed some gratitude."

"Gratitude? For what? A troop of armed men threatening to board my ship?"

"Pay the new rate, Rand. Save yourself the trouble."

"This glut won't last forever, Brega. You know that. I'll not be locked into a higher rate with no assurance what the future holds."

"Well..." Brega put a hand to her chin as if thinking, but Geth had no doubt she'd already thought it all through. "In that case I'd be willing to take a sum each time you port. Say, seven kingshead gold. That would be close enough."

"Seven kingshead? You think I don't know my sums? One. Not a round more."

"Five. And count yourself lucky, Captain."

"Three's too many. How will I turn a profit?"

"Let's call it four. Last offer."

Brega stretched out her hand. Rand eyed it, flicked a glance at Clydon and the rest. He loosed a sigh and took the lady's hand in a limp shake.

"You're a real barracuda, Brega."

"Four kingshead." The lady said. "Each shipment now, no matter the size. And don't try docking on the riverside. You don't want another visit from me."

"I hope I never see you again." Rand turned to leave.

"Not so fast, Captain. I believe you owe me four kingshead."

The captain swore. He dug into his belt pouch and slapped the shine into Brega's hand, muttering still as he turned back for his cabin. "Thieving whore."

Chapter five

The lady left happy. So did Geth. The day's work was done with no need to so much as draw a blade. What's more, he'd received his weekly wage. Half a week's, in this case, but it felt good in his belt pouch nonetheless.

The sun was still up when he reached the Netmender's Daughter. Phelan had yet to return so Geth claimed a table, ordered an ale. The gods only knew what the little bastard was doing with his time now that he had some coin. Wenching, gambling—some of each. It could have been worse.

Phelan didn't like to talk about it, but Geth knew he'd spent some years with a band of highway men before they first met on the streets of Sorn. Geth reckoned that's where he developed a taste for thievery. How else could a boy survive among such company? The common room was dark, lit only by the glow of a smoky fire, by the time Phelan slid in.

Geth ordered him an ale. "Well, I see you've still got your shirt, so I reckon it was women today and not dice."

A barmaid with overflowing cleavage set a foamy tankard down in front of Phelan but he hardly noticed. "The gods should be so kind."

"That bad? Shit."

"Shit is right." Phelan took a long pull at his ale. "But I'm not talking about women or dice. It's Palladine. He's here in the Golden City, looking for the likes of you and me."

"Already?"

"He must've used hounds. Or a damn good tracker."

Geth spared a glance around the rickety benches and wine-stained tables. Local boys mixed in among Iyrunds with oiled beards and Halicarners in baggy breeches. What notice would anyone take of one mustachioed Turian and his local friend? "We won't be so easy to find in this town."

"Palladine's offering ten kingshead to anyone who turns us in."

"Ten golds? Thram's wilted cock! You're kidding."

Phelan sucked down the rest of his ale and called for another.

"I probably should have waited that night to finish him off," Geth said.

"Maybe."

Geth took a pull at his ale, thinking. Phelan waved the barmaid down and ordered two more. He slid one across to Geth and drained his own in one draught.

"Take it easy."

"I'm nervous, Geth."

"We've got no enemies here. I can't see how he finds us without someone turning us in."

Phelan nodded. "Either way, I'm glad I kept those two mangy horses."

They took the evening meal in silence. Geth left Phelan with the busty barmaid and turned in early. Brega had gained an appreciation of him. She'd be putting him to more use, he reckoned, and he didn't want to disappoint. If all things went well, the threat of Palladine would fade, Geth's standing would rise, and Phelan would return to the fold. *One day at a time.*

Clydon's scowl the next morning affirmed Geth's hopes. The master-at-arms had been sent to make the pick-ups while Geth and a hand-picked trio of bodyguards accompanied the lady on her errands. With one tough on each side of her piebald mare, they escorted Brega to a plush inn called the Handsome Dowry to meet a potential client.

But everything about these sorts of meetings bored Geth. From the sweet pleasantries to the bitter negotiations. The client, a vintner called Eago, had brought nothing more threatening than a sharp-nosed bookkeeper with him. The lady made no headway either, her mouth stretched in a thin white line.

"Do give it some thought," she told Eago as he rose to leave. "More land means more wine."

The merchant drew on his cloak like he was late for the door. He sidled past the tables and out, Sharp-nose right behind him.

Clydon strode in the other way, maw stretched wide in a grin.

"Ah, here's the master-at-arms," said Brega.

"Here I am indeed, my lady." He knuckled his brow, giddy almost, the bastard.

"You have something good to tell me?"

"That I do. And profitable, no less."

He leaned close to whisper in Brega's ear. The lady blinked. Geth couldn't make out a word though.

He watched the master-at arms like a venomous snake. The lady flicked a glance up at Geth, her smile reassuring. No, time was on his side, whatever Clydon might have to lay at her feet. Sure enough, she waved Geth over a moment later.

"We have a meeting in the Kingswood."

"Yes, my lady."

Clydon stepped up, almost between them, to pull back her chair and Brega rose. "Send a man for my huntsman and his bows" she said. "We may take a hart if we see one while we're there."

Geth knuckled his brow. Bold. *Poaching in the bloody Kingswood*. He loved it.

Clydon left to confirm the appointment. Once the huntsman and his quiver-man arrived, Brega started them toward the Greater Gate and the swathe of wood protected by king's edict just north of the Kings Passage. It stood west of the city, outside the walls. The king's gamekeeper made a point of looking the other way when a rendezvous inside the city just wouldn't do, so long as the right heft of coin landed in his palm.

A sizable troop of bodyguards met them outside the gates. That got Geth's curiosity up. The master-at-arms had yet to return, but nearly all the lady's toughs trotted along, cudgels, daggers, swords at waists. Brega herself rode that piebald mare by his side.

"We may yet have a profitable day," she said, smiling down at him. The huntsman and his retainer rode behind her, bows strung across their laps. Geth crossed under the Greater Gate, past the same guardsmen he'd hassled just days before. Even the gaggle of beggars was the same.

"Sir! Please, sir! A crust! A round!"

One woman's voice followed Geth until he turned.

"Anything, sir!"

It was the blurry-eyed beggar woman he'd 'wed' to Phelan to help them sneak inside the city. He cursed, reached for a copper. Brega's guards snickered behind his back.

"Thank you, sir!" But she grasped his hand and held it as she took his coin. "It's my husband you see. He's taken the horses. He said it was a good thing he kept 'em. He said the time had come."

Geth blinked. "He said what?"

"Something like that." She released his hand with a shrug and disappeared among the dusty throngs coming and going through the city gates.

"Crazy as they come." Geth forced an exaggerated laugh for the toughs beside him. He stole a glance back the way they'd come. Sure enough, there was Phelan with the two horses, tucked in among the cartmen and foot traffic on the road. Their eyes met. Phelan's face was sober.

"Thram and bloody Awer," Geth mumbled.

What the hell was he up too? The time had come? What did that mean? *Little bastard decides to up and leave, just when things start looking good?*

Probably landed himself in hot water again, Geth decided. Burning hot, by the look on the little man's face.

But why send the beggar-woman to sneak him the news? That had cost at least a few silvers judging by the way she'd fleeced them the first go around. Simpler to leave a note with the barkeep at the Netmender's Daughter. *So why, damn it?*

"Perfect day for a hunt, eh?" Clydon's voice startled Geth from his thoughts. "It's rutting season, you know."

The bastard wore a grin even wider than before. Geth hadn't noticed his return, but gods all be damned if something wasn't afoot. His warrior instincts cried the alarm.

But they continued without incident, their column veering off the road, leaving the procession of cart-toting farmhands and ox-drawn wagons to strike toward a dark line of trees that marked the Kingswood. Brega had used the cover of that forest as a clandestine meeting place more than once in the past, nothing out of the ordinary there.

"I do love the autumn leaves," she said. "The reds, the yellows. The golds especially."

The golds. Geth's mouth fell open. He had to force it shut.

If not for the lady's greed, she might have gotten away with it. Realization hit the big warrior like a punch in the gut. The sly delivery of Phelan's message made all the sense in the world now, and his arrival with those two horses. The lady had sold him out to Palladine for the price of ten golds.

A wagon train of curses piled up on the tip of Geth's tongue, but he swallowed the lot. Clydon's jeers made perfect sense now as well. Rutting season indeed.

"Goddamned gold."

The sting of betrayal misted his eyes, but he drew it back in with a deep breath, formed a simmering hot anger of it. All of his labors, the bone-breaking, the bloodletting. None of it, in the end, amounted to the ten kingshead reward.

Of course it didn't. He snorted a grim laugh. What gutter-born bastard was worth a handful of gold? He'd been a fool to think otherwise, to imagine life could be any different, under the lady or anyone else.

Beside him, Brega and the master-at-arms chatted about the weather. Geth stole another look over his shoulder near the spot where they'd left the road. Phelan would be waiting for him there.

But what to do? Geth knew why Brega had chosen the Kingswood, the ruse of going hunting: she'd need those bowmen. No one wanted to cross blades with him, least of all these sonsabitches. They knew what he could do.

They drew deeper into the forest. Geth pretended to search the undergrowth for signs of game. A great meadow nestled less than a mile inside the woods if he remembered correctly; that's where they'd do it. Better sightlines for the bows. Palladine would be waiting for them, a score of lilies at his back.

Lifting his eyes, Geth found Clydon watching him. "Fine day to take down a beast." Geth breathed deep through his nose. "Ah." He turned toward the companions behind him with a fake smile. The huntsman had already nocked an arrow.

But Palladine must have wanted Geth alive. Otherwise, the big warrior knew he wouldn't have lasted this long. The quiver-bearer had a bolt ready as well.

Those two bowmen were all that stood between him and escape, Geth reckoned, assuming Phelan still followed behind with their mounts. That's how the pieces had been laid. No one else was mounted and none of these cowards would fight too hard to keep him cornered, knowing how he swung a sword. But he had to act before they reached that meadow, before they reached Palladine.

Geth dropped back alongside the huntsman's young quiver-man. "How about a drink, friend?" He flicked his chin toward the boy's water-skin. "I'm about as thirsty as a sand-digger in the Iyrund lands."

The lad stiffened but passed over the skin as asked. Taking several large, sloppy gulps, Geth started to hand it back, pretended to fumble the skin and clutched at it as it fell to squirt a good amount onto the lad's stomach and all over the arrow and bowstring.

"Watch it, man!" He wanted to say more but thought better of it.

Geth hurried back up the line. One bow was down. The boy patted his pockets for a spare string to replace the wet one, cursing all the while. That left only the huntsman himself, a hollow-cheeked bastard with leathery hands and a leathery reputation.

Geth stepped up alongside the man. "My grandfather swore he could smell a deer from a hundred paces," he said, voice conspiratorial.

"It's the other way 'round. It's the deer that smell us first."

"That right?" Geth's hand was already on Pockface's knife, hidden under his tunic.

Old Leather spit. "Your grandfather was a lying whoreson."

Geth supposed he had no choice but to defend the honor of his grand-pappie, no matter he'd never met the man. Now was better than later. He lunged for the huntsman's throat with the little blade. The old bastard's hand snatched at Geth's as it slashed his windpipe and arteries, eyes gone wide, but Geth pulled the blade clear to spray gore all over the both of them.

"Ahh!" the man cried. The smell of blood sent the lady's horse snorting and rearing. Chaos erupted along the column.

"Grab him!" someone yelled.

Geth was already bowling over the toughs behind him, sprinting headlong back the way they'd come. There was no time to draw his sword. An arm caught him by the elbow, swinging him halfway around. A second tough dove for his knees and he went down in a tangle of limbs. He rolled and punched, shaking loose only to find Clydon bearing down on him, cudgel raised.

"Slippery mutt!"

Something whizzed past Geth's ear and a resounding crack sounded. The master-at-arms crumpled like a limp sheet. A second whiz and the man nearest Geth dropped alongside Clydon.

"This way!" Phelan cried, crashing through the brush on that old horse, sling flapping in hand. The second horse came galloping behind on its tether.

Geth sprang to his feet and ran. Curses echoed behind him. He swung into the saddle, thundering beside Phelan like mad through the trees.

Chapter six

If there was one thing Geth had learned in his riotous, inconstant, often miserable stomp through life, it was that shit runs downhill. From the fighting-pits of Adamar, to the untamed Mog-lands, to the Sworn Realms on Longsea. And it was a tough climb out of the offal when you were born in the gutter. Clerk or cleric might tell you otherwise, but only when they wanted their taxes and tithes.

Or their enemies killed.

And still Geth hoped for better. *Fool that I am!* Just days after their return to Paellia, he and Phelan were on the run again. A grey autumn sky hung over his shoulders. Any satisfaction at his escape couldn't last long.

"You were right," he told his friend. "Keeping the horses, I mean."

Phelan took a sip from his water-skin, passed it over.

Geth sucked in a mouthful, swished dust from his mouth and spit. "Less than a year with Brega and we're on the outs again. Why can't we just find someplace and stick?"

"It's not our fault, Geth. It's Brega's. I warned you about her. You didn't want to listen. Let's face it, I've always been the better judge of character."

"Sure. Or maybe it's someone else's fault, someone who landed himself in a steaming pile of shit with a lily called Palladine. You ready to 'fess up to how this whole mess got started?"

"Brega didn't have to turn you in. She's a coin-grubbing sow."

"A few shots of White Adus spirits and you'll spill the truth. Hold on to it for now if you want."

Phelan eyed him smugly and laughed. "What you may be wondering is how I knew Brega was going to hand you over to Palladine. Keep your friends close and your enemies closer, eh? Well, ever since I found out Palladine was in town I started keeping tabs on him. Plenty of street-boys willing to watch for some coin."

"How much did that cost us?"

"Whatever it cost, you better believe it was worth it."

"You've got a point there."

"Right. So, there I am, perched on a rooftop watching the lily bastard myself when who should saunter over? Your dear friend the master-at-arms. It all happened fast after that. When the huntsman showed up, I knew they'd do it in the Kingswood. I barely had time to gather our things and beat you to the gates. Once I saw my dear ex-wife, I figured she'd be happy to pass the message. I just wasn't sure it would penetrate that thick skull of yours."

"In my business, a thick skull comes in handy."

"You must be the handiest bastard carrying a sword then."

"I'd throw you in a next stream if you weren't so useful. So, what's the plan going through your little mind right now?"

Phelan turned serious. "I figure we've got two options; ride these miserable beasts into the ground or sell them to pay for passage."

Geth left the unspoken question on the air, the same argument they'd had at the Netmender's Daughter. Just where in the hell would they go? A thin spit of rain began to fall.

"Let's find someplace to hole-up," he said. "Stick to the backcountry for tonight and after that head for Sorn."

"Sorn?"

"It'll be a long while before we can return to these parts. And no one will expect us to double back toward the Tower of the Moon when it's the one place you're trying to avoid."

"I don't suppose Brega will bother chasing after," Phelan said, "but Palladine has probably sent a man in each direction already. It won't be long before he winds up in Sorn. Better we moved on."

Geth shook his head. "I can't believe he hasn't been shamed out of the king's service. Especially after what we did. Must have a rich uncle somewhere. Either way, between Brega and Palladine, we have no choice after Sorn but to leave Pellon."

In the wake of the Affliction, a stretch of overgrown fields was sure sign of an abandon homestead, the perfect place to hide a pair of fugitives for the night. Phelan rambled on about dice, women, and the like, but Geth stewed over where this latest shitstorm would land them. He'd been across three of the four Sworn Realms, to the outlands and back. There was nothing left for him in any of those places. Except the graves of dead friends and the swords of living enemies.

He stared up at the leaky thatch above. Simple farm folk had once lived here, before the Affliction killed them or scared them away. No fault of theirs. And was it any fault of his he survived when his friends had all perished? The gods knew he'd never betrayed a one of them, never run from a fight. Yet somehow their spaces lay empty, like this farmer's cottage. Maybe this was his curse. Maybe the gods liked to watch him suffer.

They reached Sorn the next day. As a precaution, they circled wide around it to arrive from the north, coming down the King's Passage as if out of Turia or distant Umbel.

"Look, there's your inn now." Geth pointed to the Tower of the Moon as it came into view. "Got anything with a feather mattress and a good view?"

Phelan snorted a laugh.

It was Geth who was nervous. Across their path, the Sorn road ran west to east. The King's Passage headed nearly due south at that stretch. The prison stood on a lofty rise northeast of the crossroad, the town itself a few furlongs to the south and west. Geth had been born there. He knew the crawlspaces beneath every brothel, the rooftop of every moonshine cellar.

Among the streets of Sorn, shopkeepers had raised their awnings for the day's business and the smells of baked-goods and spices mingled with the earthy scents of woodfire and sweat. Past the row of respectable hostelries on the main drag, they veered onto narrower streets, dismounting to lead their horses down winding alleyways honest men seldom traveled. Phelan didn't approve, but it wasn't on account of the grit, that was sure. He held his tongue until they arrived before a ramshackle inn called the Acorn and Branch.

"I hate this place."

The garish red paint peeling from the beams matched the colored lips of two women lazing about the entrance. One was just a wisp of a girl, despite the exposed cleavage. The second was a man-sized creature with a heavy jaw, dyed yellow hair, and plenty of powder on her aging cheeks. She threw out a hip and flashed a smile.

"It's me, Mother," Geth said. "No point looking so happy."

The big woman squinted. Her smile vanished. She spit on the wooden porch. "Well, look who it is. What's that mustache about? And I see you've brought that good-for-nothing footpad of yours."

Phelan scowled. "I'll go look for news." He headed off the way they'd come.

"It's good to see you too, Mother."

"If you cared at all about me, you'd turn up more than once every few years. And don't start on about my line of work, you with all that blood on your hands."

"It's not—"

"I like what I do." She threw back her shoulders to emphasize those enormous breasts. "And I'm good at it too."

Geth winced. She smelled of liquor as usual. From up close he could see the circles under her eyes, the deepening creases on her forehead. How long had it been since last he'd passed through? The woman was barely in her forties.

"So, what do you want, boy?"

Geth reached out to take her hand, but she brushed it away. He rested it on his hilt instead. "It looks like I'll be leaving for a while. I just wanted to see you. It may be some time before I'm back."

"Leaving again?"

Geth could see the wheels turning behind her eyes. "I wouldn't leave if I didn't have to."

"Well, it's good you're here at any rate. I need help with something. You know I'm no good with money. It's a long story, but you'll do a favor for me, won't you?"

"Anything, Mom."

She took the hand from his hilt, held it against her cheek. "That's my boy."

Geth spent the next several hours at a watering hole aptly named the Dog's Den, a dump of an inn trolled by the inglorious ladies of his mother's trade and frequented by their clientele. By then he imagined he smelled even worse than she had. Three empty tankards formed a shield wall in front of the fourth in his hand. Phelan broke the defenses to peel it from his grip when he arrived.

"You need something to eat," he said.

Geth rubbed his nose. "Go on and say it. Why do I bother?"

"I'm not saying anything. Despite the risk of coming all the way over here."

"You had a better idea?"

"A lot of them. There's opportunity out there for men such as ourselves."

"And what kind of men are we?"

"Survivors."

Geth closed his eyes. He leaned all the way back in his chair to rest his head against the wall behind.

His body called for sleep, but that would have to wait.

"At least you didn't book us at the Acorn and Branch. I'll take this place over that one, seven days a week. They know how to feed you in this joint."

Phelan waved for the barmaid. He ordered two bowls of stew and a loaf. Geth couldn't deny he was hungry.

"Did I ever tell you about the east, how the Mog reckon each man slain in battle becomes the slave of his killer in the underworld?"

"I don't like where this is going."

"I need to take care of something before we leave. *Someone*. For my mother."

"This is why I didn't want to come here."

"What kind of son doesn't help his mother?"

Phelan exhaled a long breath. Like he hadn't gone along with such things a hundred times before. "Look, we don't need to take any chances. That's all I'm saying. We need to be on the first ship outta this place."

"I'm doing this Phelan. Now gimme back my drink."

"Fine, as long as we can finish it tonight. It's only a few miles to the Arm River and back down to the Golden City. From there we may be able to find a ship headed to sea."

"First one we find. I promise." Geth straightened up in his chair, leaned across to take his tankard back. "Once I'm done, we can go wherever you want."

A stew of pork and carrots helped clear Geth's mind. He left with a bottle of White Adus spirits nestled under his arm. The strong stuff. It cost them, but Phelan paid without question.

A long meander through night-quiet streets took them to the moneylender's district on the opposite side of town, a thin sickle of moon the only light. Geth halted them across from a tavern whose sign read the Golden Gander. Firelight spilled out the open door onto patrons coming and going in twos and threes.

"This is the place," said Geth.

"I take it the liquor's not for a celebration."

"What burns quicker than White Adus?"

Phelan smirked. "Lighting more than a prayer candle, are we?"

"Just go around back and flush 'em out. I'll find my man in the confusion."

"Then we leave, you hear me, Geth? You've seen her. You've done what she asked. Soon as your man hits the floor, we're gone."

"Soon as he's dead."

Phelan turned for the back alleyway behind the Golden Gander, padding across the cobbles and around the corner. Geth tucked himself into the shadows of a nearby doorway. He waited. The smell of smoke hit his nose as the first shouts erupted.

Phelan slunk back into the darkness beside him. "How much does she owe?" A faint orange glow backlit the *Golden Gander's* façade.

"Does it matter? I don't much care for moneylenders. Especially these days."

"Crooked bastards." Phelan spit. "What's his name?"

"Oram."

Voices rose inside the inn. A throng gathered out in front, some fleeing, others attracted by the commotion. Men shouted for water. Several toughs sprinted down the street, buckets in hand, just like Geth knew they would. The first bells rang.

Smoke hit their noses and worried shouts turned to cries. Phelan licked his lips. "You see him?" Flames clawed out the windows at the night sky. The last man to emerge from the inn was a fat-jowled scratch with soot on his face.

"There he is."

Geth shouldered through the crowd, one of the few pushing forward, not away. The first buckets of water sizzled as they hit the flames. Fire lit the street daybright, made him squint. Swirling smoke and embers only added to the confusion.

"Master Oram?" Geth called, sword drawn beneath his cloak.

"Now of all times? Fetch some water you fool! Can't you see my tavern is burning?"

"Got some payment you're owed. Interest and all."

Oram's eyes narrowed then widened, too late. Geth's blade gleamed orange. He closed the space and thrusted home.

"Ahhhh!"

Fresh screams echoed the moneylender's dying cry. Two bodyguards dropped pails and drew cudgels to rush Geth. He sidestepped the first, cutting under his swing to lay open the man's side. The blade came free in time to parry a blow from the second.

A gust of acrid smoke in the face blinded Geth before he could finish the man, but his mind's eye knew where he must be. He swung low, drew a block, kicked out toward the man's middle. His boot found the bodyguard's stomach. The clatter of something wooden told Geth the man had dropped his club. Geth stole the chance to backpedal a step, blinking furiously. He looked up. The bastard had already turned to flee.

His fellow lay moaning on the ground to one side, a hand at his ribs. Geth whirled but no one ran toward him, only away. Phelan appeared by his side, grabbed him by the arm.

"Watchmen!" He pointed up the street.

Geth spared one last glance for Oram. His eyes had already glazed over. He let his friend pull him down the street as a half-dozen lilies converged on the mass of bodies around the inn.

"Haha!" He swung his sword overhead in circles.

Phelan cursed his name. "Run, you crazy asshole!"

Chapter seven

The Tower of the Moon shadowed over Geth and Phelan's exit from Sorn. Running until they were breathless, they reached the Sorn Road's juncture with the Arm River at dawn. A row of barges and rowboats lined the banks. Phelan haggled a price for the horses at the trader's square, swearing at the meager proceeds

"Vorda's withered tits. This isn't even enough to buy passage to Rath, let alone anyplace else." He cast a sidelong glance at Geth. "If we weren't in such a hurry, I could've got twice as much."

"Quit your cryin'. The deal was I kill Oram, then we leave. You knew that meant we'd be leaving on the run."

Phelan muttered under his breath but didn't press. They were both tired. And Geth's head throbbed from the night's drinking. He already had half a mind to throw Phelan's ass in the river.

"Let's just catch the first tub headed to Paellia," Phelan said. "See what we can afford once we reach the quays."

For a king's ransom, a weasel-faced boatman was happy to ferry them south to the Golden City. From Paellia's river docks, they hustled across town to the seaport, hoods up, eyes scanning for Paellian white and Brega's people as well. They boarded the first ship that would have them.

"Umbel." Phelan groaned as the vessel shoved off. "I can't believe we couldn't find something to Rath or Iyre."

"What did you expect this late in the season? And don't forget we're saving on coin."

Phelan couldn't argue with that. In exchange for their help on deck and at the oars, the woman captaining the Windskimmer had agreed to forgo a fee for passage. Phelan grumbled that she'd surely get the better end of that deal, but hers was the only vessel headed to sea.

By Geth's reckoning, the destination suited them as well. Westerly Umbel had a backwater reputation, but the shared language, ancestry, and customs that carried throughout the Sworn Realms would certainly grease the landing. And they'd been to each of the other three Sworn Realms already, racking up enemies along the way. Not so in Umbel.

The journey across Longsea would last ten days, moving west and north toward Umbel City. Unfavorable winds forced every man to the oars for the better part of the first day, but it beat three ass-sore weeks in the saddle, Geth supposed. When the day was done and the oars drawn in, he huddled under the stars beside Phelan.

"So, this can drive a man mad?" Geth stared up into the tiny lights smeared across the sky. He'd forgotten just how bright the stars glowed above a dark sea.

"You mean at the Tower?" Phelan shrugged. "It's not the stars that drive a man mad, but the moon, so they say. And the darkness."

"I like the night. Moon, stars, and all. That tower wouldn't be any problem for me. Not unless it was as cold as the deck of this bloody ship."

Phelan shook his head. "Had to be Umbel…" he muttered.

Geth shivered. That was the one thing they hadn't considered. Soaked through by spray, the cold would be a misery those ten nights. He turned his head toward a shuffling sound as a dark lump raised itself from the far end of the deck.

"You eastern boys caught a chill?"

"What's it to you?"

By his accent, the sailor was from Umbel, a grinning bastard with lank hair hanging over his forehead. He eased himself down beside them, a bundle under one arm. "Gimme' five rounds and you can take my second blanket. It's oiled to keep out the damp, but the two of you will have to share."

"Or how about I throw you overboard and take them both," Geth said.

The sailor snickered. Phelan talked him down to three and Grin-face tossed them a frayed but serviceable cover. Lying close, the blanket spread just far enough.

"Many thanks," Phelan said. "If every Umbelman is so generous, it's a true paradise where we're headed."

"You won't like it. I didn't either, that's why I jumped on this raft. But if our Rondah says we're bound for Umbel, Umbel it is."

He rose to shuffle back up the deck. Waves slapping against the hull were the only sounds until his voice drifted back down toward them.

"Name's Addie. For two rounds, I'll buy that blanket back when we reach port."

Halfway through the second day they knew every sailor's name. A dozen more Umbelmen and a pair of Iyrunds rounded out the crew. Geth and Phelan helped out where needed, mostly at the oars. Rondah didn't have to ration their food, the crew shared freely. Still, it was Addie who spoke to them most.

"Wouldn't usually set sail so late," he told them. "Winter storms beginning to brew and all. But the captain got word of problems back home and gave the order. We lost a couple lads who didn't care to be on the sea this time of year."

Geth nodded. "Worked to our advantage."

Phelan despised the Umbleman. Probably because they were so similar, Geth reckoned. The yellow hair, the crooked antics. They diced and cursed and topped each other's tales. Geth listened and watched, gleaned whatever he could.

"You said yesterday you didn't care to head back to Umbel," he told Addie. "We gonna regret this trip?"

Addie shrugged. "It's cold, but it's not that bad. I'm just not one to sit still. Now in Paellia, even sitting still, you're moving. So many folks from every-which-where. So big. Umbel City's nothing more than a sheep-shack compared to that."

"What sort of troubles are they having?"

"The dying sort. It's been a while in these parts, but the Affliction just passed out that way."

"That right?"

"So I'm told. I reckon the captain wants to get back to her family."

Phelan held his tongue until Addie disappeared below deck. "I've been listening in on the Iyrunds. Seems King Aeldan's among the dead. His son too."

"Yeah?" Geth raised an eyebrow. "That's got the makings of a civil war."

"Nah, Aeldan had a second son. He's taken the throne. But he's young."

"Well, if Umbel's anything like Pellon after the Affliction, they'll need men to work."

"Squirrel-face says he knows some folk that may have need for men with our talents."

"I thought you hated the man?"

"I do. But our silver won't last forever. If there's easy work to be had for a man with a sword, who are we to say no?"

Geth didn't argue. Not yet. There was no such thing as easy work for a man with a sword. But he'd agreed to follow Phelan's lead after settling his mother's debts. Neither of them had guessed where that would take them.

Hugging the coast, their ship rounded into the Bay of Umbel a week later. Geth caught his first glimpse of Umbel. Foam roiled on the rocks and washed up on hide-colored beaches. Fishermen plied their nets from small boats on the water, hailing them as they passed. White-fleeced sheep dotted the hills overlooking Longsea.

Turning back toward the deck, Geth found Captain Rondah watching him. She held her hat down over a head of pale red hair, shot through with white. The wind tossed a few loose strands across a craggy, sea-weathered face, but there was something sure about that unflinching gaze. Something honest.

"Always wanted to see Umbel's Oathstone," he told her, flicking a head toward the shore. "Addie says we won't like the place though."

Rondah squinted out over the waves. "You might. Nothing like Paellia, with her dust and her crowds and all the riches in Wide Eria. But Umbel's a rich country too. If you know what you're looking at."

"I'm listening."

She spoke with reverence of Umbel's green fields and rolling pastures, all of it carved down the middle by the mighty North River. The woodlands teemed with game. Vineyards and orchards grew lush upon the hills.

"And if all that bores you, there's the Ilars further north to fire your blood."

"Ilars?"

"Tribesmen from the forests. Been at odds with the folk of Umbel since the first Aturians came over the mountains they say. Something like Pellon and the Mog."

Geth rubbed the tattoos on one forearm. "The Mog aren't so bad once you get to know them."

"Neither are the Ilars. When they're not trying to stick a blade in your guts."

Geth smiled.

Rondah's stark face never cracked. "I didn't ask what you two were running from and I don't care. I reckon it wasn't good, but you'll have a clean slate in Umbel. Don't waste it."

"Believe me, I don't intend to."

The first gleam of Umbel City's pale walls peeked out through the distance on the eleventh day. I grey-white fortress overlooked the sprawling settlement from atop a bulky rise, a stone crown planted on a hill of green turf. Erehan Keep they named it. From there, Geth was told, it watched over the mouth of the mighty North River. That lay out of sight on the far side of the great mount, but below the keep's grassy surrounds, the thatched rooftops of the city spread like a brown skirt down the hill, circled by grey-white ramparts.

A small harbor crowded with masts received them as the Windskimmer glided into port. Prayers of thanks were offered to Uro, moorings wrapped in place amid the banter and back-slapping of the crew. Geth drew a breath of crisp, clean air. He gathered his few belongings and stepped over the rail. Looking past Phelan, however, he saw Captain Rondah frowning over the gunwale as she spoke to a man on the docks. Her eyes found Geth. She turned in his direction.

"Through there." Rondah pointed under a great gate in the harbor wall leading toward the city. "The Oathstone. You can't miss it."

Geth followed the line of her hand. "If not for those sworn oaths, I reckon a pair of shabby Paellians might not be welcome in these parts."

"Look after yourselves just the same. The harbormaster says things have been a bit loose around here of late, folks blaming the ships for spreading the Affliction's humors. Blaming foreigners too."

"I'm no stranger to catching the blame."

Rondah grunted. "Even so, play it straight. You just might do well here after all."

Reaching out a hand, she gave him a shake. Geth looked down as he came away with a gleaming silver in his grasp.

"Wages. For the oars." She winked and disappeared down the pier.

Phelan watched the exchange with a grin. "And I thought I was the charmer. I won't ask when you snuck away to bed the old lady."

"A gentleman never tells."

"A gentleman, ha!"

They started down the quays, Geth's heart as light as he could remember despite the captain's warning. They might not have planned on a visit to Umbel, but because of their arrangement with Rondah, they had coin to hold them over. He thought of what she'd said about starting clean. Galleys and skiffs bumped together in that little harbor, dappled in light as the sun peeked through a scattering of clouds.

"Phelan, look." Geth gestured inside the gates where a gleaming black shard twice the height of a man sat on a pedestal at the center of a cobbled court.

"The Oathstone."

Story went, that slab had been wrenched from the parapet of Tower Greynor some centuries prior, the fastness of a bygone enemy. In that spot, the four realms of Pellon, Turia, Rath, and Umbel bound themselves with oaths of allegiance. Geth studied the faint reflection of cloud and sky in the stone's glassy surface. No god-like monarch chiseled there, brave stare glossing over a life of tyranny. Just a plain, dark chunk of rock.

"I think I might like this place."

Phelan snorted. "How 'bout we discuss it over a drink?"

The tidy placard of an inn called the Journey's End beckoned from across the cobbles. They plopped into chairs under the curious eyes of a few merchants and seagoers. Phelan set a line of rounds down on the tabletop and a smiling barmaid with yellow curls arrived, two foamy brown ales in hand.

"Ah." Phelan licked his lips, peered into his mug, studied the color and swirl of the drink. "Now that's an ale. A bit clean for me, this place, if you know what I mean. But we can afford one night among our betters I suppose."

Geth turned from the departure of their barmaid's swaying hips. "How much we got? A fair sum from the horses and now another silver from the captain. That should hold us a while."

"I've got a meet set up with Addie tomorrow just the same."

"When did you start trusting him?"

"When he offered to find us work."

"For a fee, I reckon."

Phelan shrugged. "Business is business. But if he did offer to do it for free, then I wouldn't trust him."

Geth muttered a curse. He took a swig of ale.

"We got no ins here, Geth. That's all I'm saying. Let's work with what we got."

"Or we could be patient, keep our heads low and see what comes our way. At least 'til the shine runs low."

Phelan snorted.

"Look," Geth said, "if you want, I'll hold the purse. That oughta keep it safe should you happen to fall headlong into a game of dice."

"I don't know what you're worried about. I always win. In fact, if I didn't, we wouldn't have ended up on the run in the first place."

Geth had a choice reply in mind, but across the common room, the barmaid caught him looking and flashed him a smile. She had an adorable gap between her front teeth and the sort of curves he just couldn't stop staring at. He hurried to down his drink so he could call her over for another.

"To Umbel." He lifted his cup. "To starting fresh."

"To the best ale I've had in at least eleven days."

Geth waved the barmaid over. She came with an ale already in hand.

The Oathstone's shadow stretched long and uneven across the cobbles by the time Addie arrived to meet them the next day. Phelan cursed him but Geth's mood had yet to sour after a night with tender Morisa.

"You're late," Phelan told Addie as the Umbelman sauntered up.

"Came as soon as I had an answer," Addie replied. "You got the shine?"

Phelan cursed some more.

"Just pay the man and let's see what he's got," Geth said.

"That tumble last night sure put *you* in a good mood. You might benefit from keeping a mistress. Or at least a working girl."

Addie chuckled. "Someone's got to support the industry."

Geth let them have their fun. He supposed Phelan wasn't wrong, but as much as he enjoyed a woman's warmth, he wasn't about to settle down with the first barmaid that had a thing for big men with foreign accents. Addie waved them to follow and they started through the city.

Geth dropped back beside Phelan as they walked. He flicked his chin toward Addie. "Did he ever mention what sort of work he found?"

"Dunno. Bodyguarding maybe?"

"That's something I guess."

"We could always go on our own if it doesn't pan out."

Geth snorted through his mustache.

"Alright, alright. But with all the dead, who knows? Maybe we'll find an inn or tavern for sale. You work the door; I'll manage the coin."

"Be serious."

Addie pulled them to a halt in front of the torn awning of a ramshackle wooden edifice with no signage to speak of. Geth's hand moved to rest on the hilt of his sword. Judging by the closed shutters and crooked pavers, he reckoned it the sort of neighborhood where folk didn't read anyway.

The reek of piss and stale alcohol hit him as a swaying drunk pushed out the front door. Geth relaxed a hair. Another watering hole of some sort, no ambush. Addie waved them in. He peeked over the man's shoulder into a dim room scattered with benches, tables, and shabby locals.

"I'll tell you this up front," Addie said as they stepped inside. "The woman we're here to meet is a witch."

Geth shared a look with Phelan. From birthmarked virgins who convened with the dead, to men that controlled wild animals, they'd seen their share of witchcraft. Sorcerers, shamans, god-speakers and diviners, Great Eria was full of mysteries he'd long since given up on understanding.

But it wasn't all bad. Geth had once fallen in love with a woman whose mere touch could raise the sick or injured. He'd traveled for months and befriended a man who could see inside your very soul. And Phelan himself had that inexplicable talent for speaking any tongue.

"What sort of witch?" his friend asked, echoing those thoughts.

"The sort that's hiring."

Addie claimed them a table and ordered a round amid wary looks from the innkeep and his shifty-eyed patrons. The room wasn't big enough to hide anyone and Geth didn't peg any of the serving girls or red-nosed female clients for a witch. Addie had racked them up a healthy tab before a cloaked woman with a pair of toughs behind her hushed the place with her entrance.

"Mind your manners," Addie whispered. "They say she's a lordess or some such. From northern parts."

The two bodyguards ushered the woman to a table in the corner. Geth studied her as her hood came down. Big dark eyes caught the firelight, but fine lines at the corners of her mouth betrayed her age. A loose bun of wavy fire-red hair rested above her straight, slender neck.

They let the party settle in before Addie approached, knuckling his brow. Geth couldn't make out what was said, but the woman hardly spared the Umbelman a glance, gazing past the sailor to run a keen eye over Phelan, then himself. Something passed between her and Addie. He straightened from the table, turned toward them with a wave and shuffled out the door.

"What the hell?" Phelan's glare flicked from Addie's exit to the empty mugs he'd left on the table. The lady motioned them over before he could say more. Her minders pulled up two chairs and Geth and Phelan rose with their drinks.

"Evening, m'lady," Phelan said.

"You are the Paellian mercenaries?"

"We're from Pellon," Geth said.

The lady nodded. She motioned to the chairs. Didn't bode well that Addie had introduced them as mercenaries by Geth's reckoning, but he'd give the woman a listen just the same.

"I am Pythelle. They call me a witch in these parts, but only because they don't understand my methods. If you have any questions of me, ask."

"We've heard you're hiring," Phelan said. "Addie didn't tell us more."

Pythelle nodded. "I'm an heiress. My husband died years ago. With the current unrest, it isn't wise for a woman in my position to be without protection."

"Unrest?" Geth frowned.

"The Affliction took many lives. Including both the king and his heir. The queen succumbed to grief shortly after. Hadean, Aeldan's younger son, sits the throne now. But he is untried. And these are difficult times."

Geth mulled that over. Her story seemed likely enough. But by all the sideways glances, her bodyguards seemed a better fit for the likes of Brega than any noblewoman and her household. Or maybe those two were just nervous about taking the lady to such a seedy inn. Geth could only imagine what they might make of his own heavy knuckles and weather-worn cloak.

"So it's bodyguards you're after," he said. "We've got a bit of experience in that area."

Pythelle nodded. "Some work around the manse, perhaps, but protection mostly. For me, it's that or a new marriage."

"Why us? Why not hire some of your own people? I'm not saying it's right, but I've heard there's little love for foreign folk around here."

"Simple minds always fear outsiders. But the truth is, there's a shortage of hands around Umbel these days. I'm sure you experienced the same back in Pellon after the Affliction."

Geth flicked a glance at Phelan and back to Pythelle. "Perhaps you're hiring for work no honest man would take."

"There's some brain in there among the muscles." The woman smiled, a dangerous, seductive turn of those lips. "You aren't a fool to ask. I need men. Proven men. The sort that know which end of a sword to grip. I was assured you have the right qualities. By the look of you, I believe it."

Phelan shifted in his seat, frowning. "So, you need men like us. Well, I'll tell you now, we don't come cheap."

"Straight to it then."

They went back and forth, haggling over the wage. The lady was firm in her offer, but the coin was far below what they expected. It really was a pittance.

"A silver will carry you much farther in Umbel than it did in the Golden City," said Pythelle. "No doubt you've already surmised as much."

"Still," Phelan said, "my friend here is like three other men in a fight. And my skill with the sling doesn't disappoint."

"Perhaps you'd be willing to give a...demonstration?"

Geth bit down a growl. "I don't wet my blade for the fun of it."

Pythelle shrugged. She kicked back her chair and rose. "I think you'll find my offer quite generous, by standards of these parts. Ask around if you like."

Geth flicked a glance from the lady to her bodyguards. No eagerness there, but he reckoned that a good sign.

"Give us some time to think."

"Of course. But not too long. We leave for Greenfell in three days' time."

Chapter eight

Geth left Phelan snoring at the Journey's End the next morning to walk the Oathstone's wide plaza. He left out the gates, headed up the length of the harbor and back down again. He didn't miss the sideways glances of shipwrights, fishmongers, and dockhands as he made his circuit, but it was a fine morning just the same. He spoke to no one except to buy a loaf for breakfast. His mind was on Pythelle's offer.

He weighed Addie's warning against the possibility of stable, familiar work. The times called for men with a hard edge, men like himself. But was that a fresh start? There was no way to be sure what the woman might ask of them, who her enemies were, what her designs might be. And they had the coin to wait on something better.

The air was good for him, but it decided nothing. *Gods but it'd be nice to stand atop the ramparts and think!* He joined Phelan at midday in the common room of the Journey's End.

"Food's important at an inn," Phelan said between mouthfuls of bacon and boiled cabbage. "This place does it right."

"Maybe *all* the food is good here in Umbel." Geth licked grease from the corner of his mouth. "How should we know? This is the only place we've eaten."

"What did you think about that dump Addie brought us to? Bet you wouldn't want to eat what they're serving."

"I'm just trying to understand why a highborn lady would hold a meet at a place like that."

Phelan shrugged. "Maybe she really is a witch."

Morisa arrived with an ale in each hand, smiling that cute smile. "Two more for my friends."

Geth flashed a smile in return. "And thank you, m'lady."

She turned back to her duties and Phelan rolled his eyes at her back. "Are we still considering Pythelle's offer, or did you decide to settle down with your barmaid now?"

"Vorda's tits, you of all people?"

"That's not an answer."

Geth set down his drink. "Morisa's a good woman. A widow, Phelan. For her, I'm just someone to fend off the loneliness. You think a person like that would settle down with the likes of me?"

"What about Pythelle's offer then? I'm in no rush to head farther north than I already am, that's for sure. But otherwise, the job's perfect."

Geth mopped up grease with a bread crust, frowned down at the empty plate.

Pythelle's offer? Time was when he wouldn't have thought twice about taking her up on it. Here in Umbel though, it felt like a wasted opportunity. He looked across the table at Phelan. His friend wasn't humming with enthusiasm either.

"We've still got a couple days to decide," Geth said. "In the meantime, I raise my cup. To Umbel."

Phelan lifted his drink. "To us."

The day wore on. The common room began to fill, merchants in embroidered tunics shouldering up beside sweaty laborers and country folk. A pair of fishermen stole the two empty chairs from their table as the seats ran out. Lively banter floated beneath the low beams, but the crowd of locals left Geth and Phelan to themselves.

"The thing is," Geth said, "Brega's turned me sour. I know I come from the gutter, but I don't need every pock-faced sergeant to remind me."

Phelan drained his cup. "I hear what you're saying. You know, if we play it tight, we may just have enough shine to hold out 'til something really good finds us."

Geth nodded.

But experience told him it was a risky proposition with Phelan holding the purse. They were never more than a dice game away from broke. Geth couldn't claim to be any better managing coin himself.

"We just need something before winter," he said. "We don't want to be sleeping under the stars when the freeze sets in."

Phelan snorted a laugh. That brought a grumble from a huddle of patrons forced to stand to one side of their table. By their dress, Geth pegged them for sailors or dockhands. He'd never understood why that sort were always the first to stir up trouble.

But the windows hadn't even darkened, the evening too young for the kind of rough stuff that came naturally when men and their cups mixed. A trio of green-cloaked soldiers a few tables over would be enough to keep the peace either way, Geth reckoned. He ordered another round, as happy with the drink as the weight of Morisa's hand on his shoulder.

The dockhands didn't like that either.

"...petting that foreign mutt."

"...belong in the stables. Or better yet, in a ditch somewhere."

Morisa squeezed Geth's shoulder, spoke low. "Never you mind them. They're just jealous."

Her eyes flicked to the trio of soldiers. With a pat she hurried off back to the bar. Geth sipped his ale and held his tongue.

Phelan eyed him from across the table. "Gimme your sword."

"I've got no intention of starting trouble."

"Then hand it over."

Geth unbuckled his sword belt and passed it under the table. "You know, if it's fresh starts we're at, I think I'd like a portion of that silver for a new blade.

The balance of this thing is all off. Piece of shit could shatter at any moment."

"Just don't make any problems in here, alright?"

Phelan had spoken low, but not low enough.

"Listen to the little rat. Maybe it's time to leave and make room for those that belong."

Laughter echoed from the cluster of dockhands, a good half dozen heavy-handed laborers. By the smirk one lantern-jawed braggart wore, Geth reckoned it was him that had spoken. Much as he wanted to crack his knuckles on that bastard, he supposed it was better they left.

He flagged down Morisa. "How about we settle up."

She opened her mouth but ol' Lantern-jaw edged in first. "Yeah, get 'em gone and out of our seats, foreign-loving whore."

Geth's jaw clenched, but Phelan laid a hand on his arm before he could speak. "Geth—"

He heard nothing else. Geth turned to meet Lantern-jaw's eye.

"Has someone trained his horse to talk out of its ass? I hear some muttering, but all I smell is shit."

Phelan blew out a sigh. Geth smiled at the sudden quiet that fell over the tables nearby. Lantern-jaw lifted his tankard to his lips for a calm pull before jabbing a crooked finger at Geth.

"You. Time to get your manners righted."

Geth's smile only went wider.

Every tavern had its brawler, who knew it better than him? Whether a mischief-maker or just a bad drunk, certain folk couldn't resist a fight. And in each tavern or inn there was always one scratch who considered himself the resident tough-man. By the rubbing of hands and whispers all around, Geth reckoned ol' Lantern-jaw held that title at the Journey's End. The innkeeper pleaded with the three green-cloaked soldiers, but the bastards just grinned.

"Raeg, please." Morisa said.

"This outland whoreson's about to pay for that smart mouth."

The innkeeper hurried in between them. "At least take it outside!"

Geth kicked back his chair and started for the door. "You coming, horse-face?"

A ruckus of hoots drowned out Phelan's protests. Geth edged through the crowd toward the door. Out on the cobbles, he waited. The Oathstone's shadow stretched across the wide court. A small throng already gathered on the far side of the plaza, but an exodus from the Journey's End soon matched it for size as her patrons jostled to get a view of the spectacle.

Phelan struggled through the crowd to join him. "Damn it, Geth! We haven't arrived two days ago! You wanna make us outlaws again?"

"So, it's only alright if it's you that lands us in the clink?"

"Don't be an ass."

"You think this will be the first bar fight in the history of Umbel?" Raeg had emerged from the inn and Geth flicked his chin in that direction. "With a bully like him, half these bastards will be happy to see him get thrashed."

Phelan kept spluttering but Geth ignored him.

He took stock of his adversary. He was a big one, Raeg, as tall as Geth and heavier besides. Quick too, Geth imagined. Strength was never enough alone. The bloodshot, pig-eyes that watched him indicated a nasty streak as well.

But judging from the stench, Big Raeg was even drunker than Geth. That would slow him.

"You ready to take a beating, foreign mutt?"

"Come and try me."

Raeg didn't waste any more time on words. He skipped forward with a series of jabs. Geth ducked the first, sidestepped another and caught one on his raised forearms. There was force there, but not enough to do real harm. Shouts of encouragement rang out for the local boy.

Geth countered with a straight-armed right, then a body-blow left. Raeg ducked the first punch, absorbed the second in his paunchy middle with a grunt. That pissed him off.

Spectators spit curses at Geth. There was some commotion at the back of the crowd, but he kept his focus on that lantern jaw. Raeg threw another series of jabs. Geth just kept circling, sidestepping, drawing Raeg into throwing more punches. It couldn't be long before the bastard grew tired and lost his patience.

"I'm here, horse-face. Can't catch me?"

Those words were enough to goad one final, vicious haymaker out of Raeg. Had he made contact, Geth figured that punch would've about knocked his head off. But it was just the opening he needed. Ducking under the right-handed swing, he darted inside at a crouch to unleash a ferocious upper cut, catching Raeg square under the chin. That blow, the one that rattles the teeth from the bottom up, made the bastard's eyes roll.

Geth stepped back, waiting for the man to drop. There he stood though, dazed and staggering, refusing to go down. Instead of the dramatic one-punch knockout, Geth was forced to crack the bastard one more time, a straight jab that broke his nose and sent him flat on his back.

Catcalls and jeers mixed with hoots as Geth turned to counter the inevitable rush of Raeg's fellow dockhands. Dropping to one knee as the first of them charged, he sent the man hurtling overhead into the onlookers, using momentum against him with a wrestler's toss. The second managed a kick in his ribs before he could turn. Geth groaned, but caught another kick at the ankle, giving the leg a twist that sent the bastard down to his side. By then, the landing of the first dockhand had ignited more tempers.

A full-scale brawl broke out as old scores were settled across the cobbles. Punches and curses flew. It seemed the dockhands had the most to account for.

Geth howled for joy. Morisa wailed. Phelan kept his wits about him.

"Look out!"

Geth turned in time to see steel flashing his way as Raeg came charging with a knife. There was that nasty streak.

"Bastard!" Raeg yelled.

Geth twisted to avoid his barreling weight, letting knife and body fly wide, one foot stuck out to send Raeg tripping past him, sprawling to the ground. Before he could rise, Geth stamped down hard on the back of his neck.

"Ha!" A hurled tankard made Geth duck and he left the big bastard where he was. He turned to confront his assailant, but a voice rang out, halting all combatants, some with fists still raised.

"Stop! In the name of the king!"

Green-cloaked soldiers had Geth by the arms before he could protest. Phelan, the three dockhands, and several others were shoved up against the storefront or wrestled down to the cobbles as soldiers swarmed the place.

A red-bearded captain marched through the crowd, seething. "What in the name of Uro's wrinkled asshole?"

"Easy now," Geth told the soldiers to either side. "Just a little tussle."

But someone noticed Raeg still laid on the ground. The innkeep rolled him to his back. "I think he's dead."

Geth started to disagree until Raeg's neck lolled to one side. "Thram's balls."

All eyes turned toward him, not least among them a stern pair from the red-bearded captain.

"Hang him!" someone cried. "Murderer!"

The trio of soldiers who'd been there from the start moved toward Geth, jabbing fingers and accusations.

"Hang him! Hang him from the outwall!"

"The filthy foreigner's killed one of our boys!"

Red-beard cuffed the first of them across the back of the neck. "To the keep with these three. And strip their cloaks."

He moved on to question the innkeep. Geth shook his head, amazed by how fast a bloody army had descended on the place. Over the heads of the crowd, he could just make out a mounted party clustered beneath the Oathstone. Fine cloaks and well-bred steeds indicated their station. A second group beside the monument donned odd fur-lined leathers, sat shaggy, outland beasts.

"Look, there's the knife! It was self-defense!"

Thank the gods for Morisa. She shouldered up beside the innkeep to give the captain a hurried account. He nodded as she spoke, mouth twisted like he'd got a mouthful a rotten fish. His eyes flicked from Geth to the dockhands to the weapon still resting on the floor not a pace from Raeg's limp hand.

"It's the dead man that drew the first steel." Phelan said.

"Lying foreign bastard!" one of the dockhands cursed. "That was the Turian's knife. Hang 'em!"

"You'd hang a man right here," Phelan said, "beneath the bloody Oathstone? A sworn ally, for Thram's sake?"

"Shut them up! All of them," the captain said.

His green-cloaks pushed Geth, Phelan and the others down to their knees. The captain marched back the way he'd come to entreat the mounted party looking on from beside the Oathstone. Words passed between an older man and a younger. Red-beard waved and the soldiers dragged Geth and everyone else to their feet, marched them in that direction. Geth spared a glance over his shoulder as the patrons of the Journey's End began filing back inside. He caught one last sight of Morisa, arms crossed tight, eyes wet, standing over Raeg's motionless form.

"To the keep with the lot of them," the captain said.

Geth leaned in toward Phelan. "What's going on? Who are they?"

"Those are Ilars. Guests of the king. I heard the innkeep say they brought them here to see the Oathstone. I guess we just showed them something about sworn-oaths."

Red-beard stamped over to stare him down. "Shut your mouth before I hang you myself. You're lucky it's Hadean that's king."

Chapter nine

Geth pounded the floor beneath him with a fist, cursed each of the gods in turn. One minute he was at sea, the open sky above him and dreams of new beginnings in his head. The next he was shoulder to shoulder with the wretches and drunks of Erehan Keep's dungeon.

A good week had passed, Pythelle and her offer long since gone north. At least Phelan had turned that accusatory stare elsewhere. Just inside the door of the jail room, the deposit of a new prisoner in their midst started a buzz among the assembled criminals. Geth watched until his friend returned to plop back down beside him.

"Things are happening out there," Phelan said. "That's why they've kept us so long. Unless that toothless old fart is lying."

"Like what?"

"Like someone's made an attempt on King Hadean."

Geth whistled. "Tried to kill the king?"

"That's what he says. Remember that young lordling back by the Oathstone? On the horse? That was the king. The other was his uncle."

"Well, it was probably the uncle that tried to off the lad. Plot solved."

Phelan scratched at the floor with a dirty fingernail. "You'd think. But they say it was his uncle that saved him. Killed the assassin himself."

"Funny, I don't see *him* in here, jailed for murder."

"Could have been worse. I reckon they'd have lynched us if the king hadn't been so close at hand."

Geth supposed his friend was right. "Have they caught the traitors? The ones who tried to kill the lad? Or is this the beginning of something worse"

"Could be. Toothless over there says the boy's got plenty of enemies. Not just the Ilars. Lords, cousins."

"Every bit as nasty as our lot, these blue bloods."

"You thought different?" Phelan snorted. "Anyway, things have started to quiet down again. We'll get our trial by tomorrow midday."

A trial. *Uro's puckered asshole.* Back in Pellon, a trial amounted to nothing more than a bit of fancy speech, a hefty bribe, and a pardon. So long as you had the coin to splash. Geth never did.

But if their surrounds were any indication, things might be different in Umbel. The dungeon itself sat beneath one of the four towers of the king's own keep. There were mice of course, but no rats. And the bread they doled out was only a few days old, the water fresh from the well.

The latrine stank, however, leaving Geth to ruminate on this latest predicament amid a heavy odor of piss and shit.

Beside him, Phelan kept scratching the dirt. "All this while his Ilar guests are in town, poor lad."

"Hadean?"

"They say he's been trying to tie down a peace agreement. An assassination attempt won't help his cause. I reckon your antics didn't help much either."

"Come on, you enjoyed seeing that bastard knocked out as much as me. I bet you didn't mind that I killed him either."

"Well, I mind being locked up for it."

Geth grimaced. He didn't feel good about that part. But several green-cloaks arrived at the door to haul his friend out almost at that very instant.

"What's this?" Geth sprang to his feet, fists balled. "Where are you taking him?"

"You stay." The guard moved a hand pointedly to the hilt at his waist. "This one's free to go. Apologies from the captain and all that. They say you were just a bystander. We'd have had you out sooner if we could."

Phelan balked halfway out the door. "What about my friend?"

"He gets his trial tomorrow. If he's innocent, he'll walk. If not…well, that'll be for the Asp to decide."

Geth spent more than a few hours wondering about 'the Asp.'

And well he should, with a moniker like that. Who wanted their fate decided by a cold-blooded creature of venom and fangs? The sounds of horse hooves and watercarriers in the ward above faded as the day drew to a close, but sleep didn't come.

He inspected the doorframe of his prison, peeked through the bars, up the stairway while the other prisoners snored. There was no picking the lock or cracking the hinges. A quick rush might overpower the morning guards and break him out, but then what? A bloody charge through countless warriors in the keep? And if—against all odds—he survived, what then? A life on the run, friendless, in a strange land?

"So much for a fresh start."

When the first noises of the new day filtered down to the dungeons and the guards came for them, they came with a full dozen, squashing whatever was left of that plan. They hauled the prisoners out at intervals, through the low door and up the spiral stair. The other miscreants went first, then Toothless. They came for Geth last.

"Your turn, Paellian."

This once, he prayed.

Red-handed Awer, if you're listening, don't let them string me up. There's more blood to be spilled in your name and there's few that can spill it like me. The gods all know the butchery I've commited for the beast called War. Give me a warrior's death, dammit! On some rainy field or in some rich bastard's halls. Give me that at least!

A guardsman clamped irons over his wrists and all twelve green-cloaks escorted him across the grassy inner ward of Erehan Keep. The tall doors of King Hadean's great hall yawned open. Inside, shafts of sunlight diffused down from narrow windows to light a small crowd gathered inside beneath the dais. Soldiers mingled with plain-clothed folk while a knot of straight-necks watched from one side. The leather-clad party Phelan had named Ilars joined them.

The guards marched Geth past white-stone columns, down the length of the hall. He passed Toothless coming the other way. "Please Lord, mercy!" the man cried.

A soldier at each elbow dragged him out. A third green-cloak followed, rope in hand. Geth muttered a curse.

If that wasn't enough, the three soldiers from the Journey's End and several of Raeg's friends waited up ahead. The crowd parted as they arrived. Beneath the gilded chair of Umbel's kings, a balding man with a thin neck and bony nose sat behind a table strewn with parchments.

"That's the Asp? Looks more like a worm to me."

One of the guards snickered. A stern look from his sergeant cut him off. Geth was relieved to find Phelan, Morisa, and the innkeep from the Journey's End's clustered at the front of the crowd.

The sergeant thrust Geth forward before the judge's table. "Master Melagus, this is the Paellian charged—"

"I know who he is." The worm tapped his parchments. He turned toward a scribe seated at a second table that had been concealed by all the standing folk. The worm waited for the man to dip his pen. He turned back toward Geth.

"You are charged with murder. What is your name?"

"Geth, my lord."

"Son of…?"

"Just Geth, my lord."

The worm's nose wrinkled. "Geth…of Pellon."

The scribe's quill scratched, and the trial began.

"You have been accused of murder, Geth of Pellon. Under King Hadean's rule, every man has the right to a trial. Even those of foreigner origin. We will hear all accounts. If you are found guilty, you will be hanged."

Geth looked up at that bony, stern-eyed face. Somehow it encapsulated all the haughty, hateful, self-assured higher-ups Geth had ever known. He thought of poor Toothless, dead already perhaps. And now his own fate rested in this callous bastard's hands.

The trial began with the account of his accusers. One by one the three dockhands gave their version of events. According to them, Geth had picked the fight and even drew the knife that Raeg had tried to kill him with. The part where he stamped on their friend's neck, they got right. Geth stared fire at them all the while.

The innkeep spoke next. The man had the decency to admit Raeg had started more than a few brawls in his establishment, though he couldn't say how this particular scrape began. Or who drew the weapon. Of

Geth's character he could only say he was a man who paid his tab.

Morisa, gods bless her, did him true. "Raeg was jealous. He called me names, called Geth here names as well. It was him that started the fight, came with that knife too. I saw it and so did everyone else. That's Neyna's sweet truth."

The worm listened well as she spoke. She met Geth's eye for only an instant, then hurried to be gone, arms crossed tight across her chest. Geth watched her exit and sighed. A good woman, he reckoned. Too good for the likes of him.

He didn't dwell on that for long. The arrival of one of the three green-cloaks that had watched the fight turned Geth's eyes forward again. Dare he count on the word of a fellow warrior, a brother in arms?

Not him. This green-cloak, a sergeant no less, lied even worse than the rest.

"...and may the gods curse me if it's not true," their sergeant finished, "but this foreign fellow had been thrashed so bad he knew he was beat, so he pulled his knife on the other. I saw it all, Lord Melagus. I tried to stop it then, but they wrestled until he came out on top, stamped down on the other sending him to Vorda's cold arms."

Geth spit on the ground toward the green-cloak's feet. "Lying cunt."

Phelan's voice carried over the murmur of the crowd. "Easy now."

"Is this what happened?" The worm's eyes found Phelan. "Speak if you are a friend of the accused."

The green-cloak cast a sideways glance in Phelan's direction and stepped back. Phelan gave him a glare as he moved forward to take his place. He bowed for the worm, groveled almost.

"My lord, let me tell you what kind of man you've shackled and accused."

Geth cocked an ear, half curious, half terrified where the little rogue might be going with this. Phelan began with the good deeds, a list of lies so long Geth reckoned he must have rehearsed them. He wished Morisa could have heard. From feeding beggars to saving widows to tending to the sick back during the Affliction. He made sure to mention how the big warrior stood up for one poor, derided barmaid, as well. A local girl, as it happened.

All out of lies, Phelan frowned.

"We've heard—" the worm started, but the little man cut him off.

"There's more."

He ventured into parts unknown to a tongue like his; the truth. Like the months Geth had protected a gravedigger priest, even lent a hand at the shovel while the cleric followed his humble but sacred calling. Phelan told the worm about the time Geth freed the human cargo of an Iyrund slave ship. He finished with the time he saved an orphaned country boy from hunger and abuse on the hard streets of Sorn.

Phelan's eyes were wide and blue as he finished that one. If Geth was an emotional man, he might have squeezed a tear. But the worm was watching, and a helluva lot of other people. He snorted the itch from his nose and lifted his chin, proud for once. The lot of these Umbel bastards be damned.

The court went silent for a moment until a chorus of angry shouts erupted all at once. The sergeant's natural authority won out. "Lies, my lord. Plain and simple."

"Let us hear his own account," the worm replied. "Afterward, I shall give my judgment."

A hand in the back shoved Geth forward. He glared over his shoulder, straightened up to face the worm.

"Well?" the bony bastard asked.

"I didn't start the fight, m'lord. And I didn't draw that blade either. I was only defending myself. That's not a crime in these parts, is it? As for these men, they're all liars. Two men don't pick a fight with four, my lord. That's common sense."

"Is this all you have to say?" The worm arched an eyebrow.

"You've heard the truth three times now. Isn't that enough?"

The worm ticked off fingers. "Once from the barmaid and once from your friend. I'm afraid I cannot accept your account with the dead man unable to give an account of his own. That's two. With four accounts to the contrary."

"Four sets of lies from four shitless liars. Isn't it a crime to lie to one such as yourself?"

"It is."

"That man's a killer!" The sergeant stabbed a finger at Geth. "Don't be fooled, Master Melagus. You've heard the words of four Umbelmen. The three others may have been friends of the fallen, but

I myself am friend to neither side, just an honest steward of the realm."

"Steward of the realm?" The worm's mouth twisted. "One of the same three stewards who stood by and did nothing to intervene?"

"Now—"

"I trust you've been reprimanded by Captain Utrand already. If not, may his justice come swiftly."

The sergeant melted back into the crowd.

"So, I must weigh the tale of a barmaid and a foreigner against the word of a sergeant and three other witnesses."

"My lord," Phelan said. "I think there may be one more witness."

The crowd stirred as a well-appointed woman in her middle years shouldered through to bow before the judge's table. Geth blinked. Robed in her finery, he hardly recognized Captain Rondah.

"My lady."

By the looks of it, the worm already knew her. The scribe's quill scratched before she'd given so much as an introduction. Rondah spared Geth no more than a glance.

"I'm here to speak on behalf of the accused."

The worm nodded. "Did you know he killed a man? He doesn't deny it."

"I know he rowed for me all the way from Pellon without so much as a peep. He never once shirked or complained. And I'd have him back in the spring should he wish to return to sea."

"Did he mention why he left Pellon in the first place?"

"Does it matter?"

"It might tell us something of the man's character."

Rondah turned toward Geth, met his eye. "He said he wanted to see the Oathstone. But perhaps we've shown him the truth of those bonds. A foreigner's word counts for little here, even those of a sworn ally."

The worm heaved a sigh. "I do appreciate your contribution, Captain Rondah, but I'm afraid your testament to his character has little bearing on the true order of events. I must weigh the account of seven witnesses and the foreigner who stands accused."

The foreigner. That bony face turned toward Geth. In that moment he knew he would hang. The worm had heard enough. *The Asp*. He wasn't going to take the word of a lowborn foreigner and a barmaid over the word of four of his own subjects. Two against four. It was simple math.

The Asp looked down to straighten his parchments. "If there are no more witnesses, we must move forward. We have a full docket of grievances to attend to. The matter here is decided. Murder was committed and this man—"

Geth threw an elbow to either side of him before he could finish, stunning the green-cloaks beside him. Their grip loosened enough for him to twist free. In one bound he was at the Asp's table, throwing a leg up to slide over the surface and land directly on top of him. He dragged the bony bastard to his feet with him as he rose, manacle chain stretched around his neck.

Swords rasped out of scabbards. Shocked cries rang out. Some at the back of the crowd fled.

"Everyone back or the judge dies!"

"Help!" The Asp struggled for a brief moment, then went limp.

"Kill the bastard!" the sergeant cried. Green-cloaks crept closer. Geth's grip on the Asp tightened.

"Wait!" Phelan forced himself between them as Geth backed himself up against a wall. "Make reason! Otherwise, the king's counselor dies!"

As if he'd heard his name, the king himself parted the crowd. Geth knew him by the circlet around his head, realized he must have been among the highborn off to the side. The hall went quiet. Young, hazel eyes met a world-weary dark pair. Behind the king, a middle-aged nobleman clutched his sword. Several more green-cloaks and those leather-clad Ilars followed behind the pair.

"What's going on here?" the king demanded.

"Ask him," Geth said, flicked his chin at the hostage pulled up against his chest. "He was about to hang an innocent man."

The king looked to his counselor. Geth loosened the chain across his neck to allow the little bastard to speak.

"The trial of a murderer—"

A chorus of shouts drowned him out. "He killed a man!"

"He's innocent!"

"No, he's not!"

"That man tried to stab him!"

"Silence!"

The king stepped over to the scribe and his record. He wasn't stupid, young or no. The same red-bearded green-cloak from outside the Journey's End joined the king along with the older nobleman. Geth strained to hear their words over the counselor's wheezing. The captain whispered furiously in the king's ear, but the young man shook his head. He turned back toward Geth.

"You killed a man and do not deny it," he said. "How is it you claim to be innocent?"

"That man tried to kill me first."

"Can you prove it?"

Geth frowned, thinking. *The soldiers.* "There were two other soldiers with the sergeant that night. They saw the whole thing. They know the other bastards are lying."

"Are they here?"

A pair of wide-eyed green cloaks were hauled up from the back of the crowd. The red-bearded captain took the first by the collar.

"Speak the truth now to your king. Thram be my witness, I swear I'll have your hide if you lie!"

"Tell him, you bastard!" Geth flexed the chain around the counselor's neck. "Tell him or this one's done. I'll be damned if I die at the end of a rope."

The king met Geth's eye, hands raised. "Calmly now. How can we expect the truth while you threaten the counselor's life?"

Geth looked up. Dozens of swords tilted toward him, waiting. He searched that young face. Nothing there but sincerity. The chain came over the Asp's head and Geth shoved him forward into the king's arms. "My life is in your hands now."

"Dear gods!" The counselor rubbed his neck and gasped like a two-copper whore.

Soldiers growled, edged forward. But the king silenced them with a glare, sent them back before they could rush. He turned to the two wide-eyed soldiers.

"You. You've saved my counselor's life, and I commend you for it. I absolve you of any wrongdoing. Now tell me what you saw."

The truth tumbled out of these green-cloaks. Melagus looked like he'd swallowed a goat's turd, but tensions eased throughout the hall. Phelan broke the silence.

"So, are we free?"

The red-bearded captain gestured toward Geth with his sword. "He's still killed a man, my king. I was there."

King Hadean's brow furrowed. "But it seems it was in self-defense."

"And that bastard over there meant to hang me for it," Geth said.

"Where is the sergeant?" said the Asp, quick to shift the blame. "And those duplicitous dockhands."

The four of them had slunk away, leaving captain, counselor, and king frowning at one another. A trill of laughter sounded from the leather-clad contingent. Red-beard muttered a curse. "Find them!"

Geth noticed for the first time there was a woman among the Ilars, clad the same as the men, standing taller than some. But the older nobleman stepped up close to the king just then, speaking under his breath.

"I'm told this man arrived in Umbel with a sword among his possessions." He flicked a meaningful glance toward the Ilars a few paces off.

King Hadean nodded. "A man has been killed," he said, loud enough to carry. "We can hardly release you without some reparation. And yet I see no weeping widow. Therefore, let your debt be paid to the realm."

"To the realm?" Geth's eyes narrowed. Phelan's eyes went wide.

"You will serve your penance with Lord Eldric's men at the Boundaries," Hadean said. "For a year and a day, as is the custom."

Geth opened his mouth, but the Asp struck first. "It will be winter soon. Maybe that will be enough to cool your temper."

Chapter ten

Captain Utrand produced a ring of iron keys and removed Geth's manacles himself. "You stay within the walls of the keep. If you leave, you're a deserter. No trial for that, just the rope."

Geth nodded. Red-beard disappeared out into the ward and the entire gathering melted away, leaving the big warrior standing with just Phelan at the center of the great hall. The little man knuckled his brow at the last departing green-cloaks.

"I can gather our things from the inn," he said out of the side of his mouth, "and we can be on our way by nightfall."

Geth shook his head. "I'm not leaving on the run again, Phelan."

"Well, I'm not partial to crawling up the Hoarwind's ass. You heard that snake, it'll be winter soon."

"You still got any silver?"

"You serious?"

"There's a lot of possibilities for you if you've still got coin. You don't have to do this."

Phelan's mouth opened, intent to curse Geth to Eria's bowels, no doubt. But something caught him short. He cursed himself instead.

"Oh, what does it matter? It's over. We've been conscripted."

Geth smiled. "Thanks, Phelan. And hey, who knows? Maybe you'll like it."

"That's not funny."

They turned to follow the exodus from the hall, past white stone columns and dour-faced kings on faded tapestries.

"It won't be so bad." Geth said. "We've done soldier's work before."

"I didn't come here to dig ditches. Or take a blade in the gut from some savage. I've heard things have got pretty hairy upriver. Raids and the like, the odd homestead burned."

"Where'd you hear all that?"

"I spent the last couple days in the city's taverns."

"So, you *don't* have any silver left."

"I was looking for Rondah, you ungrateful jackass. To get you free. I ended up having to go through Addie to catch up with her. That wasn't cheap."

"Thanks for that."

Geth turned for one last look at the hall as the great doors swung closed behind them. Melagus's table and parchments stood unattended, likewise the great gilded chair of the king. Rondah's words hadn't hurt, but it was young Hadean that had saved him.

"Did they really try to kill the boy?" he asked.

"The king?" Phelan nodded. "They sure did. Never heard if they uncovered the plot though."

"Could have been the Ilars. Then again, who would take the throne if he were gone? They might prefer an untried lad wearing the crown."

Phelan shrugged. They emerged into the ward. The comings and goings of a busy keep flowed around them. Across the grassy expanse, the king and his Ilar guests milled around beside a stable, preparing their steeds for an outing of some sort.

"He seems a fair lad, this king," Geth said

"Fair to you, weak to them."

Geth followed Phelan's gaze to the party of Ilars, fur-lined cloaks thrown open to catch the sunshine. There were fighters among them, but they were a mismatched bunch, standing a little apart as if to emphasize the point. That big woman for one, sword slung casually at her side, plain and yet haughty and beautiful at the same time. A great, yellow-bearded Ilar stamped around like he was in charge, but a handsome fellow with a sharp chin and clever eyes looked the brains of the company. A stumpy, middle-aged Ilar wandered the ward like an errant child as well, huge dog following on his heels, at least half wolf unless Geth was mistaken.

"You should have heard 'em," Phelan said. "They're licking their chops. Division among the Sworn Realms, a tender boy-king on the throne..."

Geth's eyes swung back to young Hadean. How would it sit if the boy that saved him got himself drawn into a war all because his enemies had witnessed a show of pity for a downtrodden foreigner?

"I'm not allowed to leave the keep," he told Phelan. "But you should head back to the inn."

"Fetch our things?"

"Yeah. But not so we can leave."

Phelan sighed, started off.

"Oh, and Phelan—" Geth waited for his friend to turn. "Don't forget my sword."

A troop of green-cloaks hauled the lying sergeant from Geth's trial through the keep's high gates just before sunset. They'd stripped him of the green, standing him up before Utrand. Geth and Phelan watched from a sunny patch beside the walls.

"Looks like they caught the scratch," Geth said.

"Lying bastard."

Captain Utrand dressed him down good. Geth whistled loud enough to be heard. That drew a hateful stare.

Utrand followed the ex-sergeant's eyes until they found Geth. He stabbed a finger directly at him and motioned toward the center of the ward. Geth grimaced.

"These Umbelmen waste no time," Phelan muttered.

Utrand assembled a line of men alongside the disgraced sergeant. Young men mostly, the usual sort. The Asp's scribe hurried over with a ledger and ink. The drum of horse hooves announced the arrival of the king himself, trailed by the older nobleman, Eldric, King Hadean's uncle by the looks of it.

"Hadean himself is gonna swear us in?" Geth could hardly believe it.

"Twice in one day, this scratch."

"Have you ever even stood this close to King Elius?"

The king swung out of the saddle. Captain Utrand and the Lord Eldric flanked him as the line of recruits were directed to take a knee. That bastard sergeant knelt beside them, renewing his oaths all over again by the looks of it. King Hadean stood near Geth at the center of the line.

"Today in the keep of Erehan the Young," Hadean said, "you receive your cloak. Before all the gods, you will swear allegiance to Umbel, your king, and Lord Eldric of Greenfell. Serve them with honor."

He stepped to one end of the line. Utrand draped a fresh cloak of forest green over the first man's shoulders. The king drew his sword. Standing the blade on its point, he clutched the wide-eyed recruit's hand against the hilt.

"Do you swear your sword and your life to me? To Umbel and Lord Eldric of Towerrock?"

"I-I swear it."

"Let the gods and all those gathered bear witness."

The soldier rose. Hadean continued down the line until he came to Geth. He sheathed his own weapon and motioned the big warrior to draw his own blade, to stand it point-down in the earth. The king's hand closed over Geth's on the hilt. He met those unwavering eyes.

"Do you swear your sword and your life to me, Geth of Pellon? To Umbel and to Lord Eldric?"

"I swear to you." Geth rose with the green wool of Umbel across his shoulders.

Hadean helped him to his feet. He congratulated each of his new recruits, and the scribe penned their names into his ledger. Thick wool sat heavy and warm over Geth's arms. It was done, a new start.

Geth looked down the line at the other new-sworn soldiers. Not a one had any idea what was in store, he reckoned. Except that bastard lying at the end.

Geth bent an ear to catch the ex-sergeant's name as he spoke to the scribe. *Gylfric*. He wouldn't forget it.

A curse from Phelan distracted him before his imagination could get too carried away with the different ways he might get even. The little man adjusted his new cloak over his frame. "Need to get this bloody thing hemmed."

Geth opened his mouth to taunt him, but the crunch of boot heels turned them both. Lord Eldric studied the pair with a sober eye.

"M'lord." Geth took a knee. Phelan followed suit.

"Rise. You're under my command now. I have no use for men on their knees."

Geth stood.

"I have no use for men who turn and run either," Eldric said. "Should I worry about you running?"

"No, Lord."

"I won't chase you. But you'll be an outlaw. If you are caught, you will be hanged. This realm's not as big as Pellon so better you didn't bother with running at all."

"I understand Lord."

Eldric nodded.

Geth studied the king's uncle in turn. There was no doubting the family resemblance. He stood of a height with young Hadean, shared the same chiseled features and hazel eyes, though his close-cropped hair had gone more salt than pepper. Geth reckoned this one had seen a dust-up or two. The way those hazel eyes went to the sword at Geth's waist confirmed it.

"You know what to do with that?" the lord asked.

Geth dipped his head. "I've used it before."

"And you're good with your hands as well if you thrashed four men at the Journey's End."

"M'lord—"

Eldric didn't let him finish. "I could use a man like you at Towerrock. If you're willing. Anyone can dig trenches and fletch arrows at the boundary forts."

Geth blinked. He flicked a triumphant glance at Phelan. "It would be an honor to serve, lord."

"Good. Take your rest. Your footman too. We set out at dawn."

Morning broke over Erehan Keep. Horses fidgeted as cinches were tightened, baggage stuffed. Men shivered in the cool air as two dozen riders assembled on the grass of the ward. Geth, Phelan and the rest of the new green-cloaks ate biscuits and drank well-water as they waited on foot.

"I still can't believe we've landed in the bloody army," Phelan said.

Geth licked crumbs from his fingertips. "Could've been a lot worse. Hadean's a good boy—a good man, I should say. And as for Eldric, he's a tough one I reckon, but decent. Done right by his nephew."

"He thinks I'm your footman. He actually called me that."

"It would be good to have a manservant, I'll not lie."

Phelan glared at him.

Geth laughed.

The company formed up near the gates. Geth slung his satchel over one shoulder. Phelan muttered his usual curses and followed suit. A baggage train of two covered wagons filed in behind the mounted green-cloaks, leaving the pair to walk among the other new recruits at the rear.

"Did you ever stop to think why we came here?" Phelan asked.

Wagon wheels creaked. They began their descent.

"To avoid the Tower of the Moon?"

"Don't be a wise ass, Geth. Not this early in the morning."

"I thought you liked the idea of starting over?"

"All I'm saying is, what's here for us? Especially after the Affliction. Nothing but farmland and locals who hate us."

Geth held his voice low. "Come on, Phelan. I didn't make you take that cloak. You chose to. And it's you that chose Umbel in the first place."

"It was the only ship—"

"Did you really expect to find another Golden City waiting? Dice and liquor and whores 'til we used up our coin or drank ourselves dead?"

"I haven't had a decent drink in weeks. Or a she-cat to tumble, now you mention it."

"Those things are just fine—you know I've enjoyed my share. But we can't live off that. These cloaks on our backs will give us the means to earn a few silvers. That way you can pay for your women and your ale."

"Coppers, not silvers. A pittance."

"Don't you worry. My sword will win us favor. Your wits as well. We'll be at Eldric's right-hand within the month, watch and see. That'll bring gold. That's what you really want isn't it?"

"You think you know me so well?"

"If gold's not enough, wait 'til I tell you what I've heard about the lands upriver." Geth cast an exaggerated glance to either side. "They say the Ilar women are like spring flowers. And none too virtuous, if you understand me."

"Thram's balls, you're a terrible liar. But women of all lands do tend to forget virtue in my company."

Geth grinned. Phelan puffed out his chest, straightened his belt, and they shared a laugh. They had each other and now they had work. For Geth, that was enough.

Down from Erehan Keep's knobby hill, past the first thatched-rooftops shops of Umbel City, they crossed under grey-white ramparts of the outwall and into the surrounding countryside. A wide track scored by hoofmarks and wagon ruts led inland. Eldric drew them to a halt as a second party joined them.

Phelan's eyes narrowed. "Is that who I think it is?"

It was. Geth shielded his eyes to get a better look. No mistaking those leathers and furs, that handsome woman with the sword, the stumpy scratch with his wolfdog.

"Ilars."

Phelan whistled. "Didn't see that coming."

Eldric started them up again, the tribesmen swelling their ranks with dignitaries on shaggy steeds, retainers padding along behind. Their road shadowed the North River's lazy curves through autumn-colored hills, green pastures, and fresh harvested fields. Lush. Peaceful. Idyllic almost.

But Phelan's skepticism wasn't misplaced. Geth twisted to have a look over one shoulder. Gylfric trudged along behind them, a man he'd sooner strangle than fight alongside.

Up ahead, Lord Eldric made nice with their enemies, riding next to that handsome, clever-eyed Ilar, but the other outlanders spurred their steeds in distinct clusters along the column. No accord even among them.

Phelan eyed the Umbelmen as they made camp. "Each to his own it looks like." Eldric and his officers lit their own fires while the Ilars separated to kindle four separate campfires as well. Lower ranked green-cloaks made their own set-up. Gylfric and most of the other new conscripts formed yet another circle.

Geth dropped his satchel and marched off to gather wood while Phelan picked their spot. Geth returned to find them set up between the Ilars and Umbelmen. The little man bent an ear toward the tribesmen as he arranged the kindling.

With a few strikes at his flint, the fire took. He made a show of dusting off his hands.

"Well?" Geth whispered. He tore off a strip of the dried salt-beef that had been doled out and handed a piece over.

"They aren't friends, these Ilars."

"That right?"

"With each other I mean."

"I could have told you that much."

"They're all from different tribes. If they're anything like the Mog, that'll mean plenty of bad blood."

Geth adjusted his legs to lean a little closer. "What I want to know is this: if you were gonna set us up by these Ilars, why not get us closer to the woman instead of that ball-scratcher and his dog?"

"That sow? I'll never understand you."

Geth ignored him. "You seen that beast? At least half wolf I tell ya."

"It is. And that Ilar fella talks to it too."

Geth blinked. He knew what Phelan meant. "Can *you* talk to it?"

"I don't know. But I'll tell you one thing, that man's a sorcerer. Talking to a wolf isn't the only thing he can do."

Phelan's gift with languages wasn't something they ever spoke about, but when it came to such magicks, Geth reckoned his friend knew a thing or two. He eyed the stumpy northerner. Course brown hair, shot through with silver, had been molded into spikes that stuck out in every direction. Deep lines crisscrossed his forehead and the white in his beard gleamed red in the firelight.

"Wolfie there," Phelan went on, "he represents one tribe. The woman, the pretty man, and that big, yellow-bearded prick each represent their own.

Yellow-beard's feeling strong now that Umbel's got a scraggle-bearded youth on the throne. The woman too. I can't say for certain about the others."

"That must be why these Ilars came south," Geth said. "To size Hadean up. Explains why Eldric's moving fighters north as well."

Phelan prodded the fire with a stick to send a chimney of bright embers up into the night. Geth watched them swirl and burn. *All the right ingredients.* And here they sat, right beside Umbel's age-old enemies, green-cloaks across their shoulders.

Not that those cloaks had won them any friends. Foreign scum, mercenary bastards—Geth hadn't missed the soldiers' mutterings. And Gylfric had a score to settle of his own. Geth eased onto his back for sleep, satchel under his head. One hand never left the hilt of his sword.

Chapter eleven

A shout drew Geth's attention mid-march the next day. "What's happening?"

Phelan shielded his eyes and stepped wide to peer around the man in front of him. A fight had erupted further up the column. Best Geth could tell, three green-cloaks had jumped a fourth. The big warrior's frown reversed itself as he recognized Gylfric on the receiving end.

"Well, that's the sweetest sight I've seen since we first made land."

"Ouch! Nice kick." Phelan chuckled. "Looked like it hurt."

Eldric's second-in-command arrived within seconds, sword drawn and flanked by two grim-faced warriors. Three panting green-cloaks backed up, hands raised at their approach. Gylfric lay in a groaning pile in the middle of the road.

"What's this!" The second jabbed his blade in the direction of the three.

"He's the bastard that lied to the king. Whoreson cheated us at dice last night on top of that."

Gylfric spit blood from his mouth. "I beat 'em fair and square. Everyone knows it's all luck. I was due for a turn of luck, that's for sure."

Geth cupped a hand to his mouth. "Got a slick tongue! Watch him!" he put in.

The second's eye darted in his direction but Geth ducked behind the man in front of him. Phelan snickered.

From the sound of things, all four combatants were docked a week's pay and the column was on the march again. Geth wondered if the Ilars had seen, what they made of that. Gylfric trudged on with a swollen lip, a purple eye, friendless as a man with a cough during the Affliction.

That beating hadn't earned Geth any friends, but damn if it didn't feel good just to see it. Stands of broadleaf on the hilltops burst orange, red and yellow among a few evergreens. Cool air flowed sweet with every breath.

Perhaps it was the air, maybe the scenery, but hearts seemed to have lightened. Geth hummed as they marched. The soldiers took to singing and jest. Their road passed some village or homestead every few miles, the first sign often an abandoned cottage or plot of freshly turned earth that could only mark a grave site, but life moved briskly within each settlement. Farmwives hauled onions or prodded wagons stacked with hay while field hands harvested the last of the season's wheat. Children shepherded their woolly flocks, hailing the column with waves and shouts. In the towns, shopkeepers and craftsmen put down their tools to fetch water for those in green. That included Geth and Phelan.

"Not a bad folk," Geth told his friend after an old man in black left them with a dripping bucket.

Phelan shrugged. "As long as they don't hear our accents."

He spoke the truth. No one knew they were foreigners here. But their courtesy said something just the same. Back in Pellon, village folk were more likely to run from an approaching column of lilies than serve them cool water. And those lilies were just as likely to rob them. Maybe it was the sight of Gylfric's fat lip, or the honest sweat of a day's march, but Geth supposed Umbel was growing on him.

The column moved north without incident for two days before halting on the outskirts of a large, fortified town.

"You two stay here with the baggage train," Eldric's second told them. The column disbanded in threes and fours, headed for the town's many alehouses judging by the backslapping and grins. The Ilars joined Eldric and his men, wolfdog and all. A few others stayed behind, whether by order or not, Geth couldn't say. Gylfric was among them.

Geth resisted the temptation to throw the bastard in the river. He eyed the other stragglers, wondered what their crime could have been or if they'd just drawn the short straw. A pair of sour-faced green-cloaks tramped around the place, presumably to keep an eye on things, and a few Ilars had stayed to mind their horses. A young spear-bearer sat apart from the rest; his boyish frame swallowed in his man-sized green cloak.

Geth stepped over to plop down beside him. "Alright if I sit here?"

The boy shrugged.

"I don't want anything, don't worry. But maybe you can tell me why they hate us Paellians. First thing we see when we land in Umbel is the Oathstone, reminding us we're sworn-allies. Next thing we know, a whole tavern wants our nuts roasted."

That earned a smile. "Didn't used to be that way," the boy said. "Least I don't think so. But some say it was foreign witchcraft that brought the Affliction to Umbel. Everyone lost somebody."

"You too?" Geth already knew the answer. No other reason for a beardless boy to take up with the army.

"I like soldiering. And they've been good to me."

The lad looked away, far too knowing, those eyes on such a young face. Geth cursed inwardly. Back home, the Affliction was more than a year behind them. But that scourge had arrived late here in

Umbel. By the fresh graves and black of mourning, Geth reckoned the worst of it just months gone.

"There may be some truth that those bad airs came from afar," Geth said, "but I can tell you no one in Pellon meant to send them here. And it didn't start there either. It just jumped from man to man like fleas. We lost a lot of good folk too."

"I know it's none of your fault."

Geth extended a hand. He was glad when the boy took it. "I'm Geth. That's Phelan."

Serious blue eyes framed by straw-yellow hair flicked to Phelan and back. "Kerrel, son of Nevid. You've got one friend in Umbel now. I reckon you've still got some enemies though."

"Ha!" Geth flicking a glance toward Gylfric. "You're worth a dozen of that lot."

Kerrel smiled.

The sound of horse hooves turned them down the road. Eldric and a younger man appeared at the head of a mounted column, heading their way. By the unsoiled tunic and somber carriage, Geth supposed the second rider was a lord himself.

"...at Towerrock and the boundary forts," Geth heard the king's uncle say. "We'll need more men at Point-fort too."

"Of course."

As they came closer, Geth sensed a palpable tension between the pair.

"Every man and boy that can be found, Brant." Eldric aimed a stern eye at the younger lord. "These Ilars want only one thing. Iyngaer of Dues is set on grabbing what he can. Othwid and the Arnui share his mind. They'll accept neither gift nor gold."

"Two Ilar chieftains in agreement? I hardly believe it. You should have met them separately. Offer gold to the one and not the other and see how quick they remember their differences."

"Gold won't do this time. Iyngaer's seen to that."

"Steel then."

"It's only a matter of time."

The one called Brant spurred his horse toward the other end of camp. Eldric frowned at his departing back. Geth waved Kerrel over.

"What's the rub between those two?"

"Lord Eldric and Lord Brant? That's his son."

Father and son. "Figures."

Phelan stepped up beside Geth, pulled him out of Kerrel's earshot. "Forget the family feud, it's all this talk of gold and steel that's got me nervous."

"We've been caught up in something, looks like. Something big."

"I was afraid you might say that."

Geth flared his nostrils, drew a deep breath. "War is on the kettle, Phelan. Can't you smell it?"

The prospect of war didn't trouble Geth. The beauty of Umbel didn't lessen as they traveled either. That wolfdog dropped back in the file to loll at Geth's side. He scratched the dog's ears and hummed with each step.

Brant and a good twenty additional warriors joined them from Waterset heading north. Eldric spent more time riding alongside that one handsome Ilar than his son, pointing out landmarks, perhaps describing crops and produce. To their right, a yellow, cultivated flood-plain faded into rolling hills. To the left, Vorus, the mighty river of the North, flowed through the heart of it all.

"We'll reach the Tooth later today," Kerrel told Geth one afternoon.

"The Tooth?"

"Towerrock, Umbel's fortress in the North. Lord Eldric keeps his household there. Looks like a big white tooth from a distance."

Kerrel seemed satisfied with the explanation, but a brown-bearded fighter wagged a finger, one of the three that had thrashed Gylfric, if Geth wasn't mistaken. "That's not why they call it the Tooth. It's because it grinds up the enemy. You'll like it there."

Geth blinked, surprised but pleased to be addressed by any of the Umbelmen. Maybe Kerrel had put in a good word for him.

It wasn't much longer before they topped a rise to gaze out into the hazy distance at the great fastness of Towerrock. Brown and yellow fields stretched as far as the eye could see to either side of the gleaming ribbon of Vorus. A thatch-roofed settlement sat snug beside the banks. The fortification itself stood on a small island around which the river flowed blue-green and sluggish. It did appear something like a white, rectangular tooth from that approach. As the miles closed, Geth counted five formidable towers plus a staunch gatehouse with a wooden bridge spanning the water eastwards toward the town.

"Now that's a fortress," Phelan said. "Burn the bridge and all seven gods together couldn't fight their way in."

Geth squinted up at the ramparts. "Easy enough to withstand a siege I suppose, but hard to mount a sally. And all that water will count for nothing in a few months when the river's frozen over."

"Hadn't thought of that."

Indeed, winter had already begun to push south with the solstice still months away. Night's chill found its way into old injuries and men grumbled at the start of each day. All except the Ilars.

"I reckon it wasn't Kerrel but the other fellow who was right about why they call it 'The Tooth,'" Geth said. "This fort was built to force an invading army to lay siege, thinning out the main attacking thrust. From here, they wear down the enemy."

"And leave the countryside to fend for itself?"

"Can't fit them all inside, can they?"

"Couldn't feed them for very long, that's for sure."

Geth nodded. "And any decisive victory would still have to be won in the field."

Their path wound through countryside and eventually among the shops and the homes of the town at the river's edge. Horse hooves thumped hollowly on timber as they crossed the bridge they'd seen toward the stone walls of Towerrock. Umbel's green and white banners flew from every tower. A horn blew within and the huge portcullis jerked upward on squealing pulleys to reveal a handful of warriors and minders waiting at the threshold. A bald-pated steward, a few paunchy noblemen, and a grizzled bear of a man with a sword at his waist. Geth was content to ignore the pleasantries until he noticed the fiery red tresses of the witch Pythelle among them.

"Isn't that—" Phelan started.

"Shush!" Geth held up a finger. "I want to hear what they're saying."

The steward and noblemen finished their bootlicking, and the grizzled bear straightened his great beard to give a stiff report. He eyed the Ilar contingent warily. Geth edged forward to listen in as the witch curtsied in front of the Lord Eldric.

"Welcome home, my lord. You'll find all in order, as Master Wayan has said. I shall personally oversee the preparation of your dinner banquet."

Eldric smiled. "You have my thanks, Lady. A bath first, we shall sup together. All of us."

His look encompassed the bald steward and noblemen but skipped over the grizzled fighter. *No love lost there,* Geth mused. The bear watched Pythelle with narrowed eyes.

That look changed with the arrival of Brant. Those two embraced warmly. Eldric moved inside, crowded around by his hangers-on. Only Pythelle remained behind. She smirked at Geth as he passed across the threshold.

"A Paellian in green is still a Paellian, is he not?"

Geth bowed stiffly. "I'm Umbel's man now. I swore an oath."

"I heard about your dealings with Melagus."

Geth could see why they called her witch. He didn't ask how she'd already learned of his trial. "That's all behind me now," he said instead.

"Well spoken."

With an Umbel-style salute of fist to heart, Geth continued inside the keep. Noises of men and horses filled the ward. Phelan leaned close to one ear.

"What do you make of it?"

"Pythelle? There's something afoot. Why hire a couple foreign bodyguards unless she thought she needed protection."

"Right. No need for protection if your fingernails are clean."

Geth remembered the attempt on young Hadean's life back in Umbel City. Could it have been her? To what end? Then again, she certainly seemed cozy with Eldric, the man that had saved the king's life.

"Keep an eye open," he said. "Smells like there's more cooking here than just a war with the tribes."

Phelan nodded. "Speaking of Ilars, am I the only one thinks it strange Eldric would invite his enemies inside the fortress?"

Geth turned to watch the leather-clad contingent lead their shaggy steeds toward the stable. Greencloaks crowded thick on the walls and atop the towers above. The way the tribesmen craned their necks, they hadn't missed it either.

"I reckon it's a kind of deterrence," he said.

"My father did the same thing. He kept a big stick around, made sure I could see it."

"Didn't work though, did it."

"When I did get into trouble, I stole the stick and threw it in the woods."

"Yeah?"

"He kept a spare."

Chapter twelve

Towerrock was a staunch fortress, as staunch as any Geth had seen. He walked its walls, explored every inch he could. It occupied the whole of its river island and stood roughly teardrop shaped, the southward bulb comprised of a wide inner ward with barracks, stables, kitchens, smithies and more, all built up against the curtain walls. Four towers and that massive gatehouse watched over. A small dock and man-made breakwater protruded from the west-facing side, hidden from view when he'd first arrived. His warrior eye reckoned this a key feature in the fort's defense as a point of escape or sally. The tapering northern end, which curved to follow the contours of the lands beneath, contained a much smaller green, along with the lord's chamber and hall. Towerrock's fifth and highest tower stood at the teardrop's point, furthest north, a true keep and final bastion of defense.

Phelan had left on some excursion of his own and didn't return until nightfall. "Looks like you were right about Umbel preparing for war," he said. After a cursory meal, they spread their blankets on a rush-strewn floor alongside the other new arrivals in a barracks bereft of amenity except a single blazing hearth.

"Did you ever doubt me?" Geth asked.

Phelan knew the signs as well as anyone. Fletchers sighted their shafts in the ward, whetstones and steel made rasping music. The smoke of the smithies wafted everywhere. And there was too much laughter among the younger soldiers, too little among the older. Eldric and the grizzled Captain Wayan barely smiled at all.

"You think they'll let us range a bit tomorrow?" Phelan tucked his hands behind his head to stare up at the rafters. "I saw a few taverns across the bridge in that town. Gods but I could use a couple fingers of liquor."

"I wouldn't count on it."

Phelan sighed. "Yeah, Uncle Eldric means business. That grizzled bear as well."

It was a fair assessment. The next morning, amid a thin grey drizzle, the grey bear called Geth, Phelan, and a few other conscripts out into Towerrock's ward. A dozen fresh riders whisked Gylfric and most of the new soldiers back out the gates, headed northward. The bear beckoned the rest to follow through an inner gate and into the keep's lesser ward. He lined them up and stood before them, chest out, hands on hips.

"For anyone who doesn't know, I am Captain Wayan. I'm your father, your uncle, your worst enemy and your best friend. Every fighter in these walls belongs to me. We all belong to Lord Eldric and Umbel.

"You lucky bastards have been sent in my direction to train up. The lord seems to think you've got more in you than to swing a shovel or whittle arrows. You've got your cloaks I see. Now let's make men of you."

Geth flicked a glance at Phelan and smiled.

Wayan's underlings handed out carved hickory practice swords. A pair of man-high timber poles had been sunk into the ground. They were put to work on these first and Geth went through the motions of cut and parry. Even among this 'chosen' group, his comfort with the blade couldn't go unnoticed for long. A sergeant pulled him aside to practice by sparring with Phelan.

"I'm beginning to like this place," Geth said, jabbing his friend easily in one shoulder and then the other.

"Ow! Quit showing off."

"I'm just saying, we could do well here."

"If eating stale road-bread and getting bruises is doing well, I wonder what you call doing bad."

"Don't make it so easy for me. Put your back into it. If you want to turn some profit from our stay in this land, best thing to do is to earn it."

"Earn a kiss on this ass."

The little man tried a sudden jab, but Geth knocked it aside. The big warrior landed another crack, this one against the ribs. Phelan cursed and dropped his waster, a hand at his side. Geth snickered but

Phelan's glare turned to a look of warning as the master of the yard came sauntering toward them.

"Don't kill the little runt," the bear growled. "Even he might prove useful when the Ilars come."

"Sorry sir, don't know my own strength sometimes."

The yardmaster eyed Geth up and down. He bent to pick up Phelan's waster. "Maybe you need a go at something big enough to bite back."

Geth swallowed a curse. Barrel-chested and as tall as Geth besides, Wayan was a big one alright. That thick grey beard lent a wild appearance, but Geth reckoned he hadn't earned his place through mere savagery. The scabbard at his hip was worn with age, his hands callused from years on the hilt. He squared Geth up, weapon level.

"M'lord, I couldn't—"

"Raise your sword or get thrashed anyway."

Geth smoothed his mustache to hide a scowl. *Why do I always attract these bastards?* There was nothing for it but to let the man crack him.

"Lord." Geth stretched out his wooden blade to touch the end of Wayan's.

The yardmaster lunged straight for Geth's sternum, hard enough to break bones. Geth reacted out of pure instinct, parried the blow aside. His eyes widened and he staggered backward as Wayan followed up with a flurry of slashes and thrusts.

Parrying furiously, Geth backpedaled, twisted, ducked and skipped. Another lunge took Wayan past him a few steps, but the yardmaster only squared Geth up again. The big warrior cast a glance to either side, cursed inwardly. The entire yard had stopped to watch his humiliation.

"Not bad at all." Wayan tossed his blade from hand to hand.

Cocky bastard. "Barely keeping up, lord."

Geth knew it was better to concede early, before things got ugly. Wayan came at him with another slash. He deflected it wide, but dragging a foot, allowed the yardmaster an opening to thump his hamstring with a backhand as he passed. Wayan seized the opportunity, leaving Geth wincing as he hopped on the other leg.

"That's gonna hurt a week from now," Phelan said, loud enough to make the other soldiers hoot. Geth thanked him silently.

But Wayan just licked his lips, stance coiled. "Need to work on your feet."

He sent a probing thrust out. Geth responded with an exaggerated shift of each boot. Wayan bought it. One more blow, that would be enough. The yardmaster faked a high swing, swerving to chop down at a foot. Geth left the boot planted and gritted his teeth.

Pain shot up his leg like fire as the blow landed. "Thram's shriveled…!"

"Ha!" Wayan's hand went to his midriff as he laughed. "Did I say he needed better footwork?"

Geth sucked in air through his teeth. Green-cloaks chuckled all around. That strike was sure to have blackened a few toenails. At least the yardmaster seemed pleased.

"I concede, my lord." Geth threw up his hands.

But the grizzled bastard was having too much fun. "I'll give you one more chance to land a blow."

The bear flicked out his blade to touch Geth's and set himself once more. Geth blew out a breath, forced his emotions down. The yardmaster watched him over the tip of his waster, eyes lit by a smile of pure evil. Geth set himself on his two aching legs.

Wayan rushed as he had before, one strike faster than the next and harder besides. Geth wielded that practice sword with desperation, turning blow after blow. The back of his right thigh burned. The toes on his left foot cried out with each step.

The yardmaster only pushed harder. Sweat beaded Geth's forehead. Wayan's bearded grin filled his vision. He thought he heard Phelan's voice begging them to peace, but Wayan just kept coming. Pain turned to burning anger, traveling up from Geth's toes to the center of his chest. His grimace turned to a snarl.

The bear's next slash set it up perfect. Geth turned his body to give the appearance of an opening the yardmaster couldn't ignore. As Wayan made the lunge in, he took a quick, painful step sideways to come from behind, smacking the old warrior's hamstring just as had been done to him moments before.

No more than a grunt escaped the old warrior's lips, but the significance of that blow was unmistakable. Jaws fell open. The sword-yard went silent as the grave.

Wayan's eyes narrowed to thin slits. If he'd looked evil before, he looked like death itself now. "Seems we've got a fox among the chickens."

The yardmaster circled warily.

Geth felt no remorse, shifting on aching toes. He was going to give this cocky old bastard a lesson in his own yard, a lesson he'd shudder to remember. Not waiting for Wayan's next attack, he charged.

The bear must have seen it coming. He was already retreating as the blows rained down, knocking one after another aside, skipping backward all the while. Geth never let up. He was no fox, but a blood-hungry mastiff.

The rhythm of a well-matched duel set in. The yard echoed with the sound of wood cracking against wood. Just for the sake of it, Geth tried the same fake the yardmaster had used to chop at his boots. Wayan saw that coming too. But Geth knew the bastard had spent himself already trying to humiliate him.

Geth wore away at the bear's defenses, his attack relentless. Cut, thrust, parry, thrust. Wayan's face went red. His mouth hung open. Geth pushed even harder until the bear finally stumbled. A solid whack took the sonofabitch across his exposed ribs.

"Agh!"

A wiser man would have let it end there. But Geth followed with a kick that sent the yardmaster down to the turf. He skipped forward to tower over the downed yardmaster, waster raised overhead in both hands.

"Enough!"

Eldric's voice caught Geth a heartbeat away from smashing Wayan's head in. He blew out a long breath to master the bloodlust, lowered the length of hickory, and backed off. Wayan, on the other hand, loosed a string of expletives, wiping spittle from his mouth, scrambling to rise.

"Master Wayan!"

The command in Eldric's voice froze him. If not for that, Geth was sure the old wretch would have gone for his sword. *The last mistake he would've made.*

But that wasn't what Geth wanted either. He blew out a hot breath, thanked the gods for the lord's good timing. Eldric shot a warning look at the big warrior, then stepped past him to dust grass from the yardmaster's back.

"The best swordplay I've seen in years." He turned back toward Geth. "You're the first person I can remember to come within a foot of landing a touch on the captain. Did you know that?"

Geth bowed his head. It was all he could do not to curse Wayan to Vorda's deepest hell.

The yardmaster starred daggers at him. "Ten years ago, I'd have strangled you with your own guts, boy." Under Eldric's eye, he forced a smile. "But don't worry, lord, I'll turn his sword to face Ilia."

And turn my back toward yourself, Geth thought.

At the insistence of Towerrock's lord, Wayan left the balance of the day's training to his second and departed at Eldric's side. Exercises in the sword-yard resumed. The thump of wooden wasters filled the air, interspersed by murmurs. No one spoke to Geth, but he could feel the eyes on his back. Phelan shook his head, eyed him over the tip of his own practice sword.

"Well, you haven't lost your knack for making friends."

Chapter thirteen

If not for Eldric, Geth had no doubt he'd have been locked in the pillory straightaway. Or worse. News of the fight with Wayan spread like fire through summer-parched fields. From the barracks where they slept to the hall where they broke bread, the eyes of soldiers, serving folk, and laborers followed him. Some watched darkly. Others offered a nod. When he passed, all of them whispered.

Even that Ilar wolfdog took an interest, trotting up to him the next morning in the greater ward.

"You too?"

The beast just sniffed up and down his pant leg.

"He likes you."

Geth turned to find the dog's spiky-haired master standing right behind him. *How the hell...?* Across the ward, the rest of the Ilar contingent had emerged from the stables ahead of a file of horses and baggage. Geth watched the Ilar with narrowed eyes, remembering what Phelan had said of him.

"Leaving this day." The Ilar flicked a glance toward his countrymen. "To Iyngaer, Chieftain of Dues. And home."

"Best of luck with that."

"We will see each other again. Mmmm?"

Geth didn't know what to make of that odd hum, but he didn't like the sounds of the Ilar's prediction. "Keep your magicks to yourself, you hear me?"

"No magicks," the Ilar smiled. "Call me Agrem."

Geth searched the tribesman's face. Deep green eyes, like a cat's, watched the big warrior like he already knew him, this conversation just a formality. Geth had never much cared for witcheries and the like, but there was something honest about the straightforward approach.

Or maybe that was one of his powers.

"You can call me Geth. So long as you keep your magicks off me."

The Ilar grinned. "Friends, Geth and Agrem. Not enemies. Mmmm?"

"Not yet."

A woman's voice turned them both toward the throng of tribesmen before Geth could say more. "Agrem!"

It was the tall Ilar woman who beckoned.

For a moment, Geth meet her stare, bright, sharp and as strange and hostile as Agrem's was familiar. She scowled and turned back toward the train of shaggy horses. Behind her, that big, stomping yellow-beard and the handsome, sharp-eyed Ilar waited beside their footmen. Eldric and Pythelle watched somber-faced from the stable doorway.

"We will see each other again," Agrem said, leaving Geth wondering what he'd wanted in the first place. The Ilar column mounted up and cantered toward the gates. Agrem may or may not have meant what he said about being friends, but that stomping yellow-beard made his feelings clear. Pointing to the walls, he spoke loudly in his own language and spit. The leather-clad warriors around him grinned.

Geth thought of Hadean, of Umbel, as the file of shaggy beasts and men disappeared out the gate, hooves thumping hollowly across the bridge. These bastards wanted to tear it all down, take what belonged to the king, the man that had saved his life, one of few that had ever given him the benefit of the doubt. He started for the sword-yard with fresh determination, Wayan be damned.

Crossing under the gate leading to the lesser ward, he found the yard full of green-cloaks already. And there was the yardmaster. The bear left a cluster of recruits and marched straight in Geth's direction.

"Peace." The yardmaster raised both hands, teeth bared in something like a smile.

"Captain." Geth knuckled a brow.

"I have good news."

Here we go...

"You know how to swing a sword. No doubt about that. The lord thinks you've got the mettle to lead as well."

"To lead?"

"Here's your chance." The yardmaster thumbed in the direction of the green-cloaks behind him. "That right there is your file. Keep 'em alive if you can."

Geth knew an ass-ram when he saw it. He looked from Wayan to the cluster of soldiers and back.

Nothing false about the bastard's smile this time. The yardmaster had given him the ten most unlikely warriors Geth'd ever seen. There were greener recruits up north maybe, but none were more pimpled, knock-kneed, or just plain uglier than this lot. There wasn't a strong chin or a determined brow among them.

Wayan clapped Geth's shoulder and left. Phelan arrived, still licking his fingers from breakast.

"What'd I miss?"

"Them." Geth flicked his head toward the file. Huffing a sigh, he straightened up and headed over.

It wasn't until then he noticed young Kerrel among his men. That, at least, made him smile.

"Back together again, eh?" He slapped the lad on the back.

"The Lord Eldric gave me leave."

"Then I've got one true soldier already."

Phelan eyed the ten-man file dubiously. Geth moved on to the next soldier.

"And you, sir. What do they call you?"

One by one they gave their names. Geth remembered none of them but gave a firm nod to each. He took Phelan aside.

"What do we do now?"

"How would I know? I didn't see this coming."

Geth muttered a curse. *Keep 'em alive,* Wayan had said. That wasn't a bad place to start. Geth nodded once more, as much to himself as to anyone.

"Alright, pick up a waster, boys. Let's see what you know."

For the next hour, he paired them up, bellowing instructions, stopping to watch each man's stance, swing, and parry. There wasn't a natural fighter among them, except maybe Kerrel. Geth offered the best advice he could. After his spar with the yardmaster, they hung on his every word.

Phelan watched with an odd look on his face as Geth waved his pupils toward the well for a water break. "Not bad, Captain."

"I'm not even a sergeant. Not yet anyway."

"Well, I was pleasantly surprised."

"What's that supposed to mean? I've led men before." Geth ticked off fingers on one hand. "Turia, the Mog, that Iyrund slave-galley."

Phelan ticked off his own slim digits. "Bloodthirsty Turians, easterner savages, a ratty tangle of escaped-slaves. This is different."

"Well—"

"Listen, a beast will submit to the meanest animal in the pack. Upright creatures though, it takes a little more. Looks like you've got 'em all fooled."

Phelan winked but Geth didn't rise to the bait. He looked to his file. The farm-hands and cobbler's sons under his charge were all watching him, eyes a little too wide.

Phelan left him for the mess hall, leaving Geth to pick up wasters by himself. He cursed the little bastard, but no sooner had he stooped to snatch up the first weapon than he felt a pair of eyes on his back. He turned.

Across the sword-yard, Pythelle watched him, arms folded across her chest. Their eyes met and she beckoned with a flick of her head, disappearing under the stone archway leading to various living chambers that housed Towerrock's stationed folk. Much as he knew better, curiosity got the better of the big warrior. He followed.

"What is it, m'lady?"

"We should talk."

Geth trailed her down a set of stairs where she pushed open the door to a small, candle-lit cellar scattered with trunks, a few chairs, a table. And a bed. "M'lady, I—"

"Don't worry, I don't bite." Pythelle laughed and stepped inside.

She wasn't old, and she wasn't homely either. Geth set his jaw before stepping inside. "I have duties, my lady. Speak your piece so I can get back to them."

Pythelle seated herself on a stool in front of the table and turned to face him. She crossed her legs, took a moment to arrange her skirts. "Seems you're a man on the rise, Geth of Pellon. My instincts told me as much the first moment we met. People will flock to you like crows to dead flesh."

"Dead flesh?" Geth snorted. "What do you want from me, woman? You had your chance to hire my sword. If the price had been right, you could have sealed it then and there."

"I don't think so. In any case, I merely wish to warn you."

"About what?"

"Success breeds jealousy. You know that. If you think you have enemies now, you can be sure you'll have more before long."

"I don't have any enemies, not in these lands."

"Melagus, that soldier, Gylfric, the yardmaster...need I continue?"

Geth bit down a curse. "Is that why you lured me here? To goad me?"

Pythelle leaned forward, eyes narrowed. Geth still stood near the door. From that angle, his gaze slid straight down her cleavage. He forced his chin up.

"We both need allies, Sergeant. We're both outsiders within these walls. Just remember that I warned you, that I scratched your back. We could help each other."

"If that's it, I'll be going now."

"I have something else for you."

The hairs on the back of Geth's neck stood. He should have been gone already. He reached for the door. Pythelle sprang up to catch his hand on the knob. Her grip was smooth and cool but firm.

"Don't you want knowledge?" she asked.

Geth took a step back. "Information, you mean?" If someone's got it out for me, just say it."

"I don't know. *Yet*. But we can find out together."

She turned back toward the table. Geth scanned the surface, eyes well-adjusted to the dim light now. A bowl and a pitcher rested on the table behind her, no shrunken heads, curved knives or knotted rope, thank the gods. She poured something dark from the pitcher to the bowl, mixed in a pinch of ash, and moved the candles close to the brim.

"Look. Here." She dipped a long fingernail into the surface and turned it in a slow circle. "What do you see?"

She wanted something more than a back-scratch, Geth was no halfwit. A man with a sword-arm like his could only expect the highborn to use him.

But better to play the tame ox than the angry bull, he reckoned, take what she offered on the end of her pitchfork, lull her—and all the others—to sleep.

"I see…"

He frowned. At first Geth saw nothing. The bowl's contents flowed in a gentle arc, dark in patches, orange, yellow or gold where it caught the candlelight. He blinked and it all went white. A field of snow, trees heavy with the stuff, and dark tracks crunched through the surface.

"Trees." He sucked in a startled breath. "In winter."

"Ilia." Pythelle's voice was a whisper. "Good."

The vision moved, soared like a bird over the white canopy, swooped down through a smoke-hole and inside a long, low cottage of sorts. A woman with grey hair in a thin ponytail looked up. Her face stretched in a grandmotherly smile. Even so, Geth recoiled. If this was Ilia, the woman was an Ilar, an enemy. Someone else's grandmother, not his. The gutters of Sorn didn't raise him a fool.

With an effort like pulling himself up out of a cold lake, Geth wrenched his eyes from the water and stood straight. Pythelle ran a finger down his back.

"You see," she purred, "Ilia waits in your future. Is that not something worth knowing?"

If it's true. Geth stepped back out of her reach, scowled. "And who was this woman?"

"Perhaps you have allies there, allies where you least expect."

He didn't answer, his head still a little light. Pythelle watched him with smokey eyes, but he backed further away until his shoulder blades touched the door. Thanking the gods, he turned, pulled the handle. A thin slice of light found its way in from above, and his senses cleared.

He straightened his tunic and ran a hand through greasy hair, started out of the room like Pythelle had just bedded him indeed.

"Be careful, Geth of Pellon," her voice sounded from over his shoulder as he hurried up the stairs. "And don't forget your friends."

Phelan had snuck out of the barracks the previous night and he'd already slipped away again by the time Geth returned, leaving the big warrior to muse over Pythelle's snare alone. What had she really wanted? And what did the vision in her bowl mean? *Bloody magicks!* Gods but he was tired of being used.

Ignoring the rumbling in his stomach, he went hunting for his friend in the watering holes across the bridge in the town of Greenfell. Plenty of soldiers mixed in among the townsfolk, spending their wages on ale and dice and women of the trade. But if Phelan was there, he'd seen Geth coming and slid out the back. Geth only caught up to him back in

Towerrock's moonlit ward. The space had gone quiet, soldiers, groundkeepers and the like turned in for the evening. Phelan lounged against the wall beside the barracks, bottle in hand.

"Looking for me?"

"You know damn well."

"Look, I can't just swing a sword all day and sleep like a baby at night. I need to get out, get some air from time to time."

"I missed dinner because of it. You better have a good reason."

"Bet you were surprised not to find me across the river, eh?"

"Just come out with it."

"Alright fine. It's like this: while you've been chopping away, trying to make warriors of those walking dead men, I've had my eyes open. There're currents swirling in this fortress. If we don't want to get sucked under, we better mind them."

Geth frowned. He reached over to snatch the bottle from his friend and downed a long pull.

Phelan ignored that. "Like getting a file of men when Captain Wayan hates you. He's got plans for us, none of 'em good."

"What was I supposed to do, say no?"

"We need a better lay of the land. That's all I'm saying. Makes no sense to wait for trouble to find us then try to cut our way out."

"So, you found an excuse to creep through somebody's window."

"We are running a bit low on shine, now that you mention it. But don't worry, I didn't take much."

"Phelan!"

"Shush! Stay focused, man. A little lift or two isn't what we're talking about. It's bigger than that. There's Pythelle for one."

"Yeah, she—"

"She's up to something more than warming Eldric's bed, I'll tell you that."

"Lord Eldric?" *Crafty bitch!* Geth felt even more the fool, even though he reckoned he'd more or less escaped her web.

Phelan was too busy looking smug to notice Geth's scowl. "That's a young catch for the old hound, eh? And the worm has got himself an old woman too. Not a looker either. But the goddess of love is blind, right?"

"So they say."

"Eldric and Pythelle, now that's the one to watch. The lord's trying to make good with the Ilars. She's helping him somehow, I think."

Geth wondered if that magick bowl was the trick. "You reckon they're trying to turn the Ilars against one another, favoring one tribe, divide 'em up? Eldric's son said as much back at Waterset."

"That's what Pellon did against the Mog."

Phelan reached for the bottle. Geth pulled it out of reach and took another swig. The little man snorted, folded his arms.

"Nobody's talking about it," Phelan went on, "but the crown's not sitting so easy on young Hadean's head either. It's only a matter of time before we're at open war with at least a couple Ilar tribes. Is he really the man to lead?"

"What are you saying?"

"They've already tried to kill Hadean once. That's what I'm saying. And did they ever catch the scratch? Not that I've heard."

"Eldric killed him. You told me that."

"He killed an *assassin*. But who sent the man? There are rumors going around, rumors that Hadean's got a target on his back."

Geth muttered a curse. "So where does this leave us?"

"A couple of friendless foreigners in a fortress preparing for war? Up a shit creek I'd say. With only our hands to paddle."

Phelan's words opened Geth's eyes. The signs of fractures within the kingdom were all around him. Preparations for war had only become more obvious, but newly arrived troops eyed the locals sideways. *Currents.*

And the grizzled bear watched Geth's every move. It was a blessing when his file began taking their share of watchman duties along the walls. Young Kerrel joined him one night, the stone ramparts moonlit, the only sound the whisper of wind and the noise of Geth's whetstone against his blade.

"What's its name?" the lad asked. "Your sword."

Geth considered the question. "Fesi," he said.

"What's that mean?"

"In the tongue of the Mog, in the eastern wilds, 'Peace of shit.'"

Kerrel smiled.

"Isn't much of a sword." The big warrior held up the chinked metal, the plain crossguard and counterweight to demonstrate. "But it does the job. Seems like I go through swords like cuckold through wives."

The lad chuckled.

"Wouldn't mind to have a better one someday."

"You will. When I took my leave to join you, Lord Eldric gave me mine. I call it 'snake-fang.'"

Kerrel passed over his own weapon, a work of solid sword-smithing. Geth whistled. Eldric had given it to a mere lad. An orphan. Umbel may have spawned such bastards as Wayan and Gylfric, but it also birthed true gems in the likes of Towerrock's lord and his nephew, King Hadean.

Geth passed the sword back and Kerrel turned in, his watch done. Phelan replaced him, cloak pulled close around his shoulders. Geth stood to scan the horizon to the north one last time, hair tousled by the wind at those heights.

Phelan leaned up against the merlon beside him. "Cold up here."

"Colder out there I'd wager."

"The Ilars don't seem to mind."

"Maybe they do. Maybe that's why they're so keen to take a bite out of Umbel."

"Well, they've got to get through the dead-man dozen first."

Geth rested a hand on the pommel at his waist. "Next chance I get, remind me to find a better sword."

Phelan might have replied but for the slap of footfalls further down the ramparts. A pigeon-keeper had emerged from the coops at a dead run, hurrying toward the nearest stair. He pounded down the steps, three at a time. Geth watched him dart across the greater ward and disappear through the gates leading to the inner keep.

Phelan mouthed a curse. "That's a message for Eldric."

"What do you think it means?"

"I'm about to find out."

Phelan hurried down from the walls, across the ward. He was back again in minutes. He arrived breathless beside Geth, his cloak thrown back.

"The message came from Point-fort. They're surrounded."

Geth's grip on his hilt tightened. "Surrounded by who?"

"Ilars, who else?"

"Gods all be damned. Already?"

Phelan snorted. "You're the one that said war was on the kettle. Had to come to a boil eventually."

Chapter fourteen

Only the king's most trusted captains were invited to war councils of course, leaving Geth no choice but to wait till morning to learn more. He arrived in the sword-yard at dawn, hoping to catch Lord Eldric with news on his way down from his quarters. The grass crunched under his boots, stiff with frost.

A huddled pair stood close together across the ward, Towerrock's lord and the yardmaster in a hushed exchange. "...never know what they'll do," Eldric was saying.

"We aren't dealing with—" Wayan cut himself short as the sound of Geth's footfalls betrayed him. "Well, well, we may just have a volunteer for the job right here."

Geth saluted with fist to heart. But by the yardmaster's tone, he got the feeling he'd stepped into something other than frost. "My lords."

"Ever eager to be at it. That's a good man." Wayan went on. "There's been a bit of action up north."

"Action, sir?"

"It's true." Eldric watched him, weighing.

The bear flicked a glance at Towerrock's lord, picked up where he left off. "Seems there's a band of Ilars roaming the hills near Point-fort. The garrison's closed themselves in."

Geth tried to look surprised. "Must be they reckon the enemy too many to engage."

"Indeed," Eldric said.

Geth looked from the lord's sober face to Wayan's half-hidden smirk and back again. They wanted something from him, that was obvious. He went ahead and bit, gods all be damned.

"Whatever I can do, just give the order."

Wayan smiled. "There is one thing. The garrison at Point-fort has called for more men."

"To seek out and confront the Ilars," Eldric added. "But we believe it could be a trap."

"An ambush." Wayan said. "They want to draw us out and hit us hard. Could be we're wrong and they're just out for a bit of plunder, but we can't risk good lives to find out."

Good lives. "So, you need someone to head north and check it out."

"Point-fort's gone quiet," said Eldric. "Too quiet for my liking. We should have heard back again by now. The man courageous enough to spy it out would be commended."

Geth nodded. "I'll do it. I just need my footman and a couple horses."

"Take your file," Wayan said. He cracked that evil smile of his. "They could use some experience."

Amazing how fast the yardmaster provided twelve horses after that. They were across the bridge and cantering northward well before midmorning. Geth looked from the line of awkward soldiers behind him to Phelan riding at his side. "I guess we're headed up that shitty creek you were talking about."

Phelan kept his eyes straight forward. "This is my fault. No, I mean it. I've been praying for some excitement. Now we're as dead as these straw dummies."

He hooked a thumb back in the direction of the file. Geth followed his gaze and frowned. The boy, Kerrel, met his eyes. Geth forced a smile.

Keep 'em alive. He hadn't drunk with them or faced anything like a fight, but these were his men. What were their talents, their uses, if not swinging steel? Even after a week, he realized he had no idea. He drew them to a halt and turned his horse to face them.

"Who among you knows the parts? Anyone?"

A lanky fellow with farmer's woolens under his leather jerkin pulled off his iron cap. A bright fall sun gleamed off his silver hair.

"I do, sergeant."

"Right. Pardon if I've forgotten your name, soldier."

"It's Neary, sir."

"How far to Point-fort, Neary?"

"Better part of a day for us, moving at a clip. Not more. Longer with wagons and the like."

Geth turned to Phelan, voice low. "That doesn't leave us much time. I don't want to run into these Ilars before we've got a plan."

"You already know my thoughts on it," the little man said.

"Right. Steer clear of them altogether."

But they still had to ride within sight of Point-fort at least. Otherwise, it was all for nothing. Geth pulled at the end of his mustache. If it was indeed a trap, Wayan could care less if they sprang it. He probably preferred that they did. And if the message from the garrison was any indication, that would land them sword-to-sword with a hungry warband of Ilars. Geth didn't need to survey his men again to know how that would end.

"Neary, describe the road ahead best you can. All the way to Point-fort."

The lanky oldster nodded. "The road keeps winding straight up alongside the river a few more miles, then it veers east through the hills for a stretch. Back to the river again after that 'til you come up on the fort."

Geth looked from Neary to Phelan. "You hear that?"

"Better we avoid those hills, I'm thinking."

"Pretty clean sight lines other than those hills, Neary? Open country? If the yardmaster's right, the Ilars could be waiting for us up ahead with a sharp surprise."

Neary's eyes widened. Behind him, a murmur rose from the boys. "That'd be the place, I suppose. Lots of turns in the road up through those hills. Perfect place for a bit of banditry."

"And this is the only way to Point-fort?"

"Well, if we cut out east, we could swing in from that way, but that'd take an extra day at least. A boat or two would have come in handy. We could've poled up the river. No hiding on the water though. The fort sits on a great chunk of rock just beside the eastern bank."

Eastern bank. The same side they were already on. That got Geth's wheels turning.

Phelan must've been thinking the same thing by the way he looked at him. "You hear that?"

Geth nodded, turned back to the old Umbelman. "Tell me there's a ford nearby, Neary. Some other way to cross the river without a boat."

Neary smiled. The old bastard wasn't dumb. "Well, there sure is."

At Neary's direction, the company veered off the road a few miles up, following a well-worn track down to the water's edge. The great North River flowed wide at this stretch, but Geth was assured it wasn't deep. Dismounting to lead their horses, they arrived cold and wet but safe on the other side within the hour.

Neary led them west and away from the river a fair distance before turning them north again toward Point-fort. "If we want to cross back, we'll have to leave the horses and swim, but if this route doesn't fool these Ilars, nothing will."

"They won't expect us to cross the river?" Geth asked.

"That," Neary said, "and they won't be looking for us coming down from the north."

Geth blinked, working that out. "So, the next place to cross takes us *beyond* the fort?" He twisted in the saddle to grin back at Phelan.

"Not bad. I gotta say it."

But the plan wasn't without flaws. For one, they were shivering already. And which of his men could swim? What use was it to arrive half-frozen and three-quarters-drowned at Point-fort that evening? Geth reigned in alongside Phelan as they rode.

"I wonder if we could see the fort from across the river without ever having to cross?"

"Something tells me that's not gonna cut it."

"It's worth having a look."

Geth went silent for the rest of the ride, thinking. Best case scenario, the Ilars held Point-fort under siege, the lack of communication due to messenger birds being brought down. A view from across the river would suffice in that case. Then they could ride for home. He muttered a half-hearted prayer it was so.

It was late in the afternoon by the time Neary judged them parallel to the fort. Geth put him in charge of the boys and crept off with Phelan toward the riverbank. They kept their heads low, but with the sun behind them, anyone across the river would have had a hard time spotting them anyway.

"You see anything?" Geth asked. The square stone spire of Point-fort thrust up from a rocky outcropping beside the river, no more than a longbow shot away.

Umbel's green and white banners flew from the ramparts.

Still, something wasn't right.

"Where are the watchmen?" Phelan squinted across the water. "I don't see any Ilars laying siege, but still, there should be watchmen."

"Thram's pimpled ass."

According to Neary, the best place to cross was another two miles upriver. They rounded up the file and made the distance at a trot, leading their horses to avoid injury as darkness fell. Geth left the old soldier and the rest of the boys a half mile inland from the banks.

"If we're not back by dawn," Geth told him, "get your asses back downriver and inside the walls of Towerrock. You hear me?"

"But what—" Kerrel started.

"Don't worry about me." Geth rested a hand on the lad's shoulder. "It could just mean I've decided to hike north into Ilia to add a few knuckle bones to my collection. But with a sergeant or without, you ride for the fortress at dawn."

Kerrel saluted, fist to heart. Neary and the rest of the gang jumped to copy the gesture. Geth returned it and waved Phelan down toward the water. They left their cloaks hanging on a bush to wade and swim their way across the cold, moonlit river.

"Bloody Umbel." Phelan cursed between shivers. "Had to be Umbel."

"Keep your eyes open," Geth told him. "We're in enemy territory now."

The need for haste was almost enough to keep Geth warm. And the danger. The oft-raided stretch between Umbel and Ilia known as the Boundaries belonged to the tribesmen these days if reports were true. Umbel's boundary-forts strung east to west across those lands, but in the past year, the last holdout cottagers had all been killed or driven off. The wind tousled the waist-high grass and crackled dry leaves among the brambles as they crept out of the water, southward, shivering with each step.

The tower of Point-fort peeked into view beside the river some mile or so down, all grays and blacks in the moonlight. Geth's warrior-eye studied the defenses. More of a stronghold than a true fort, the main structure stood a mere three stories, surrounded by a man-high stone fence that enclosed a small ward and a few slate-topped barns and sheds. The whole compound crowned a weathered stone lump beside the river, making it accessible only from the east. The moon's low position left corners and stretches of the wall in darkness, but if anything moved on the ramparts, they would have seen it by now. They circled wide through the tall grass on hands and knees until they faced the entry.

"Looks like—"

"Shh!" Phelan reached for his waist. He drew out his sling and set a stone.

"Where?" Geth whispered. "I don't see anyone?"

"That's why I'm in charge."

Phelan motioned for quiet and crept forward. He stood suddenly, jerked his arm twice and loosed his stone. A thud sounded, followed by silence.

"It's alright," Phelan said. "He was alone."

Geth followed his friend toward the gate, hand on hilt. He almost tripped over the man Phelan had brought down before he saw him. Reaching down, he rolled him on his back, dead as dirt.

"Ilar." Phelan spit.

No mistaking those fur-trimmed leathers, but if there was some way to determine tribe or station, Geth didn't know it. The man wore knee-high boots of supple suede, tied by laces. A bone-handled knife swung from his hip, no sword. A bow and quiver rested against the wall where he'd been hiding.

"Must be a scout," Phelan said. He knelt to rummage the dead man's pockets and pilfer his knife.

Geth took a breath and froze. A breeze kicked up, whisking the rancid smell of death past his nose. It couldn't have come from the fresh kill at his feet. Phelan looked up. He'd smelled it too.

"You ready?" Geth squeezed the hilt of his sword and turned toward Point-fort's gate. Heavy timber doors creaked open with just a push and a swarm of dark shapes launched themselves into the air, the noise of flapping wings and rasping caws startling the quiet night.

"Bloody crows."

"Had to be Umbel." Phelan nocked an arrow on the Ilar bow he'd filched. "Vorda's withered tits."

Without a lantern or torch, vague lumps across the small ward only hinted at the carnage. The reek, however, left nothing to the imagination.

"Dead. To a man," Geth said.

"But how'd they get in? No way they stormed the walls."

Geth gave it some thought. He knelt beside the nearest corpse. Cold as ice and stiff besides.

"These men have been dead a while. What if the Ilars sacked the place and sent that pigeon themselves?"

Phelan wiped his hands on his pants. "Then whoever did this is about the cleverest bastard we've come up against."

A noise caught Geth's attention before he could say more. His sword rasped out of his sheath in an instant as two more Ilars came charging through the open gates. They screamed as they came, swords pale streaks in the dark ward.

Geth lurched forward to meet the first Ilar's swing with a vicious parry that smashed the sword clear from the bastard's hands. Forward momentum took the tribesman right into him, but weight and size won out and the shorter, slighter Ilar bounced off him to land in the dirt.

The second Ilar closed the space and stabbed low for the guts. Geth skipped to the side, let the strike pass but tripped over the first Ilar to join him on the ground. "Oof!"

Geth scrambled to raise his sword, braced himself for the inevitable slash coming. But the twang of a bowstring saved him as Phelan dropped the Ilar standing over him with his countryman's bow.

That left only the first, dazed tribesmen. Phelan froze that one where he sat with a word in the Ilar tongue, another arrow nocked and leveled.

Geth rose to dust off his pants. "What are you waiting for?"

Phelan barked at the Ilar again in his own language. Squinty, hateful eyes flicked from that nocked arrow to Geth and back, but his mouth stayed clamped shut. Geth stepped toward the dead tribesman beside him then turned to eye his living countryman from over one shoulder.

"You watching this?" Raising his sword, he severed the corpse's head with a ferocious two-handed chop.

A string of curses erupted from the Ilar. He rose to his haunches, but Phelan hissed an order and froze him there.

"Whatever you were asking, Phelan, ask him again," Geth said.

Phelan smiled. The Ilar sighed, made like he was scratching his head, then chucked his iron-studded helmet right at the little man.

Phelan's arrow slipped from its notch. He swore. Geth lifted his blade, but a twist and roll took the bastard out of reach. In two stride he was gone, kicking up loose turf and gravel, sprinting for the gates. Damn but he could run. The last thing Geth saw was his pasty bald head bobbing through the darkness, moving south.

"Shit."

"It's alright," Phelan recovered the arrow. "They did it like you said. Bastard never admitted it, but I could tell from his face. They snuck up on the place and killed the garrison then sent that pigeon to Towerrock themselves."

"Thram's crooked cock."

Geth could think of nothing else to say. He turned to gather the live Ilar's sword and the dead Ilar's head before heading for the gates. It was a mark of Phelan's nerves he didn't argue for staying to rummage more pockets.

Outside, Geth tested the stolen sword on the neck of the dead scout, bringing his grisly collection of trophies to two. "Not a bad blade."

"I'm not carrying one of those," Phelan said.

Geth waved him to follow and they headed back north at a run. "At least we'll have something to show for our troubles." They ran all the way to their crossing point, steeled themselves for the plunge into cold river water, and waded back the way they'd come.

Neary jumped up at their return to camp, startling the sleeping horses. "Sir!"

The boys rose as well, grinning from ear to ear, swearing they never doubted a swift return. Eyes widened at the sight of the two Ilar heads, but by Geth's reckoning, it was just the sort of introduction to war they needed.

"Point-fort's been sacked," he told them. "Dead to a man, best I could tell."

A murmur passed through them. Kerrel cursed like someone twice his age.

"Do we head back then?" Neary asked.

Geth recovered his cloak and pulled it around wet shoulders. He looked at Phelan. It was nearing daybreak, and it had been a long day and night. He shivered under it.

"First, some rest."

Tying the Ilar heads to his saddle by their hair, he plopped down for an hour of shut-eye. He must have needed it. He slept until midday.

They started moving south again at an easy pace. "Forget about hurrying back," Geth told Phelan. "The garrison will still be dead whether they get the news tonight or the day after."

"Let me talk to Neary," the little man said. "Together we should be able to plot a course that keeps us well out of sight."

Geth left him to it. If the Ilars caught them on the road with those trophies, their vengeance would be swift. After a few words, Neary waved them westward, away from the river. Phelan jogged out in front on foot, scouting the path ahead.

Winding from thicket to thicket, avoiding hill crests and scanning the horizon in every direction, they rode until nightfall. Neary judged them a good day's ride from Towerock still. He volunteered to take first watch as the rest of the bunch dismounted and made camp. Phelan came over to crouch next to Geth as he stretched himself out.

"They would have expected us back at the Tooth by now," he said. "Or at least to have received a message by pigeon. They'll know something's happened."

"Probably think we're dead," Geth said. "And so much the better. When we do come home, they'll receive us like princes."

Phelan worked that out for a moment then smiled. "You're not as dumb as you look, you know that?"

Geth's first thought had only been to keep the boys safe, but arriving back at Towerrock with those heads… He nodded grimly to himself. True, they would come bearing the ill news of Point-fort's sack, but they'd ventured to the fringes of Ilia itself, smelled the reek of battle, and would soon come home to tell the tale. There couldn't be many at the Tooth who could claim to have done the same.

The dead-man dozen had been gone a full three and a half days when the jagged grey walls of the Tooth appeared in the distance. It was like a weight lifted off their shoulders. Behind Geth, Neary and the boys started singing.

"You hear that?" Phelan nudged Geth with an elbow. "Job done and every one of them still alive. It's a miracle."

They crossed the river again by way of ferry and reached the muddy outskirts of Greenfell. Plowmen and shopkeepers offered grim but approving nods at the sight of the two Ilar heads bobbing from Geth's saddle. Horse hooves thumped across the timbers of Towerrock's bridge.

Geth rolled his shoulders back, spared a glance at Phelan.

"Let's enjoy the moment." Up ahead, the gates stood open and soldiers atop the walls hailed them with welcoming shouts. Neary and his entire homely lot answered back with salutes of fist to heart. Pride made up for any fierceness looks or stature might have denied them. "Gods, but it's been a long time since I was greeted like this."

Word of their return spread quickly. Green-cloaks mobbed them with shouts and grins as the company dismounted beside the stables. Geth edged through, ignoring questions, letting the two heads dangling from his grip speak for him.

Wayan appeared from under the gate to the swordyard and Lord's Hall. "You live."

Geth couldn't help but look smug. He bowed just the same. "Point-fort's been overrun, my lord. Dead, to a man."

"Not all dead." Wayan flicked his grizzled chin to one side. Geth followed the gesture to find Gylfric leaning up beside the stable doors, head bandaged but every inch the living bastard Geth remembered.

"He escaped?"

The yardmaster grunted. "The sergeant led the sally, fought his way out. Him and a few more. Arrived back here not half a day after you set out."

The sergeant. Geth didn't miss the significance of that. "We didn't have time to count the bodies." Geth lifted the severed heads. "Ran into a few tribesmen ourselves."

The grizzled bear spared a glance for the heads, nothing more.

"We did manage to question one of 'em," Geth said. "It was the Ilars that sent the pigeon south. We learned that much."

Wayan's eyes narrowed. He opened his mouth, but a voice sounded from over his shoulder before he could speak.

"A provocation."

Geth looked up to find none other than King Hadean striding toward him. Beside him came his uncle, Eldric, trailed by that worm of a counselor, Melagus.

"My lords." Geth bowed best he could with those two heads still dangling from his grasp. He looked up to meet the king's gaze. Such somber eyes on his young face. It was like the boy had aged another year since Geth'd last seen him.

"You were at Point-fort?" Hadean asked. "You ran into the Ilars there?"

"Just some scouts, lord. Nothing more. We circled wide and came down from the north to avoid any other force."

"No doubt they lay in ambush further south. You did well to stay clear. With numbers great enough to overwhelm Point-fort, your file wouldn't have stood a chance."

"He seems proud nonetheless," Melagus put in, nose wrinkled at those severed Ilar heads.

Geth wanted to slap that look right off his face. But standing there, with those grisly tokens in hand, he felt exactly the barbarian he'd often been called. They hung heavy in his grasp all of a sudden.

"We'll speak of this later," Hadean said. "I expect many a war council to be had in the coming days."

"Let's not rush to judge," Eldric put in. "It seems clear the Ilars were after more than plunder. But which Ilars?"

"They meant to take soldiers' lives, don't you think Uncle? And then to draw us out and take more. How can we answer with anything other than our swords?"

Eldric frowned. "In every conflict there will be casualties, a few sacrificed to red-handed Awer for the good of the many. Those that died at Point-fort will be remembered as heroes."

"Would you counsel peace?"

"I counsel patience. The chieftains of the Ilars are wont to act on their own, whatever alliances they claim. Let's not charge headlong into war without first knowing who the culprit is. Gutted forts and severed heads benefit no one."

Hadean looked from the bloody trophies dangling behind Geth's knees and back up to meet his uncle's eye. "Either way, the boundary forts must be abandoned and Towerrock reinforced. Be ready, Uncle. If the sack of Point-fort was not a provocation, those heads are."

Chapter fifteen

Geth cursed himself all the way to the mess hall and clear through supper. Men clapped him on the shoulder. They plied him with questions, applauded his kills, drank to his name. Never mind it was Phelan that had done the killing. Or that they'd possibly dragged the entire kingdom into a needless war.

Gylfric had his fair share of admirers as well. Captain Wayan appeared to be among them, judging by the way he grinned and hoisted cups. Geth didn't miss the sideways glances the pair directed his way between jests.

Phelan plunked a fresh ale down in front of him "Thram's balls, you look like a jilted dairymaid."

"What's that supposed to mean?"

"This is your chance to make a friend or two. Lift your tankard, for Neyna's sweet love."

"Easy for you to say. You didn't see the look on the king's face when he saw those heads."

"Would have made me happy, if it were me."

"Eldric thinks they may be able to avoid a full-on war. But Hadean said that beheading those two Ilars might be the spark that sets it all alight."

"And since when were you scared of a little dust-up?"

Geth heaved a sigh. "Look, Hadean doesn't need a war right now. You said it yourself, he's already got enough bastards trying to kill him."

"Seems like that crown is his curse."

"Shit on that."

He'd spoken louder than he meant to. Nearby soldiers looked up, but Geth's glower turned them away just as quick. For once in his life, a man of station had taken his word, given him a chance and treated him fair. More than fair maybe. But a flock of vultures circled over that young man's head. Geth knew the feeling. He leaned in closer and lowered his voice.

"Listen, when have you ever rubbed elbows with a highborn like Hadean? If his countrymen want his crown, and the Ilars want his realm, I'd say he's got his back against the wall. And a part of that is my fault. I can't abide it."

Phelan frowned. "If it's war these Ilars are after, Geth, they'll have it. Even I can tell you that. That oughta' given you ample opportunity to make amends."

Phelan was right. Weariness had caught up with Geth after a hot meal and a few ales, he sacked out like a dead man. He was almost ready to forgive himself in the morning when Melagus arrived to fetch him from the sword-yard.

"Your presence is required by the king."

Neary and Phelan exchanged looks. Geth swore under his breath. He dropped his waster and fell in behind the counselor.

"Where are we headed?"

The worm spoke as he walked, not bothering to turn. "It's a king you'll be speaking to so mind your manners. You may hail from Golden Paellia, but I know pot-iron from rare ingots. I'll be watching your every step."

Nothing veiled about that.

On the other hand, why the warning if Hadean intended to lock him in irons like he probably deserved? Geth followed the worm through the broad door leading to the Lord's Hall, Towerrock's innermost keep. Among the tables and benches where Eldric and his best folk took their meat and drink, a solitary figure sat waiting. Geth's boot heels clicked on the stone floors, echoed off the high rafters.

Hadean stood up at his approach. "Good morning, Sergeant Geth. I wanted to be the first person to call you by your new title."

Geth hesitated. "My lord?"

"That's right. Your errand into Ilia brought your situation to light. Who gives a man a file to lead but withholds the title of sergeant? And the pay that comes with it. Especially when that man has completed a very dangerous task."

All the tightness left Geth's chest. In fact, he felt he was floating. He didn't mention the fact he'd been calling himself sergeant the whole while. "You are generous, my king. I thank you."

"Where did you learn your swordcraft? In King Elius's army?"

"I did spend some time in white, m'lord."

"Well…"

Was Hadean blushing?

"I do have another reason for calling you here, sergeant. A selfish one. I must ask your service once again."

"My lord," Melagus cut in, "a king need not *ask*, only command. I remind you, this man was sentenced to service. All the more is he obliged."

Hadean's eyes flicked from the worm back to Geth. "I've come to think your sentence a harsh one. But also fitting, given your talents. The crown must hold to the law, as my father always said. And the punishments for breaking it."

"The king *is* the law," Geth replied. "That's what they say back in Pellon."

Hadean shook his head. His brow furrowed but he held his tongue.

Such a pensive face on so young a lad. "M'lord?"

Hadean began to pace, searching for the right words maybe. What could the king want from him? Geth didn't miss it as Hadean's eyes scanned the corners of the hall for eavesdroppers. That airy, proud feeling had melted away, but whatever the king needed of him, Geth was already determined to do it.

"My kingdom is in danger, Geth. My rule as well. The Ilar tribes unite just when we are weakened by the Affliction and robbed of our greatest leaders."

Melagus pushed close to the king. "You are a great leader, my lord. Don't discount yourself."

Geth gave a firm nod. And meant it.

"I can only do what I think is just," Hadean said. "What is right. And to trust those who have the experience to help me. I never expected to find myself here after all."

A look passed over that young face, anger mixed with grief. He'd lost both parents and his brother all at once, Geth suddenly remembered. He had lived through similar losses himself. He couldn't say he'd handled it as well.

"You have your uncle," Geth offered. "A true ally. And your cousin Brant."

"One good uncle and enemies by the score."

Melagus shuffled nervously but the king continued.

"They may not show their faces but they're here, waiting for me to step wrong. Ambitious, calculating men. Worse than Captain Wayan even."

Geth blinked. The king cracked a smile.

"I heard what you did to him. He was my instructor once and I still hate him."

"A...misunderstanding, lord. Nothing more."

Hadean chuckled.

Geth found himself fighting down a smile himself, but Melagus huffed in annoyance. "Please, my lord, what is the purpose? You trust this mercenary, this masterless man, with close counsel. If you need counsel, confide in your captains. Confide in *me*. You don't know anything about him. He's not even an Umbelman."

"Don't you see it, Melagus? That's the point. I thought you were supposed to be clever?"

"Explain to me the wisdom in it."

"Geth isn't part of all these plots. How could he be? He's not from Umbel. What's more, he was in prison when the attempt was made on me. Who better to confide in?"

"Who better—?"

"As for his merit, when sentenced to the boundaries, not only has he stayed rather than running off—like many of our own folk have tried—he's made a name for himself. If it's true he's a mercenary, as you supposed, I'd be a fool not to take advantage of such experience."

Melagus took an exaggerated breath, gathered himself visibly. "With respect, my lord, this *man*—" Geth was certain he'd wanted to call him something else— "hasn't run away precisely *because* of the fact he is a mercenary. It's clear he knows which is the business end of a sword. But let's not be naive. That doesn't make him loyal."

"I'm loyal." Geth scowled. "If I haven't proved it yet, give me the chance. I promise you I will."

"You—" Melagus started.

But the king cut him off. "Here is your chance. The reason I summoned you was to ask your help. I want you to personally instruct me at swordplay."

Melagus's voice went up an octave. "My king!"

"Take another breath, Master Melagus." Hadean turned from him back to Geth. "You said it was only a misunderstanding between you and Captain Wayan. But there was no misunderstanding the outcome. Wayan was considered the best swordsman in all the land. Until now."

Geth didn't know what to say. He knew he was good—damn good—but better than the best swordsman in a whole kingdom? And to instruct a king? "I…"

The king watched him expectantly. Geth straightened up tall, wrestled the words out.

"I will teach you, lord. Gods all be damned, but I'll do my best."

Geth caught up with Phelan in the mess hall that evening.

"Where the hell have you been?" Phelan scowled. He pierced a hunk of salted pork on its platter and slapped it down on his plate.

Geth slid onto the bench beside him, voice low. "Training the bloody king! He's made me his personal instructor. And let me tell you, that boy's got an arm."

"You're leaving me?"

"What's that supposed to mean?"

"You expect me to play soldier all by myself?"

"This is better than anything we could have imagined, Phelan! Sure, we started off wrong in Umbel. But we're working directly for the king now. If that's not a fresh start, I don't know what is."

"Fresh start. Right. All's well and good until that king gets toppled and us along with him."

Geth glared at his friend. He reached out, snatched Phelan's ale, pulled it back out of reach. "You're a real cheery bastard, you know that?" He drained the cup and passed it back, none too gently.

"Take it easy, man. I'm just saying, it's no accident Hadean's asked you to train him. You're one of the only people he can trust. They're out to get him, his own subjects. I'm not talking about the Ilars."

Geth loosed a sigh. He turned his attention to the pork, tore off a joint for himself but just sat there looking at. The king had pretty much confirmed what Phelan had been saying for a while now. Hadean had as many enemies within the realm as without.

"All the more reason to help," Geth said finally. "You'll be in charge of the file while I'm with Hadean."

"The file."

"Don't make that face, it'll only be a few hours a day. And you've got Neary to share the load."

"You serious?"

"There's experience under those grey locks."

"Ancient bastard…"

Geth ignored that. "So, Hadean's got enemies." He took a bite at last, spoke as he chewed. "Who stands to gain most from a dead young king? Someone who wants the crown, I reckon."

"There's a few names been bandied about, downriver lords, mostly."

"That right?"

Phelan nodded. "When Hadean called the muster, not everyone answered. Somebody called Towdric from Turey Hill, another scratch from Sirona. A few other places I never heard of."

"I never heard of any of them."

"One of the mountain forts to the west I think."

"Those lords would be suspect," Geth agreed. "But does any of them have a claim on the throne?"

"There's no love lost between Hadean and Lord Brant," Phelan offered.

"His cousin? He's here with his men now. Unless it's just for fear of his father's wrath."

"No love lost between those two either. You saw them on the ride north."

He had. Geth swallowed a mouthful and let it all set in. There was just so much he still didn't know.

"And the assassin?" he asked. "You learn anything about that?

"Some nobody from upriver."

"Not downriver?"

"Kind of goes against everything else, eh? Unless that was the whole idea. Throw off the dogs, so to speak."

"Thanks, Phelan." Geth waved a lad over to refill his friend's ale. "I'm not gonna ask how you manage it, but thanks."

"Thank me later. In the meantime, here come those ten ugly bastards of yours. Drink an ale with them. Let's see if you can't learn a thing or two on your own."

Chapter sixteen

Geth spent the better part of the next few days training with the king. He worked under the eyes of Eldric or Utrand most times, though neither stayed as long as Melagus. The counselor seldom left Hadean's side. If he did, he might miss a chance to question Geth's methods, undermine him, or outright belittle him.

"Let's keep on with all the different weapons," Geth told the king. "You never know when your sword might break or get lost."

Hadean nodded. Geth had brought in wasters to spar with the lad, mixing in knives, spears and the occasional axe or mace. They went to work straightaway.

"Talent for the Red God's work, now there's a thing can't be bought or chose like a sword or shield. But don't fret, you've got a warrior's arm. That's plain as day."

"I suppose it's a good thing," Hadean said. "We're in such times. I'll not ask men to fight while I hide in the back ranks."

"Well said. But you'll need a new blade." Geth flicked a glance at the weapon at Hadean's waist. "That thing's all wrong."

They sparred at half-speed, Geth's shoddy weapon, Fesi, clanking off Hadean's ill-fitted one. Hadean needed more of a challenge, in truth. But the rote motions helped Geth's mind work through the tangles of intrigue he'd only begun to uncover.

Phelan had promised to keep digging as well. That would lead him onto barstools, into bed with gossipy whores, and through open windows—the kind of job he couldn't turn down. Geth had no doubt they'd both live to rue the day, but no one knew which keyholes to peek through, which cracked door to listen beside, better than Phelan.

The sight of that Ilar wolfdog curled up outside the barracks at day's end sent Geth looking for the little man. He found him inside the dark barracks among the other sleeping soldiers. "The Ilars are back, and you didn't tell me?"

Phelan turned in his blanket, pretending he'd just woken. "Ilars?"

"Drop the act, Phelan. You haven't gone to sleep before midnight since...well, ever. And I know you've got your boots on under those covers."

"You wanted me to spy things out, didn't you?"

"As long as you've got them on, let's walk."

Geth started for the door. Phelan grumbled but followed behind. He spared a glance over each shoulder as they slid into the shadows under an eave.

"Tell me what you know about the Ilars. I've been with the king all day. I never saw them once."

Phelan shrugged. "It's Agrem the Seer, come alone. He met with Eldric earlier, probably catching up with Hadean now."

"The Seer? You weren't wrong when you named him a warlock, were you?"

"When am I ever wrong? But that's not the point. Point is, Eldric's made one last gambit for peace. He's gonna try to buy it, a trade for land."

"Why didn't you tell me this sooner?"

"When was I supposed to do that? Between chasing down these rumors and leading the file, my plate's full."

Geth snorted. "Neary already told me you left him with the boys all day, Phelan."

"I can't be in two places at once, can I? You're the one who asked me to nose around. Anyway, the reason I didn't tell you about Eldric's deal sooner is because it's not going to happen."

"You sure?"

"Hadean's against it."

"What?" Geth frowned. "Why would Hadean stand in the way of peace?"

Phelan threw up his hands. "I don't know. Maybe your training has gone to his head. Wouldn't be the first time a young man went itchin' for a fight."

Geth thought that through. A wolf howled somewhere in the distance. That Ilar half-dog perked up its ears.

"You gather anything else?"

"Just this: the boy's nervous. If you watch close, you'll see he's got his uncle or Captain Utrand nearby at all times. Or you."

"You think he knows more than he's letting on? What if he already knows who's after him?"

"Ask him. You're his personal ass-wiper nowadays."

Geth ignored the jibe, but not the advice. Phelan was right. He met the king in his hall the next morning, pushing aside the tables and benches. The first order of business, however, was getting the right sword in the boy's hands.

"No."

Geth eyed the blade Hadean had favored the past week and shook his head. It was a gift from his brother, something he was loath to part with. But the weapon had been sized for a child, not a man. Let alone a long-limbed fighter like Hadean. Geth put sword after sword into Hadean's grip after that, only to scowl at each and send for a new one after a few bouts.

Melagus watched from a bench stacked high with parchments. "Foolishness."

Hadean paid him no mind. He swung the latest blade through the air a few times and looked to Geth for his opinion. Melagus sniffed and left the hall. Geth thanked the gods for the sight of his back.

"What do you think?" Hadean asked.

Geth flicked a glance to make sure the counselor was gone before turning back to the king. "I think this a good time to talk about your enemies. Knowing your weapon is well and fine, but only if you know who you're gonna point it at."

Hadean opened his mouth then closed it. Geth sheathed his own sword, spared a glance over his shoulder and stepped closer to the king. "I'm talking about the traitors. There's a snake in your cupboards, that much is clear. And if it's my job to prepare you for combat, better we started with the enemies closest to home."

Hadean met Geth's eye. He turned and began to pace. "My father warned me of it."

"A traitor?"

"More than one even. I just couldn't believe how close they could get."

Geth nodded. "Tell me how it happened."

Hadean gave an account of the assassination attempt that rang all too true to a seasoned bodyguard like Geth. A solitary bath, a silent intruder, and a dead king—nearly.

"My father warned me," Hadean said again, "but it was my brother's words that saved my life. 'Be aware of anything out of place, anything out of the ordinary,' he told me. I had noticed an unfamiliar face among the servants, just an ordinary looking fellow. It was him that slipped in my chamber with the knife. I think they'd poisoned my meal as well, but when I saw that strange face carrying the tray, I didn't touch it. I had plenty of strength to defend myself."

"He came while you were in the bath?"

Hadean nodded, looking down into his hands.

"Of course he did." *Standard assassin's work.* "But you kept a weapon close by, didn't you?"

"Well, no."

Geth raised an eyebrow. Was the king blushing?

"All I had within reach was my undergarments and a towel. I threw them in his face when I saw the knife. That bought a second to get out of the tub and fight for the weapon."

"Saved by your dirty drawers?" Geth cracked a smile. "Uro's wrinkled ass, that's a tale."

"Uh, I guess so."

They shared a laugh. Only Hadean knew how lucky he'd gotten, though. Even through the grin, Geth's mind worked over all he'd heard.

"Whoever was behind it, that man is close enough to sneak an assassin inside your keep. But he's also far enough that he can't do the dirt himself. Or he's incapable. If there's any man—or woman, for that matter—who strikes you as that sort of enemy, tell me. Think hard."

Hadean's brow furrowed. He shook his head. "I just don't know."

"Don't know what?"

A noise sounded over Geth's shoulder. He whirled, hand on his hilt. but it was only Melagus. How the bastard had arrived so quietly, Geth couldn't say. The counselor's face was solemn as he moved toward Hadean, a scabbarded sword across his arms.

Hadean's eye trained on that plain black sheath, watching as his counselor stretched it out toward him. The lad made no move to take it. Melagus drew several gleaming inches and turned it to present the hilt. The counterweight was set with a large green gemstone, the crosspiece engraved with a pattern like wings.

"Now that's a bloody sword," Geth muttered.

Hadean took the grip. He drew the blade free in one ringing motion. "My father's sword."

"It has long since been time." Melagus said.

For once, Geth didn't begrudge the worm's contribution. Hadean swung the blade through the air a few times. Geth could already tell it was perfect.

"What's it called?" he asked.

The king looked up. "Vingil. It means 'Vigilant' in Old Aturian. Eres Longhair gave it to his brother Erehan the Young, the first king of my line, bidding him be ever vigilant against the Westing hordes that sacked Umbel in those years. According to my father, anyway."

Geth eyed its flawless, shining length. "Prince Eres, eh? Then it would be Turian steel. The finest."

"Only now it must keep vigil against the North, not the West."

Geth flicked a dark glance toward Melagus and back to the king. "Every direction, m'lord. Every direction."

Chapter seventeen

Hadean spent the next two days holed up in Towerrock's war room. Geth watched the message-runners, captains, and ranking ministers come and go. Eldric, Wayan, Utrand, Pythelle, Melagus of course, and Brant. Geth had his reservations about that last one, but if Eldric was there, Hadean was safe. Turing back to the sword-yard, he found Neary and the boys making a farce of the time-honored tradition of swordplay.

"Dear gods, is this what Phelan's been teaching you?"

Neary's red nose got redder. "Haven't seen Master Phelan in days, sir. He left me in charge, said you'd sent him on an errand. I've had to train the boys up myself, best I know how."

"Thram's balls."

Geth put the boys to work with wasters in the morning then mocked up a shield wall clash after the midday meal. His mind wandered to Hadean, but it was the ten men under him he'd neglected worse. War was coming. And Vorda would have the lot of them if he didn't do something quick.

Phelan slipped in among the file around sundown, scoundrel that he was. He picked up a waster. For once, he swung that hickory blade with a purpose. That got Geth's attention. He sidled up alongside as they left the training ground.

"Spit it out. Did your favorite whore get the grippe or did someone catch you cheating at dice?"

"Nothing so serious." Phelan managed a half-hearted smile. "The Ilars have put together an army on the fringes of the forest. Three tribes at least."

"That explains why Hadean's been at council so long. I guess Eldric's deal for peace fell through."

"We're balls deep in it now."

"It had to be war. Sooner or later."

"You haven't noticed the fresh supplies though?" Phelan asked. "The Stonemasons on the walls? Carpenters on the bridge?"

They reached the mess hall and eased onto the benches. Geth looked back the way they'd come, out the open door. A wagonload of grain crossed the ward followed by a second lashed up with barrels. The voice of a sergeant echoed as he marched a new company into the Tooth.

"Part and parcel of the business. What am I missing?"

"Only the whole damn point, Geth. Building up stores, moving green-cloaks inside the walls. They've even piled straw under the damn bridge."

Geth's eyes narrowed.

"That's right, Mister Sergeant. It's not a war we're in for. It's a siege."

A messenger from Hadean arrived in the sword-yard the next morning to fetch Geth back to training. Happy as he was to get back to work with the king, one look over the shoulder was enough to spoil it. A murmur passed through the dead-man dozen as he tramped off. News of the Ilar muster had long since reached every corner of the Tooth. They knew what was coming.

The worm did nothing to brighten Geth's mood. He watched down the length of his nose as Geth put Hadean through the paces. Even the king seemed off, silent, pensive, hacking down imaginary foes with more force than finesse.

"Easy, lord," Geth told him. "Hard as you swing, you're not gonna cut a shadow in half."

"I've got a lot on my mind."

Geth eyed Hadean, pushed his luck. "The Ilars? Or the siege?"

Hadean flicked a glance to Melagus and back again. "If this war is really here, then I need to go out and meet it."

"Folly," said Melagus, almost off hand.

"Is it?"

Geth clamped his mouth shut and opened his ears.

"To chase the Ilars is to fight them on their terms," Melagus said. "It's exactly what they want, to draw us out into the open. May I remind you they have amassed four full tribes, some twelve thousand men at least."

"And by my count we have nearly the same. And more horse as well."

"Our recruits are green. The Ilars are savages, born to kill."

Hadean shook his head. "You really don't see the danger in sitting idle? I can't afford to let the tribes grind themselves to dust against the Tooth."

"My lord, what you can't afford is an untimely death."

"I need to secure my rule." Hadean smacked a fist into his palm.

Melagus breathed a sigh, softened his tone. "My king, losing your head in the field hardly secures your rule. Drawing our army out is exactly what the Ilars want. Why else massacre the fort?"

"It was Vriana that did it, if Sergeant Gylfric's account is true. Not Iyngaer. These Ilar chieftains never cease in their efforts to outdo one another."

"Vriana," Geth said, frowning. "That would be the Ilar warrior-woman?"

Hadean nodded. "My uncle says she's known for being a rogue. Iyngaer probably intended to sack the fort himself. But Vriana beat him to it, just to thumb her nose at him."

"You mention your uncle," Melagus put in. "That alone should be enough to give pause. Does your uncle counsel that we march? No, I believe he doesn't."

Hadean looked like a trapped animal. He sheathed Vingil and turned to pace. Geth would have been cursing, he imagined, had it been him.

"Sometimes destroying your enemy is the only answer," he offered. "But either way, my sword is at your side."

The worm eyed Geth with the same smugness he'd seen so many times from so many other haughty bastards. "The only answer? Quite the thinker, aren't we? Do you suppose your one mighty sword counts for anything against four blood-hungry tribes?"

"That's enough." Hadean turned a hard eye on his counselor. "I need meat and bread. Go to the kitchen and fetch a platter and some ale."

Melagus hid his scowl with an obedient bow. No sooner had he disappeared than Hadean pulled Geth up a set of stairs and out onto the ramparts overlooking the sword-yard.

"C'mon, I need some air."

The king didn't stop there. Trading his fine cloak for a weatherworn mantle, he ducked his head low and led Geth past the sword-yard and all the way to the stables.

"Where are we going?"

Hadean took two horses at random and in moments they were outside the keep, across the bridge and on the other side of Greenfell, among the tents where yet more soldiers and supplies were housed.

"I like the open air," Hadean said. "Especially when I need to think."

"Can't say I disagree. That way you can see the enemy coming."

Turning left at the river road, they cantered another several furlongs away before Hadean dismounted to tether his horse near the riverbank. Geth followed suit. Behind them, the Tooth thrust up from its rocky seat, white and formidable, into dull grey skies.

"The way you hustled us out," Geth said. "I reckon some few won't appreciate we've gone."

Hadean smirked. "Melagus doesn't like to let me out of his sight. He also doesn't like me talking about the traitors within our ranks."

Those traitors were never far from Geth's mind. He held his tongue though, let the king speak.

"There's more to my push for battle than some fool's idea of glory. Melagus, Wayan, my uncle—they all want to burn the bridge and hide inside Towerrock, leaving the Ilars to freeze outside our walls."

"That right?"

"But allowing the tribes free reign over the countryside only shifts the bloody business from our armies to the people. We both know the rape and plunder that would bring. And even if we eventually did claim the victory, the only true winners would be those that want me dead. They'd unseat me with no trouble after I left my own folk to fend for themselves against four Ilar tribes."

"Wouldn't the people flee south?"

"Some would. But how would they survive the winter with no food and no home?"

Geth frowned. "I heard Lord Eldric had one last plan to buy peace, at least until spring."

"He planned to gift away the Raven Dells," said Hadean, "to trade land for one more winter during which we might prepare for the war. But there was never any guarantee the tribes would stop there even if they agreed. Perhaps I should have backed him in that, but I just didn't trust the Ilars to uphold their end of the deal. Look what Vriana did to Point-fort? With so many unguarded villages just a few miles south, how could they resist sacking a few?"

"So, we march to war." Geth nodded, as much to himself as to the king. "A knife in the back kills as swiftly as a sword in the front. Better we go out and meet it as you say."

"Am I a fool? Do I march our soldiers into danger simply to preserve my rule? Can we even win?"

"If our numbers match the Ilars, we can win."

"The others are against it. Eldric, Melagus, all of them."

Geth laughed. "Shit and piss, m'lord—pardon the saying—but it's you who's the king. The decision is yours."

If Hadean meant to reply, the rumble of horse hooves cut him short.

"There he is!" someone shouted.

Geth hadn't been wrong when he figured they be missed. Hadean just clapped him on the shoulder and smiled.

"Here I am!" He waved to a column of green-cloaks led by Captain Utrand and trailed by none other than Melagus. "And safe!"

Utrand's mount skidded to a halt in front of Geth, the captain glaring down from under those red eyebrows. Geth saluted with fist to heart. Melagus came huffing up next, awkward on his horse, wispy hair blowing, a drip of snot running from one nostril.

"You call yourself a soldier of the realm?"

"I follow my orders. And I trust the judgment of the king."

"You led him unguarded into danger, that's what you did."

Geth ignored him, climbing into his own saddle.

But the voice of the worm trailed after. "Time will tell what all else you've done."

Chapter eighteen

Melagus wasn't wrong. He'd done it.

News of Hadean's decision spread through Towerrock the same evening. Swords rasped against whetstones in the barracks and men drowned their fears with ale in the mess hall. On the morrow, they marched for war.

"You're in charge of the file," Geth told Phelan. "Remember what Wayan said. Keep 'em alive."

"Vorda's withered tits, man, how am I gonna do that? Who's gonna stand in the first rank, Neary?"

Geth tasted bile in his throat. He had no answer. But how could he leave the king alone for this, his first taste of combat?

"Look, Phelan, if there's anyone who knows how to survive, it's you. See if you can't rub a little of that off on the dozen."

The little man muttered a string of expletives and wouldn't speak for the rest of the night. Horns woke them soon after.

The day had arrived. Boots pounded the floors. Torches lit the dawn red in the Tooth's greater ward. Even the air tasted liked war.

The beating of drums ushered Umbel's soldiers across the bridge, into the streets of Greenfell. Outside the town, more companies joined until their column stretched a good mile long. Geth rode with Hadean's contingent, a jacket of scale armor on his back, a gift from the king. He'd even found a scabbard for the Ilar sword he'd taken at Point-fort. He left Fesi behind. Ahead, Hadean gleamed in well-polished plate and mail. Eldric, Wayan, Pythelle and Utrand crowded nearby. Umbel's green and white standard waved overhead.

Beside their banner-bearer, Brant and two more captains, newly arrived from the south, joined the king's bodyguards. Geth couldn't help but wonder which, if not all, of these was the traitor. And then there was Melagus, speaking urgently with an old woman that must've been the concubine Phelan had uncovered. The weight of the worm's armor bent him almost double. A scabbard hung at his narrow waist, but Geth suspected it held nothing more than a parade sword.

Hadean spurred his mount northward behind the vanguard. Geth looked over his shoulder more than once, though his file was too far back to see. *Deadman dozen indeed.* His stomach went tight at the thought of Neary and Kerrel in the shield wall. Even Phelan was in danger. This was the real thing after all.

"Not long now," Hadean called out. He flicked a glance over his shoulder, met Geth's eye briefly. Girt for war, the lad looked every inch the warrior-king. But the stiff set of his shoulders betrayed his nerves. Geth offered a firm nod, saluted with fist to heart.

Best he could tell, they numbered five hundred horse and another ten or twelve thousand on foot. Each rider carried sword, spear and round shield. The ground force bore larger shields and pikes. Mail and breastplates mixed in among hardened leather. Some wore swords or daggers as well, though Geth cringed to see many with no more than a cooking knife at the belt. The green cloaks of Umbel hung from every shoulder.

They didn't stop marching until past midday. The Ilars had been spotted a few miles ahead. Geth cocked an ear as Eldric rode up alongside the king.

"The vanguard has already clashed with their outriders." Towerrock's lord pointed to a line of low moors. "Just over those hills. We'll meet the enemy on the other side."

Hadean looked back to beckon Geth with a wave.

"Can anyone see them yet?" Geth asked.

Hadean shook his head. "Not from here."

Geth spurred his mount and left the ranks, ignoring the protest of the sergeants that rode up and down the front of their line, forming them up. His steed climbed the hill, passed the last scouts to peer down from the crest. Below him, the tribesmen had assembled a bloody horde.

"Vorda's withered tits."

Some half a mile off, a seething mass of fur and leather and iron jostled as the enemy made their lines. Horsemen trotted up and down the length while companies of archers stood in loose clusters behind.

Spears bristled like dragon spines. A quick estimate put their numbers well over fifteen thousand.

That explained why the green cloaks were being arrayed just eight men deep, not ten or twelve—to match the length of the Ilar line. Geth swore again. Heading back, he took a place directly beside the king.

The order came, and Umbel's lines marched step by step up to the crest. The whole army drew a collective breath at the sight of so many enemies down below. Shitting their pants, Geth reckoned, more than a few. He knew what had to be done.

He pounded hilt against shield, screamed the first challenge. "Arrrggghhh!"

It was a meaningless noise, but the seasoned fighters among the ranks raised their voices as well. They'd seen war. They knew it was only by animal savagery that a man had any hope to survive. Soon the entire army bellowed its defiance.

The Ilars screamed back. Geth had to appreciate the determination in their answer. They clattered their own weapons against shields. Some even stepped out of rank to hurl what must have been feces.

But the way those leather-clad fighters wrestled for position reminded Geth of the merciless yet disorderly warriors of the East. The Ilar lines wobbled forward and back again despite attempts to marshal them. These men, Geth suspected, were accustomed to fighting in small warbands, not a huge army like this. As individuals they would be confident killers. But as a mass, their greatest weapon was intimidation more than any tactic.

"What happens next?" Hadean whispered toward Geth.

"There." Geth pointed to the center of the Ilars where four bannermen and a good dozen more tribesmen broke ranks to ride forward. "Time to meet the enemy face to face."

Eldric barked out orders and Umbel's own standards marched to the fore. Wayan stayed behind, but Eldric, Hadean, Utrand, and Melagus all spurred their mounts. Geth fell in among the king's grim-faced bodyguards.

They met the Ilar contingent near the center of the field. Agrem was there along with that big, stomping yellow-beard they'd traveled north with and several other important-looking Ilars. The Seer, as Phelan had named Agrem, played translator. He stepped up between the two parties, motioning to each of his countrymen as he introduced him.

"Iyngaer, Chieftain of Dues. Othwid, Chief of the Arnui. Chieftain Ceter of Thiring tribe." A helmet came off a warrior in the back to release a tumble of brown hair, streaked with gold, and a set of piercing hazel eyes. "Lady Vriana of Laer."

Geth's mouth parted. He forced it closed. Clad in shining mail, chin held high, Vriana sat her mount like the image of some war-goddess out of Mog legend. Forget that she'd gutted Point-fort and slaughtered the garrison. Or that she'd happily murder Hadean and the lot of them, given the chance. It was hard not to stare.

The one Agrem named Iyngaer spoke first. Here was a man in his prime, and one of the tallest bastards Geth had ever seen besides. His thick russet beard glinted red, his locks free-flowing, but well kept. Under his arm rested a burnished helm and his armor was of scales like Geth's. But steel rather than bronze, and not a one was missing. There was steel in his eyes as well, even if Geth couldn't make out the words as he began to speak.

Agrem translated the throaty language of the Ilars. The usual demands and insults shot back and forth. Eldric spoke for Umbel. Iyngaer may have started things off, but the second chieftain, Othwid, spit curses and demands of his own.

It was all for nothing of course. Hadean still had the Raven Dells to bargain with, but why would the Ilars make a deal for land when they already stood in a position to take it? A deal for gold wasn't on the table either, Geth reckoned. If a treasure had been hauled up with the army, he would have seen it.

That big, yellow-bearded scratch said something, prompting an argument among his countrymen. The words flew between them so fast Agrem didn't even attempt to translate. But the way Big Yellow slapped the axe at his waist and smirked at Umbel's fighters could only mean one thing. Geth spurred up closer to the king.

"He's made a challenge."

Hadean looked suspicious. "Does that mean what I think it means?"

"They've offered to settle this the old way. Single combat. The only question is do we accept?"

Big Yellow dismounted, ignoring the protests of a few holdouts among the tribesmen.

"Champion against champion." Geth said. "Winner takes all."

"That's ridiculous," Melagus cried. "Take all of what? Northern Umbel?"

Eldric, Brant, and a few others shouted various opinions, all at the same time. Would the Ilars honor the deal if they lost? What exactly were they agreeing to in the first place?

"Why take the risk if we've nothing to gain?" Melagus said, louder than anyone.

Big Yellow just stood there in front of them, chuckling.

"Because." Geth slid down from his saddle. "No one laughs at my king."

Chapter nineteen

"Wait!"

Geth had been laughed at enough in one lifetime and the battle-lust ran hot through his veins. But Melagus of all people had climbed down from his saddle to rush out in front of him.

"First the agreements!" He turned toward Agrem. "If we win, we demand the tribes remove their army from Umbel's soil until spring. Furthermore, no tribesmen or chieftain shall raid or molest any of King Hadean's subjects. Do we have an accord?"

Agrem translated. Othwid rolled his eyes, but Iyngaer grunted his assent. Ceter the Old, the white-haired chieftain of the Thiring tribe raised his voice for the first time.

"And should we win," he said, speaking better Aturian than Agrem, "the tribes claim all the lands from the forest edge to Towerrock in the south."

The Seer eyed him queerly but translated his words back to the Ilar tongue for the other chiefs. Before any of them could speak, Melagus shouted over them all.

"We need to exchange hostages! To make sure the agreement is honored. Give us Iyngaer and we will give you Lord Eldric in exchange, to hold until the terms have been met."

The very idea sent an uproar through the tribesmen. Eldric didn't look pleased either, but Geth smiled.

Melagus wasn't stupid. With so many Ilars already on Umbel's soil, what was to stop them from attacking regardless of who won? Not that the counselor expected them to hand Iyngaer over. No, the whole point was to probe the cracks in this Ilar alliance, Geth was sure of it. To get them arguing, weighing their own importance, one against the other.

Vriana's voice rang out over everyone else. Geth reckoned someone had finally seen through the ploy.

Her scowl flashed from Melagus to Geth and back to her countrymen. She said something else and Big Yellow swung his axe through the air a few times, squared up toward Geth.

"No one is fighting anyone!" Melagus said. "Not until we take Iyngaer!"

The Ilars ignored that, wheeling their mounts back a few yards to clear a space. Geth drew his sword. Melagus muttered a surprisingly filthy curse and tramped back the way he'd come.

"I've done my part," he told Geth as he passed. "Now you do yours."

Geth ignored him, looking to Hadean instead. He offered an Umbel-style salute and unslung the cavalry shield from across his back.

"You don't have to do this, Geth," Hadean called out. "Melagus is right. Without an exchange of hostages, there's no point. They won't honor the agreement."

"Then I'll fight just to put one more enemy in the dirt."

He turned toward his foe. Snorting up a nasty bit of phlegm, he spit on the ground in front of him. Big Yellow smiled, swung his axe in a lazy arc overhead.

Hadean had missed the point. Sure, it meant nothing for lords and chiefs. But for those poor bastards with kitchen knives thrust through their belts and turds in their shorts already, this duel could be the difference between life and death. Out in front of them, the Ilar horde writhed like some giant, malevolent beast. Umbel's green-cloaks needed something to believe in.

And Geth could give it to them. Stepping out from between the two parties, he turned to face the long ranks of Umbel's spearmen, the archers behind, horsemen at the flanks. He raised his sword until it caught the light and howled.

A deafening cry answered, surged through his chest, into every limb.

The Ilars replied with thunderous encouragement for Big Yellow.

Geth sized him up as he stomped back and forth, soaking it in. He was a monster, this scratch, tall and thick with a touch of madness around the eyes to boot. No tavern brawler here. This bastard would know how to fight.

He carried no shield, just that axe. Geth eyed the broad silver head as they stepped closer, working out how things would develop as they fought. He hefted the shield in his left hand, prayed its maker knew his craft.

But he wasn't afraid. Dark days in the pits of Adamar had prepared him for such moments. He readied himself for the rush. This fight would be over in seconds if he didn't move fast.

"Argh!"

Big Yellow came with a yell. Geth had already noted he was right-handed, and as the tribesman delivered his first two-handed swipe, he sidestepped to his own right, away from that crunching blow. He absorbed the weakened, half-contact on his shield. The Ilars jeered his retreat, but Geth hurried back the other way when the yellow-bearded bastard switched to come at him from the opposite direction.

"Fight! Fight!" the Ilar shouted.

This, apparently, was the extent of his Aturian. He kept repeating it. Geth flicked out a darting stab, still well out of the reach of that axe. The full contact of it, even on his shield, might break an arm. That's exactly what the bastard intended. The only way for Geth to land a thrust would be to goad a sloppy swing from the man. Or survive a direct hit and get inside the bastard's reach.

"Come on, big boy! That all you got?"

Geth flicked out another stab, but Big Yellow used the iron-studded handle of his axe to parry with ease. Geth thrust his neck forward, tried to invite a hasty swing. He jeered and cursed to no avail.

Too quick, this scratch. Too tidy.

Big Yellow wasn't about to over-commit and Geth knew it. There wasn't going to be any counterattack without first bearing the brunt of one good chop. He had to see to it somehow that the blow was weakened.

"Come and get it!"

Geth flicked out a thrust, caught the big tribesman in the upper arm with the tip of his sword. It wasn't more than a prick, but it pissed him off. That axe whooshed through air as he stepped back, spitting what had to be curses.

That made Geth smile. He stretched for another precise stab, snagged a bit of leather, nothing more, as the Ilar backpedaled. But the pattern was clear. The tribesman's axe had less reach than the big warrior's sword. And Geth was going to poke him to death with a thousand little pricks if the bastard let him.

"Fight!" Big Yellow growled.

"Come and catch me!"

The Ilar came. He had no choice unless he wanted to let his enemy keep sticking him. Geth didn't try to parry that axe head. He danced and dodged, backpedaled himself, skipped to either side. The watching tribesmen jeered him. Hadean called his name, but Geth didn't stop until both he and Big Yellow were panting.

"Geth!" the king's voice sounded.

But he ignored it, looked directly into Big Yellow's puffy red face. *Now.* He squared the Ilar up, drifted within reach of that axe. The weapon went up and Geth hefted his shield, braced for the impact.

The crack of splintering timber rang in his ear. The jolt sent him staggering. But it wasn't the full-blooded swing it might have been before Geth's little game of chase. Big Yellow was tired. Shield and bone held.

"Argh!" Before the big bastard could raise that axe again, Geth lunged forward with his own weapon.

Inside the Ilar's defenses, his sword stretched far enough this time to puncture mail, leather, and flesh.

Big Yellow shrieked. Fear replaced the madness in his eyes. Geth twisted his blade free and leapt back out of reach of that axe as a backswing came at him.

The Ilar staggered, swinging for Geth with desperate arcs. The big warrior skipped out of range easily. The tribesman stumbled, red foam huffing at his lips.

"Just die, you bastard."

Another curse was all Big Yellow had left. He dropped to one knee, hand at his wound. He tried to rise again, swayed like a falling tree, and finally toppled over. Geth stepped forward, ran his blade through once more just to be sure.

He turned to face the long ranks of green-cloaked fighters, both arms raised. "Umbel! *Arrrrgggghhhh!*"

A ground-rumbling roar answered. The chieftain called Othwid spluttered, cursed and wept. Two of his men dismounted to retrieve Big Yellow. The white-haired chieftain of the Thirings kicked his mount forward as Iyngaer and Vriana moved to restrain Othwid. White-head met Geth's eye, the corner of his lip twisted in a smile, and a shiver passed through the big warrior, like the Dark Lady herself had tapped him on the shoulder.

Geth shook it off. He wiped his sword off on his pant leg, sheathed it, and climbed back into his saddle.

"The matter's been settled." Melagus dusted off his hands. "Take your armies and go."

Agrem frowned. "They don't think so, mmmm?"

Iyngaer made some incomprehensible gesture. Vriana laughed. That brought a hateful glare from Othwid, but as a group, the Ilar contingent turned their mounts to leave. As if it needed explaining, the Seer lingered to make things clear.

"This war now begins, Iyngaer is saying. Othwid too."

"You'll regret this!" Eldric slapped his pommel.

But Hadean watched their exit, calm as could be. "Let them go. We knew they'd never hold to the outcome. The battle was always coming. At least we've drawn first blood." He shot a grim smile toward the big warrior.

"Thank you, my king."

Hadean led them all back to the ranks. More shouts and shield-banging erupted as the lines parted to admit them.

"King's man!"

"Champion!"

"Umbel's Paellian!"

Many a seasoned fighter hailed Geth or clapped his shoulder. Not least among them Utrand and Hadean's closest bodyguards. The ranks closed around them. They took their place, well in the rear, among the reserves.

But the sight of so many staunch warriors only sent Geth's thoughts back to Phelan and the boys. "Thram and bloody Awer." He spurred his mount toward Hadean, tried to smooth a scowl.

"M'lord, have I earned a favor from you today?"

"Name it, Master Geth. You've proved your mettle. Yet again."

"You've got your uncle here, my lord. And Utrand. And all your best fighters from Umbel City. But there's ten men down the line somewhere that might not live out the day without my help."

Hadean understood. "Your file."

"Yes, m'lord."

The king looked out over the green-cloak ranks and back. He smiled. "Go."

Chapter twenty

Geth spurred his horse down one flank and then the other until he found Phelan and the boys. Cheers echoed in his wake, stirring a pride he hadn't felt since, well, the gods only knew when. The ten ugly bastards under his command hooted louder than anyone when they saw him slide down from the saddle.

"Get back into line, you slouches!" He smiled even as he said it. "You thought I'd let you have all the fun?"

Phelan snorted. Geth handed him the reins and pushed him out of file.

"It's your lucky day. You get to keep an eye on Hadean while I do the real work."

"Keep an eye on Hadean? Doesn't he have a whole army for that?"

"Forgot about the traitor already?"

Phelan frowned. "You reckon they might try to bump him in all the confusion?"

"It's your job to make sure they don't. The shield wall's no place for such a pretty face as yours anyway. What will the whores think if your nose gets broke?"

"You want me to leave, Sergeant, you don't have to ask twice."

Phelan offered a mock salute.

Geth snorted.

Across the field, the Ilars started pounding their shields again.

"Phelan…" The words stuck.

"Take care of yourself." The little man climbed into the saddle. "I know you will."

Geth watched him gallop down the line. His smiled returned, if only for the moment. He'd gotten one friend out of harm's way. That left only ten more.

Squeezing shoulders, offering a nod here and there, Geth edged back up to the front. By the murmurs that followed, these fools thought he could slay the gods. At least he'd given them some confidence. When the two armies came together, he'd give more than that.

But the battle hadn't even begun. The pounding of fifteen thousand shields continued some few furlongs off. Geth took Kerrel's pike and sent him to the rear of the file first thing.

"I need someone to watch our backs. Are you that man?"

Kerrel set his chin. "I can do it."

"Good. Keep your head low and your shield high."

In truth, the boy was as good with a blade as most of the others. And a hell of a lot better looking. But Geth wasn't taking any chances, not with him.

"Don't worry, I'll tell you all about that duel tonight."

Kerrel grinned. If the boy was scared, it didn't show.

Neary was another story.

"You fight behind me," Geth told the lanky oldster. Cover my ass. Can you handle that?"

"'Course I can."

It was a brave reply, but he gripped his pike white-knuckled.

"How'd you end up soldiering at your age anyway? The Affliction?"

"It took my wife, took everything. Should've took me too I reckon." Neary croaked a hoarse laugh. "What better place for a dead man than in the army?"

"Well, I for one am glad you didn't die."

Neary's eyes drifted across the field and back. *Not yet*, they seemed to say. He'd heard the Ilars outnumbered them—they all had. He wasn't stupid. Could anyone blame him for being scared?

"You've got nothing to worry about," Geth said. "Except to watch my back. Stay behind me and you'll come out the other end just fine."

That wasn't something Geth could promise really, but Neary needed to hear it. The rest of the boys as well. Horns started blowing across the field. The Ilars began their slow advance.

"Remember your training!" Geth shouted. "Shields touching, stay close. Second rank, cover the man in front of you. And for the love of Thram, don't panic! They're coming for us and they're coming hard. But if we hold firm through that first charge, it's only a matter of time before they crumble."

Determined noises answered from either side. *Gods bless the lot of them.*

A glance to Geth's left and right showed what he'd expected regarding their formation. A line matching the length of their enemies stretched about as far as he could see. Two companies of riders comprised the flanks. Archers had already strung bows behind the ranks, alongside Brant and a hundred or so reserve fighters. The king, his uncle, and a third company of horse hung back as well. Lurking somewhere among them was one crafty little slinger.

"When will they charge?" Neary asked. "Will they charge soon?"

As if in answer, a dark cloud of arrows went up into the sky, launched from behind them. An answering hail twanged out from the Ilars and the battle cries began.

"Right about now." Geth braced himself. "Shields up! For Umbel! For glory!"

Eldric's strategy was a simple one: absorb the Ilar charge, mire them down long enough for Umbel's cavalry to win out on the flanks, and circle behind to catch the Ilars between a hammer of the horseflesh and the anvil of the shield wall.

But if it had been left to Geth, he would have charged first.

"Glory, men!" he shouted. "Gods and Glory! Stand firm!"

The arrows thumped down. His shield was close to those around him, and none slid through, but men screamed and fell here and there among the ranks. For Geth, there was no fear, just the rush of blood, the surge in his chest, the feeling that this was what he was born to do. He watched the glittering blades flash in the sun as the enemy rushed. He set his pike and dug his boots in.

"Cover my back, Neary!" The tramping of the enemy's charge reverberated up from the ground. Ilar war cries filled the air. It was going to be like a battering ram to the gut, the force of that charge. "Stand firm men! Stand firm!"

The ocean of enemies smashed home with an ear-splitting crash. A spear point slammed into Geth's shield with enough force to rock him off his feet, but the press of Neary and the rest of the men behind held him up until the shaft splintered and careened overhead. Geth felt his own length of ash split as the first Ilar shield smashed into his and battle began in earnest.

"Come and die!" he yelled over the rim of his shield.

A savage-eyed Ilar screamed something back.

Geth dropped his pike shaft and drew his sword. He'd done it so many times before, the grunting, the pushing. He knew how to slide his blade, over, under, between shields to stab a man's thigh or puncture his gut just under the hem of his jerkin.

Swords struck his armor in return. A deflected blow from the left clanked off his helm and another sword stuck fast into the iron rim at the top of his shield. He worked his blade in between the shields while that bastard struggled to free his weapon, and another enemy fell. His fellow tribesmen dragged him out of the way and the next snarling attacker rammed into Geth's shield.

Sweat and blood ran down into the big warrior's eyes. His arms grew heavy, his legs burned, but it was fight or die. The man to his right cried out and stumbled. Geth pulled him back by his belt before another blow could land. Another Umbelman hopped into the breach.

By the shrieks and the sickening thunk of weapons finding flesh, men were dying on both sides. Geth spared a glance around. Their line had wobbled, bowed by that first mad rush, but for now it held. They were doing their part. He had no idea how the rest of the army fared.

"Eat that!" Neary kept yelling from over his shoulder. "Eat that!"

Lanky arms hacked over Geth's head, ringing helms, distracting Ilars before they could double up to attack him from two sides. Whatever fear Neary had harbored before, it was gone now. Geth reckoned he'd enlisted the right man for the second rank. The pressure against his shield subsided as the tribesmen backed away, finding no give in that stretch of the line. Geth spared another glance up and down the ranks. Eldric's plan was working.

The braying of Ilar horns sounded. "They're retreating!" someone called out. In front of Geth, a pasty-skinned tribesman made one last, futile slash against his shield and took several steps back. Geth searched past him for Umbel's horsemen slamming into the rear ranks but found none.

"We press!" he shouted, waving his men forward. "We'll finish this ourselves!"

"Eredan's dead," was all the man next to him said.

Geth waited for the call to advance but the horns never sounded. "Awer's bloody cock!"

Turning from the Ilars, he glanced around to find more than just Eredan laid out, whoever that was. Moaning fighters sat or knelt beside others who lay still, strewn across the field like rag dolls. Only a thin line of warriors remained to hold a wall of shields facing the enemy.

Neary reached out to lean heavily on his shoulder. Ahead of them, slipping farther away with each step, the Ilars spit, waving their swords and daring any man to come for more. They dragged their dead back with them. For all the taunts, Geth knew they could be crushed, obliterated, right then and there.

Scanning the field, he looked for Hadean and Brant's reserve. But Umbel's lines had taken a beating everywhere he looked. Horsemen and archers mixed in among the pikes, sure sign they'd been thrown in to shore up the ranks. A paltry rain of arrows went overhead toward the retreating enemy but nothing like the killing thrust the moment called for. Across the trampled, blood-splattered field, the Ilars disappeared over the hills, unchallenged.

Chapter twenty-one

Geth left Neary in charge and sprinted down the line to find Hadean, Eldric, Wayan and Brant already in counsel.

"Why don't we press?" He smacked a fist into his palm. "Crush them now and end this. It's not too late."

Hadean looked up but Wayan spoke first. "Sergeants don't give orders around here, Paellian."

Geth felt a tug at his elbow. Phelan hissed in his ear. "C'mon, damn it!"

He let his friend pull him away. "It's good to see you too."

Phelan grinned. He hauled Geth a good distance off before passing over a waterskin. Geth took a pull, choked on the first swallow, then gulped down the half of it.

"Where in the hell did you get wine?"

"Hits the spot, doesn't it?"

"But why celebrate? We should be routing those bastards right now, ending this war."

Phelan threw up his hands. "Look around, Geth. Our boys are too busy counting their limbs. A fair few of them have come up missing."

They started walking back toward the file. It was the same everywhere Geth looked. Umbel's ranks had only narrowly held it together, even if it was the Ilars that first sounded the retreat.

"What happened?" he asked.

"With the king? He got sucked into the action pretty early. Nearly got himself killed too. Brant arrived with his boys before things could turn ugly."

"Brant, eh? Guess I underestimated that one."

"Hadean though…" Phelan whistled. "He broke the lines. You would've been proud. Got himself surrounded quick, but the boy can fight. Whatever you've been teaching him, it worked."

Geth swelled, hearing that. Hadean had not only survived but acquitted himself like a true warrior.

"So, what forced the Ilar retreat then?"

"Our horse won out on the flanks. Eldric's plan nearly worked; we got behind them. But their warlocks did something to frighten the horses."

Geth raised an eyebrow.

"Ilar witchcraft."

The silver-haired chieftain, Ceter, came to mind. Geth shivered. "Magicks?"

"Whatever it was," Phelan went on, "it bought them enough time to pull back and regroup."

Geth surveyed the battlefield once more. Field-surgeons had arrived with bandages and poultices. The order was given to set up tents and untie bedrolls. Men lit fires, passed around drink. They would camp atop the hill overlooking the battleground for the night.

"So that's that."

The living hauled off the dead. A massive grave was dug, the fallen interred with prayers to Vorda that they might be welcomed into her cold halls.

The Ilars they left for the crows.

By morning the army was limping back toward Towerrock. A feast stood waiting for them. Geth led his file into the great hall to join the throngs of bandaged warriors gathered around the tables, stiff and sore but alive.

All but one. "Drink, Eredan," Geth poured out the first cup into the rushes. His mind went to Old Mather, Khyr, so many others he'd lost through the years. The boys watched him. Fighting in the first rank, he'd saved their lives and they knew it. Still, he cursed himself. He hadn't even known Eredan's name.

"Don't think, Geth." Phelan swiped a carafe from a passing servant and refilled Geth's cup. "What's it you always say? There was never a man born that wasn't meant to die."

Geth turned to one of his dozen, a crater-faced scratch with a bloody wrap around one arm. "You were there. How did Eredan die?"

"Spear, sir. Came right over the top. I hacked the head off before the bastards could get anyone else, but it was too late for Eredan."

Geth nodded, as much to himself as anyone else. "He died a hero, saved a fair few of us. Not to mention the women and children back home."

The boys grunted their accord.

"To Eredan," Geth lifted his drink. "And to Hack."

He clapped crater-face on the shoulder. That earned a few smiles. Wine and ale went down hoarse throats. The more battles he survived, the better Geth got at this kinda thing.

"And you there," he asked another soldier, "how'd you get that cut on your cheek?"

"Arrow, sir. I think."

"Close one, eh Dodger?" Geth winked.

One by one, he nicknamed each of his men. There was Neary and Kerrel of course. And Hack and Dodger. And Bird-man and Red-eye. Sweaty, Blink, and Baby. They were a motley crew, this dead-man dozen. But they'd tucked in at Red-Awer's banquet and survived to sit at this one.

"That was a close one," Phelan told Geth. He gestured with the lamb shank in his hand. "None of em ran for it though. Can't hardly believe it."

"Brave, these ugly pricks."

"Well, eat your fill. They've slaughtered the fatted calves and tapped the best ales. Ask around and they're calling it a victory."

Geth lowered his voice. "You know as well as anyone Eldric's already preparing for a siege. Ask me, better we were up north hounding those leather-stinking bastards than feasting here 'til they come back."

"Shit, Geth, it's cold out there. You should be happy. Far as I'm concerned, the last thing I want to do is chase Ilars through the frozen trees."

Geth poked at a hunk of mutton and bit off a mouthful, but he couldn't argue.

As usual, Phelan made good sense. Winter was coming, even if the fires blazed in the hearth of Towerrock's great hall. Outside on the grass of the ward, the sound of lutes and singing drifted in as another file cracked the doors to join them.

"Look." Neary pointed down the hall toward the door. It was none other than Hadean arriving. Melagus, Eldric, Brant, and Pythelle trailed in his wake. A cheer went up from the benches. Men shouted and banged their mugs. By then all had heard how their king had fought. The lad had made a name for himself.

His entourage split up, moving from table to table, patting shoulders, toasting each man's bravery. Many an homage of liquor was poured out on the rushes. Geth stood with fist to heart as Hadean reached his file.

"Master Geth."

"My king."

Hadean spoke loud enough for his voice to carry. "The Kingdom of Umbel commends your valor and your swordcraft. You spilled the first blood of the day. I raise my cup to you."

A hearty cheer went up from the file, echoed by neighboring tables. "We all fought well, my lord. None better than you, I'm told." *You made me proud.*

How he wished he could say it out loud. He met the king's eye, willing those unspoken words into Hadean's ear. Melagus shuffled up before Geth could think up some way to imply the fact without embarrassing the lad.

"We must keep moving to your other subjects, my lord." To more important subjects, the turn of

Melagus's lips said. Hadean frowned at the worm before turning back to Geth and the file.

"You've covered yourselves in glory," he said. "One and all."

More cheers. Hadean rested a hand on Geth's shoulder for a moment, then turned back toward the Lord's Hall. Geth eased down onto his bench. Neary and the boys slapped his back and clanged their mugs against his.

Geth watched Hadean's exit. That fallish, wood-smoke scent blew in as he stepped through the doors. Geth loved that smell. Downing his cup with a long pull, he glanced around the high-ceilinged chamber, crowded with warriors. With *friends*. Battered shields and cloven horns hung from the walls, interspersed by tapestries of hunting scenes. He'd hardly noticed before.

"Another round!" He stood, cup hoisted overhead. "Alright, who thinks they can drink me under? That's a challenge, you cowards!"

An air of victory pervaded Towerrock in the wake of the battle. Copper Ridge, as it was being called, had settled matters, the men in the ranks all agreed. Conscripts and volunteers would soon be headed home.

Companies from downriver had already begun the exodus, starting with Brant. Geth watched his column disappear down the river road from atop the walls, singing their triumph. But he knew better.

"Why are they leaving? I always reckoned that bastard for a traitor."

Phelan huddled beneath his cloak beside a merlon, not even pretending to keep watch. "Because it's bloody cold. You and me, we've been sleeping indoors with Eldric's men. That lot were camped outside of town. Can you blame 'em for not wanting to spend the winter in a tent?"

"I'd like to know what Eldric had to say about that."

"It's too cold for war now anyway, that's what they're saying. Not even the Ilars would try it."

Geth wasn't so sure.

Hadean invited him to resume exercises the next day. The king wasn't so sure either, Geth reckoned.

The Lord's Hall served as their practice yard as always.

They went straight to work with live steel, Melagus watching from beside his customary stack of ledgers. Hadean's first taste of war sparked plenty of questions, from simple matters of swordplay to the complexities of strategy. Geth had never commanded an army, but he'd been in the butcher's business long enough to provide the answers.

"Is it often two armies clash with no clear victor on the day?" Hadean asked between bouts.

Geth reached for a pitcher on the table and drank straight out of it. Melagus muttered something about 'tattooed barbarians.'

"No." Geth told the king. "When you look back on how things play out, there's almost always a winner and loser. It just takes a while for the one side to bleed out."

"By the look on your face, I'd say you fear it's Umbel that might rue the outcome of Copper Ridge."

"Could be. If it turns out we've bled the tribes enough that their accord falls apart, maybe it's us that have won. If these chieftains are anything like the chieftains I've known back east, that kinda failure will shake things up."

"Or it could harden their resolve."

Geth blinked. Hadean stepped over to take the pitcher, pouring himself a cup. He drank it down and set empty cup and pitcher back down on the table.

"In either case," he said, "your lessons saved my life."

Melagus snorted. "Yes, he gave you the foolhardy idea to break the lines, which nearly got you killed. Gods be praised for your cousin Brant."

"And where's Brant now?" Geth asked.

"Never you mind Brant, Geth of Pellon." Still plenty of venom in the Asp. "Leave strategy to better minds."

Hadean breathed a sigh. "No, it's true. He's gone."

"I don't like it," said Geth.

Melagus waved it off. "Should we ask his fighters to winter in their tents? Here, on the fringes of Ilia? For now, the war is done."

Hadean eyed Melagus sideways. He reached for the pitcher again, dripping the last of their water into his cup, drop by drop.

"Fetch us drink, would you Master Melagus? And bread and cheese from the cellars."

Melagus eyed Geth first, then the king. He wasn't stupid, but how could he refuse? Soft shoes brushed the floor as he disappeared toward the kitchens.

Hadean waited until the doors closed behind him. "This war is not over. You're right."

Geth blinked.

"There are things I've learned. Not everyone knows these things. I'd like to keep it so."

"I'll tell no one. You have my word."

"Good." Hadean began to pace, lips pursed, eyes on the floor. "We have a spy in the forest."

"A spy?"

"The Lady Pythelle has a contact."

Geth pulled at the end of his mustache, remembering her witcheries. A contact, or a *means* of contact, he wondered. "Can she be trusted?

"My uncle believes her spy speaks truth."

"What truth then?"

"The setback at Copper Ridge hasn't hurt the Ilar alliance as much as we hoped. Iyngaer wants land, glory. They all do. That hasn't changed."

Geth thought back. *Iyngaer.* The tall Ilar chieftain, impossible to forget. And the leader of the Ilar alliance by the sound of it.

"They know our forces will dissolve with winter," Hadean said. "Iyngaer, for one, intends to take advantage. He's invited the three other tribes to his stronghold, Dues, for a counsel in four weeks' time. Smaller tribes as well. They will gain allies, and they will come south again."

"Lord Eldric knows all this?" Geth asked. "Why don't we march?"

"It's too dangerous to fight under the trees. That's what he says. Whole armies have been lost in Ilia in winter. And such an attack could be just the thing to cement Iyngaer's coalition if we failed."

"Plus, we've lost men. It makes sense."

Hadean nodded. "My uncle is of a mind to do nothing, hole up in Towerrock and let the Ilars lay siege if that's their intent. They'll never breach the walls, that's for certain."

"Grind them down."

It was the same argument as before. But if they did hole up, the countryside and all her folk would fall under the sword. Towerrock could only hold a few thousand souls, no more.

And there was another problem Hadean may not have realized. Hiding behind the walls played right into Iyngaer's plan to gather more allies. With the whole north of the realm plump for the taking, who could refuse? The promise of plunder would draw hungry warbands like flies to shit.

"Your uncle can't see how that plays into the hands of your enemies? Inside the realm and without?"

"We spoke of it. 'One problem at a time,' he said. In the past, Ilar invasions have fallen apart under the bickering of the chieftains once the spoils ran thin. Come spring, we could be looking at two tribes, or even just the one."

"Iyngaer strikes me as a better leader than that," Geth said.

Hadean frowned. "There was some talk about giving land, but this only buys peace for a season. Then we'd have to flush them out again. Iyngaer's not stupid, he knows that."

"Plus, he can take the land right now if he wants."

"How can I call myself king if I leave my subjects to fend for themselves while I hide behind these walls?"

Hadean sank into a chair. Poor lad had no one else to talk to. There was Eldric, but it seemed their opinions differed. The king of Umbel had no choice but to confide in an outsider. Geth was just glad it was him.

That sparked an idea. "Has the realm of Umbel no friends, my lord?"

"Friends?"

"Her sworn allies, the Sworn Realms. Perhaps we send out for aid. Think what a hundred horsemen could do? If we did hole up, at least we could mount a hit and fly campaign, hit the Ilars while under siege. Harass them, give hope to the countryside. Better than nothing, right?"

"We tried. The pigeons have gone out, but no troops have come the other way."

Geth muttered a curse. He looked to the door. No sign of Melagus yet. Hadean followed his glance.

"Melagus did have one other idea," the king said.

Geth waited.

"He thinks that if we parley and offer gold to one tribe, we just might disrupt the alliance, at least until spring. Brant and the like can be recalled by then."

Geth thought it through. Brega had used gold to divide her enemies with some success. And Brant had voiced the same idea on the trip north to the Tooth. There was the matter of the gold itself, of course, and the danger involved if the Ilars refused.

Geth hadn't forgotten the attempt on Hadean's life either. The longer this war dragged out, the bolder his enemies would become.

"Can it work?" he asked.

"Maybe. Or they could just kill the messenger. And how much gold? This isn't a good time to levy new taxes."

"Perhaps Pythelle's spy can look into it?" Geth offered, "Find out if there's one chieftain that might crack easier than the others. Forget the gold. By my reckoning, yours is a rich land. You'll not lose anything you can't earn back in time."

Hadean stood. "I'll ask her. In the meantime, we sit tight."

"Grind them down?"

"Not if there's any other way. I've got half a mind to march straight to Dues, hit them hard before they gather, before we lose more men like Brant."

Geth wanted to slap him on the back. He grinned and slapped the hilt at his waist instead. The door cracked at the end of the hall and Melagus came hurrying in, tray and pitcher in hand. His eyes flicked from the king to Geth and back. By the scowl he wore, he didn't like what he saw.

New companies began moving inside the keep the next morning, crowding the ward with tents, the barracks with soldiers. They hadn't removed the hay from under the bridge, but it didn't take a strategist to surmise that the higher-ups had changed tack. By Geth's reckoning, Hadean had told his uncle and all the rest his dissatisfaction with the plan to sit tight and weather a siege.

Eldric moved through the halls with faraway eyes. Melagus stared daggers through Geth's heart. No doubt he'd found someone to blame.

But he wasn't there to harass Geth when next the big warrior received summons to the Lord's Hall to train. Hadean spoke freely of his plans, moving through each exercise like a weight had been lifted off his back. Geth flicked glances over each shoulder just the same.

"We'll wait another day to hear back from Pythelle's spy," the king told him as they sparred. "If the idea to drive wedges between the tribes seems unlikely to work, we march north."

Geth faked a thrust and circled the king. "Straight to Dues. I hear it's got nothing more than a wooden palisade. We should have the numbers to overwhelm a single tribe, palisade or no."

"The concern is that they flee and draw us into the trees."

"Then we don't follow. We steal everything that isn't nailed down in Dues and burn the place to ash. Then we march straight back. Let them worry about where they'll house their women and livestock for the winter. That will keep them busy."

"Busy enough to hold off their advance until spring?"

"Busy enough to push Iyngaer's council back. A defeat like that might be enough to upset his alliance all by itself."

Hadean swung his sword. Geth parried. He let the king drive him back a few steps. Sidestepping quickly, he flicked a swat at Hadean's ribs, but the king pivoted to parry it wide. He jumped back, out of reach before Geth could press.

"Good."

Hadean sheathed his sword, motioned toward the table with their drinks. "Better for us if the Ilars stand and fight."

"I'm praying for it."

A pitcher and loaf rested on the table. No cheese or dried fruit, though Melagus couldn't be blamed for the austere offering this time. Geth poured a cup of cool water for each of them.

"Where is the old worm anyway?" Geth muttered. He looked down the length of the hall out of habit only to meet the eyes of a young serving woman watching them from around the corner of the back hallway. She ducked back at the sight of him and disappeared like a frightened doe.

"I haven't seen him all morning," Hadean replied. He raised the cup to his lips, but Geth lunged across the table to slap it from his mouth.

"What the—"

Geth didn't wait to let him finish, sprinting down the hall toward the back. His boots skidded around the corner, and he charged down the hall, pushing open every door he passed. The girl was gone. By the time he got back to the Lord's Hall, Melagus had come in the other way.

"What's going on here!" he demanded.

Hadean stood beside the table rubbing his jaw. His silver cup lay in a puddle among the rushes.

"That water was poisoned," Geth said, still panting. "Did you drink any? Throw it out, the bread too."

Melagus eyed Geth like a madman. "What makes you think—"

He ignored the counselor, turned to the king. "Do you remember what you told me, lord? It's Melagus who usually brings your drink. Before we've even begun. But he was gone and there was a serving girl watching us this time. I couldn't catch her."

"You really think it was poisoned?" Hadean's hand froze on his jaw.

Geth nodded. He reached over the table to spill what was left in the pitcher on the floor. A red welt showed on Hadean's chin, whether from Geth's slap or the burn of something harsh in the cup, the big warrior couldn't say. The boy's eyes went from the bread on the table to his upended cup.

Melagus shook his head. "You rush to such a conclusion at my first absence? How will you prove it? You've just broken the king's lip and emptied out your only evidence on the floor."

"Eat this if you don't believe me." Geth snatched up a slice of bread from the table and thrust it into the worm's hands.

Melagus took one look at it and dropped it like a live spider.

"Not so sure anymore, eh?" Geth's snorted. "Or maybe you already know the answer."

"How dare you!"

"Calm now, both of you!"

Hadean opened his mouth, but one of the keep's many hounds had scurried over at the sight of the fallen bread. Three sets of eyes widened as the beast dipped its neck.

"Don't—" Hadean started, but there was no need. One sniff curled the animal's nose. She left that bread where it sat.

Chapter twenty-two

"Slinking bastard." Geth took a long pull at Phelan's bottle and passed it back. Harsh White Adus spirits burned a trail down his throat, the only heat of any kind up there on the ramparts. He didn't bother to ask Phelan how he'd gotten his hands on the stuff.

"Maybe you shouldn't have accused him. I mean, he was counselor to Hadean's father for Thram's sake. The boy trusts him. And he's got a helluva lot more authority than you do."

"I'm a fool."

Geth reached for the bottle again. The wind in his face froze his lips in a snarl, but it was the only place he felt he didn't have to look over his shoulder. Phelan was right about Melagus of course. The worm hadn't wasted any time exercising his authority. Two days gone and Hadean had yet to summon him for training. A trip to the Lord's Hall earlier that afternoon ended with Geth turned away by the guards.

"They didn't say it, but I know it was that slithering shit that gave the order." He took a swig and passed it back. "Don't tell me there's nothing suspicious in banishing me from the king just when they've taken another swipe at him."

"Anything's possible," Phelan said.

"Smacks of just the sort of thing a worm would try."

"Poison?"

Geth shook his head. "Using an assassin. Too weak to do the deed himself but close enough to sneak someone within striking distance. At no risk to himself, cowardly sonofabitch."

"Maybe it's bigger than him?" Phelan said. "Maybe he's got allies. You ever thought of that?"

Geth swore. "I knew this would happen. I always said it could happen again."

"Hard to imagine the man taking the throne himself, that's what I'm getting at."

"Anything's possible, that's what you said."

Phelan nodded. He pulled his cloak a little closer, eyes narrowed, thinking. Geth waited. He passed over the bottle in case it might help.

Phelan took a swig and grimaced. "I'll tell you what," the little man said. "If Melagus really is the traitor, I reckon I know what his next move is."

"What's that?"

"He'll blame you."

"Me?"

"You were there, right? No one else. Who's to say different?"

"Hadean was there. He won't turn his back on me."

Phelan snorted. "Hadean's young. Green. Easy meat for a fork-tongue like Melagus."

"The lad's no fool."

"I'm just saying, blaming you, the foreign sellsword who happened to be in the room, well, there's no better way for Melagus to distance himself from the crime. If it was, indeed, him."

"I hear ya. But the idea of me using poison doesn't even make sense. If I wanted the king dead, I could just run him through while we practiced."

Phelan took him by the shoulders. "You don't have to convince me, brother. Just be ready. If Melagus blames you, all hell is about to come down on us."

Geth wasn't gonna wait for that to happen. Night had fallen, but he knew the counselor stayed up late. *Stacking and unstacking his parchments, worthless scratch.* Geth headed straight for his chamber.

The door to the Lord's Hall would be guarded but striding the ramparts around to that side of the great fortress, Geth made his approach from above. A night sentinel saluted in passing. Slipping down onto the roof of the hall, it wasn't a difficult climb down the side to the nearest window. Once inside, Geth padded empty hallways until he stood outside the worm's chamber.

He knocked. A curse sounded, the noise of a chair scooting back. The door cracked.

"Who's there?"

Geth pushed door and counselor back and forced himself inside. "Your worst nightmare."

The light of a candelabra inside lit the worm's face as it turned from surprise to scorn. "You give yourself too much credit."

Geth returned a wicked smile.

"Well, what do you want?"

"I know you want the king dead."

"Ha! I want the king dead. And you propose to offer your services?"

"You wish."

Melagus cocked his head. "Oh, I see. The foreign butcher now fancies himself Hadean's protector."

"Why is it you want a trusted sword so far from the king's side? Answer me that."

"Trusted sword?"

"That's right."

"You think some clever bladework and one day in the field can make a home for a masterless dog like you? Didn't you ever learn not to trust a stray?"

Geth felt the heat rising in his chest. Memories of bitter betrayals, of lashes and manacles, lent a weight to those words. He took an involuntary step forward. He could have crushed Melagus's windpipe right then and there. No one would have been the wiser.

He sucked a breath, reined in his temper instead. "Never you mind who I am, except that I'm a loyal servant of the king. One who's willing to kill or be killed for him. Not some scraping toad-shit like you."

"Blood and glory's all you care about. It's as plain as that oft-broken nose on your face."

Geth leaned over him. Melagus must have seen the fury in his eyes, smelled the liquor on his breath, but to his credit, that wisp of a man stood firm where stouter men often crumbled. "I know your role in this," Geth hissed.

"Me? Ha! What about you? It's you that put fool ideas in Hadean's head that almost saw him killed at Copper Ridge. It's you that hatched this suicidal plan to march into Ilia—I've yet to dissuade him from that deathtrap. So, who's to say it wasn't you that poisoned his cup as well?"

Geth's eyes narrowed. He opened his mouth, but the Asp wasn't done spitting venom.

"Do you think I haven't been watching you, Paellian? And your sneaking footman, filling our young king full of vainglorious aims and dangerous plots."

"I only want—"

"And isn't it strange how your arrival coincides with the burglaries we've suffered all of a sudden?"

"That's a lot of accusations all in one night."

"It's you that came knocking at my door."

"That I did."

"Well, don't be surprised if someone comes knocking at your door next."

Geth didn't like the sound of that. The night wore on but Phelan never returned to the barracks. Geth went out looking for him. He found him at the dice table of the Bottom of the Cup, good and drunk with a tavern wench on each knee.

"Uro's shriveled nuts, man, what's wrong with you?" Geth took Phelan by the elbow, staring down the protests of the other players and scattering his lady friends. He dragged him off into a corner.

"I was winning!"

"I should rip this skinny little arm off. What did I tell you about stealing on the job? Melagus is complaining of a wave of robberies and he's figuring to pin it on you."

Phelan lifted a finger, regarded Geth with watery eyes. "He'll never catch me in the act, I promise you—"

Geth smacked him across the mouth.

"Hey, that hurt, jackass!"

"If you don't want another one then listen. Melagus will have you hanged if you're caught with something stolen. Me too probably. Whatever you've got, dump it. If it's coin, hide it. We're outsiders here. We've got enemies. And in a matter of days, we could be stuck on the inside of a fortress under siege."

"I barely—"

"No more lies! I don't want to see you jerking at the end of a rope, alright?"

"Alright, alright." Phelan rested a hand on Geth's shoulder. He shook his head to clear it. "I'll straighten up."

"Do it."

"I said I would! Thram's crooked cock!"

"Alright." Geth softened his tone. "Hadean's a good lad, that's all I'm saying. We're lucky to call him lord. So don't shit where you eat. And dump anything that doesn't belong to you before Melagus comes nosing around. Got it?"

"Got it. Dump the stuff and don't eat any shit."

Dawn had broken by the time Geth made it back across the bridge, into Towerrock's greater ward. Phelan's White Adus spirits had left him with a dull headache. Melagus's words did nothing to relieve the pressure.

Groundskeepers and laundresses hustled about their business. The first soldiers had already emerged to begin a day at training or a turn upon the walls. Geth wanted nothing more than to sack out for an hour first, but a sly smile from Gylfric in passing stopped him short of the barracks.

"What are you looking at, shit-stain?"

Gylfric only half-turned to utter a reply. "A dead man walking."

Geth started toward him until he caught sight of Wayan and several green-cloaks coming the other way. The yardmaster bared his teeth in that fake smile of his, but grim faces on the men at his back told another tale.

"Sergeant Geth, just the man I need."

"On my way to the sword-yard, sir. Can't be late."

"How about a stop in the Lord's Hall first? Got some questions about what happened the other day with the king."

"I've already told Utrand and Melagus all that I know."

"Maybe we need to hear it all again."

Geth felt his jaw clench. "There's nothing else to tell. Did they find the girl I saw? If not, I'm not going anywhere."

"Is that right?" Wayan's eyes narrowed. "Looks like you still wear the green, don't you? You'll go where you're told."

Geth sucked in a breath, but it did nothing to calm him. "Did that sneaking counselor put you up to this? You really think you can put that poison job on me when I was the one who spilled the bloody cup?"

"Maybe now is the time to tell your side of things. Let us judge what you have to say."

"You and Melagus?"

Wayan bared that fake smile again. "C'mon now, lad." But Geth had already been sentenced by Melagus once.

"I would never turn on Hadean. That's all you need to know." He started past, but the yardmaster's hand shot out to grip him by the arm. He leaned in close.

"You think I don't know what tattoos like yours mean? You're a savage-lover, that's what you are. Maybe even a half-blood. If you'll side with the Mog over your own people, who's to say you won't turn against Umbel?"

Geth felt the blood pumping in his head. "You know nothing about my marks. Or the men who gave them to me. Honest men, not lying, backstabbing bastards like you."

"Filthy little—"

They went for each other at the same time, pushing and pulling at close range, fighting for leverage. Shouts rang out. Geth gave ground, tried to set up an overhead throw, but a pair of arms caught him from behind.

"Hold him!" someone cried.

Wayan tore loose, managed a kick into Geth's midriff, but by some luck the clasped hands of the man behind him took the brunt of the force. The soldier swore. Geth seized the chance to break his grip, ramming an elbow backward into the bastard's stomach and lashing out at Wayan with a straight kick of his own. A second soldier lunged at Geth, but a well-timed jab collapsed him back into the yardmaster.

"Get off me!" Wayan cursed. "Don't let him go!"

But Geth still had a few friends in Towerrock. And a reputation. Green-cloaks scattered as he dashed for the gates. He ran into Phelan on the bridge coming the other way, back from town. His friend took one look at him and followed at a dead run through the muddy lanes of Greenfell.

They pulled to a panting halt behind a row of thatch roofs. "I'm gonna puke." Phelan breathed.

"You were right." Geth said, sucking air. "They mean to blame me. They—"

The sound of footsteps sent his hand to his hilt, but it was Kerrel who emerged from around the corner, skidding to a stop beside them. "Where are you going? I saw you fighting the captain. I saw you running."

"Well…"

"Are you leaving?"

Geth caught his breath, put a hand on the lad's arm. "I have to. Wayan's got it out for me. Neary's in charge of the file for now, alright?"

"You're really leaving?"

"Not leaving, not really. It's just… The king's got a secret errand for me. Right, Phelan?"

Phelan managed a nod.

"Not even the yardmaster knows of it. We've been sent east to gather allies for Umbel. We've still got some friends in Turia. Be back with a hundred swords faster than you can whistle."

Kerrel frowned. "Can I come?"

"Who'd be left to look after Neary? And keep an eye out for the king as well?"

"I guess—"

"Remember, it's a secret." Geth rested his hands on the lad's shoulders, looked him in the eyes. "I need you to carry a message back to Hadean too. A very important message."

Kerrel knuckled his brow. "Right."

"Tell the king… Tell him I haven't forgot what he's done for me. I'm his man."

"That's the message?"

"And one more thing. Tell the Lord Eldric to keep an eye on the Asp. He's a real snake alright. You tell him that."

Kerrel looked confused but Geth didn't wait for an affirmation. He clapped the lad on the shoulder and sent him back the way he'd come. Shoving Phelan in the other direction, he started them moving again.

A light snow began to fall. They hustled through back alleys and out into the fields beyond the town, the only sounds the smack of boots on wet ground and their own ragged breathing. They didn't stop until they reached the River Road.

"So, we're really heading back east?" Phelan asked.

"Wayan wanted to put me on trial. You know how I feel about trials."

"And you're serious about gathering allies for the king?"

"We still got a few friends, right? Whether the Tooth falls under siege or they march for Ilia, more swords can't hurt. By then this will all have blown over."

"Of course." Phelan rubbed his hands together. "Good idea. Gets us out of that siege too. If it takes a season or two to drum up allies, so be it."

A season or two. Damp ground passed underfoot. Geth looked back the way they'd come. Towerrock sat dull and grey under snow-laden skies, but there was no denying the grandeur of it. Green and white banners waved from each of her five towers.

Phelan smiled beside him, eyes already turned east. It wasn't so easy for Geth. Somewhere inside that keep, Hadean trained alone. Or sat in counsel. Maybe he was just getting news of Geth's fight with Wayan, his humiliating exit. Maybe the Asp whispered in his ear, explained how the vile mercenary must surely have been at the root of his poisoned cup. Why else would he flee?

Geth cursed the gods. He could only hope Eldric would guard the king's back in his absence, that this latest failed attempt on the lad would buy some time. And then there was the matter of the Ilar tribes. In three weeks' time, Iyngaer's counsel would begin to gather. In four weeks, the bastard would be headed south with an army at his back.

The siege would begin. Northern Umbel would fall under sword and fire. Plunder, rape, enslavement. Hadean would take the blame, just the sort of thing to embolden a traitor.

Geth stopped in his tracks. "Wait."

Phelan raised an eyebrow.

"We're going north."

"What's north?"

"Iyngaer's council with the other Ilar tribes. While we're out east drumming up a few measly dozens, he'll be drumming up whole tribes."

Phelan blinked. "You're saying you want to go to his council?"

"No, I want to spoil the soup before it starts cooking."

Phelan eyed him like he was mad.

"Melagus had a plan to send an emissary north, right? To offer gold and land to one of the tribes, force cracks in Iyngaer's alliance."

"Yeah?"

"Divide and conquer, the oldest trick in the book. That could be enough to stave off an attack on Umbel. Or better yet, set the tribes at each other's throats instead of ours."

"You serious? We aren't Hadean's emissaries, Geth. And we don't have any gold to offer."

"They don't know that. Melagus thought it could work. We both know what a clever sonofabitch he is. The only reason Hadean didn't send someone north already is because he thought they might kill the messenger."

Phelan blinked. "Did you even hear what you just told me?"

"I know these tribesmen, Phelan. The way they think. They're not so different from the Mog. They'll hear us out."

"And kill us afterward." The little man snorted. "You go on if you have to, I'm out."

"I need you to translate! You know damn well I don't speak Ilar."

"It's cold, Geth! It's snowing right now for shit's sake! And you want me to march further north? To certain death?"

"Would you rather go back to Towerrock and 'fess up to what you stole? Or go back home, straight into Palladine's jaws?"

"Got a better chance in Pellon than bloody Ilia."

"Not without me to watch your back. And I'm headed north, so gather your balls and let's do this."

"You wouldn't."

"Look me in the eye."

Phelan looked like he might take a swing. "You're a real asshole, you know that? Real nasty sonofabitch."

"I knew you'd come around."

Phelan opened his mouth, but Geth started walking, waving him to follow.

"C'mon. We've got three weeks. Or it's all for nothing."

Chapter twenty-three

"We can pick up supplies at Point-fort," Phelan said. "The Ilars didn't steal everything."

Geth smiled. "How was this city boy ever gonna survive in the woods without you?"

"Well, you probably weren't. I should've just let you try and went my own way. Mention of Palladine must have unmanned me."

"You never told me how you landed on his shitlist."

"A tale for another day. A few flagons of wine and some harp music would dislodge it, I reckon. They do have wine and harps in Ilia, don't they?"

Geth just shook his head. They marched at a sharp clip despite exhaustion dragging at each limb, hoping to make the shelter of Point-fort's empty walls by nightfall. Geth flicked a glance over his shoulder from time to time, but no one came after them. Nor would they, he realized. He was gone. Both Melagus and Wayan would be content. No need to waste lives on his sword as long as he never came back.

At midday they reached a rise overlooking the site of Copper Ridge, the ground still stained and trampled. Memory of the duel against Big Yellow put a smile across Geth's face but they kept moving. They reached Point-fort just after sundown.

Blood stained the ground here too. The king had ordered the boundary forts abandoned at the start of the war and the place stood empty, but a mound of freshly turned earth marked where Hadean's men had buried the slaughtered garrison. The gates opened with a shove.

Geth looked up. A low moon lit the underside of thick, low-hanging clouds. "Glad we made it. There's snow on the air."

"I'll gather what we need," Phelan said.

Geth chased a squirrel out of the hall and stacked some wood in the hearth just in time for Phelan's return with flint and tinder. The little man struck a flame, rolled out a couple bedrolls. The fire threw shadows off a low-beamed ceiling, walls lined with empty racks for weapons and moth-eaten hangings.

"Got waterskins, socks, gloves," Phelan said. "Everything we need except drink."

"We might want to eat at some point too. There was a squirrel in here. You still got your sling?"

"Dried fruit is gonna have to suffice for tonight. I'll make another pass tomorrow when there's more light but that's all I found. Hadean's boys probably overlooked something. Hopefully they left a cookpot too, in case we bring down a dove or a hare."

Geth snorted. "I'm sure you'll find a few tidbits to hang on to as well. You know, some silverware, an earring. Maybe a stray brooch."

"Actually, I was thinking to bury a thing or two. For safe keeping."

He reached into his belt pouch, pulled out a handful of glittering coins and at least a few rings. Geth sat up from his bedding to get a better look.

"Thram's balls, Phelan."

"You still want me to dump it?"

"Now that you mention it, that shine just might come in handy in Ilia."

"Ha! Admit it, it's a good thing I set us up."

"You've got a real short memory, ya know that? Your sticky fingers are half the reason we've been run out of Umbel."

"What about your little dust-up with Wayan? That bloody temper! Anybody looks at you sideways and you want to squeeze his throat."

"That's not—"

"And Melagus. Vorda's tits, man, when are you gonna learn how to kiss some ass?"

"You can kiss their asses if that's what you're about."

Phelan tucked his haul back into a pocket and laid back down, eyes up on the rafters. "You're not gonna pin this all on me, that's all I'm saying. You made yourself plenty of enemies along the way. And this is where it's landed us."

The combination of cold air and exhaustion meant Geth slept like the dead. He wasn't particularly inclined to move the next morning until the sun had driven off the worst of the chill. Phelan's indictment still rang in his ear.

The surly bastard was right.

I'm a fool. Geth cursed himself. They were on a good run, had really made a go of starting fresh. Until he ruined it. He'd let down Phelan and he'd let down himself. And now Hadean was gonna pay for it.

"Let's go, lazy-ass." Geth stood with a grimace, nudged Phelan with one foot.

"Alright, alright."

"See if you can find something to eat, would ya?"

Phelan made a crude gesture and rose to shuffle off toward the chamber that once housed the fort's captain. Rummaging sounds echoed through the open door. Geth watched as he wandered from chamber to chamber, muttering.

A pristine white scene greeted Geth as he finished the bedrolls and stepped outside. Fresh snow blanketed the yard. A wind blew, creeping under his neck. He pulled his cloak tighter.

Phelan appeared with a small pot in hand. "We're in luck."

"Anything else?"

"No fillets or custard pie if that's what you were expecting, but I found a half-barrel of salted venison." He passed over a finger-length strip of cured meat.

"Venison it is."

Phelan looked out toward the gate. "So, what's the plan?"

"What do you know about Ilia? Besides the fact it's a little to the north."

"You're asking me? This was your idea. You tell me how this is gonna go."

Geth bit off a chunk of meat, worked it with his molars. "Well, once you take Iyngaer off the list, there's only three options. But which one of the three tribes is most likely to take the bait?"

"I bet you want to start with that big woman we came north with."

"Sure, give her one of those rings. What woman doesn't like jewelry?"

"One that carries a hand-and-a-half sword."

Geth laughed. "Speaking of ladies, I never had a chance to tell you what I learned from Pythelle."

"Pythelle?"

"She lured me into her cellar."

"This sounds interesting."

"Don't get excited, it was all business. She wanted to show me some kind of witchery that allowed her to look into Ilia."

"She what? And you never told me? If she lured you into her cellar for a bounce on the bush-rat, that's one thing. But she's a witch, Geth. What if she put an enchantment on you?"

"Sorry, brother. I guess I was just a little shook."

"Are you sure she *didn't* magick you?"

"If she did, would I know it?"

"Maybe I should smack you a few times, shake the spells loose."

"Yeah, yeah. But listen, this is the point: Hadean mentioned Pythelle had a spy in Ilia. I reckon she was using the same trick she showed me to speak to someone up there. The king planned to use her spy to decide which tribe to offer the gold to."

Phelan frowned. "I'm still trying to figure out where she fits in all this."

"You said she was getting cozy with Eldric. Doesn't that make her an ally of Hadean as well?"

"Maybe."

"Well either way, I never learned which chief her spy was closest to. That would have made the choice a lot easier."

Phelan looked back out across the yard. "The way I reckon, we haven't got a choice. Straight north and we run into the lands of the Duei, Iyngaer's tribe. I don't think we stand much of a chance sneaking clean through to reach the Arnus tribe north of Dues. But if we cross the river, we can reach the lands of the Thirings, Ceter's people."

"Ceter." Geth tried to remember. "Wasn't he that white-haired scratch?"

Phelan shrugged.

"Ceter it is, I reckon."

Geth stripped a green and white banner from one of the walls inside and stowed it in a pack along with the rest of the gear they'd gathered. The better part of the morning was gone by the time they started north, but after crossing the river at the same ford Neary had shown them, they were done for the day anyway. Frozen hands somehow struck a fire to warm them and dry their clothes. A narrow ravine shielded them from the wind.

After an hour almost on top of the flames, Phelan mustered the energy to bring down a rabbit with his sling. Geth skinned and gutted. Phelan used his pot to make a stew. It beat the hell out of chewy venison, but Geth's mind kept going back to Hadean.

From what Melagus had told him, they'd talked the lad out of marching his army north. It was Iyngaer's move. In a matter of weeks, once the big chieftain had wrangled all the tribes into line, he'd loose his mob on Umbel. For Neary, Kerrel, and the rest of the boys, that meant weathering a siege. For Hadean, it could mean death.

Geth had them up and marching early again the next morning. He squinted against the bright, sunlit snowscape. It was only a few inches that had come down—not enough to hamper them, thank the gods—but even so, Phelan stalled when the forests of Ilia came into view.

"We really doing this?"

"Iyngaer's council meets in a few weeks."

Geth didn't wait for his friend but plunged ahead. Row upon row of snow-burdened pine welcomed them, white and leaning like old men. Perhaps it was just a trick of the mind, but rather than being warmer there, with the trees to shield them from the wind, the chill seemed to deepen.

Phelan knew the woodlands best and Geth dropped back to let him pick the path. They kept a course alongside the river, driving ever north until they struck a well-used road. It ran west, away from the banks. Geth reached in his pack to unfurl Umbel's banner.

"We march until someone picks us up. That's the plan. You do the talking."

"Do we have any other choice?"

Geth used his Ilar sword to hack off a tree limb and fashion a pole for his flag. They started down the path. Phelan marched with gritted teeth, but they weren't five miles in before the barking of dogs rang out.

A company of tribesmen appeared from the trees, surrounded them with bows and swords. A man and woman in their middle years stepped forward, blades in hand. They wore the same fur-trimmed leathers as every other Ilar Geth had ever seen, but a burnished silver brooch on the man's cloak and several rings on the woman's fingers indicated some station. Geth lifted his banner, raised his free hand palm open in a gesture of peace.

"Do your thing, Phelan," he muttered.

The Ilar tongue rolled off the little man's lips like he'd spoken it since the day he was born. That was his gift. If there wasn't some magick in that, there was no such thing. He went back and forth with the pair of Ilars. Magick or otherwise, it worked.

"Give 'em your sword," Phelan said. "They agreed to take us to Ceter in his hillfort at Thiringia."

Geth exhaled a breath he didn't realize he'd been holding. "We're in."

Chapter twenty-four

The journey took two full days. Geth's mind went to Iyngaer's looming counsel. There was just no way to move faster.

Phelan marched beside him, eavesdropping best he could on the tribesmen. They followed the same wagon-rutted road through an endless forest of snow-matted evergreens. Queer black squirrels skittering among the boles and branches reminded Geth just how far they were from home.

On the second day, they reached a wide meadow, stumbling on some animal that resembled a huge, lumbering deer. The Ilars hooted and gave chase. Geth craned his neck to see but the hunters were soon out of sight. The creature had been skinned and slaughtered by the time the main party caught up. His mouth watered, wondering what a roasted hock of that might taste like.

The smell of woodsmoke was Geth's first indication they'd arrived. "You smell that?"

Phelan nodded.

Their road emerged from the trees into a broad white valley, sliced by a frozen river and dotted with low, thatch-roofed dwellings. As they neared the first homestead, Geth eyed small herds of some breed of short, tamed deer clustered in pens beside long-haired goats and woolly sheep. Shielding his eyes from the bright, noonday sun on the snow, he followed the curve of the river to a hillock topped by squarish ramparts.

"That must be it. Thiringia."

The Ilar woman fell in stride beside Phelan, eying him sternly and slapping the hilt of her weapon as she gave some instruction. Phelan nodded, repeating that strange humming expression of the tribesmen Geth had heard back in Umbel.

"That was a warning," Phelan said.

"Well, it wasn't a welcoming speech, that's for sure."

The path wound between more log dwellings until they walked beneath the eyes of spear-toting sentries on the walls. Geth reckoned it a man-made hill, the stockade of timber with at least three ornate gatehouses and several high-peaked buildings within. Iron-bound gates stood open, pierced by a muddied track, though little actual traffic flowed along its length.

"So, what's the plan again?" Phelan asked.

"Tell them we're Hadean's emissaries and offer them the sun. Whatever it takes for Ceter to part with Iyngaer."

"You sure they won't just kill us?"

Geth didn't answer. Their escorts halted them there at the gates. An Ilar with an impressive mustache came clunking down the stairs from the gatehouse tower above them.

He dismissed Phelan with a glance, but his eyes lingered on Geth. These Ilars were something different, that was sure, but everything about them recalled Geth's days among the so-called wild men of the east. If the tribes were as similar to the Mog as he suspected, he reckoned he might hazard a guess at how they thought, what got their blood up, what might make them laugh.

Still, Ilia was its own place—remote, one of a kind in all the wide lands of Eria. The mustachioed gate captain waved the Ilar couple off, taking Geth's sword from the man and motioning several of his own guardsmen down from the parapet. The Ilar woman barked something in return, but Mustache just laughed. His men arrived, circling around Geth and Phelan, eyeing them with hungry grins.

Mustache stepped in front of Geth to utter something stern in his own tongue.

"He's telling you to mind your manners," Phelan said. "Or don't, and see what happens."

Geth nodded. Mustache thrust Geth's confiscated sword back into his arms with a snort. His men prodded them up the hill. Geth flicked a glance over his shoulder at the gates, noted a stable with a few shaggy northern horses nearby, counted the men on the walls. A tall, steep-roofed structure with ornate carvings like something from the bow of a ship loomed ahead.

"The palace," Phelan whispered. "That's what the scratch with the mustache called it. The chieftain will be waiting."

Geth set his jaw. Mustache's men pushed the weatherworn doors open and motioned them inside. At first, he could see nothing aside from a huge fire burning in a central hearth. The ceiling was low, and smoke swirled among the rafters except where a shaft above the flames drew it out. As Geth's eyes adjusted, he made out Ilar men and women in twos and threes seated on lush fur pelts, sipping from mugs, working needle and thread, honing blades. There were only two chairs in the wide chamber, both on the other side of the fire, near the center of the hall. Geth picked out the chieftain, Ceter, by his white hair seated on the one. As he drew closer, he recognized the sharp-eyed Ilar who'd ridden north with them on the other.

Mustache's sentries ushered them around the fire to the far side to stand before the chieftain.

"Start talking," Geth told Phelan. The little man bowed. Geth copied the gesture.

"O Ceter Govende," Phelan began.

The Ilar language floated off his tongue as he worked through the introductions. Geth held his makeshift banner so they could see it. Every eye in the room was on them. If the Ilars didn't accept them as Hadean's true emissaries, they were as good as dead. He made note of an exit at the back of the room, who wore a sword, where the sentries stood.

He studied Ceter as well. Aside from deep-set, knowing eyes and those snow-white locks, he really didn't look so old. Ornate stitchwork decorated his leathers. The fur at his collar was rich sable, and gold studs gleamed in each ear. Geth blinked, realizing the sharp-eyed Ilar at his side wore a matching set.

The chieftain nodded when Phelan was done. Sharp-eye leaned in to utter something to Ceter, flicking a smug glance at Geth.

"He remembers your trial," Phelan said, "with Melagus, back in Hadean's keep."

Geth felt his cheeks go hot.

But Ceter never smiled, eyes intent on the big warrior. "Seteng tells me you were almost hanged by your own people."

Aside from a queer accent, the chieftain spoke perfect Aturian. Geth nodded.

"I watched as you stood for your king in single combat. And now you cross the miles to stand before me. It's a dangerous path you've trodden. Either you're very brave, or a desperate fool."

"King Hadean says you're a man of reason," Geth lied. "Of sharp wit. That you alone in Ilia will see the real merit in what I have to say and welcome it."

"Welcome? I'm afraid you might find me a terrible host. The meats are the freshest here, but we've got nothing to drink except berry wine."

Geth tensed, but Ceter smiled. He was toying with them.

Geth forced a smile of his own. He turned to Phelan, whispering under his breath. "Tell me you've got a flask hidden somewhere."

His friend grumbled something about "worst idea ever" but reached behind his back to produce a tin. Geth unstopped it and took a whiff. White Adus. The good stuff.

"I was saving it," Phelan hissed. "To celebrate once we get home."

"I'll need something from your belt pouch too."

Phelan's jaw clenched. Geth went easy on him. From that pouch he took a single gold ring.

"Accept this," Geth told Ceter, stepping closer, "a token from King Hadean."

He passed over the flask. Ceter sniffed it. He closed his eyes.

"White Adus."

Phelan muttered curses behind him, but Geth ignored that. He turned to Seteng, Ceter's lover, he reckoned.

"And for you." He held the ring up to be seen then reached forward to slide it onto the tribesman's hand.

Seteng admired his gift. He turned to utter something to Ceter in their tongue. They shared a smile.

"Senteng says you did us all a favor ridding Ilia of Othwid's foul-breathed brother. The braggart with the fair beard I mean."

"Big Yellow? Glad to do it."

That seemed to have sealed it. Ceter laughed out loud. He rubbed his hands together. Tension in the room melted away. Lounging tribesmen went back to their needlework or meal.

"You've traveled far. Take some rest. After, we shall speak."

The chieftain motioned to an attendant and pelts were rolled out on the ground. Young Ilars brought wash basins for both Geth and Phelan, followed by a tray of cheeses and some tart berry wine. Ceter stood. He started toward a door at the back of the hall. With a trailing hand, he led Seteng along with him. Light flooded the dim chamber as they stepped out into the snow.

Geth settled onto one of the pelts and rinsed his hands. Those cheeses stared at him. He wanted to savor them but ate fast instead, before Phelan could claim the bigger share.

His friend sat cross-legged on the other pelt. "You didn't need me after all. The old scratch speaks Aturian better than you do."

"That Ceter is something special, that's for sure."

"Seems to me he's bored. You think it was an accident he gave us an audience right away? Bastard's got nothing else to do."

"That won't help our cause. This war will be something to excite him, get him off this windswept dung pile. I don't take him for a warrior though. Iyngaer and the other chieftains, sure. Not this one."

Phelan stuffed a slice of cheese in his mouth and spoke around it. "Well, if there's one thing about old men I've learned, they didn't get old by accident. They're careful. They don't take chances."

Geth snorted. "Not with their own lives anyway."

"Sounds like something you could learn from."

"It's that wit of yours, Phelan. I need you more than you realize."

Phelan rolled his eyes. He took a pull at his wine and puckered his lips. Geth sipped at his own cup and grimaced. An acquired taste, berry wine, no doubt about that.

"So, Ceter may or may not want a war," he said, "but he's gotta want *something*."

"Besides rolling with that pretty kitten of his?"

"Maybe we have to convince him that the tribes will lose if it comes to a war? Tell him Hadean's got more troops coming up from the south."

"I don't reckon he'll be fooled so easy." Phelan shook his head. "He may not be a warrior, but he's got other...talents."

Geth eyed his friend sideways. "What do you mean? Like the Seer, Agrem?

"I don't know. Something. He's not from here, you know."

"That accent." Geth nodded.

"You should hear his people whisper. He's an outsider for sure, even if he holds the reins."

Geth thought that through. If Ceter wasn't a tribesman, didn't think like the other tribesmen, that could change everything. "Keep listening, Phelan. And let me know what you hear. Our lives may depend on it."

Ceter's spread was almost worth the march north. Young tribesmen with baskets of sweetbreads, platters of steaming meats, cooked snails, and river trout moved throughout the knots of seated Ilars. There were vegetables Geth didn't recognize and a huge slab of ribs that might have belonged to an animal like the one his escorts brought down the previous day. Geth wasn't about to let his guard down on account of one delicious meal, but it *was* delicious.

They sat between the chieftain and the central fire, a place of honor. The wind howled outside as a storm blew in, but it was cozy in Ceter's palace. The chieftain's manner had Geth's hopes up as well. He told tales of hunting strange game in faraway lands, one of Seteng's hands resting in his lap all the while. He laughed at Phelan's stories and plied Geth with questions about Pellon and the east. Phelan was right, the old bastard was bored in Ilia, no natural-born tribesman himself. That played into their hands.

"You've shared tidings of every country but one," Ceter said, hand moved to the shoulder of his mate, fingers rubbing idly. "What of Umbel? Tell me why Hadean sent you."

Geth set his cup down on the ground beside him. "Can't you guess?"

"Yes, I know. But why would he send *you*?"

"Maybe I was the only man brave enough to make the journey?"

The chieftain laughed. He turned to his man and translated. The handsome Ilar smiled.

"My king wants you to leave Iyngaer's alliance," Geth said. "And he's willing to make it worth your while."

"Of course he is."

"Not just in gold," Geth raised a finger. "But in land. And title. 'Lord Ceter of the North.' You'd be recognized as more than just a chieftain here in Ilia. You'd be nobility in Umbel. And that means nobility in all the Sworn Realms."

Ceter's hand rested on Seteng's forearm, one finger tapping thoughtfully. Geth had made it all up on the spot. He had no idea if Hadean could do such a thing.

"Lands in the south." Ceter pursed his lips.

"Beside the sea if you like. That's what King Hadean's willing to give in order to seal this pact with you."

Geth pushed on. "And what's Iyngaer promising? Glory? Plunder? Take this deal and you can get gold for your men without leaving this valley. And as for yourself, you could march south any time you like for some proper wine and sunshine on your face."

Ceter breathed a sigh. "The offer tempts me. But you don't understand the Ilar mind. Glory? Plunder? My men can't resist it. A loaf stolen tastes much sweeter than the one you bake yourself."

"This is your tribe, isn't it?" Geth said. "Unless I'm getting something wrong. You tell these men which way to point their spears. If it's a dust-up they want, join us in the fight against Dues. But Hadean isn't even asking that much. He only asks that you leave Iyngaer's alliance. Let that tree-top bastard fight for his own glory."

Ceter frowned at his cup. Geth flicked a glance at Phelan. He lounged on one elbow, drink in hand. Geth knew it was no accident how he cocked one ear toward the chieftain.

"Do you like a strong drink, Master Geth? I've recently come upon some White Adus Spirits. I might be inclined to share."

Geth dipped his head. "Gracious of you, my Lord."

He downed his berry wine and held out his cup. Ceter rose to pour him a finger of clear liquor. Phelan looked up expectantly, but the chieftain poured for himself and his lover and settled back into his chair.

"Ahh." Ceter savored the first sip.

"Do we have an agreement?" Geth asked. "Where I come from, you don't drink 'til after the work is done."

"And where is that? You're not from Umbel. I hear it in your words. Nor Turia, despite the mustache."

"And you, Lord Ceter, are no Ilar."

The chieftain smiled. "No. I'm a citizen of the world, like you."

Geth snorted a laugh and looked down to swirl the clear spirits in his hand. Ceter leaned forward.

"Hadean's plot is an old one," he said. "But I am old as well. He'll make promises today and break them tomorrow. Or his lords will break them. Or his sons. He'll divide the tribes, turn on them, one at a time. Like the sunlanders have always done."

"Hadean's different."

"How can he be? We are what we are."

"He saved my life. Any other lord would have let me hang. Just ask, Seteng. He saw the whole thing."

Ceter flicked a glance at his mate but held his tongue.

"Hadean's different, better. Like you said, 'you are what you are.'"

"You believe that don't you, about this king?"

"I do."

The chieftain met his eye. A moment passed. Another. It was like the bastard was looking through him, into his head. Geth shivered.

Maybe Phelan was right. Maybe Ceter was a warlock like the Seer. Maybe Geth had just been magicked and the sonofabitch knew his every thought.

Not good.

But perhaps it worked both ways. Geth looked at the chieftain, there beside his pretty man, and it all became clear. He *was* bored. This whole meeting was nothing but a diversion.

Ceter had no intention of leaving Iyngaer. He didn't believe in Hadean the way Geth did—or didn't believe the boy's rule would last long enough for it to matter. No, Ceter was a cat with a couple of mice between its paws, batting them around. When he was done, he'd eat the pair.

Geth leaned toward Phelan, whispered in the tongue of the Mog. "Be ready."

Phelan coughed on his drink, faked a laugh to cover it. Geth stood, lifted his lacquered wooden cup. He'd never been very patient. And this might be his only chance to catch the cat on his back feet.

"A toast," he said, "to our arrangement."

Ceter cracked a wry grin. He lifted his cup. Geth flicked a glance to either side of the dim chamber to find only a handful of servants standing as well. Clamping his eyes shut, he splashed his spirits into the fire.

The heat of it washed over him, followed by a collective gasp from Ceter's people. In one step Geth had a hand on Setengs's collar, delivering a vicious chop to his throat with the other before tossing him full onto the chieftain.

Shouts erupted throughout the room, but three long strides carried Geth to the hall's back exit. His sword came free. A guard hoisted his own blade, but half-blinded by the fire's flash, he missed the arc of Geth's weapon and fell with a hand at his spurting neck. Phelan threw a pelt into the face of a second guard. Geth could *feel* the outrage trailing him as they dashed through the door.

Wind and snow hit him like a slap in the face. At first, he saw nothing, only felt his boots hit fresh powder. He dragged one hand against the side of the building to follow it back around toward the front until his eyes adjusted. "This way!" he yelled over his shoulder.

He sucked in snow with every cold, burning breath. It came down in a swirling mass. Only the sound of Phelan's footsteps told him his friend still followed.

Geth led them back down the hill toward the stable he'd seen at the gatehouse. Fortune was with him that night, he reckoned. A white owl couldn't have seen ten feet in that snowfall. Everyone in the entire hillfort had taken shelter inside anyway.

Geth didn't slow until they reached the stables he'd seen earlier. Distant voices sounded, nothing more.

"What now?" Phelan asked.

"Steal some horses and get the hell outta here. With any luck, Ceter will hang around to nurse his man. That'll give us a head start."

Phelan didn't argue. Geth pushed through the door slowly, chased out a stable boy, and led two shaggy horses back out. They mounted bareback, spurred their steeds toward the gates.

"Ho!"

Mustache appeared under the arch of the exit. His eyes widened but he had no chance to draw his sword before Geth hacked him down.

Chapter twenty-five

Nights were long that time of year in the north and they rode blindly away from Ceter's fastness for what seemed an eternity. Darkness cloaked them. Snowfall covered their tracks. What's more, the chieftain would stay behind with his injured lover at least 'til daybreak, Geth reckoned. That gave them a generous lead.

They rode with their heads down, teeth gritted, even as the clouds finally parted to admit a bright morning sun. Geth was tired. And hungry.

"I wish I would have eaten more."

Phelan grumbled beside him. "The gods really hate me. We had a roof over our heads. A fire. Meat. I know you like meat."

Geth didn't look up. "Ceter was gonna kill us."

"How's that?"

"I just know. The longer we stayed, the more time for him to catch us with our guard down. Poison maybe. Sorcery. A knife across the throat while we slept."

"If you're right, I owe someone a big apology."

"The gods? Ha!" Geth snorted. "They still want something from us, that's all."

"Like what?"

"Blood, I reckon. What else am I good for?"

"Maybe it's the Ilar gods that sent that storm." Phelan said. "We're in Ilia after all. Maybe they hate Ceter. Either way, it's hard to feel any love at the moment, for the gods or anyone else."

Geth couldn't argue. The sun was out, the air still and cold but tolerable. But what happened when they stopped moving and night fell? Or if another storm blew in? They'd left with the cloaks on their backs, little else. No tent. No foodstuffs. Not even a saddle. Geth's ass was already sore.

"You're right," he said. "There's no love. They've set us on the run again."

"I'm starting to get tired of running."

"Well damn the gods. I'm not doing it anymore. I'm done running."

"Then what is it we're doing now?"

"Heading north."

Phelan chewed his lip. "I was gonna mention that. I thought it might be some daft attempt of yours to throw off the chase."

"It is. Partly. But we aren't doubling back. I said I'm done running and I meant it. We're marching north, to the next tribe."

"Now I know you've really lost it, friend."

"Have I?" Geth pulled his shaggy mount to a halt. "We only need one tribe to split from Iyngaer. One tribe. That's enough to give Hadean the upper hand in this war."

"Uro's wrinkled ass, Geth. You do remember what lies north of here, don't you? Laer, Vriana's lands. The woman who gutted Point-fort and tried to lure more troops north to be massacred."

"She thinks like a warrior. Maybe I can get through to her."

"How? With gold? We can't offer her land. How would she even get to any lands in Umbel? Ceter's in the way. No chance that woman sides with Umbel, not now."

"There are rifts between these tribes up here, Phelan. You heard Ceter; Umbel's been using those rifts to its advantage for years. And there's a rift between men and women even when they share the same bed."

"You think that'll be enough?"

"I'm just saying, that woman's got a chip on her shoulder the size of the Oathstone."

"Well…"

"I reckon it's been hard for her, sitting in the chieftain's chair with all these hard-knuckle types all around. You can bet your ass she's been looked down at by more than a few."

"I bet she made 'em regret it."

"I bet she has." Geth nodded grimly. "But it's Iyngaer that leads this bunch, right? The other chieftain's won't appreciate him taking all the glory, getting the biggest piece of the pie. And no one will resent him more than Vriana."

Phelan frowned. "I think I smell what you're cooking. We promise her an alliance with Umbel, take down Iyngaer together, and set her up as the top dog."

"What have you got left in that belt pouch besides coin?"

"A couple rings, that's it. The one has a nice ruby in it."

"We give her that ring then, a marker of the contract. What woman doesn't like jewelry?"

They dismounted and walked the horses for several miles, partly to rest the beasts, partly to keep their own blood pumping, their eyes open. Phelan steered them deeper into the pines, away from the few winding cart-paths they found. They settled down underneath a rocky outcropping beside a frozen creek, far enough in the hills to risk a fire.

"Thank the gods you held tight to that flint."

Phelan shook his head. "In this country? I'm sleeping with it in my under-drawers."

With a fire, it was cold but tolerable. The horses huddled close and the lay of the land sheltered them from any wind. Geth was hungry of course. No getting around that. He sat with his back to the stone, knees pulled up under his chin and cloak drawn tight. Phelan dug stones out from under the snow to pile them round the fire. He took off his boots and rested his stockinged feet on one of them, just inches from the flames.

"Ahh." The little man closed his eyes. "Take those cold boots off and put your foot on one of these. Once these rocks have soaked up some heat, we can kick 'em over and curl up around them to sleep."

"You're full of tricks, aren't you."

"I am. Here's another one I know you'll like."

Limbs shifted beneath the snow-flecked green wool of Phelan's cloak. A hand emerged from the fold holding a hunk of yellow cheese.

"Ha!" Geth grinned.

"I knew you'd try to eat most of it, so I cuffed a wedge while you were getting your cup filled."

"I do love you, brother." Geth put the whole thing in his mouth, savored the salty flavor. He swallowed and patted his stomach. "I was about to butcher one of the horses, I swear."

They shared a laugh.

Geth slept straight through the night and they were back on the move again early the next day. Phelan dug up a handful of edible tubers. It was better than nothing, but after a day on only frozen roots and snowmelt, Geth started eying the haunch of Phelan's mount in earnest.

But Vriana's people found them before the beast could come into any real danger. Phelan did the talking. As before, the Ilars demanded their weapons, agreed to escort them to the chieftess. A bandy-legged scratch with a greased mustache led them, eying Geth askance all the while.

Phelan listened in as best he could. Vriana's Laeri folk shared no banter though they did provide fire and a tent each night. Apart from the fact that they were headed toward Vriana's fortress, Bandy-legs gave away nothing. Geth caught the man watching them more than once.

Boots crunched across snow-crusted valleys, through an endless procession of drooping pines. Vriana's realm was much the same as Ceter's as far as Geth could tell, though the forests seemed denser, the Ilar villages fewer and farther between. Even the air was colder, a match for its frosty mistress. Either that or they'd reached the ends of the earth, where the Hoarwinds blew their miserable breath down on all of Eria.

Two days laboring through snowdrifts and stinging wind brought them at last beneath the wooden walls of a hillfort much like Thiringia. Geth counted on one hand as they rode. Iyngaer's council would meet in sixteen days. That didn't leave much time.

"We're here." Phelan flicked his head toward a steep-roofed hall peeking up from beyond the walls. Like her lands, Vriana's stronghold reminded Geth of nothing so much as a wilder version of Ceter's hillfort. The gates swung open and hails rang down. Inside, no more than a few dozen longhouses clustered around the steep-roofed hall at the crown of the tor.

"She's coming down to meet us," Phelan said.

"More than the old man bothered with. That seems promising."

Vriana arrived on foot, grey fur cloak swaying. Brown hair hung free to her shoulders, glowing like burnished copper where the sun touched it. But the hard set of her eyes ruined any beauty in it. A half-dozen grim Ilars trailed her, armed to the teeth.

"O Vriana Govendis." Phelan greeted her. He fell to one knee.

Geth followed suit. The introductions were made. His hands itched, wishing for something official like the green and white banner he'd carried before, but Vriana didn't seem to care.

She turned a honey-brown eye in his direction, uttered something matter-of-fact in her tongue. Her people made noises of accord. She'd recognized him from his duel as Hadean's champion, Geth reckoned. By the looks of it, they mourned the bastard's loss about as much as Ceter had.

The chieftess said something to Phelan. He dipped his head, turned to Geth to translate. "So far so good. She seems impressed we made it this far, but she wants to know what for. She's hasn't invited us inside either."

"Tell her our message is not a matter for open air and open ears."

Phelan translated. Vriana pursed her lips. Before she could reply, Bandy-legs pushed up alongside.

"O Vriana Lonegas." He slapped the hilt of the sword thrust through his belt. Geth's sword. A finger stabbed in the big warrior's direction.

"Mmmm." The chieftess looked thoughtful.

"What was that?" Geth asked.

Phelan muttered a curse.

Bandy-legs prowled over to stand in front of Geth, ire plain now he had the men to back him. He stood a head shorter, probably weighed less than half. Remembering how he'd gestured with that sword, however, Geth finally recognized him as the Ilar scout who'd escaped them on their first mission to Point-fort.

"Son of a..."

Bandy-legs uttered something in his native tongue. It didn't sound nice. Before Geth could ask for a translation, the little bastard spit full in his face.

Geth sucked a deep breath, grappled with his temper. They were outnumbered ten to one. Or more. Vriana's escorts had all inched closer, eager for a fight. But he was here for Hadean, not blood.

He wiped spittle from his eye and forced a smile. Vriana watched, stone-faced. Bandy-legs uttered something else and turned toward Phelan. He started to reply, until Bandy-legs smacked him full across the face.

"Little shit!" Geth had him by the back of the neck and down on the ground in the space of a heartbeat, face smashed into the snow. Those bandy legs kicked, arms floundered. It took a fury of blows from the other tribesmen to dislodge Geth before he could finish smothering the bastard.

It was a free-for-all after that. Several Ilars dragged the big warrior up, still throwing kicks, jabbing with spear butts. Geth roared, tore at hands, threw two Ilars off him with a surge of anger-fueled strength, dropped a third with a straight punch. Vriana's high-pitched laughter punctuated the grunts and curses. Several more tribesmen piled onto Geth from behind until he was crushed back down onto all fours. Even through watering eyes, he laughed at the sight as Bandy-legs struggled to his feet, snow caked on his face like sugar on a goddamn pastry.

Four Ilars were finally able to subdue the big warrior, to pin him down on his stomach, well-thrashed, panting, exhausted. Bandy-legs stepped toward him, drew his sword. Words flew back and forth between the cowardly wretch and his mistress and somewhere behind Geth, Phelan shouted in the Ilar tongue.

Whatever he said, it saved Geth's life. Bandy-legs sheathed his sword and snarled one last curse.

My sword, Geth reminded himself. *That's mine.*

Bandy-legs said something to the tribesmen at either of Geth's sides and they pulled him up to his knees.

"How do you say mouse in Ilar?" Geth asked Phelan.

"Katare. But Geth—"

"I'm gonna kill you some day, little Katare." Geth met the tribeman's eye. The Ilar's cap had come off to reveal a bald pate, demon-white even after the tussle.

Katare flicked a glance over his shoulder at Vriana, hissed something back at Geth in Ilar. With one hand gripping that sheathed sword below the crosspiece, Katare drove the hilt into Geth's ribs, doubling him over and back down into the snow.

Chapter twenty-six

They dumped Geth like a sack of manure in a windowless hovel with no hearth and a dirt floor. Agonizing pain shot through his side but he clenched his teeth, never uttered a sound. At least they hadn't left him outside the palisade to freeze in the snow.

Phelan tumbled in after. He cursed the Ilars in their own tongue. A pair of guards clamped fiddle-shaped wooden restraints around their ankles and slammed the door behind them, leaving Geth to blink in the darkness.

He put a hand to his side and winced.

"Uro's wrinkled ass," said Phelan. "You alright?"

"Broken rib. Maybe two."

"Shit."

Geth scooted across the floor to lean his back against the wall. The silence stretched. This wasn't what he'd hoped for when first they set out from Towerrock; Ceter wanting them dead, Vriana throwing them down a hole. *Gods all be damned!* Had he really led them all the way up the Hoarwind's ass for nothing but a frostbitten cock and an unceremonious death?

"Look, this is all my fault," he told Phelan. "I'm sorry."

The little man scooted over beside him. "You should have seen them. You broke one bastard's nose and a couple fingers on another one's hand. They were still slapping that other scratch back to consciousness last I saw."

Geth started to laugh, then groaned. "Damn, that hurts."

"Feels good though, doesn't it? To hear it?"

"Yeah. But what now?"

"You asking me?"

"Iyngaer's council meets in two weeks. We're running out of time."

"I don't know." Phelan loosed a sigh. "If the bitch won't even see us, how are we supposed to spin our lies?"

Geth didn't have an immediate answer. A sliver of light filtered in under the door, enough to study their surrounds now that his eyes had adjusted. It was one of those dug-out longhouses, walls sealed by clay, thatched roof overhead. Some kind of storage room, a pile of untanned skins in the back. Otherwise, it was empty.

"I don't suppose you've still got your flint?"

Phelan shook his head. "They took everything."

"We could tear through the thatch on this roof easy enough, but we wouldn't get far." Geth tapped the fiddle around his ankles.

"True." Phelan frowned. "Then there's the guards. Even if we slipped past, the cold would get us in a day or two. And the hunger."

"Gods but I could go for a drumstick about now."

Phelan ignored that, face gone pensive. "Why didn't she just kill us, though? I don't get it."

Geth shifted where he sat, grunted. The pain in his side had made him sweat. Now that they'd settled down, the chill set in. "Maybe she's curious."

"I reckon you're right. That's it."

"Am I? Well…"

Phelan nodded. "She's playing hard to get. She knows we want something. And she wants the upper hand when negotiations start."

"Maybe."

"It's always a negotiation when it comes to a man and a woman. Am I wrong?"

"Maybe she actually wants us dead, Phelan. Have you thought of that? Otherwise, I'd say she's gone a little over the top with the 'hard to get' thing."

"You beat the piss out of half of her men, Geth. You gave her no choice but to take it up a notch."

Geth frowned.

But Phelan had always understood women better than he did. People in general, for that matter. "So, what's her next move?"

Phelan stretched out his legs. "We wait. She'll pay us a visit before long."

Voices outside announced Vriana's arrival the next morning. Their door burst open to admit the blinding glow of sunlight on snow. Two shining spearheads inched under the lintel, followed by a pair of dour-faced tribesmen.

The pain in Geth's ribs had him swallowing curses as he rose to shuffle outside. Vriana stood a few paces off, arms folded, gang of toughs at her back. Geth's eyes flicked from the sword at her waist to the hard set of her mouth. Nothing like Ceter. But exactly what Geth had expected of a tribal ruler.

"Just translate," he told Phelan. "Follow my lead."

Vriana spoke before he could start.

"She wants to know why we're trespassing on her lands," Phelan said.

"Tell her she's a fool if she can't figure it out."

Vriana snorted before Phelan could finish relaying the message. She answered in Ilar, flicked her head toward her men, then met Geth's gaze, one eyebrow raised.

"She's says it's obvious we've heard of her and want to join her warband. That's why you had to, ya know…"

"What? Speak plain, Phelan."

"Yesterday, the fight. She says you were showing off."

Geth scowled. "Tell her if I wanted to show off, I could make this hill run red."

Phelan passed the message. Vriana looked bored. She gave them a flat look.

"She says she knows we aren't Umbel's true emissaries, Geth. I told her we are but she's sure of it."

"Tell her I know she remembers my duel as Hadean's champion. She knows I stand close to the king."

"She says that even if we had any authority, she doesn't want either friendship or gold from Umbel."

Vriana added something, gestured with a hand snatching air.

"What she wants," Phelan said, "She takes."

The chieftess crossed her arms. It was only then Geth noticed that ring with the ruby gleaming on her hand.

Geth cursed. *Think like the Mog!* He resisted the urge to pull at his mustache, mind working.

"You say you don't want our gold?" he said finally. "What about your warriors? Did any of them get a ring yesterday? I bet they wouldn't turn down some easy coin. Tell her that, Phelan. Say it loud. Make sure they all hear."

Phelan obliged. Vriana didn't look so bored anymore.

Geth pressed before she could start in on the threats. "And what about your enemies? Gold could buy swords. Warriors. Power. You can't tell me a woman with your reputation is satisfied with a fort of twigs up on this dunghill in the middle of nowhere."

Phelan translated. The way Vriana's eyes went tight, Geth thought maybe he'd overplayed it, but the woman reined herself in with admirable control.

"She says she'll ransom us," Phelan said. "A man so good with both his tongue and his blades should fetch a good price. She says that will give her all the gold she needs."

"Tell her that Hadean—"

Vriana cut him off, speaking rapidly in her tongue. Her look said it all before Phelan passed the message.

"She's done."

But she wasn't done talking, only listening. *Typical*. Phelan relayed her words.

"When the ransom gold is spent, she says she'll march down and take more. While our shrinking people hide on their river-island. She'll march south on vacation, take her winter in the warm south."

Geth met her eye but didn't bother with a retort. She wouldn't hear it. She was still talking, throwing Geth's own words back at him, punctuated for emphasis.

"Gold," Phelan translated. "Warriors. Power." She made that snatching gesture again, turned and started off up the hill. Geth just sat there watching her go, side aching, out of ideas.

A handful of her guardsmen remained though, among them Katare. He smiled. That mustache bristled as greased and proud as ever. The spear-toting guards ushered Geth and Phelan back inside their prison and a baby-faced Ilar moved forward to deposit a basket and a bucket just inside the doorway.

Katare uttered something and laughed before following in the wake of his mistress. Their door closed. The noise of a bar falling into place echoed under the frame.

"Vorda's withered tits." Phelan swore.

Geth examined what Baby-face had left. A single frozen river trout sat lonely in the bottom of the basket. There was no mistaking the reek of fresh piss wafting from the bucket.

Vriana left them there for days. The baskets of fish kept coming, but also the buckets of yellow snow that served as their drink. Compliments of Katare. From another bucket in the corner, the stink of their own excrement wafted up to the low ceiling.

"How can she know Hadean didn't actually send us?" Geth mused. "A spy? Pythelle's witchcraft?"

"Maybe the witch is working it both ways, trading info to the Ilars for her own gain. Or maybe the Ilar sorceress gleaned as much without her knowing."

Geth sighed. "Who knows. I don't like it either way."

"Do you really think she means to ransom us to Hadean?" Phelan asked. "It would take a good week just to get the message down to Towerrock, another to carry the answer back. You reckon Umbel would even pay for the likes of you and me?"

"We can't afford to wait two weeks."

"Not on dried lake trout and Ilar piss, that's for sure."

Geth snorted. "Makes Ceter's berry wine seem like the nectar of the Elder Race."

Phelan forced a laugh.

But Geth's thoughts had gone to Hadean. How did he fare? Had the Ilars planted a spy somewhere in the Tooth? A traitor still lurked those corridors, that was certain, an assassin as well perhaps. *Melagus dies first*, he vowed, *then Wayan and anyone else who turns a dark eye on the king.*

The thought of that made Geth smile. With Iyngaer's council just ten days off though, how did he expect to get back to Towerrock anyway? Would the chieftess even bother ransoming them with war just on the horizon?

"We can't wait any longer," he told Phelan after another day passed. "We need to force a meeting with Vriana."

"Force a decent meal too. What? I'm just thinking of you."

"But how?"

Phelan didn't answer, just watched, waited.

"Violence," Geth said at last. "A show of strength. That's the only thing these tribesmen understand."

"You're not wrong about that."

Geth gave it a think. Studying the fetters at his feet, he supposed they could be broken, given time. Through the thatch and out on the hill after that, he could crack skulls until Vriana had no choice except to sit up and take note.

But she might take a bit more than that, like his head in retribution. Or Phelan's. Or one of their hands. He didn't want to test her ingenuity.

"There could be one other way," he mused aloud.

Phelan frowned in the darkness. "What's that?"

Geth laughed but there was no mirth in it. After all, Vriana was doing the same thing with them right now. "We take a hostage."

The aching in Geth's ribs had only somewhat subsided, but he wasted no time. Their door opened just once each morning when the baby-faced Ilar dropped off their basket of fish. Hiding beside the entry, Geth had both hands on the poor bastard almost before he could scream.

The pair of sleepy-eyed tribesmen escorting Babyface came fully awake, but Geth already had the lad turned around to face them in a wrestler's chokehold. His left forearm pressed the young Ilar's throat, his right barred both elbows behind him. Geth forced his way outside onto the snow, using his captive as a shield. It wasn't easy with those fiddle-clamps around his ankles. Phelan shuffled out behind him.

"Tell them we demand to see their mistress," Geth said. "Or I'll choke him out right now."

Phelan barked at the wide-eyed tribesmen. One of them sprinted off to a nearby longhouse. He returned to deliver an armful of foodstuff in seconds. Phelan hissed another command and each of the two tribesmen took off his cloak and passed it over.

"The chieftess, Phelan!"

"You'll thank me later."

A second exchange and the first guard ran in the direction of Vriana's hall. A crowd of tribesmen had gathered, some spitting curses, others laughing. *Smug bastards.* Vriana arrived and their numbers swelled, Katare once again among the throng of scowling toughs at her back.

"We demand to be released," Geth said, not waiting to let the woman speak. Phelan translated in a rush. "We've come bearing a message of peace, but your hospitality is shit. Were you beaten when you visited Umbel? Jailed and starved? No, King Hadean treated you with the highest respect."

That cut some of the curses short, but Vriana didn't waste time voicing her reply through Phelan. "That was in a time of peace. This is a time of war."

"You're no chief." Geth spit. "Nothing noble about you at all. You're no one, just a bitch with a sword. Release us, otherwise the boy dies."

Vriana's cheeks reddened. Her fist clenched. This once, inconvenienced and insulted at such an early hour, Geth thought she might crack.

He was wrong. She mastered her emotions.

"Kill him, she says. She's used to men fighting over her."

A snicker passed through the Ilars behind her, Katare's loudest among them. Geth cursed under his breath, scrambled for some other words to shame her.

"What of our ransom then? You don't really want me to kill this boy. You don't want all those rats behind you to know how little you think of them."

Vriana snorted.

"She says she's trying to bid us up." Phelan translated. "Turns out we're not worth as much as she hoped."

Geth opened his mouth but the chieftess kept going. Phelan held up a finger, listening.

"In a season, she says, they'll have all the gold in Umbel. Four great tribes and three smaller ones will cover the sunlands like a blanket of fresh snow. What have you got to stop us, she asks? A few thousand men and one island fort?

Geth smiled. He made a show of laughing out loud.

"Prying for information, are we now? Tell her this: we've got ten thousand fresh troops waiting in the south. Four tribes? We've got the strength of four sworn realms balled like a fist, ready to strike. You may take the north for a few months, tell her, but you'll never set a foot south of Waterset. Come spring, Hadean will put your army to the sword. You won't have a serving man left to empty your chamber pot. If you survive at all."

Vriana hardly blinked. Damn but she was good. Phelan relayed her reply.

"Hadean will do nothing, she says. Kill the boy, she doesn't want him."

Geth licked his lips, thinking furiously. His ribs ached. Sweat rolled down his side. She'd like nothing better than for him to kill the boy, he reckoned. That would give her the excuse to order another beating, maybe even kill him. He opened his mouth, but Vriana didn't let him reply. She rattled something off in her language, eyes on Phelan as she waited for him to pass the message. She ended with that odd Ilar hum, a question of sorts, calm as you like.

"She says 'I give you food, drink, a roof above you. If you've been beaten, it's because you had a fight over a stolen sword, not because of me. Give up the boy or kill him now and have done.'"

"Kill him? Maybe I will."

Geth squeezed a little harder. Baby-face whimpered. Vriana said nothing, just watched.

"He stays with us," Geth said at last, "to make sure the warmth of your hospitality doesn't grow cold."

Vriana studied him. Wheels turned behind those honey-brown eyes. She shrugged and started back up the hill with a few Ilar words in parting.

"What'd she say?" Geth asked.

Phelan's voice went flat. "Enjoy the cloaks."

Bloody cunt. Geth watched her go, that grey fur of hers swaying. He shouted up after.

"Pray Hadean's more merciful than I am! When we have you in chains, I'll cut you up and feed you to the catfish!"

She never turned. Katare, however, stopped in his tracks, came all the way back down to stand among the handful of guards that remained, hands on hips.

"Hadean?" the mouse repeated.

Geth adjusted his grip on Baby-face, ready to use him as a shield if the bandy-legged bastard made a move.

But Katare just shook his bald head, lips curled in a smile beneath that greased mustache. "Hadean dead," he said in plain Aturian.

"What did you say?"

Katare answered in his own tongue. Phelan listened, eyes gone wide.

"Lying son-of-a bitch." Geth spit. "Wipe that name from your mouth."

The Ilar grinned, switched back to Aturian. "Sunlander king dead. Boy-king dead. Soon, you dead too. Mmmm?"

Chapter twenty-seven

There was no point standing out in the cold forever. Geth and Phelan ducked back inside their prison. Geth shoved their hostage toward the rear and sank to a seat on the floor.

Hadean dead? He didn't believe it. How could the Ilars even know? The door slammed shut leaving them in darkness.

But what if Vriana had a spy in Towerrock? She knew Geth was no true ambassador of Umbel. What else did she know? Perhaps it was Hadean's demise she'd been alluding to all the while, calling them false messengers. How could they claim to represent the king if he'd already been killed?

The silence hung heavy under that low ceiling.

"Say it, Phelan. Is it true?"

A deep breath sounded from across their dark prison. "Umbel called a parley to buy the peace, that's what Katare said. The Ilars doubled-crossed him. That's his story."

"They lie. He's just trying to get into our heads."

But it rang true. Gods, but it rang true. Hadean had himself mentioned a plan to parley with the Ilars to offer gold for peace—Melagus's idea, the way Geth remembered it. And what better way to be rid of the king than partner with his enemies and leave them to it?

"Lying, shit-stinking, cowardly bastard!" Only the pain in Geth's ribs cut him short. "Treasonous snake!"

"Geth—"

"And Katare... I'll cut off that mustache, lips and all. I'll gut him with a rusty butter-spread and hang him by his own entrails."

"Well, I won't stand in your way."

Something ran warm down Geth's cheek. Inwardly, he cursed himself, his rage unable to swallow the other emotions, not this time. Hadean dead? He loosed a ragged sigh, thanked the dark for hiding his weakness.

"They lie," he said, voice horse. "But I'll punish the mere thought of it. I'll bleed the north dry, Umbel as well if I have to."

A rustling sound echoed from Phelan's direction. Geth's eyes had adjusted, and he looked up to see his friend sorting through the goods they'd extorted from the guards. Phelan's pale hand stretched out.

"Eat. It's cheese. There's dried fruit here too, some bread, a leg of mutton I think."

"You did well, Phelan."

His friend flicked a glance at their captive, huddled with his legs up against his chest in a corner. Phelan spoke in the tongue of the Mog lest the Ilar understand. *"I know. But more importantly, I watched where they got it from. We'll need a lot more if we're gonna make good our escape."*

Escape. Geth couldn't think of that right now. His thoughts were of his king, sparring, sharing cutlets and aged cheese, the way the lad's cheeks colored every time someone mentioned the word marriage…

The hours wore on. Geth drifted to sleep at some point and woke up hungry. "Pass me that leg of mutton."

Phelan obliged. "Well, now is as good a time as any, I reckon." He breathed a sigh.

"For what? Mutton?"

"You still wanna know how I got Palladine stuck to my ass, don't you?"

"Well—"

"It was weighted dice."

Geth just listened.

"Good times. I was on a helluva run. Before I got sentenced to the Tower anyway."

"Sure."

"It started out as some simple dice games. Working for Brega had me so bored. I just needed an out. I didn't intend to be gone long. But I was really raking in the shine, moving from tavern to tavern with those dice, working it real careful. Then I hit this spot near Selel's temple. Who should I run into but Prince Gahalus himself."

"I think I know where this is going."

"Hey, it's him that wanted to mix it up with the common folk, not the other way 'round. I just reminded him why the highborn hate us."

"Ha!"

"But honestly, he was alright. Got a hollow leg when it comes to his wine. And he never suspected a thing."

Geth shook his head. "Or he didn't care."

"Maybe. He sure didn't push me away, I'll tell you that. We went from tavern to tavern for a good week."

"A few brothels too, I reckon."

"They call them 'Pleasure Houses,' Geth."

The big warrior snorted.

"We were winning. Every night. Drinking and singing and winning. That never gets old."

"He had to suspect, Phelan."

The little man tapped his lips, frowned. "I suppose you're right. But that didn't stop him from fleecing his own friends. I asked him to get me in on a bigger game, with some real shine involved, and he didn't disappoint."

"High-brows?"

"The highest, a whole table full. This lot had gold up to their ears. And gods all be damned if I didn't try to take it all."

Phelan grinned. It was easy for Geth to share the laugh now, so many months after. He breathed a final sigh, bit into the cold mutton in his hands. Gods but it was delicious.

"Thanks, Phelan. I needed that. Nice work with the cloaks too."

There was no point hanging on to their captive really. They released him back to the guards outside with a bang on the door. Vriana wasn't interested in reprisals, thank the gods. She wasn't much interested in them at all at this point, Geth reckoned.

"No hard feelings, eh?" he called after the lad.

The Ilar frowned in their direction and hurried out onto the snow.

"We couldn't afford to feed him," Phelan said. "That's for sure." He muttered to himself, counting on his fingers.

"How's that?"

"The way I reckon it, we'll need all these provisions and more when we break out."

Geth grimaced.

Phelan had come to the only possible conclusion. With Hadean dead, who would even consider paying a ransom for their release? Eldric, perhaps, but like as not, Towerrock's lord had met the same fate as his nephew by now. It was only a matter of time before Vriana grew bored with them and executed them both. Or simply let them starve.

"Nothing for it," Geth said. "You're right. We're gonna need every scrap of food we can carry if there's any hope of making it out of Laer."

"So, you think you can get us out of these?" Phelan tapped the fiddle at his ankles.

"I can break yours. It's gonna be harder for you to break mine. Starving to death is what we'll want to avoid. Or freezing to death out there. And that's assuming we don't get nabbed a mile off this gods-forsaken hill."

"We have these cloaks now. And the boy's flint. I could probably pull some threads and use a fish bone to stitch a few of those hides back there into a sack for our food."

"You're a godsend. You'll make fine housewife someday."

Phelan snorted. "And now, thanks to your betrothed, we know where to get more provisions as well."

"But how do we get away?" Geth mused aloud.

Phelan shrugged. "I still can't believe we escaped Ceter's fort, even with the horses."

He was right. Geth went silent, thinking.

It was mention of the white-haired chieftain gave him the idea eventually. He laughed out loud.

"That's it. Don't you see?"

Phelan frowned. "See what?"

"We need a snowstorm."

A grin bloomed on Phelan's face, a light in the dark. "Like in Thiringia."

"Exactly. And it can't be long before we get one in these godforsaken parts. So, pray for it, Phelan. Pray for it like our lives depended on it."

"They do, don't they?"

Geth had never been one for prayer. Thank the gods? Occasionally. Curse them? More often than not.

But pray?

He started with Awer, red-handed god of war. After that he prayed to the Red God's wife, Vorda the Wise, keeper of souls. That pair knew him well. He'd given them plenty of business.

Phelan sat by the crack under the door to catch what light he could, working on that sack for their supplies. Geth looked over their stores: a wedge of salty cheese, some dried apples, a stale loaf, one river trout. And a half-gnawed leg of cold mutton. Quite a spread compared to what they'd grown used to.

But it wouldn't be enough if they ever made it off Vriana's hill. A body needed fuel, especially when it was cold. Not to mention the hunger brought on by miles of trudging through snow. Geth ran things over in his mind the best he could. *Break the fiddles, tear through the thatched roof, steal more food, sneak over the walls.* The cloaks and flint would go some way to keeping them warm in the wild. Phelan and his woodland know-how would have to do the rest.

Two days passed. They rationed a portion of their daily trout, though it smelled like Katare had started pissing on that as well. Geth dug a small opening through the thatch overhead to keep a watch on the skies. Cold and blue during the days, star-scattered at night. Not a cloud to be seen.

"Did you ever read the Omnibus?" He asked on the third day after their meeting with Vriana.

Phlean looked up from the untanned hide in his hands. "Don't be an ass."

Geth felt his cheeks go warm. He'd forgotten, Phelan could only read a few words. His friend had been raised among a band of highwaymen, learning the ways of the woods. And of thieves. No holyman's Omnibus among that lot. And no kindly old cleric to indulge him with the written word.

"I didn't mean it that way. It's just I've been thinking of Old Mather. He made me read almost the whole damn thing. The stories stuck. The habits, the virtues? Well…"

"Not so much, eh?"

"You reckon it's the Ilar gods we should be praying to? That's what I'm saying. This is their domain after all."

Phelan chuckled. "Pray if you want to, brother. Or save your breath. This far north, we're bound to get a snowstorm before long."

Geth supposed he was right.

Phelan went back to his hide. He'd long since finished the bag for their food and had started on a pair of sleeping-sacks. Geth whispered prayers to unnamed gods of a foreign land as he studied the fiddle at his ankles. He thought of Hadean's betrayal, of Melagus, of Katare. He had no choice but to escape. He'd promised Awer a river of blood in return for that storm. But there could be no vengeance unless they broke out.

Praying to the Ilar gods, Geth reckoned, had been a mistake. Shouts and the stamp of horse hooves sounded from out on the hill the next day. Phelan lay down on his stomach to cock an ear at the crack under the door, but his report only confirmed that the gods of those lands hated Geth as much as all the others.

"Are you sure it's Ceter?"

Phelan dusted off the front of his shirt and sat up. "It's him, old cocksucker. Like a beehive that's been kicked out there. Sounds like he's got a damn warband with him."

"They friends, Ceter and Vriana?"

"Neighbors. So, they hate each other, of course."

"So, why would she let him inside the gates at all? Especially with men and weapons."

Phelan had no answer. Geth frowned, working that over until it hit him.

"Vriana's found a buyer."

"For what?"

"For a pair of unlucky bastards, that's what. She's never meant to ransom us to Hadean. She already knew he was dead. She's ransomed us to Ceter."

Phelan swore.

Geth watched him pace the length of their prison in silence. If he wanted to blame the man who'd killed Ceter's lover, who led them into Ilia in the first place, he had the heart not to.

He came to a halt. "How can we be sure, Geth?"

"It's the only thing that makes sense."

If Phelan still doubted, Katare arrived to confirm it, grinning beneath that proud mustache. "You dead soon, mmmm? Sunlander dead. Very dead."

Phelan shot something back in the Ilar tongue. Katare started in on a hateful reply until the baby-faced Ilar tugged at one arm. Words were exchanged. Katare put an end to that with a backhand across the young tribesman's cheek. He spit a final curse at Geth, locked them back in, and turned back the way he'd come.

"You were right." Phelan said, voice flat. "Ceter's agreed to pay for us."

"I wonder how much we'll fetch."

"A fair price, I reckon. Katare says the old man's already bragged about skinning us alive, feeding our nuts to his dogs. The usual."

"But what was all that with Baby-face?"

"He told the bald prick Vriana didn't want us to know about the whole ransom thing."

"She's no fool. More than I can say for Katare. Time is against us. Now we know it."

"He also mentioned a feast. Hatred or no, seems Vriana's more inclined to break bread than break bones."

Geth blinked. "Well, there's some good news at least."

"How's that? We show up, we get buckets of piss. The silver fox shows up, he gets a feast. Any way you look at it, we got the short end of the stick. Or the sharp end, whatever you want to call it."

"Think, Phelan. The wine will flow. They'll have music, stories."

"Distractions." Phelan rubbed his chin, nodded slowly.

"That's right." Geth nodded grimly in turn. "We make our move tonight. It's now or never."

Chapter twenty-eight

As Ilars went, the baby-faced tribesman, wasn't half bad. The noise of their bar lifting announced the lad's arrival. He offered a bulging water skin, uttered a few words, and locked them back in.

"Clean water?" Geth asked.

Phelan took a swig and grimaced. "Worse. Berry wine."

"His heart's in the right place."

"He said if this is to be our last night, at least we can enjoy it."

"You think he told on Katare? Do you think Vriana knows that he let slip about Ceter?"

Phelan shook his head. "I doubt it. He wouldn't want to get hit again."

Phelan passed the skin over. Geth took a good long swig but saved the rest. If they made it off that hill, they'd need it.

And there was work yet to be done. He started with the fiddle on Phelan's legs. No point waiting, the next visit would likely be from Ceter.

The fiddle itself was a simple thing, two carved boards held together with a dowel at each end. Geth didn't bother with the dowels.

"Stand up, Phelan. Legs apart as far as they'll go."

He raised a foot. Phelan nodded, rose, back turned to Geth as he braced himself against the wall. "Hard, you bastard. Otherwise, it'll break my legs."

Geth didn't count off or give warning. He leaped up and came down with all his weight on one heel. Aged wood snapped like a dry twig.

Phelan stumbled and fell. "Shit that hurt!" The fiddle around Geth's legs had grazed Phelan's calf, but when he stood, he was only encumbered by the remains of the broken restraint.

"Now mine," Geth said. He turned and stretched his stance as far as he could. The noise of Phelan practicing sounded behind him a few times.

But it all came to nothing. His strike bounced off the wood, leaving them both cursing.

"Try again. You can do it, Phelan."

"I'm not heavy enough."

"Just try! I can't fight like this!"

Phelan ignored him. He reached down to his own mangled restraint, tearing a piece off the splintered wood. He rose with a shank as thick as a man's finger.

"Size and strength, that's your game." Phelan tapped his head. "I've got this."

"Just do it, whatever you've got planned."

Phelan dumped their daily ration of piss-water and used the bucket like a hammer against that wooden shank, tapping out the dowels on the big warrior's fiddle. Geth cringed at the racket, but it worked.

"I'll be damned." He slapped Phelan's shoulder as the two halves separated neatly.

Using the bucket and wooden shank, Geth returned the favor, removing the broken restraint still clamped around Phelan's ankles. They gathered their stores, sat and waited. Phelan cut a strip of leather for what looked like a headband if Geth didn't know better. They didn't wait long. Vriana's feast for Ceter began before the sun went down. The rhythm of drums and the whistle of bone flutes floated down to their prison, along with the mouthwatering aroma of roasting meats.

Geth ignored the hunger in his belly, focused his mind instead on his thirst for revenge. "First Melagus, then Wayan. Then Gylfric, Katare…"

"I think I want to buy an inn." Phelan said out of nowhere.

"A what?"

"An inn. Not a tavern. It's gotta have guest rooms. That way we can have working women."

"An inn?"

"I can pour the liquor, manage the girls. You work the door. Maybe deal with the cook. Who appreciates food better than you? We'd have a back room for the serious gamblers, cellars full of ale…" He trailed off, clutching that blunted little shank of wood.

Geth watched him through the dim light. They'd been through so much. He realized he wasn't ready to die yet either.

"C'mon."

Geth reckoned the back of the longhouse would be the best place to dig through the thatch without attracting notice. Phelan crouched in the dark. He carried the bag full of rations in one hand. The sleep sacks he'd fashioned were rolled up under the other arm. Geth took the wooden shank, the only weapon they had.

The sound of voices in song drifted down to them, laughter, shouting. How long dared they wait? Could he even get to the guards before they cried the alarm? The odds were long. Very long. He touched the end of his wooden shank. It didn't even have a point.

"Phelan, if we—"

"Wait."

The little man held up a finger, cocked an ear. The intensity in his voice, or something else, raised the hairs on the back of Geth's neck. Phelan hustled back toward the door to listen at the crack.

"Whatever happens, Phelan, you just get over the wall and run for it."

"They're at it!" Phelan sprang to his feet.

"What?"

Phelan hooted. A faint cry reached Geth's ear, and his eyes widened. He hollared for joy. The noise grew louder, steel clanging off steel, punctuated by shouts and cries.

"Couldn't resist!" Phelan said. "Hated each other a little too much. Maybe the old bastard got cheap in the end, didn't want to pay for the goods?"

"Shit on the reasons, man! This is our chance!"

Vriana's feasting hall wasn't close to their hovel, but by the sound of things, Geth reckoned the fighting had escaped those walls. An inexplicable wave of fear washed over him, threatened to freeze him where he stood. With a shiver, he shook it off, pushing Phelan back toward the rear of their prison. He tore through the thatch with both hands. In a few heartbeats they were out.

Moonlight off snow lit the night, gleamed off metal helms and flashing blades clustered around the hall up at the crown of Vriana's tor. Curses and the ring of blade against blade filled the nose-chilling air. A nearby roof took fire with a whoosh. Old Ceter's shining hair caught the light from the thick of the melee, surrounded by his men. Not an eye turned toward Geth and Phelan.

"Go!" Geth pointed toward the palisade. "There's a ladder there, get over the wall!"

"Geth!"

He'd already started toward the action, running at a half-crouch. Phelan cursed behind him. Ahead, Ceter and his lot hacked their way downhill toward the gate.

But the chieftain wasn't Geth's mark. He didn't have to search long for Katare's bald head. The bastard came sprinting toward him, the only sonofabitch in all of Laer that hadn't forgotten about them.

Geth stood from his crouch and ran with that tiny splinter to meet him. If the rage in his blood were the sea, it would have drowned them both. Katare raised his sword, eyes wide with fury. Geth cocked his arm to throw the shank—his only play—but Katare stumbled and doubled over before Geth could release.

Geth looked over his shoulder.

Phelan still stood beside their longhouse, that length of leather dangling from one hand. "Hurry, man!"

Katare moaned, laid out on the snow on his side. Geth went down to his knees and straddled him, shank high overhead. "Your turn to die." He drove the blunt shard over and over into the Ilar's chest until it slipped from his grasp for all the blood on his hands.

"Uro's puckered ass!" Phelan came all the way back to yank at his arm. "Let's *go!*"

Geth wasn't done. He rose, still breathing hard, and snatched up the Ilar's sword. *My sword!* He laid it across the dead man's neck.

"Your job in Vorda's Hall will be to wipe my ass."

He raised the blade high. Katare's head came off with one clean motion.

Katare's head went over the lip of Vriana's rough-hewn palisade and Geth jumped down after. He tumbled through the snow, came up spitting powder. Phelan landed beside him with a yelp. They lurched like drunkards down the hill, stumbling and cursing, encumbered by knee-high snow and arms loaded with supplies.

They didn't slow until they reached the surrounding woods. Geth led them north at first, the opposite direction Ceter had been driving for. He spared a glance over his shoulder. No one followed.

Not yet at any rate. But footprints behind them left a trail plain for any eye to see, even at night

Phelan turned them east. "Don't look back. They've got enough to keep them busy for now. Let's just put some miles between us."

Geth held Katare's head upside down by the jaw, two fingers thrust in his gaping mouth. "Watch us escape, bastard. Nothing you can do about it now."

It felt good to murder the scratch. It felt *great*. But aside from being the one to taunt them with Hadean's death, Geth knew Katare meant nothing. He'd killed the messenger, no more. It was Melagus who had to die. Only then would the world begin to feel right again. Snorting a wry laugh, Geth slowed to a stop. He dropped Katare's head on the snow and emptied his bladder on the bastard's face, into his open mouth.

Phelan came to stand beside him when he was done, looking down at the grisly trophy. "How's that taste, eh?" He nudged Geth with an elbow, chuckled. "Man, I wish I had to shit."

They left Katare and hurried on. In addition to the tribesman's sword, Geth had taken the sword-belt with the scabbard Hadean had commissioned for him, along with a pair of gloves. He pulled these on.

As the initial rush of their escape faded, the cold settled in. Despite Phelan's words, the big warrior spared plenty of glances back the way they'd come.

They pushed on through the night and into the morning with no sign of pursuit. It finally hit Geth. Vriana wasn't coming. Not that he reckoned she'd been killed during the fight—nothing so fortunate—she just didn't care. How many times during the past week had she summoned them to be questioned, visited their prison, even just stopped by to gloat? None. When they wanted to speak with her, they had to capture Baby-face to force a meeting. She had the horses and hounds, trackers who knew the lay of the land. If she gave the order, they'd be dead. Looking back, however, it now seemed clear the only reason she'd kept them alive at all was to ransom them to Ceter.

Phelan turned them south by and by, slowed the pace. They rested during the day, rising again to march under the relative cover of night.

"Keep moving during the coldest hours," Phelan said. "That's the best way not to freeze." A light snow began to fall the second morning after their escape, the storm they'd prayed for.

It came down thicker and thicker, heavy white flakes, until Geth could hardly see a yard ahead. "We can't hike like this."

"And neither can anyone who might try coming up behind us." Phelan pointed to the trees. "There. Under that spruce."

The little man dug them a shelter under the mass of sagging limbs. They finished off the mutton, cheese, and lake trout. Geth watched the snow sheet down. There was some good in it: at this rate the blizzard would cover their tracks. Exhaustion, cold, and the first whiff of safety he'd had in weeks had him asleep within minutes.

He woke to an inexplicable uneasiness though, thoughts gone to the warlock, Ceter.

Phelan stirred beside him. "You feel that?" he asked.

Geth met his eye, nodded.

"Me too. I felt something like it at Vriana's place. Made me go stiff sort of, like a ghost had tapped me on the shoulder from behind."

"What do you think it means?"

"He's close."

Phelan didn't need to say who. Geth grumbled a curse, pulled his cloak tighter. If a creature like Ceter could cast out a spell to stalk them across the miles, what else could he do? They sat quiet, like a clutch of rabbits in their hole. For the moment, Geth reckoned it was better to hide than run.

They waited. Geth ate and slept, ate some more. By the time the feeling passed, it was night. It was cold beneath their tree boughs and Geth's stomach seemed to have folded in on itself. He reached for Phelan's sack with the food.

"It's empty," the little man said. "What? Don't look at me like that, it's you that ate the last apricot."

"Let's get moving. But if you see so much as a squirrel and don't bring it down, so help me Thram, you just might make the return trip in my belly."

They broke camp and toiled on. Geth fueled himself with daydreams of Melagus's bony neck in his hands. They came within sight of a frozen watercourse sometime before dawn. Vorus, Umbel's mighty North River, still and snow-covered in the moonlight. Phelan led them with greater care after that. There would be villages along those banks, attention they didn't want to attract.

But they never crossed so much as a cart-path. It was a wild country, Vriana's realm, Laer's sparse population spread thin among the valleys and hills. No chance of stealing a loaf, even if they wanted to. Geth collapsed onto the seat of his pants as the sun rose, leaving Phelan to set up camp.

"Even if I could get a squirrel or some frozen grubs," Phelan said between strikes at his flint, "it won't be enough to keep us going."

"It has to be, Phelan. Ceter's still behind us somewhere."

Phelan cursed, blew at his tiny flames, cursed some more, and finally got a fire going. Geth stretched out his hands as it took light, licked the sharp, cold forest air. A wolf howled in the distance. His fingers soaked up the heat but without a pot over it, a fire could only do so much on its own.

He stared at the flames, blinked to shake off the exhaustion, to think things through. What next? Phelan hadn't lied. Without food, they wouldn't make it much farther. But dare they slow the pace long enough to hunt up, slaughter and cook some game? No, not with Ceter somewhere in those woods.

So, it was starve and freeze to death, or wait for Ceter to catch up and skin them alive.

Chapter twenty-nine

A noise woke Geth. He must have dozed off. He turned his head and looked into a pair of yellow eyes.

"Get outta here!" he yelled.

Phelan started at the sound. Geth was already out of his sack and on his feet, but the wolf had only skittered off a few paces. It lowered its head, sniffed in Geth's direction.

"Wait a minute," Phelan said. "Isn't that the Ilar wolfdog that came north with us?"

It was. Geth swore. He stretched out a hand. The animal came forward to slide his head under it, gliding past like a cat so Geth rubbed his whole back. It circled around again, faced Geth with those yellow eyes, tongue lolling out.

Phelan watched the surrounding woods warily. "What do you think it means?"

The beast started off at a trot, turned, eyed Geth, and started off again. He circled back, repeated the process.

"He wants us to follow."

"I know that. But do you really think it's a good idea? He belongs to the tribes."

"They say that old Ilar is some kind of sorcerer, right?"

"Seer," Phelan said. "They called him 'Agrem the Seer'"

"Well, if that's the case, I reckon we'd already be dead if that's what the scratch wanted."

"Agrem is Iyngaer's man. Don't forget that."

"You saying you'd rather stay here and starve?"

"Don't think with your stomach, Geth. The man's an Ilar and a warlock. We haven't had much luck with either sort lately."

"You want to want to wait around for Ceter then?"

Phelan rolled his eyes.

Geth pulled on his boots and packed up his sleep-sack. "I like dogs. I'm going."

Phelan cursed but followed suit. Half a day's journey south and west brought them to the edge of a clearing surrounded by a white wall of snow-crusted trees. The wolf trotted between an opening in the boughs toward a campfire at the center. A low tent of animal hide sagged under a fresh blanket of snow. Three pelts had been arranged around the blaze, but the clearing stood empty. The wolfdog skipped past the fire, through the tent flap, emerging a moment later with Agrem in his wake.

The Ilar rubbed his arms and pulled the folds of his cloak around his shoulders. "Cold, mmmm?" He sat cross-legged on the nearest pelt, waving them forward with some sort of biscuit in his hand. Geth watched, mouth watering, as Agrem took a bite himself and patted his belly.

"Wait—" Phelan started.

Geth had already decided. He sank onto the pelt next to the Ilar and swallowed the proffered biscuit in three bites. Berry wine washed it down. Agrem laughed, taking the skin back to have a swig himself. He reached inside his cloak to produce more biscuits. Phelan uttered something foul but hurried over to claim his share.

"Wait," Agrem told the smaller man. He turned back inside his tent and fetch a smaller skin. He took a sip and grimaced. It was Geth's turn to laugh. Agrem passed it to Phelan. His friend took a hearty swallow, blew out a hot breath, and passed it to Geth.

"It's not White Adus, but it's doesn't need a spark to catch fire."

Geth took a cautious sip, swished the hearty liquor in his mouth. "Probably distilled from the same berries as the wine."

"Good, mmmm?"

That Ilar hum could mean yes, no, or maybe, best Geth could tell. He had no reply.

And what did the Ilar himself mean, feeding them, inviting them to share his fire? Geth studied the man. He looked older than Geth remembered, the lines in his forehead deeper, the grey in his beard more pronounced. Those course locks still jutted out in every direction, waxed into spikes like some kind of trap to catch unwary prey. But he stroked his wolfdog under the chin like any ordinary man.

"I was waiting for you." The Seer looked down at his dog, cooed like a mother with her babe. "Sent him to find you."

"And he did," Geth said. "But last I checked, we're at war. Isn't it treason to aid an enemy at war?"

Agrem shrugged. "War is bad. Ilars don't need war. Don't need land, don't need to fight Umbel." He snorted a wry laugh. "Don't need enemies. We have each other."

"Everyone has enemies," Phelan said.

Geth couldn't argue with that. He looked back at the Seer. "You don't want this war?"

"Neither do you, mmmm?"

"Is that you talking, or your chief? Seems like Iyngaer wants this war more than anyone."

"There are winds in the air that want this war." Agrem eyes went far away. "Ancient things."

Geth flicked a sideways glance toward Phelan. His friend watched the Ilar close until the old tribesman blew out a sigh.

"The sickness came," Agrem said. "Many died. More meat for the survivors, mmmm? More bread. More land. Iyngaer doesn't need land, mmmm?"

"Glory," Geth said. "Who's got the bigger cherries. That's all it's really about."

Agrem muttered something and reached for the smaller skin. He took a swig of the strong stuff and passed it across to Phelan. "Ilars are people of the forest. You know this."

Geth nodded.

"Hungry men—Othwid, Ceter, Iyngaer too—these men like war. Like to take southern lands."

"I'm listening."

"This is not wise. If the tribes win the lands, what, mmmm? We Ilars are people of the forest. Win sunlands and become sunlanders? Win war, win land, but lose *ourselves*."

It made sense. In the Lows, east of Pellon proper, some among the Mog had lived alongside the Paellians so long they no longer wandered. Their tattoos faded. They sold horses, herd, and tent for plots to farm. Maybe that was just the way of things.

"You want to go south now," Agrem picked up where he'd left off. "Mmmm?"

"That's right."

"Don't go. Many dangers. Ceter is looking for you. And no Vriana here to protect you."

"Vriana?" Phelan said. "Protect us? This one's funny."

Geth ignored that. "How am I supposed to get back to Umbel if I don't go south?"

"Don't go to Umbel," said Agrem. "Not now. Ceter's net is open. You will die."

"We made it this far," Phelan shot back.

"Came here almost dead, mmmm?"

"If we can't go south, where is it you want us to go?"

"To Iyngaer."

Phelan took a sip of that Ilar liquor, cursed and wiped his mouth. "Have you lost it, man?"

Agrem turned to Geth. "You killed Othwid's brother. Killed Ceter's bride. Killed Vriana's man. You came to speak for Umbel, mmmm? Not a good start."

"Well, uh…"

"Iyngaer is the only chieftain left."

Geth gave the Seer a hard stare. "You're saying you want me to go to Iyngaer and talk him out of a war he started?"

Agrem nodded.

"Now I understand that crazy hair."

Phelan made noises of agreement, but the Seer's face was sober as the grave. "Cross the river into Dues. With me. I will take you to Iyngaer. Ceter can do no harm there."

"It's not Ceter I'm worried about."

"What else can you do, mmmm?"

The Seer looked to Phelan, said something in the Ilar tongue. They went back and forth. Geth heard 'Iyngaer' and 'Govendi,' but he understood nothing more. The wolfdog came and laid down against his leg. Geth reached down to rub his ears.

Phelan snorted one final curse and folded his arms against his chest. Agrem huffed a sigh. It was all a bit much for Geth so soon after escaping one chief's clutches, the idea of hopping right into the arms of another. He looked up to find the Seer watching him.

"Well?" Geth asked. He looked down at the wolfdog beside him. "What's the wolf's name?"

"Wolf?" Agrem snorted. "Not a wolf."

"Alright, what's the *dog's* name?"

"Eko."

Phelan muttered a curse, but Geth took the bait. "Eko. Sure. And what does that mean?"

Agrem smiled, reached for the liquor again. "Wolf."

He was a wily bastard, Agrem. But at least he had the decency to leave Geth and Phelan to talk things over in private. Rising from his pelt, the Ilar uttered something in his own language and disappeared into the woods. Phelan sucked down the last of the man's liquor.

"You get used to this wine after a while," he said, wiping dribble from his beard.

"Big strings attached to it. Hey, don't pass out on me now, I need you to help think this through!"

"Right. Give it a good think."

Geth grimaced. The fact that Phelan agreed so quick made it clear he was gonna have to do the thinking on his own after all.

Was it really so hard though? Or did he only trust Agrem because of the meal and the friendly dog? The whole idea was crazy, but as the saying went in Adamar, when your shoes are on fire, you piss on your toes.

"If Agrem wanted us dead," he reasoned aloud, "he could have just left us to die on our own. We had one foot in the grave and the other kicking dirt on it, eh? For that reason alone, I think we can agree he doesn't mean us any harm."

Phelan laid back in the snow, stared up into the cold blue sky. "It's one thing to mean us harm, another to lead us into harm's way. He wants something, Geth, you know that. What does it matter to him if we risk our lives for his ends?"

"Still got a few wits floating on that liquor, eh? You do make a fair point. One hell of a risky proposition, marching into Iyngaer's lair. No risk to the Seer, mind. That's all on us."

Phelan waved his hand vaguely.

"What were you two talking about anyway?"

"Iyngaer, what else."

"And?"

"And how he's a bloodthirsty sonofabitch. They say he can cut a man in half with one swing. From what I heard after Copper Ridge, I don't doubt it. But Agrem claims he's got a devious kind of wit, that he can surprise you at times."

"Agrem thinks we've got a chance then?"

"That's what he says."

Phelan was fading. Geth stood, peered through the trees. The Seer's tracks disappeared over a low rise, the tribesman himself nowhere to be seen. "Where'd the scratch go anyway?"

"To check some snares he said."

Geth nodded. He threw another log on the fire and settled back down on his pelt. "I wish it was Melagus waiting on the other side of that river."

"That's your plan? Make it south and kill the Asp?"

"You got a better one?"

"Not really." Phelan yawned. "It's warmer down in Umbel. But after that, then what? Without Hadean around, it's only a matter of time before Wayan makes a run at you."

"I'll deal with the yardmaster. He's part of the plan."

The Seer arrived with a white-haired rabbit dangling from his fist before Geth could think on it more. They cleaned, cooked, and devoured the animal in less than an hour. Agrem didn't press about Dues.

Three grown men and one big ass dog all crammed into the Seer's tent as night fell. The Ilar snored like a cave bear, but Geth hadn't been so warm in a month. He turned on his side, watched the tribesman's chest rise and fall. If something stranger could have happened on this tour of Ilia, he couldn't think of it.

That inexplicable fear woke Geth some time before dawn. Phelan moaned in his sleep. Agrem had already risen. His eyes glowed, wide and bright.

"Ceter."

The Seer pulled on his boots and cloak to step outside. Geth poked his head out the flap, watched as he paced from one cardinal direction to the next, pausing at each to snap a twig and utter something in his own tongue. With a half-burned stick from their fire, he scraped a blackish circle in the snow around their camp. Geth wrapped himself in his own cloak and crawled out of the tent to take a seat on one of the pelts.

"Protection?" he asked.

Agrem sank onto another pelt. Moonlight washed his features grey. "Mmmm."

A string of muttered expletives sounded, preceding Phelan through the flap of their tent. His eyes went from Geth to Agrem to the ring of char. "Piss and shit! Ceter again?"

"Guess we never did shake him."

Phelan's mouth closed but Geth could see the wheels turning. Ceter or Iyngaer?

Eko slid out through the tent flap last. The beast settled in the snow at Geth's side, looked up at him expectantly. The answer was plain. He scratched the beast's ears, looked down into his big eyes. "Guess we'll be traveling together a little while longer."

Chapter thirty

There was no more discussion. They broke camp and turned east at dawn. Toward Dues.

Agrem claimed he could hide them from Ceter until they reached the river and Iyngaer's lands. The warlock would not dare touch them there. Eko hauled their tent on a small sled strapped to his shoulders with a leather harness. The scrape of that sled over hardened snow set the big warrior's nerves on edge, but Agrem hummed as he marched.

Geth didn't let his guard down until they crossed the frozen-over North River. *What are we walking into though?* He cast a glance at Phelan, trudging along, grimace frozen to his face. Agrem must've sensed Geth's hesitation. He fell in stride.

"In three days, we reach Dues. On time for Iyngaer's great *misa*."

Iyngaer's council—Geth didn't need Phelan's talent to understand that. He pulled them to a halt.

"You hear that, Phelan? The gods have some sense of humor. We've trekked all across the forest trying to convince Ilar tribes not to join Iyngaer's council. Now we're headed there ourselves."

Phelan snorted. "Sounds like a great time. Nice reunion with all the friends we've made in Ilia."

Agrem reached under his cloak to retrieve his waterskin. He took a drink and passed it to Geth. "You are good sunlanders. Come all the way to Ilia to try to stop war."

"I did it for Hadean." Geth said.

"Mmmm. I am sorry for him."

"Why should you be sorry? He's an enemy. And *you* didn't kill him."

"But I knew they betrayed him." Agrem shook his head. "They sent him north to die. I tried to make Iyngaer stop it, but…"

"But what?"

"He…surprised me."

Geth looked away. It was Iyngaer that killed Hadean? His hands squeezed Agrem's waterskin. He thrust it at Phelan and started hiking again.

"Hey, slow down!"

Geth's boots crunched through snow like it was bone breaking beneath his feet. Vengeful thoughts flashed through his mind, images of twisted entrails and eyeless sockets. The Red God called.

"Geth!" It took all Phelan's strength to yank him to a halt. "Where you going?"

A fire burned in Geth's belly. His nostrils flared with each breath, but no words came out.

"I know what you're thinking, Geth. I do. But I'm not dying in this gods-forsaken country just so you can settle that score."

"Hadean…"

He didn't even know what to say. The lad had believed in him where lesser men had scorned him, used him up and cast him aside when they were done. No, every fiber of Geth's being demanded vengeance, a rusty blade through Iyngaer's eyes, across his throat, and up his ass.

But what would that do for Hadean?

Nothing.

Geth let out a ragged sigh. He had a long history in the revenge business. The venture never paid out like it promised.

"Geth—"

"No, you're right. A few heads separated from necks—" Geth ground his teeth. "That's a far cry from the justice Hadean deserves."

Phelan looked him in the eye. "So don't waste your life—and mine—getting even."

Agrem watched from a few paces off, Eko beside him. Geth looked from the wolfdog to the Ilar and back. The answer stood right before him.

"Three days 'til Iyngaer's council?" he asked.

The Seer nodded.

There it was. Geth laughed like a mad man. Agrem's errand to Dues offered more than safety from Ceter, more than a path out of Ilia. It offered a way forward. *The gods!* It was one last chance to serve Hadean, he realized, his people, and all that he cared about. Revenge alone could never do that.

"We can't leave Kerrel and the boys in the middle of a war now, can we?"

Phelan smiled. "The dead-man dozen would be…well, dead men."

"You're right. We march to Dues, tell Iyngaer to call off the war. Killing the sonofabitch will only piss the tribes off more."

"Not to mention getting us chopped to pieces."

Phelan straightened Geth's cloak where he'd grabbed it. "Can we just survive this bloody forest and make it back alive?" he went on. "Promise me you'll do your best to get outta these parts. Otherwise, I swear I'll take my chances with Ceter and make for Umbel on my own."

Geth laughed. "You think I wanna die up here?" He started walking again. Phelan's voice came up from behind.

"I'm holding you to it, you bloodthirsty prick!"

Three days hiking through uninhabited wilds brought them to a region dotted by snow-blanketed homesteads, crisscrossed by muddy cart paths. Travelers hailed the Seer with reverence, eying Geth and Phelan with curiosity, nothing more. One last bend in the road delivered them into the broad vale of a tributary of the North River. The great whitened tor of Dues rose in the midst of it all.

"Now that's something," Phelan said.

Timber palisades similar to those in Laer and Thiringia crowned the hill, but on a grander scale. Muddy tracks like brown streamers ran out through tall gatehouses thrust up into a clear blue sky. Even at a distance, Geth could make out the spearheads of sentinels on the ramparts, flashing in the sun.

"What's our angle at this council anyway?" Phelan asked, eying the armed tribesmen ahead.

"What have we got to work with?"

"Well, let's see." Phelan ticked off fingers. "Ceter hates us. He doesn't want peace either, we've already been through that. Vriana couldn't be bothered whether we live or die. She doesn't love the old warlock, but judging from what she did to Point-fort, she wants glory as much as any of them."

From a few paces ahead, Agrem turned. "No man can know Vriana. You know a woman's mind, mmmm?"

"He makes a good point," Geth said.

Phelan waved that off. "So where does that leave us? A bunch of smaller tribes should be at this council as well. Eldric said Iyngaer hoped to add to his army by signing them on."

"And you're forgetting the chieftain Othwid, of the Arnus tribe," said Geth. "I killed his brother. Can't imagine that makes him an ally."

"Mmmm." Agrem slowed to walk beside them. "Othwid and Iyngaer never friends. But Othwid is very important to Iyngaer."

Geth flicked a glance toward the Seer, mulled that over. It made sense the two most powerful Ilar chiefs, Othwid and Iyngaer would be rivals. Might this offer the angle they needed? If Othwid could be convinced that this war benefited Iyngaer more than him, could that be enough to separate one of the four great tribes from the Ilar alliance?

"If only I hadn't killed Big Yellow," Geth muttered.

"What were you gonna do, tickle him into submission?" Phelan shook his head. "I'll tell you one thing though, the way these folk all knuckle their brow at Agrem here, I'm starting to think we stand a chance."

Clusters of tents stood like tiny villages outside the walls, the first sign Geth had seen of Iyngaer's misa.

Warriors hunched around fires watched them pass. Judging by the dark looks, more than a few recognized Geth. These weren't Agrem's countrymen either. They paid the Seer no special regard, nor he them.

But the hails ringing down as they came within earshot of the walls came from friends. Agrem and the gate captain clapped each other's shoulders and grinned. Eko ran circles around the pair.

"They sent a boy up ahead to prepare us a meal," Phelan said, translating the small talk. "And an audience with Iyngaer."

A muddy gravel road carried them uphill through concentric rings of longhouses to Iyngaer's massive hall at the summit. The savory smell of cookfires hit Geth's nose. The din of smiths, sunlight on snowy rooftops met his ears and eyes. One look at the age-darkened doors reminded him he was in a foreign land though—enemy territory. A skull like a dog's but bigger had been nailed above the lintel. Hide banners stretched on man-high crosses to either side stood watch like tortured prisoners.

"This is it," Phelan said under his breath. "I hope you've got a plan."

Geth reckoned he did. An inkling of an idea had come to him, the perfect means to plant suspicion in Othwid's ear without coming within knife range. Geth eyed the Seer. They'd trusted the man this far. He had no choice but to trust him a little further.

"Iyngaer is waiting for us," Agrem said. He nodded, waved a pair of sentinels off and pushed through the doors.

Geth turned to Phelan. "Keep your ears open. Tell me everything they say. And pass my words back exactly as I say them."

"Don't get us killed, alright?"

Geth straightened his shoulders and followed the Seer inside. Circles of leather-clad warriors around low braziers packed the dim room. Most sat cross-legged or stretched out on pelts. A few squatted on sawed, polished tree-rings. Ladies in beaded leather dresses and flowing hair laughed among the men while youths weaved in and out, filling cups and drinking horns, passing platters around.

No sooner did they step across the threshold than the whispers began, the glowers, the considering looks. Geth followed Agrem toward the massive stone-ringed hearth blazing at the center of it all.

"Geth," Phelan's tone was urgent. "It's Ceter."

The *misa* had begun indeed. Ceter turned to watch their approach, face smooth. Geth didn't need an outward sign to recognize the animosity smoldering under his skin. Beside the warlock, Othwid made no attempt to hide his own feelings, eyes wide and angry, spitting curses in his own tongue. An old woman rested a hand on the chieftain's shoulder to calm him while a handful of self-important tribesmen eyed the new arrivals from the wings. Chiefs of the lesser tribes, Geth supposed. Only Vriana was missing.

None of them mattered anyway, pouting children under the stern watch of their minder. Iyngaer presided over the gathering from a huge wooden chair on the far side of the fire. A thick cloak of yellow-white fur draped his wide frame, a golden band across his forehead. Thinking of Hadean, Geth fought down the urge to draw his sword and hack the bastard to pieces.

Agrem raised his arms. "Iyngaer Lonega!" He circled to the right around the fire, just under Ceter's nose. The seer was all smiles as the greeting went back and forth, but Iyngaer's expression was cool.

"Yes, I remember him," he said, speaking perfect Aturian. "And you seem as proud as a cat that's dropped a dead mouse on his master's doorstep."

The great hall went quiet except for the low whispers of words being translated and shared.

Agrem cleared his throat. "You remember. Good. These men are my guests. Treat them well."

A brief delay for translation, followed by noises of outrage from Othwid. Behind him, others shouted their agreement with the chief of the Arnui.

Iyngaer flicked only the slightest glance toward Geth before turning back to Agrem. "It seems some have grievance with your guests. Why should I not turn them away from my door? Should they not pay their debts like other men, with gold or with blood?"

Geth didn't wait for anyone's help. "Blood and gold can be paid later, Chieftain Iyngaer. I'm here for your misa. I come here as emissary of the Kingdom of Umbel."

The translations were made. Laughter followed, from Othwid and others besides. Sweat rolled down Geth's side but he held fast.

"You've brought me a madman, Agrema Ehlo." Iyngaer said. "And the small one, is he a juggler? Are they part of the entertainment?"

Geth felt his cheeks go hot. He puffed out his chest, rested a hand on his hilt. "I assure you, this is no jest."

That killed the laughter.

"Something more serious then?"

Iyngaer stood slowly, calm as you like. Gods all be damned but he was tall!

That white cloak, Geth realized, must have belonged to some huge breed of bear. The length of the yellow-white arms and the great black claws had been left intact, folded over one another in lieu of a clasp to rest across the chieftain's broad chest.

"Easy now," Phelan breathed from Geth's side.

And he was right. "I stand for the King of Umbel," the big warrior said. "Nothing could be more serious than that."

"At a council of the Ilar tribes?"

"You propose to go to war against Umbel, don't you? I'd say that concerns my king. Why should he deal piecemeal with the Ilar chieftains when you're all here gathered together?"

Iyngaer snorted. But there was more amusement in it than scorn. The other chieftains took his cue, laughing, one louder than the next.

All except Ceter. He rose from the polished tree-ring beneath him, eyes on Geth. "You came to my hall offering land and gold in blunt attempt to divide and weaken the great Ilar tribes. And now you expect an invitation to our misa The king you claimed to speak for isn't even alive."

Geth lifted his chin. "I represent the kingdom of Umbel. A kingdom is greater than any one man, king or not."

"You're not even an Umbelman. You said so yourself."

"And you're not even an Ilar."

A torrent of curses flowed from Othwid in the Ilar tongue, but his ire was for Geth, not the old warlock. Phelan leaned in to translate the parts that mattered.

"Othwid says 'I have bad blood with this man. You all know how he killed my brother. And he lied to Ceter the Old.'"

"What else is he saying?"

"'Here sits a poisonous spider in our midst. Do we let it crawl off to bite someone? No, we squash it now.'"

Agrem had both hands in the air before Phelan was done. "These are my guests! And this is Iyngaer's house. A mark on him is a mark on all the Duei."

"*If* Great Iyngaer accepts him," said Ceter, "And even if he does, this is a misa of Ilar tribes. He cannot attend our council."

"Why not—?" Agrem started.

The entire hall shouted their dissent, waving arms, slapping hilts, cursing. Iyngaer frowned. Geth watched his eyes flick from Agrem to Othwid and back. Iyngaer needed the support of the chieftains, that was plain. Geth's chest tightened, wondering if Agrem hadn't just handed him over as a juicy gift, a sacrificial lamb for Iyngaer to present to Othwid and Ceter before he asked them to march beside him to war.

Bloody bastard... He eyed the exits, counted sharps, but Agrem moved closer to Iyngaer to shout above the din.

"Govende!"

Iyngaer motioned his people to silence.

The Seer's eyes flicked to Geth and back. "If chiefs cannot agree, Govendi, the spirits must decide. The gods."

Iyngaer's gaze went to Geth. The wheels were turning. Whatever Agrem was about, it couldn't be worse than trying to fight a way out of that hall.

"Does your guest agree?" Iyngaer asked.

Agrem nodded. *"Heteng Trusla."*

A murmur passed through the assemblage. Iyngaer settled it.

"Then let the Trusla decide."

Chapter thirty-one

Tribesmen and women all around went back to their food and drink. Geth blinked. He watched as Agrem took a seat on a tree-ring beside Iyngaer. The Seer turned to offer him a firm nod, a placating wave of the hand.

"What's he gotten us into now?" Geth muttered.

"A way to prove you are worthy," Phelan said. "The Trusla."

"Why don't I like the way you said that?"

"Because it's a trial."

Geth swore.

But at least Othwid, Ceter and the rest had given the sword-rattling a rest. A young Ilar led Geth and Phelan to a brazier of their own at the rear of the hall.

Meat and berry wine provided some measure of solace.

"A trial. That's wonderful."

Phelan frowned into his cup. "It's not exactly a trial, best I can tell. My...talent doesn't work that way. Maybe Agrem can explain it."

"Well, there's no better way to send a gutter-born inconvenience to his death than a trial, Phelan. You know that. Dress it up with ceremony and officiality, but judges serve the ones in power. Laws and trials... Ha! Nothing but a fancy way to squeeze a poor bastard for a rich bastard's profit."

"We're not gutter-rats here, Geth." Phelan gestured to the meat platter between them. "You're Hadean's champion. That counts for something."

"We're lower than gutter-rats. We're foreigners. And enemies."

"Don't be such an ass. We may be pieces on a game board, but we aren't pawns."

Most of that was true, Geth supposed. He already had the distinct feeling he was being used, by Agrem, Iyngaer, all of them. Then again, when was he *not* being used? He bit a piece of meat off its wooden skewer, cursed under his breath.

"Give the Seer some credit," Phelan went on. "We aren't dead yet, are we?"

Geth grunted.

"Agrem's not stupid." Phelan reached for the skewer, chewed as he spoke. "After what you did to his brother, Othwid wants you dead. Iyngaer needs Othwid's help in his war, he had to give the bastard something. Agrem got you a trial. That means we've got a chance."

"Mmmm." Agrem arrived, sinking onto a pelt between the two. "You pass this trial. I have *seen* it."

Mere mention of such magicks made Geth nervous. He flicked a glance to Phelan and back. "Everything you see comes true?"

The warlock frowned. "No, but—"

"I don't do well with trials."

"Not a sunlander trial. A test. Test of strength. Of *man-ness*. If you are strong, favored by gods, you pass. If not…" The Seer gestured with a thumb down.

Geth snorted. "We die. I get it."

"But I think you are strong."

"So, what is this test?"

"Swim lake, climb cliff maybe. Iyngaer will decide which. It is no matter. You will survive."

"When do we find out which one?"

"Later. First, we eat."

Agrem patted his stomach. Geth could never argue against eating. Steaming trays came out on the shoulders of Ilars, served to Iyngaer and his guests at the center of the hall first. By the time they reached Geth and Phelan, the meat was cold, but still delicious.

"You see 'em watching?" Phelan asked.

The higher-ups had finished their meal, muttering among themselves with more than a few calculating looks directed at the pair of foreigners. Ceter, Othwid—their animosity needed no explanation. Iyngaer seemed annoyed more than anything else. As for Agrem, their one and only ally, he'd turned to chat with a nearby circle of tribesmen before turning back.

The Seer belched once, smiled ruefully and stood. "Time to decide."

Geth took a casual sip at his wine, aware of the eyes on him. He watched Agrem trade words with the chieftains. Voices rose.

"Vorda's tits, now what?"

Phelan shushed him, ears cocked. "They're arguing over which trusla, the lake or the cliff. Agrem wants to be the one to pick."

"They're looking for a way to rig it."

Ceter and Othwid argued back and forth with Agrem. The line between Geth's friends and enemies had been drawn. Iyngaer listened, considered. That old Ilar woman leaned in at Othwid's shoulder as well. Geth's eyes widened. He realized he knew her. Hers was the face he'd seen through Pythelle's magick waters.

"Thram's balls! I saw that old hag in Pythelle's cellar."

"The one with Othwid?" Phelan frowned. "No."

"That's the one."

The little man threw in a few curses of his own. "It's her that's gonna decide your test. Seems she's some kinda witch."

Geth lifted his cup to hide a scowl. What did it all mean? Pythelle and the Ilars, Hadean's betrayal—what was her connection?

He didn't have time to think on it further. Things settled down around Iyngaer's fire, but by the flat look on Agrem's face, Geth reckoned he had more immediate problems.

"Well?"

Agrem settled back onto his pelt and drained his wine and swore. "Lake and cliff both. This is your trusla."

Iyngaer provided a longhouse for Geth and Phelan and they retired down the hill. Agrem badgered the chieftain until he'd won an extra day's rest before the trial. Geth reckoned the Seer truly wanted him to survive, even if it was only to forward his own aim of ending this war. That was something.

But passing the test of cliff and lake brought them no closer to meeting that shared aim. It only bought some time. Geth had come to the misa hoping to convince Othwid that it was his rival, Iyngaer, who profited most from the Ilar alliance. How was he supposed to get close enough to whisper in Othwid's ear now? Judging by the chieftain's insistence on two truslas, the man wouldn't stop hating him until he was dead.

At least the meal had done some good. The cozy blaze Phelan lit in their longhouse as well. Agrem would sleep in the hall with his chief, Geth supposed, but all the better. He touched his side, feeling the sore spot where Katare had broken his ribs.

"You gonna be alright?" Phelan asked.

Geth settled himself on the floor, pulled his cloak around him. "I can climb pretty well, even with these ribs still hurting. And I can swim. I'm just worried about freezing to death halfway across."

"I've been thinking about that. How is this lake not frozen over like the river and everything else?"

Geth shrugged. "Serpent Sea's all salt they say. That's what keeps it flowing. Maybe this lake is saltwater too."

"I don't know. Ilia's got to be colder than Adamar. Even Serpent Sea would freeze if it were like this I reckon."

"Has to be some trick to it then."

But what? Geth rolled on his back, looked up at the thatch of low ceiling above him. The cliff, the lake—neither would be easy. These Ilars were a tough bunch. Their test would be tough as well.

He mulled it all over again the next morning. Phelan ventured out into the lanes of Dues to learn what he could. Geth rested. Iyngaer's people sent ample food and drink, and not just salted fish and water. Hot mutton soup, wine and crusty brown bread. Geth wondered if Iyngaer didn't actually want him to succeed.

Or maybe it was Agrem's doing. Either way, when Geth poked his head out at midday for a breath of fresh air, passersby greeted him with many an approving nod. Phelan returned breathless to meet him outside.

"Big news," he said.

"Go on."

"Vriana's on her way up the hill. A woman like that's bound to shake up this hog-roast."

Geth frowned. "The last piece of the puzzle."

Phelan left to retrieve their sitting-pelts from the longhouse. He reemerged to throw them down on the snow to either side of the door, sitting on one with his legs stretched out in front of him. "For better or worse, I can't wait to see her expression when she lays eyes on us."

Geth followed suit. He drew Katare's sword—*his* sword—and ran a whetstone along its length. She couldn't avoid them. Their lodgings sat along the main road climbing Iyngaer's tor.

"I reckon we've got more allies than we had yesterday," he told Phelan, nodding to another smiling Ilar in passing.

"Folk inside the walls have taken an interest. Most of the locals are on our side."

"Guess we can thank Agrem for that?"

"Or maybe the fact that you killed Othwid's brother. He wants you to fail, but that puts Iyngaer's lot square in our favor."

"But not Iyngaer himself."

They didn't have time to talk further. There was no mistaking Vriana's long braid, that fierce brow among the dozen fur-clad tribesmen marching up the hill. Geth propped his weapon up beside him and leaned back against the longhouse, feet crossed and stretched out in front of him. She had to have seen them by then, but she did a fair job pretending she hadn't. Phelan whistled beside him like a man without a care in the world.

"Damn but I wish we still had Katáre's noggin," he said between notes.

Geth laced his hands behind his head, tilted his face toward the sun. "We could have set him right beside us. Who knows, maybe she would've appreciated the sight of a familiar face at the end of a long journey?"

Boots crunched on gravel and snow. The lady marched past without a look or a word but the expressions on the faces of her warriors spoke for her. A bright sun gleamed off the whitened rooftops. The wind was hardly a bother as far as Geth was concerned.

With the last of the four great chiefs arrived, Iyngaer wasted no more time. The tor of Dues hummed with activity. The trusla would begin.

Vriana may have feigned indifference, but the event had consumed the rest of her Ilar brethren. Warriors with sword and spear, women in braids, and even shaggy-coated dogs trailed them as they descended the fort-town the next morning. Even the wind was still, watching, waiting. Short Ilar horses had been provided to speed the half-day journey.

Geth reined in beside Phelan to talk through the side of his mouth as they rode. "I wonder if this trusla might not work in our favor. I mean, think about it: if surviving the trusla looks like a victory for Iyngaer, isn't that a good thing?"

"I'd say surviving is better than the alternative."

"I'm serious, Phelan. There's no getting close to Othwid, right? But we want to encourage the bad blood with Iyngaer, drive that wedge in as hard as we can. Well, if we can't get close enough to whisper in his ear—"

"On account of he wants your eyes out—"

"—then maybe with the trusla I can show him, without us having to tell him."

"Show him what?"

"That Iyngaer wins! He always wins. He wins in the trusla and he's set to win even more if they march south for Umbel."

Phelan went quiet, mulled that over. But in the short term, what other choice did Geth have? It was live or die.

Deep among the alders and evergreens they halted, a sheer wall of rock rising out of the trees ahead.

"So, it's the climbing that comes first." Geth eyed the cliff. Scraggly junipers clung to its crumbling face. Icicles hung from ledges and knobs.

"What do you make it?" Phelan asked.

"Forty paces?"

"I heard young men sometimes climb cliffs like this and bring down bird eggs for the womenfolk, to prove their worth. I bet they don't do it in winter. And they don't have to reach the summit to find a nest. But it's done all the same."

Geth rested a hand on his friend's shoulder. "You're more nervous than me, aren't you? Relax. I've climbed through almost as many windows as you have."

"The only difference is that I was going in for a roll. You were going in to bleed a scratch."

"I'm sure you stole something from the poor wench while you were at it."

"I only stole hearts, my friend."

Phelan smirked. Geth couldn't resist a smile.

"The key is to pick the right place to begin." Phelan turned his eyes back to the cliff. "Map out how you'll make the ascent now, from the ground."

"I'll be fine. Look, there's where I'll start." Geth pointed to a spot at the base of the rock wall. An appreciative murmur from the onlookers confirmed the decision. "See what I mean?"

The chatter rose behind him. A glance over his shoulder showed Ilars down on their haunches in knots, making wagers more than likely. Fires were stoked, the smell of hot cider wafted to Geth's nose. He drew Katare's blade to saw the fingertips off his gloves and stepped toward his starting point.

"If you've got any coin," he told Phelan, "this once you have my blessings if want to place a bet. But only if you bet with me."

Phelan looked like he might utter some retort, but Iyngaer arrived first, stern-eyed as ever. Geth puffed out his chest, rested hands on hips.

"This is the place," the chieftain said. "You must climb to the top. Take a knife if you want. No ropes."

Geth nodded. Both Agrem and Othwid's witch, Sythme, stepped past him to stand at the cliff base, uttering prayers. Iyngaer watched them.

"The gods have already decided if you live or die."

"I decide," Geth said. He brushed past the chieftain in the direction of the cliff base. Kicking through the snow and loose stones, he came within touching distance of the wall. The chatter of the gathered tribesmen fell to a whisper.

Geth turned to face them one last time, raised a fist to the sky. His eyes swept with deliberate slowness over the crowd. They met Othwid's, dark and hostile, Ceter's, cool and dispassionate, and Vriana's last. So hard, unknowable, despite the dark lashes. He turned and set both hands on stone.

Pushing off with one leg and pulling with both hands at the same time, Geth hoisted himself up the first few yards. He had the strength of arm and grip, but it was patience, he reminded himself, not power that would see him through. He'd plotted a course to the top already. His route would move sideways at times and sometimes back down a few feet. It also included places to rest.

"So far so good!" Phelan shouted up.

Geth snorted. He wasn't ten feet off the ground.

Words from an age ago rang in Geth's ear as he climbed, foot by foot, one handhold at a time. *Win the crowd, win the day.* A friend had doled out that advice and probably saved his life. He reckoned the same thing that worked as a pit-fighter in the arenas of Adamar would serve him now. Despicable creatures, human beings. They loved to watch a man suffer. And they hated an easy victory.

So, give them what they want.

He was nearly halfway up, clinging to a ledge, taking a breather. The wind pierced him at that height, his fingertips frozen numb, but he hadn't run into any surprises. Now was the time. He inched out sideways, then upwards a few yards, scraped down a handful of snow and loose stones, and hung half-limp, pretending to slip.

A collective gasp sounded from below.

"Steady!" Phelan shouted.

Jeers and a few curses rang up the cliff.

Geth smiled. He gestured with an upraised thumb. Clambering up a couple more paces, he took another break of exaggerated length. Starting onwards again, he scattered down more snow and debris. He even knocked loose a huge icicle this time. The sound of it shattering loudly as it crashed to earth earned another gasp, calls of encouragement from some, and plenty of jeers from the rest.

"Easy, Geth!" Phelan's concern sounded genuine this once. Geth reckoned he'd done the job.

He pulled up toward the summit, intent to finish. *Another twenty feet.* He was almost there. That's when he made the mistake of looking down.

It wasn't fear that undid him, but a loss of balance caused by the odd sight of looking earthward between his own legs. He leaned back a fraction too far, felt his weight going backward. His left hand slipped on an icy knob at the same time.

"Shit!"

Scrambling with his right for a handhold he caught a fingernail in a crack just long enough to get his left back firm around a cusp of stone. Noises echoed up from the tribesmen, but Geth wasn't listening. He stayed there, panting for a long minute, hugging the wall. He closed his eyes, focused, blocked out the catcalls until he heard only Phelan's voice.

"Almost there, Geth! You got this!"

Slow. Careful. One grip at a time, he climbed until it was done. He flopped over the edge and rolled to his back, breathless at the summit.

Phelan hooted from below. The sound of cheers echoed up as well. Still flat on the ground, Geth raised a clenched fist once more in triumph.

Chapter thirty-two

A handful of Ilars waiting atop the cliff led Geth back down the other side. Agrem greeted him with a wide grin and a clap on the back, but the line of Iyngaer's mouth was flat. Phelan brushed past them all.

"You did it!"

Watching tribesmen smiled and pumped fists as Geth passed. "Guess those are the ones that bet with me."

Phelan chuckled. "I should've laid down some coin myself."

But every bet had both winner and loser. Glowering faces followed Geth as he settled beside a fire for a drink and a crust, Othwid first among them. His eyes smoldered.

"It's just like we figured," Phelan said, voice low. "These tribesmen can't forget their differences. Iyngaer's folk have lined up behind you on account of Othwid and his lot wanting you dead."

Geth flicked a glance from his friend to the tall chieftain. "I don't know, Phelan. I reckon that's not all good. The more I succeed, the more we drive that wedge between Dues and Othwid's tribe. But did you see Iyngaer's face? That makes me a stone in his shoe."

"One that won't easily come loose." Phelan frowned. "He had to know our aim would be to stop his march into Umbel."

"Right. It's only out of respect for the Seer that we're still here. But at some point, he might decide it's easier to knife us in our sleep than deal with the inconvenience."

"Those fake slips didn't hurt our cause."

"You knew I was faking?"

Phelan winked. "The more these folk love us, the better our chances of staying alive."

They had no more time to discuss it. Tribesmen to either side began packing up. They were on to the next trusla.

A muddy trail winding through the whitened trees carried them to a narrow lake nestled between pine-laden hills. Dark water reflected grey skies overhead. Gentle waves lapped a beach of smooth round stones the size of saucers, meeting the snow to nibble away at it and retreat again. It couldn't have been more than fifty paces wide, but it stretched a good half mile long.

Geth marched to the water's edge to get a look. "How is it not frozen over? Even the bloody river was frozen. And that's running water."

"Balfega Meed," Agrem said, joining them. He pointed from the far end of the lake then back over his shoulder the way they'd come. "Sunrise, sunset. Beautiful. This is the place where Atram—the one you call Thram—bathed his feet after the Remaking. These waters are good for the bones."

"How far have I got to swim?" Geth had a feeling he wasn't going to like the answer.

"Follow the journey of the sun."

Longways. He cursed under his breath. Phelan took the sack off his shoulder. The little man eyed the distance to the far side, leaned in close.

"You've got this. It's not as far as it looks."

"Half a mile at least. That's not far? And freezing cold besides?"

"Did you pay attention to what Agrem said? These are healing waters. Must be something like the shrine of Neyna outside Old Crown. There's a hot spring under this lake."

"I'm not sure I'd trust this lake to do anything but give me the grippe."

"They say it's hot sulfur from Helu's forges in the underworld that warm places like this."

"Not a wisp of steam coming off the surface though. And that's no short distance."

Phelan shook his head. "Bodies float mostly, you taught me that. Remember all those poor bastards floating downriver during the Affliction?"

"A goddamn flotilla."

"Just put one arm in front of the other. I'll be waiting with some blankets and a fire on the far side."

"A nice hot fire. You hear me?"

Agrem and the witch Sythme stepped through the snow to the water's edge to make their prayers. Tribesmen and women started spreading out down the length of the shore. Some cupped hands to their mouths to holler what must have been encouragement. Others crossed their arms and muttered among themselves. An advance party tramped off for the lake's far end. The vale went quiet as Iyngaer approached Geth.

"Your second trusla."

Geth grunted. Standing this close, a part of him wanted to lunge for the chieftain, kill or be killed, end it all there. Much easier than swimming a gods-be-damned lake in the middle of winter.

Agrem hailed him before he could imagine himself into trouble and Iyngaer left to rejoin his people along the edge of the water. "You do this trusla easy, mmmm?" the Seer said. "I have seen it."

"I could have told you that." Geth thumped himself on the chest. "This bastard dies on a sword, not in some frozen drink halfway up the Hoarwinds' ass."

He threw off his cloak, let it land on the snow, bent double to stretch his legs, jumped in place to get his heart beating. His breath puffed into the frigid air like parts of his spirit making a break for it. *Rats off a sinking ship.* He laughed mirthlessly. "Gods all damn you, Iyngaer. All you bloody Ilars."

Phelan gathered up the cloak. Geth stripped down, handed him his boots, clothes, even his undercloth. His nipples tightened and his skin goosed up, but he fought down the shivers. The eyes of a hundred Ilars watching only lent him strength. Geth heard the murmurs. Hard folk like these appreciated the bunched muscles of his arms and shoulders, the pale battle scars cutting lines through dark chest hair, the blue-black ink swirling up each wrist.

"See you on the other side," Phelan said, eyes fierce.

It was too cold to reply. Geth turned to splash right in.

All effort to ready himself came to naught. He gasped like a god-sworn prude in a whorehouse. Phelan's voice echoed from over his shoulder.

"Swim, man! Before your prick turns into an icicle!"

Geth heeded those words, thrashing hard with arms and legs. That warded the cold off some. But it was a far distance. He'd never be able to keep it up.

Turning to float on his back at whiles, he conserved strength. The cold returned immediately. When he flipped back over, the distant shore had hardly come any closer.

But this was his test. He plodded forward, mind focused on the fire Phelan would have waiting, the hot food, the tent to shelter him from the wind. Thoughts wandered over the snow-covered forests of Ilia, south of Umbel's pastures, to the sun-dappled waves of Longsea. He'd lived through worse, he told himself, survived. From gladiatorial fighting pits, to the oars of a slave galley. To the battles—so many battles. Those were distant memories, sure. But they were worse than this.

He flipped to his back again, stroked slowly onward. He wasn't so cold really. Tired, but not cold. He'd be done soon. Warm and resting in a pile of furs. He closed his eyes, felt the water lap kindly against his cheek, unaware of the danger 'til the first mouthful passed his lips, sending him spluttering back to his stomach.

"Sonofabitch!" Geth shook his head to clear it. The lake had nearly got him there. He clawed forward, arms strangely numb. He looked ahead, fought down a rising panic. The far end of the lake was still a long way off.

Events of the past weeks flashed through Geth's mind. The need to avenge young Hadean, his promise to get Phelan out of Ilia alive. He *had* to make it to the other side.

Thinking of that, he remembered what Phelan had said about those waters. *Gods all be damned!*

He wasn't going to make it, not at this rate. But he had one last play. He'd live to fulfill none of his promises if the little man was wrong.

Bless me Helu. Bless me, sword-maker. I swear to repay you. Katáre's blade, the only thing I have, will be yours. Geth summoned his courage and gathered one last breath. "Bless me you bastard!"

Ducking beneath the surface, he kicked straight down with all his might. Icy water closed on him like Vorda's embrace. He shut his eyes, jaw clenched, holding his last breath. Then it hit him, melting the fog from his mind. Warm water caressed each frozen limb, the touch of a god.

The heat of those sulfurous vents had been just a few yards below the water's surface all along. A tingling sensation shot through Geth's limbs, a surge of strength through each and every vein.

Breaking the surface with a splash, Geth sucked in air. Distant voices sounded as he started forward again. Backstroking to rest, diving at times to warm up, he pulled toward the far shore. Geth's mind wandered back to Zeukon's slave ship, how that bloody adventure had unfolded, and he smiled. A knee scraped slimy stones, and he stood, shivering, out of the water. The trusla was over.

Chapter thirty-three

What did anyone really know about the gods? Geth squinted out over the lake. He'd been dragged across the sworn realms, crisscrossed Ilia, and come to a stop here, to watch a red sun rise over a frozen vale, seated beside a tribesman called Agrem, enemy-turned-ally. No, the gods had a way of toying with men, of that Geth was certain. To what end, he doubted they even knew themselves.

An Ilar he hadn't met brought him warm soup just as others had erected a tent for him the night before. He ate their soup and slept in their tent. The camp had only just begun to come to life, Phelan still snoring behind the flap, curled up beside Eko.

Agrem broke the silence. "You feel Atram here, mmmm?"

Geth followed the Seer's eyes eastward over the water. The first orange sliver of sun threw red dapples over the surface. The underside of purple-grey clouds glowed pink.

"That reminds me of something." Geth rose to fish through his belongings inside the tent. *Katáre's sword.* He made good on his promise, stepping up to the lake's edge to hurl the weapon far out into the depths.

"A worthy gift," Agrem said.

Geth turned back from the water to settled back beside their little fire. "You've got the wrong god, you know. It's Helu this lake should be known for. His fires light it's belly, whether Thram dipped his dirty feet in here or not."

Agrem shrugged. That about summed it up.

Phelan crawled through the tent flap to join them. "Well, we did it," he said. "Where's breakfast?"

"That's your job. I'm the one who had to climb that cliff and swim this lake."

"Cold in there, eh?" Phelan flicked a glance at Geth's crotch and smirked. "I've never seen such a... *retreat*, shall we say?"

"Retreat? My retreat is more frightening than your spear at full charge."

Phelan laughed. Geth cracked a smile, but Agrem didn't get it or hadn't been listening. He stood, eyeing the shoreline with a frown.

"What now?" Geth asked.

"Trouble."

Geth followed the Seer's gaze past clusters of tents beside the water. The camp had begun to stir. A throng of several dozen tribesmen marched in their direction, Othwid at the lead.

There was no mistaking the purpose on the faces of that approaching party, nor the intensity in Othwid's eyes. Ceter came beside him.

Geth's hand moved of its own accord toward his hip, prompting a curse at the notion of ever parting with Katáre's sword. *The gods and their games.* Othwid shouted something as he neared.

"What's he saying?" Geth asked.

Iyngaer appeared to accost the gathering, wrapped in that white bearskin. This was his realm after all. Phelan motioned Geth to silence as he listened.

"Othwid's demanding a *higher* trusla. Whatever that is."

Agrem hummed. "For killing his brother."

"Another trial?" Geth looked from the Seer to Phelan and back. "For killing a man at war?"

Noises of disgust from tribesmen and women near the two chiefs echoed his sentiments. But the wheels were turning behind Iyngaer's eyes.

"He's going to give him what he wants, isn't he?" Geth said.

"A man must pay for killing another man," Agrem grimaced. "Or he must die. This is the Ilar way. You cannot pay, mmmm?"

"I killed him in battle, not in his sleep. And the bastard challenged *me*!"

"Mmmm," Agrem agreed. But Iyngaer and Othwid turned in tandem toward them before he could say more. They marched almost in lockstep, the latter with a hand on his hilt. Behind them, tribesmen rushed about, hollering and waving at their friends.

Phelan swore.

"Iyngaer has agreed to the High Trusla," Agrem said, as if that needed explaining. "There can be no argument this time."

"There never is," Geth said, "when it's a duel to the death."

The charges were made. Iyngaer spoke in plain Aturian, circled around by just about every tribesman and woman that had accompanied them to Balfega Meed. Across from Geth, Othwid and his entourage glowered. Other Ilars crowded in behind Geth, spitting curses past his shoulder at the chieftain.

There was no way he could deny he'd killed Big Yellow. Not that he wanted to. He met Othwid's glare with one of his own. "Think you can do what your brother couldn't?"

Iyngaer sent the two parties in either direction. Phelan pulled Geth away. "This is no time for jokes. You're tired. Ask Iyngaer for a day's rest. Like you had in Dues."

"A day's rest? No way he'll give it. This is exactly what Iyngaer wants. The sooner I'm dead, the better. Before I can ruin his little misa."

Agrem hummed, taking Geth by the elbow. "Even better if you die by Othwid. If Othwid is happy, probably he agrees to march south."

"That settles it. All I've got to do is kill the bastard. Two birds with one stone."

A pair of Ilars had already begun marking off a rough circle in the snow. Agrem left Geth to speak with Iyngaer. The big warrior watched, but whatever the Seer said, his chieftain was having none of it. Tribesmen and women had already taken up places around the circle to watch, others moving up the surrounding hills, even climbing trees for a better view.

"So, what do we know about this scratch?" Geth asked Phelan.

"He hasn't got the reputation of Iyngaer or Vriana, but he wouldn't be an Ilar chief if he didn't know which end of a sword to poke with."

Geth ran a hand over his beard. He was tired, his mind a little fuzzy, but instinct told him something was off. Did Othwid really think he could win just because Geth was a little tired?

Agrem had the answer. "Ceter is your enemy. Othwid is nothing, just the arm of Ceter. And Ceter the Old has…talents."

Geth shared a look with Phelan

"That icy feeling," his friend said. "It was like he could get in your head, make you afraid of shadows."

Geth swallowed a curse, put on a fearless mask. He turned back to the Seer. "And just how do we counter his magicks?"

"I will do what I can. Very close, he will be strong."

"Ceter will be expecting you to help."

"Mmmm." His tone did nothing to lend confidence. "That's why you must be stronger."

Agrem left them to make some sort of preparations. Geth took stock of himself. His limbs were heavy, half-numb, but he could fight. He shook his head to clear it and peered across the snow at Othwid and his entourage.

"I'll have to do it quick."

He considered the slashing manner of Ilar swordplay, the length of the blade Othwid carried, the snowy fighting space. Things could go a number of ways, especially with two warlocks playing them like puppets.

But how many duels had Othwid fought? Geth had cut his teeth long ago on the gravel of the pits. And today he'd bloody the snow. If only he had a sword.

Damn you, Helu! Damn the rest of you too!

"Remember, you've got nothing to prove," Phelan was saying. "Stick the bastard and have done."

"One problem." Geth patted his empty scabbard, showed his palms.

Phelan had missed Geth's offering that morning, but Ilars to either side noticed. They raised their weapons and shouted, arguing over who would lend their blade. Not just any weapon would do, though. Not today. Geth pushed past them, through the crowd until he saw the one he wanted. Vriana watched his approach, arms folded across her chest.

"May I?"

Did the corner of her mouth twitch or had he imagined it? Whatever the case, she drew her blade and handed it over. Casual as you please.

A murmur of appreciation sounded from her men. Geth eyed the edge, sharp, flawless. "Thank you."

He headed back to join Phelan. His friend shook his head, handing over a skin of wine and speaking under his breath. "Uro's puckered ass, Geth, now's not the time to flirt."

Geth snorted. He knew what he was about and it wasn't Vriana's affections. Giving her weapon a few swings, he found it was all he'd hoped for. By then the familiar charms were being uttered by Sythme and Agrem. Ceter watched bluff-faced from the first row of onlookers beside the circle.

Iyngaer stepped up to call the combatants forth. "No quarter," he told Geth. He said something to Othwid in their own tongue, motioning the two men to touch blades. Geth directed his most menacing stare over the points. Othwid snarled back. A racket of catcalls and shouts echoed off the hills.

The chieftain made the first lunge. Vriana's blade reacted smoothly, turning the strike. That's why he'd chosen it. The sword she favored was as long as any other, but narrow and lighter, lending the lady quickness where a heavier blade might have slowed her down. Just the sort of weapon for a man with tired arms.

Geth circled right, watching the chieftain's hips, the end of his sword. Othwid cursed him. Geth cursed back.

"Old stallion's grown some balls, has he? Come and get gelded!"

Geth flicked a testing stab at Othwid's middle. The chieftain parried. Calls for blood rang from the spectators, Phelan's voice among them. Before Geth could press further, however, a suffocating panic took hold of him.

Time slowed. Rather than the ecstasy of battle filling Geth, it was a piss-your-trousers terror that gripped him. The sword across from him gleamed impossibly sharp. The cold air burned in his lungs. And he was already tired, so tired.

Othwid read the strain on Geth's face. He couldn't miss it. He *knew*. It was all part of the plan. His mouth stretched into a smile, and he coiled to strike.

You cannot kill what is already dead. Geth summoned those words from his first days in the pits, pounced on that fear, wrestled it down. Othwid slashed at him. Geth's arm moved, and his sword turned the strike, but barely.

His eyes flicked to Ceter, front row on the edge of the fighting circle. The chill of his witchcraft hung on Geth like lead chains. Othwid laughed and spit insults. He had all the time in the world. Geth looked for Agrem, finding the Seer's face contorted, his mouth working silently. *Whatever you're doing, it's not working!* He thought of the irony of what he'd told his friend about dying on a sword.

"And you, Awer." He cursed the god of war. "After all the blood and carnage I've spilled for you?"

Channeling his rage, Geth produced a feeble offensive, cutting sideways then overhand at the chieftain. Othwid parried the first strike, twisted past the second, but a widening of the eyes indicated the chieftain's surprise. And fear. That sparked an idea in Geth's head.

"Ready to die, Othwid?" His terror-clenched body still fought him, but Geth circled so that his back was to Ceter.

A skip forward and a thrust drove the chieftain to the far end of the circle, out of striking distance. But rather than pursue him, Geth whirled on Ceter, sword raised two-handed overhead. "Argh!"

That wordless scream, and the fury in Geth's eyes, sent both Ceter and the men to either side of him backpedaling. They fell in a jumble of fur and leather. The weight of the witch's fear slid off Geth's shoulders like a load of stones. He turned back toward Othwid. The chieftain's eyes widened, terrified.

Geth summoned his anger and rushed. Blow after blow battered Othwid's guard, tested his strength, put him off balance. A sideways slash sent the chieftain stumbling. Another spun him like a drunk. He wasn't just going to kill the bastard, he was going to humiliate him. He beat down Othwid's guard with a hard swing, stepped inside to slap him open-handed across the face. The chieftain whimpered, the watching tribesmen gasped. Geth would have made it last longer, but with Ceter sure to recover before long, he had no choice but to skewer Othwid and have done.

"Ahh!" the Ilar groaned, dropping his sword to clutch at the bloody end of Vriana's blade protruding through his stomach.

Geth let go of the hilt and the chieftain collapsed. Voices cried out in triumph and despair. Geth dropped to his knees, then collapsed in the snow as well.

Chapter thirty-four

Geth didn't know how long he'd slept but only Phelan and a handful of tribesmen remained beside the lake to escort them back to Dues. The little man cooked up another soup and packed their tent, laughing and joking with their custodians like old friends. Best Geth could tell, they were Vriana's men. He shot Phelan a look when one of the bastards dismounted to offer him a horse.

"Take it, Geth. You're still tired, I can see it in your face."

"Last time we saw this lot they were pissing in our drinks."

Phelan waved a hand. "Bygones."

Geth didn't forget so easy. But he wasn't about to refuse the horse. They set out at a comfortable pace through the hills. The great tor of Dues came into view before nightfall.

The journey provided Geth plenty of time to think. He'd won his place at Iyngaer's misa, but hadn't he also helped the chieftain by killing his greatest rival? Their whole plan had hinged on driving a wedge between Othwid and Dues. *How the hell do I break up the alliance now?*

Geth had yet to figure out the answer to that when the misa began early the next day. An overcast sky promised snow as he made the walk up to Iyngaer's hall. He couldn't be sure if that was a bad omen or not. At least he'd have snow to fill his tracks if they had to make a run for it.

Aside from Othwid's absence and the addition of Vriana, the same chiefs as before gathered around Iyngaer's central hearth. Hangers-on crowded them from the center of the hall outward, clustered in threes and fours around braziers. Agrem waved to Geth, motioned him to one of those polished tree rings beside the great open hearth.

"Are we crazy for trying this?" Geth said out of the side of his mouth.

From his seat at his side on the floor, Phelan muttered a curse into a cup full of dark Ilar spirits. Vriana sat stiffly to their left, Iyngaer to the right. Ceter took great pains to ignore Geth's presence altogether, while Othwid's successor, a man called Mereg, watched everyone from under a set of bushy blond eyebrows. The lesser chieftains eyed him as darkly as the rest.

The arrival of a tray of steaming pork joints improved Geth's mood briefly, but Iyngaer stood before anyone had finished eating to address the misa. He stalked back and forth beside the fire like the bear of his great yellow-white cloak, motioning with an ornate drinking horn for emphasis. He didn't bother speaking Aturian this time and the exact words were lost on Geth. Phelan translated promises of glory, plunder and the like. The fist waving and floor pounding of his listeners spoke for itself.

Questions flew, from Mereg, Vriana, others Geth didn't know. Iyngaer never stumbled in his answers.

Phelan shook his head. "Hashing out the details now. If you're gonna say something, better do it quick."

What was he gonna say? Geth looked at the pork shank in his hand. This once, he couldn't eat. Neither did he have any clever argument, except to tell the truth.

"Alright listen here." He stood, that leg bone still clutched in one hand. "Enough of the promises. I'm here to tell you they're all lies."

Iyngaer's mouth was a tight white line through his beard. Phelan translated for the rest.

"How many times have the tribes gone to war with Umbel?" Geth looked from face to face around the fire. "Countless. And how many times have you won? What have you got to show for it? As far as I can tell, never. You've only got these forests because nobody else wants them."

Curses flew. Fists shook. He had their attention.

"You won't win. Not for more than a season. The sunlanders will hide in their island fortress and let you freeze outside the walls all winter. The villagers are already headed south with their daughters and their valuables. Burn what you want, they're saying.

Take the empty barns and homesteads. Come spring, the king will march north with his full armies and tear you apart."

From what Geth had heard, this was the pattern that had played out in all the wars between the two regions. A united Umbel could field larger armies than the tribes; it was that simple. Geth looked to Iyngaer with a smirk. The tall chieftain raised a hand.

"Umbel is divided." He spoke Aturian now, leaving his seer and others to translate. "More divided than even you know. Who will march north? Why did they not march north already?"

"Even if they drag their feet," Geth replied, "the king has only to call on his allies across the sworn realms. That's four great kingdoms sworn to protect one another. You know that." He jabbed a finger in Iyngaer's direction, met his eye. "And who gains the most from this alliance anyway? High Chief Iyngaer, that's who."

More than a few Ilars grumbled. Geth pressed.

"The gods favored me in your truslas. They wanted me here at this misa. Fate stands against your war with Umbel. Your own seer has said as much."

Iyngaer laughed. "As always, the sunlanders' only hope is to divide us. Do we let them? Do we let our own rivalries stand in the way of a glorious future?"

Geth opened his mouth but across the pelt-strewn floor, eyes had shifted to his left. Vriana stood, one hand resting on her hilt.

Phelan translated. "You speak some truths, she says. Do we march to war to put Iyngaer on the sunlander throne?"

Iyngaer answered her in their own language. Others opined, slapping scabbards, waving arms. Iyngaer's face went red.

Geth needed no translation to read that as a good sign. Flicking a glance, he found Agrem watching him, quiet thus far. If the Seer had intended to speak though, Ceter beat him to it, barking out a few terse words.

"What'd he say?" Geth asked.

"Nothing," said. Phelan. "He's called for the desserts."

"Stalling."

Geth started to smile but Iyngaer uttered something that drew an intent look from Phelan. "I don't like the sound of that."

The tall chieftain turned back to Geth. "You say you've proved yourself in your truslas? Let me prove myself then as well. Prove I deserve to lead, to be the first among equals. But first, more food. And then some entertainment."

An assortment of warm buns baked with different fruit fillings served as dessert, but the smug look on Iyngaer's faced soured it in Geth's mouth. He sipped at the tart berry wine, wishing for the cheapest southern blend instead. Pale daylight filtered in from the high windows, but Iyngaer's guests had grown mellow after so much food and drink. A trio of flutists blew a tune. The room didn't perk up until a man with a hood over his head and wooden restraints at wrist and ankle was ushered in.

"Here is out entertainment," Iyngaer said, speaking directly to Geth. An evil glint in the chieftain's eye made the big warrior's stomach clench. The hooded man struggled against a yoke tied around his neck as he was hauled past laughing clusters of Ilars until he stood just behind the circle of chiefs and their crackling central hearth.

"What the hell is that? Phelan whispered.

Iyngaer stood to address his people in their tongue, arms flung wide, draped by that white bearskin like a raptor's wings. Phelan listened wide-eyed. Iyngaer turned toward Geth himself, glowing with triumph.

"You say the sunlanders will come north in spring, mmmm? Did you think I hadn't planned for that? Like for like, I say. Your kingdom would divide us? Let your kingdom be divided instead."

Iyngaer moved toward the tortured man and Geth knew. With a swift motion, the hood came off young Hadean's head.

Agrem made a noise like a dying man. A few Ilars cried out. Others laughed or murmured to one another, asking who he was, what it meant. Geth stood rooted to the spot, speechless, unable to move, assaulted by a torrent of warring emotions.

Shock, relief, and red-hot anger roiled inside him. His weight shifted, half a mind already decided to pounce on Iyngaer, kill him barehanded, or die trying. But the chieftain went to work, taking the fiddles off his blindfolded, gagged captive straight away.

"Hadean." Geth managed.

The king turned his head. Iyngaer untied the blindfold and Hadean's eyes found him. Geth couldn't say what the king saw, if he hated him, loved him, or didn't recognize him at all. Geth couldn't find any words, thoughts and feelings piling up on one another, jamming his tongue.

Iyngaer laughed. "I give this gift to you. And to myself."

He addressed his people once more. Geth didn't need Phelan to tell him what he said. He would split Umbel with civil war. Hadean would go free at the expense of all of Umbel. That had been his plan all along.

Chapter thirty-five

Geth retreated with Hadean and Phelan to the longhouse Iyngaer had given them before the truslas. The misa was over, Iyngaer had won. The tribes would march south. War would tear Umbel apart.

But Hadean was alive! Geth couldn't dwell on the rest, now that he had his arm around the boy. He studied Hadean out of the corner of his eye. His hair and beard had grown scraggly, his cheeks gaunt. And that faraway look in his eyes was never a good sign.

"I thought you were dead." Geth settled the lad down on a pelt. Phelan started a fire and poured drinks.

"I should have been." Hadean looked at his hands. "They surprised us just north of Point-fort. I killed one of them, wounded another, but there were just too many. I would have died fighting, but they wouldn't kill me."

"They wanted you alive. Iyngaer's a clever scratch. He could have killed you, but he decided to keep you in his back pocket instead."

"I was a fool. I insisted on the parley, didn't see it coming. I led Utrand and the rest to their deaths."

"You were young. You have counselors to point out dangers like that for you. It's a bad business when your counselor is the snake."

Hadean looked up. "You think it was Melagus who betrayed me? I really am a fool if it was."

"He's the only one it could have been. Remember the poisoned food in your hall?"

"I…" Hadean shook his head. "I just don't know."

"It was his idea, wasn't it? To parley and buy time?"

"It was. But I pushed for it too after you left. My uncle wanted to wait behind the walls and do nothing."

"Too many ways for that to go wrong. Especially with an assassin on the loose."

"That's why I pressed Uncle Eldric to set it up. I knew we had a spy in Ilia. He could use that spy to set up a meeting with Othwid of the Arnui. He didn't want to, but finally he gave in."

Geth nodded. "He was using the witch Pythelle to send messages to Sythme, Othwid's witch. Somehow Iyngaer learned of it and beat him to it. But only to use you for his own designs."

Hadean grimaced. "What now?"

"We get back home, deal with Melagus," Geth felt his ire rising at mere mention. "And Pythelle. And all the rest."

Hadean rose to pace the small chamber. "I just can't see Melagus selling Umbel to the Ilars for his own gain. Unless he thought it better if my uncle ruled. I pushed against all his counsel after all, refused to marry. And forced the battle at Copper Ridge. Uncle Eldric wouldn't have made those mistakes."

"Stop." Geth rose, took the king by the shoulders. "Don't blame yourself, my lord. And don't give Melagus too much credit either. He hasn't risked the gallows for Eldric or Umbel, I'll promise you that. He's made a deal with the Ilars for his own gain, no one else's. That bastard's probably wearing your crown already."

Phelan urged them to leave the next morning. Geth didn't argue. Distraught though he might be, Hadean looked fit to travel. And there was no point wasting time they didn't have.

"We've got to get south before Iyngaer and his army," Geth said. "It won't be safe for us in Ilia much longer."

Phelan snorted. "It won't be safe for us in Umbel either."

Iyngaer arrived before they could embark, alerted, perhaps, by Phelan's hasty search for provisions. The usual entourage flanked their chieftain plus a pair of bundle-toting servants. Geth met him outside on the gravelly path.

"You will leave today?" the chieftain asked.

Geth grunted.

"You have completed the truslas. It is just that the gods deliver your king back to you."

"Come to gloat, have you? The great god Iyngaer gives the sunlanders their king? Well, I killed your greatest rival, don't you forget it. I delivered the tribes to you. Maybe you should thank me while you're here."

"Othwid would have turned on me, that is true. Once we reached the south, in the field. That was the deal he made with the traitors in Umbel. Or something like it."

"Clever bunch, those traitors."

Iyngaer smiled. "You'll find out who they are soon enough. No need to drop a hook down this hole, I only know of the witch. Send her my regards."

"So, you *did* come to gloat."

"I came to give you these." The chieftain motioned to his men, and they dumped their bundles in the snow. Conical helms, green cloaks, at least one sword, and mail tumbled out. There was still blood in the creases.

"I see." It was Geth's turn to smile. "We'll need our own clothes. It wouldn't do if our own people mistook us for tribesmen and killed us before we could touch off a civil war."

"Nor would it do for the tribesmen to kill you before your reach Umbel. I'm sending an escort as well."

"Ceter?"

"There are some among the chiefs who are not so forgiving as I."

Hadean appeared through the low door. Geth watched him straighten up, smooth his shirt front. Kingly, even under those circumstances. Geth had never been prouder.

"Chieftain Iyngaer, it is well we meet. We have much to discuss. It's not too late to have peace."

But Iyngaer just turned, waved his people back up the hill. A lone figure remained.

"Agrem."

The Seer approached, a bulging skin in his hand and a string of sausages slung over his neck. "Breakfast."

He forced a smile. Geth took a cold sausage and bit off a chunk. At least it was something. He frowned at the pile Iyngaer had left, kicking through cloaks, helms and the odd sword. They'd need those green cloaks. Helmets too, those with nose-guards and closed cheek pieces.

"Well," Geth said, "After all of that, we're still at war."

The Seer blew out a sigh. "The hunger of Iyngaer is great."

"Have you tried your tricks? Your magick? If Iyngaer changes his mind, the alliance of the tribes ends."

Hadean nodded. "You want peace, as do I. Can the chieftain not be swayed?"

"Swayed?" Agrem pursed his lips. "Mmmm. Maybe Iyngaer feeds me to his dogs if I ask again."

As if the beast had heard mention, Eko came bounding down the hill. Geth crouched to embrace the animal, rubbing his big head, blinking under a barrage of licks.

"I'll miss you too, friend." He looked up at the Seer. "I'll need one favor. The witch, Sythme—"

"The sunlanders will not learn King Hadean still lives. Or that he returns. Not for a while."

"Thank you."

"Still, there are dangers in Ilia, mmmm?" Agrem stepped closer. "Ceter has watchers. That is why Iyngaer asked Vriana to bring you safe to your sunlands."

"Vriana?" Geth swore under his breath. "Thram's balls, why her?"

Hadean looked from Geth to the Seer, confused.

"Let's just say 'Vriana' and 'safe' aren't two words we've used together before now," Geth told him.

"Vriana and Iyngaer—" Agrem gestured with fingers crossed, "like this. If Iyngaer wish you safe, Vriana will make it so."

So, the two were lovers. That made sense. "I see."

Agrem opened his arms. Geth accepted the gesture and stepped in for a hearty embrace. They might face one another across a battlefield next they met, but today the Seer was his friend, a man who'd saved his life, even if together they'd failed at everything else. Agrem released him to bow low toward Hadean. He started to go, then paused, searching with one hand inside his cloak.

"This. For Phelan."

He passed over a smaller skin. Geth had a good idea what it might hold. The thump of approaching horsemen turned them before he could unstop it for a taste.

It was Vriana, girt for war. Bronze scale armor of the Ilar type peeked out beneath her fur-lined cloak. The sword Geth had grown familiar with hung at her hip. A good twenty warriors rode behind her, spears against their shoulders, shields slung across backs.

Geth pushed open the door to the longhouse where Phelan dithered over their baggage. "What are you still doing in there? You wanted to leave Ilia. Now's your chance."

Chapter thirty-six

The sturdy steeds of Ilia carried Geth and his friends along snowy tracks leaving Dues. They spoke only of trivial matters on account of Vriana and her escorts, soon to be enemies. The miles passed swiftly.

Two days from Dues, they cantered out beyond the last rank of leaning evergreens. A sensation of giddy triumph swept over Geth as vast blue skies opened up overhead. He'd failed to disrupt the Ilar alliance, failed to keep Hadean on his throne, but at least he'd kept one promise.

"I said I'd get you out of there, Phelan, and I have. Say goodbye to the forest."

His friend mumbled something foul. Vriana kicked her mount ahead and turned to face them. She spoke in her native tongue.

"This is as far as she goes," Phelan relayed.

"Tell her she can go back to Iyngaer's bedroom now." Geth turned his eyes to the chieftess, waited for her expression, but Vriana just laughed.

"See you soon, Trulsata."

Geth's mouth fell open. She'd spoken Aturian all the while, never mind the threat. He watched her canter back the way they'd come, sword bouncing at the curve of her hip.

Phelan had already turned his horse south. "Gods but I never thought I'd see an end to the trees."

"There were days I felt the same way," Hadean said. "You've proved yourself, Master Phelan. I won't forget what you've done for me. And for Umbel."

Hadean flicked a glance toward Geth, prompting an Umbel-style salute of fist to heart. Phelan just kicked his mount forward, muttering under his breath.

Geth spurred his steed after him. "What's your problem? It's not enough that we're outta there? That you've earned the compliments of a king?"

Phelan rolled his eyes. "Now what, huh?"

"Back to Umbel. Put Hadean back on his throne."

"And get ourselves stuck in a fortress under siege? That's mud for a pig like you, not me."

"It's not too late to fix this, Phelan. We had something good with Hadean. And we can have it again."

The little man snorted, kept moving. Geth let him go. They traveled in silence. Taking side-tracks, they steered wide of the river and Point-fort. There would be scouts there, Geth reckoned. He didn't want Melagus getting advance notice of their approach.

They rode across snowy fields, under a bright but distant sun. These were the boundaries, a wide, contested, uninhabited stretch. The first sign of life was the scent of char on the wind. They topped a low rise to find the burned-out husk of a homestead in the dell below.

"We'll be seeing more of this in the coming months I fear," Hadean said.

Geth kicked his mount down the hill. A light snow had settled over the place, but the blackened remains of a home, a barn, and several sheds thrust up through the white all around. "Not more than a week old."

"While we hide in the Tooth," said Hadean, "the tribes will have the run of the land. They'll slaughter and burn, steal everything in their path."

Geth said nothing. It was the way things, the way of war—he knew better than most. Soldiers risked their lives for glory and plunder, king and country. But the common man? That was the bone the animals fought over, pulled at from both ends, gnawed and devoured.

Just one of many reasons Geth had picked up a sword and never looked back.

Hadean stared at the destruction below. He turned his mount, smacked the hilt at his waist. "Gods be damned! Why won't they join me?"

Geth flinched. "I—"

"Lord Towdric and the rest…If we mustered all the men of the south earlier, we would have won at Copper Ridge."

"We almost did win."

"And this war would already be over."

It was true. Maybe Hadean should have married one of those girls, done something different to appease his liegemen. But to Geth, those bastards were still traitors. He had a few ideas on how to handle them once he was done with Melagus.

They continued up the other side of the vale. Hadean paused at the crest. He shielded his eyes to look south. "What am I riding into?"

"Your kingdom," Geth said. "And nobody else's."

"But how do I take it back?"

Hadean's eyes were somber. Geth felt Phelan watching him as well.

"Let's get this over with," he said. "We can't go south in search of safety, into the hands of the same lords that hung you out to dry at Copper Ridge. And we can't leave the realm altogether."

"Can't we?" Phelan piped up.

"Not if we want to do anything about that." Geth pointed at the burned homestead back down the hill.

"I won't run," said Hadean. "A king in exile is no king at all."

"You could build support from your sworn allies," Phelan offered. "Leave Melagus and his new friends to cut each other to ribbons in the meanwhile."

"And abandon the realm in the middle of a war?"

Geth nodded. "I think we may find you have allies closer to home as well."

Hadean raised an eyebrow. "Melagus will be watching who comes and goes."

"We have to move quickly, before word reaches the south that you aren't dead. But with these beards and helmets on our heads, we should be able to get you inside the town of Greenfell without raising the alarm. From there, we can get situated, find out who lives, who's friend and who's foe."

"And then?" Hadean asked.

"And then you just let me deal with the housecleaning. We sneak in nice and quiet-like and cut the head off the snake."

"Sounds risky."

"It is, my lord, but Phelan and I would take the risk. All that is required is stealth and a bit of bloodletting."

Hadean looked out over the fields, blew out a sign. "Why, Melagus, why?"

"Because he's an evil sonofabitch."

"Alright. To Towerrock then."

Geth nodded, more to himself than to the king. "And the head comes off."

The ride was quiet after that, all thoughts on what lay ahead. The air seemed to have warmed and it was decided to push on into night toward the Tooth. Melagus would have scouts watching the roads for Ilars, but the darkness would allow a small party like theirs to pass unseen. Geth judged it an hour past midnight when the lantern-light of the town and the smell of chimney smoke announced they'd arrived.

Geth looked up at the moon-washed walls of Towerrock. He smiled, thinking of Neary, Kerrel and the rest of those ugly bastards. Sure, Melagus lurked somewhere within, and Wayan, Pythelle, and others. But mostly his memories of the place were good ones. He reined them in beside the placard of the Bottom of the Cup.

"Let's get you hidden in a room, my lord. Keep that helm on, and don't look anyone in the eye. We can't let them know you're back. Phelan and I will sort out what comes next."

Geth passed Hadean their only sword, and when they had the king safely stowed in a chamber, the big warrior met Phelan in the dark hallway. They had no weapons save his friend's sling, and yet Geth supposed there was never a better pair for what he had in mind.

"Alright. You go in first, find out where Melagus sleeps, if Eldric still lives, what's happened to Wayan, Pythelle and the like. Once we have an idea of all that, I'll get inside, cut the worm in half and that's that. We've got to do it quick, before they lock this place down for war."

Phelan made a face Geth wasn't quite able to read in the faint light. "We need to talk."

"We'll talk later. Business first."

"I'm not going, Geth."

Geth opened his mouth but Phelan wasn't done.

"I've had enough. I'm not getting stuck on the inside when the siege hits. You and your king have made it back home now, but that's it for me. I'm heading back to Pellon."

"Phelan!" Geth took him by the shoulders. "We need you! I can't do this by myself!"

"You don't need me."

"Well maybe *you* need *me*! Who do you think is waiting for you back in Pellon? Palladine, that's who. You may have forgotten about him, but I guarantee he hasn't forgotten about you. Or me either, for that matter. You're staying."

"No, I'm not."

"Phelan—"

"Let him go." Hadean appeared in the doorway, eyes bright. "No man should be forced to take such a risk. This isn't going to be easy. Good men have died already."

Phelan nodded. "Well said. And I've got a lot of living yet to do. Listen, Geth, I know you're not coming with me, but once you've got the lad back on his throne, you'll know how to find me."

"Just go." Geth said. He couldn't even look at his friend. He turned down the dark hallway, started off alone.

Chapter thirty-seven

The lanes of Greenfell were quiet at that hour except for the rage-filled blood pumping in Geth's ears. The odd laborer or kitchen maid wheeled carts of firewood across the bridge into Towerrock and Geth fell in among them. His pulse quickened as he hailed the sentinel at the gate, but clad in the green and helmeted as he was, the man hardly paid him any mind.

Steady now. He moved across the silent ward. *Forget about Phelan. First thing you do, see if Eldric still lives. Then find out where Melagus keeps his chambers now.*

A survey of the great fortress showed a mere trickle of activity. Only the occasional cough or squelch of boots through the mud disturbed the night air as a handful of the keep's staff finished their duties. Geth kept his eyes down, trusting the dim light, new-grown beard, and the helm on his head to mask him. No one looked at him twice, but he recognized trouble when he saw a second guard posted beside the entrance to the Lord's Hall.

Thram and Vorda curse you, Phelan! This was where the little man could have helped, distracting the sentinel, maybe sneaking in himself. For Geth, there would be no talking a way past without giving up his identity. And even if he gave the scratch a knock, the man's absence wouldn't go unnoticed for long.

The roof then.

Geth ducked into one of the towers and started up the spiral stair. The parapet atop the curtainwall could take him alongside the Lord's Hall. From there it was a short climb to the higher ramparts, provided the ladder hadn't been pulled up.

Mounting the last few steps, Geth pushed through the door at the tower summit. The wind whipped his face as he stepped back out into the night air, ambling down the parapet's length as if he was a sentinel himself. Gods be praised, the ladder was there. He climbed the rungs to the platform above the Lord's Hall, started to congratulate himself until a green-cloaked guard appeared ahead.

"A little late for a stroll, isn't it?"

Geth froze. Who should stand before him but that lying bastard, Gylfric.

"You!" Gylfric's eyes went wide, recognizing Geth only a fraction of a second later. The Umbleman's blade rasped out and his mouth opened to cry an alarm, but Geth closed the space like cat, clamping his right hand on Gylfric throat, his left on the upraised sword-wrist.

"No smooth talking will get you out of this one," Geth whispered, squeezing for all he was worth. Gylfric's mouth moved without sound. He shook and twisted, unable to wrestle free. Geth reeled with the sweet taste of revenge.

But Gylfric hadn't made sergeant, hadn't survived the massacre of Point-fort, by accident. With the hand that had been clawing at Geth's grip on his neck, Gylfric switched tactics to pummel into the big warrior's side. A pain like fire shot through the old wound to Geth's ribs.

"Sonofa…!"

He countered by smashing his head forward, cracking Gylfric's nose and sending him dazed into the merlons. A twist of the wrist and that sword clattered to the ground. With one hand on Gylfric's groin, the other on his collar, Geth hoisted the bastard up to the lip of the rampart before he could gather his senses.

"This is gonna hurt," Geth hissed. A strong shove sent Gylfric right over the wall. His scream only lasted a moment before the gruesome crunch of bones on rock echoed up from below.

Geth eyed the length of the parapets, the ward below, holding his breath. If anyone had heard, they'd already dismissed it. He moved a hand to his ribs and winced. His breath felt shorter already. He cursed himself and his shit luck, even if he'd gladly kill that lying, treasonous bastard again.

But maybe the gods were with him? Geth bent with a groan to snatch up Gylfric's blade. He looked down the length of it and nodded, a solid work of sword-smithing. He thrust it through his belt. The nearest torchlit stairway took him down among the dim corridors of the Lord's Hall.

But what now? He could think of nothing better than to start at the quarters Melagus had previously occupied. The door wasn't locked so he let himself in, the room as quiet as the parapet above except for the low crackle of a fire.

Someone, whether the counselor or not, had been there recently. Slipping back out to hide in the same crevice from which he'd surprised Melagus weeks earlier, he shut the door behind himself and waited.

Masterless dog. That's what Melagus had called him. Geth reminded himself of all the other insults the worm had spit, how he'd bad-mouthed him to Hadean, tried to condemn him to death. Oh, how those beady little eyes would pop once Geth got hands around his skinny neck!

But the pain in his side was enough to dampen the thought. "And Phelan gone now too?" he muttered.

The scrape of approaching footfalls sounded before he could dwell on it. Peering out from his nook, his curses turned to prayers of thanks. It was none other than the counselor who came shuffling toward him, all by his lonesome except for a steaming mug of tea in one hand.

"There you are," Geth said.

Melagus's eyes widened as the big warrior stepped out to block his path. But there was no fear in them. He flicked a glance over one shoulder before practically rushing into Geth's arms.

"Quick, get inside!" Melagus pushed him toward the door. "Did anyone see you? If so, you're as good as dead."

"No, you are." Geth made no move to enter the room, face hard but grinning inwardly as the little man heaved against him.

"Yes, me too if they see us speaking! Hurry, move! He had the loyalty of the fortress already and now he's got the crown. And he isn't going to give it up without a fight."

"Who—?"

Melagus quit pushing at last. "I forget, you've been gone quite a while. But I must admit I'm glad to see you, this once. I thought they'd have killed you by now."

"They tried. I don't die so easy."

"Be that as it may, better men than you were less fortunate. Let me tell you, a dark cloud has hung over the Kingdom of Umbel this winter. King Hadean, our young king…" Melagus's voice broke.

Geth blinked. *What the…?*

Had he heard right? Could this actually be more than the utterings of a man trying to save his own hide? He stood close enough to see the tears in the counselor's eyes, the tremor in his bottom lip, even by dim torchlight. It was the strangest of squeaks that came out when Melagus finally gathered himself.

"He's dead! Young Hadean, betrayed by his own uncle!"

Geth's head spun as the pieces fell into place. *It was Eldric all along.* "Gods all be damned."

Of course! Geth cursed himself for a fool, the sort that forced Melagus into the role of traitor, mostly because he hated the bastard.

But Eldric?

Towerrock's lord had been just as close to Hadean, Geth realized, and even had Pythelle as a means to contact the Ilars and arrange the betrayal with Othwid. He had the bloodlines, the backing of the kingdom's warriors. The only thing he *didn't* have already was the throne.

"I'm a bloody fool."

Melagus sighed. "I had my eyes on Wayan. And others further south, though I did fear what Eldric might do when his nephew first came to the throne. But he did nothing but support the poor child. Why didn't Eldric just take the rule then? I can't fathom it."

"I should have known." Geth cursed himself. "I'll strangle that bastard with his own dismembered hands."

"The gods know he deserves it. But what now? The Ilars helped him steal the rule, only to double-cross him in the end. He traded a small stretch of land for the crown, but they'll have it all soon. And his head on a pike as well. He's brought war down on the entire kingdom in search of his own glory."

"Eldric's no fool. He's brought down war, but not defeat. He may sacrifice the countryside for a season or two, but he probably figures he can grind the Ilars down in the end. He comes out of it a hero, Hadean all but forgotten."

Melagus sighed. "And we have no choice, for the good of Umbel, but to stand by and wish him success." He smacked a fist into his palm. "Damn you all, gods and goddesses! Shit-eating brood of the Great Shaper! Damn you all for the games you play!"

Geth snorted a laugh. "Best ask forgiveness for that curse, friend. The god's own luck has just turned your way."

"Because a bloodthirsty sellsword has landed on my doorstep?"

"Because that sellsword has something that changes the game. That sellsword has the king."

Chapter thirty-eight

"That's right." Geth grinned in the torchlight. "Hadean's alive!"

Melagus looked like he might faint. But the noise of his curses seemed to have drawn some attention, voices echoing from down the hall. Geth was shocked to recognize the throaty growl of Wayan among them.

"Quick, inside your chambers!" Geth said.

Melagus shook his head. "No, he's coming for me anyway. Why else would he be in this hall so late?"

"Trust me then!" Without another word, Geth put both hands around the counselor's neck and gave him a taste of the squeeze he'd intended all along. The counselor's mug of tea dropped, shattered on the floor.

"What's going on!"

That from none other than Lord Eldric. A trio appeared in the ruddy light of the nearest torch, the Lady Pythelle right there alongside Towerrock's lord and the yardmaster. Geth let loose his grip on Melagus's throat and fell to one knee among the fragments of Melagus's mug.

"My lord," he said, "forgive me. I just got back, and this little worm won't take me to the king. He claims he's dead."

Eldric and Wayan shot each other a look. The yardmaster's hand eased toward his hilt, but at the slight frown from the lord, it came to rest on his hip instead. Eldric turned back to Geth. "Returned?"

"From Ilia, my lord. King Hadean sent me to break up Iyngaer's council with the other tribes. I managed to escape, but still I failed."

"Rise." Eldric said. "I am sorry that I must tell you that young Hadean, indeed, is dead."

Geth blinked, mouth twisted as if trying to mask his emotion. "Gods bless your reign, my lord," he said at last.

"Yes, I'll need it. The Ilars will be on the attack again, and soon. That's why I'm here." Eldric turned toward Melagus, whose eyes had narrowed, staring daggers at Pythelle. "Master Melagus, the scouts have returned. The Ilars are coming."

"We knew they would come." The counselor massaged his neck where Geth may have squeezed a little harder than necessary. "If not so soon. We must finalize our preparations."

Eldric nodded. "Come then. To the war room, for a counsel."

Wayan cleared his throat. "And him?"

Geth never doubted the bear's intent to finish him right there, take no chances. But Eldric's eye hadn't missed the naked blade thrust through Geth's belt. That was enough to give them all second thoughts.

"The Lady Pythelle will escort him to my own quarters," Eldric said. He turned back toward Geth. "Wait for me there. I'll be back soon to speak of Ilia."

This once, as Geth followed Pythelle through the torchlit halls of Towerrock toward Eldric's chamber, his status as an outsider worked in his favor. With Hadean supposedly dead, there was no real urgency to kill him. No loyal liegeman was he, after all. *Just a hired sword.*

And yet Wayan would certainly counsel in favor of tying off loose ends. Out of pure hatred if nothing else. And there was no telling if, or when, Pythelle might get word that Hadean yet lived.

So, what to do?

"So much has happened so fast," he told the witch, searching for something, anything, to guide his next move.

But her answer gave up nothing. "Wait here." They'd reached the door to the lord's chambers. "I'll send for food and drink."

"M'lady."

Geth bowed. A part of him begged to kill the wench and have done, but that would only put him on the run. Even if he managed to exit the fortress and gather up Hadean for a hasty getaway, then what?

No, that's what Iyngaer wanted: a kingdom weakened by an uncle and nephew dividing their tribe in a fight for the throne.

So, end this tonight.

It was the only way, Geth reckoned: kill Eldric before the Ilars arrived to begin their siege. *Simple enough, except that Eldric will surely be planning on killing me first.*

Pythelle disappeared down the hall and a pair of sentinels took her place in the hallway, shutting Geth inside Eldric's quarters without a word. The broad, squarish space featured a four-posted bed, two claw foot chairs, a sideboard, and a large hearth which lit the room with a bright fire. A few tapestries insulated the walls. That was it.

"As good a battlefield as any."

The one positive was that a bow would be useless in such tight quarters. Neither could great numbers be brought to bear on him. Geth smiled, satisfied with the gameboard, the lay of the pieces. It would take something special to kill him in there, even with Gylfric's blow to the ribs shortening his breath. This might be his one and only chance to strike. He was adjusting Gylfric's sword, thrust awkwardly through his belt, when a knock on the door sounded.

Right hand beside the hilt, Geth opened it.

"Kerrel!"

"Sergeant Geth! You're alive!" He set the tray he'd been holding down on the sideboard for a rough embrace. That sent pain up Geth's side, but he was glad for it just the same. "They didn't say it was you in here. We heard you were dead."

"There's a tale in all that lad, but thank the gods, I'm not. Bloody Awer, you've grown another six inches while I was gone!"

The straw-haired youth grinned, motioned Geth to the tray he'd brought in. A loaf of bread, wedge of cheese and a few salted sardines rested on a silver plate. Neither wine nor ale had been sent, so he settled on drinking from the lord's hand basin.

"Wait." Kerrel reached over for the bowl. "They told me to make sure and change that, said it's dirty. They're sending you a special wine."

Geth blinked. He looked down into the clear water and back to the tray. He thought of the attempt on Hadean's life.

"Kerrel, I want you to listen to me," he said. "Can you do me a favor? I need you to do it tonight, right now. It's very, very important."

"Anything for a friend."

Geth resisted the urge to muss the lad's hair. "A brother. But look, I need you to meet another old friend of ours in the town, at the Bottom of the Cup. Second floor, first room on the left. Tell him this: you were right about the skinny one all along. It was the uncle. Tell my friend to lay low and I'll meet him up when I can."

Kerrel repeated the message. Geth gave him a clap on the shoulder. "Go. And hurry!"

The lad saluted with fist to heart and rushed back out the way he'd come. Geth could only hope Hadean would heed the warning. On the platter in front of him, those dead-eyed sardines watched him. *Wondering how I'm gonna wriggle out of this one?* He hid a few of them under the bed, along with the cheese. After inspecting the bread, he ate the entire loaf. Then he waited.

Eldric had decided to take no chances, to kill him now, he reckoned. That's why he'd sent a friendly face with the food. In a matter of minutes, someone would arrive with a second dose of poison, this one in the wine. Reaching down to his belt, Geth arranged it with a knot he'd learned on the slave-ships so it might fall away easily, releasing his sword in an instant. He was glad for the advantage that would bring when Eldric and Wayan arrived a few minutes later, trailed by two grim-faced guardsmen.

"Wine?" The lord took a pair of tin cups and a pitcher from the yardmaster's thick hands. He stepped up beside Geth in front of the fire and passed one over.

"To Hadean," Geth said, raising a toast. "And to King Eldric."

He spilled a portion, watched as Eldric spilled his almost to the last. Geth put the drink to his lips, let the red liquid stain his mustache but never opened his mouth. He worked his throat muscles and sighed. "Ahhh." With great ceremony, he spilled the remainder down on the floor. "Poor Hadean. Vorda watch over him."

"Vorda keep him." Eldric agreed. "Now, tell us of Ilia."

Geth turned his eyes toward the fire. He began with the failed ploy at Ceter's hall, and then his imprisonment and escape from Vriana. He never mentioned the Seer but held nothing back regarding the truslas and his triumph over Othwid.

And why not brag this once? Either Eldric would be dead soon, or he would.

"A heroic tale," the king said. "More wine?"

Geth looked up. Wayan and those two assassins watched him, waiting for the poison to take effect. He moved from Eldric's side, near the fire, toward one of the chairs to lean on the back.

"After all that," he lied, "I stole a horse and made my way here." He made a point to dribble a little spit, wiping his chin with a shaky hand. He snorted a laugh, thrust out with his cup toward Wayan's carafe, but let it clatter to the floor as if by accident. "Ah, sorry, my lord."

A look passed between the two warriors at the rear. The yardmaster half-turned to give them a nod. Geth moved his right hand over his belly but also closer to the hilt of his sword. Those two toughs couldn't come at him more than one at a time, and even with his side aching again, he reckoned he could take them when they did.

But Wayan was another matter. There would be no wearing him down this time, now that he himself carried an injury. He swallowed a grim laugh before it could escape. That spiteful sonofabitch was gonna kill him. Unless he thought of something quick.

Damn you all, gods and goddesses! To the hell of your own making! There was no more time. The first of the two guardsmen took a step forward. Geth's hand slid toward his sword.

And then the door opened.

"Hello Uncle."

Chapter thirty-nine

Hadean stood in the doorway, face lit red in the firelight. Eldric's mouth dropped open. Wayan's two killers froze, hands hovering near their hilts as the young king stepped into the room.

But the yardmaster slipped past him to slide closed the iron latch on the door. "Do it now! Both of them!"

They reached for their swords, but Geth's was already free. The first man got run through with his blade only half-bared.

The other managed to draw. Geth thrust his staggering comrade into his path. "Damn it!" The guardsman threw out a hand to shove his comrade aside, but a merciless stab over the top took him full in the face. "Ahh!"

A second pierced the mail under his arm, sending the pair in a jumbled heap to bleed out on the floor. By the time Geth looked up, Hadean and Wayan had both drawn steel.

"Wait!" Eldric's sword gleamed bare as well, but he held it overhead. Uncle stood blade to blade with nephew, while the yardmaster squared off against Geth. *Oh, how the gods toy!*

"A little late to sue for peace," Geth said. He turned Gylfric's blade toward Wayan, pretending confidence despite the pain in his side. The grizzled bastard wasn't about to shy from this fight either.

"No, let him speak." Hadean said, facing Eldric. "I want to hear why my own uncle would betray me and sell the entire realm."

"It's you who would have sold the realm, fool boy!" Eldric shot back. "And to what end? To save a few acres of land and a farmwife or two. Yes, for a few months, even a year, I will appear to lose. But in the end, I will win—Umbel will win—grinding down the Ilars as we always have. I may have wronged you Hadean, and yet I did it to save the realm. From your young, impetuous, misguided rule."

That was the wrong thing to say. Hadean slashed at his uncle with a snarl.

But Eldric had been fighting long before the lad was ever born. He knocked that strike wide. Geth saw no more. Wayan came for him at the same time.

The old bastard lunged with snake-like speed. Geth twisted, dodged it by a hair. A wicked chop followed. A parry and sidestep sent that blow to Geth's left where it splintered one of the claw foot chairs nearly in two. Hoping Wayan's blade might get caught, Geth swung a backhand at the yardmaster, but the bastard sidestepped nimbly, freeing his weapon in the same motion. In a matter of seconds, two separate stalemates had ensued. Only the sound of shouting and banging on the doorframe disturbed it.

Reinforcements. Damn! But after that last exchange, Geth stood between Wayan and the exit.

"It's only a matter of time," the yardmaster hissed. "That door's coming down."

"You'll be dead by the time it does."

"There's only one person in this room that has to die."

Those hateful eyes watched Geth, waited. It was a moment before the big warrior realized what he was saying.

"So, now you'd rather turn me than kill me?"

"What's he done for all your troubles?"

Geth shot back his most loathsome glare.

And yet Wayan knew there was truth in those words. Geth had been through hell on Hadean's behalf. With no obvious rewards. And once the soldiers of Towerrock came through—Eldric's men—Hadean's time was up.

"We don't want you dead," the yardmaster went on. "We need you. Forget the boy, leave him to the past."

"He's the king," Geth said.

"And why should he be?" It was Eldric who spoke. The banging on the door grew louder. "Because his father was king? My father was king as well."

"You're a mercenary!" That from Wayan. "What do you care anyway?"

Ha! Geth laughed inwardly as the noise of wood splitting forced his decision. Pivoting on his feet, he redirected his sword from the yardmaster toward Hadean. "Maybe you're right."

Hadean's eyes went wide. "Geth—"

"Not so fast." Wayan gestured with an outstretched hand for Geth's weapon.

Geth snorted. "Right, a man like me isn't to be trusted. Just the same…"

He spun the weapon around to grip it just below the cross-piece, presenting the plain iron pommel to the yardmaster. Hadean could only watch. Wayan licked his lips, smiled, and another great crash shook the chamber door on its hinges.

Geth used the distraction to strike. Lunging upwards with that hilt, he caught Wayan's chin in the same tooth-rattling blow that had dropped Raeg months before.

"Argghh!"

The bear staggered. Geth spun the blade in his hand to chop the sword from Wayan's grip. Blood and fingers splattered the ground as he fell to his knees, doubled over his wrecked hand.

"You whoreson! You lying dog!"

Geth lifted his blade to the yardmaster's throat. The door quivered but held. "Never fault a dog his loyalty."

Dizzy with the ecstasy of vengeance, he dragged the tip of Gylfric's sword under Wayan's chin to let loose his life's blood in a red sheet. Hateful eyes widened as the bastard tried to rise, claw his way toward Geth with a fingerless hand. But his legs gave way. Like the beast that he was, he collapsed face-first onto the floor.

How glorious that moment, and yet Geth couldn't revel in it long. From outside, the sound of battering had stopped, replaced by a faint metallic scraping. Across the room, too far to reach in time, Eldric's eyes lit with triumph. Geth steeled himself for one last bloody fight as the lock sprung with a click.

The door swung open. Standing in the threshold, swords in hand, were Phelan, Neary and a dozen of the ugliest bastards Geth had ever seen.

"Haha!"

Phelan hooted. Eldric dropped his blade, hands raised. Geth took a step toward him, but the lord's eyes were on his nephew.

"Forgive me, Hadean. I thought I was doing what was right for the realm."

"Uncle—"

Geth struck quickly, crossing the room in quick strides to stab Eldric through the heart. A gasp escaped his lips, nothing more. Hadean lunged forward, cuaght him as he fell, eased him gently to the floor.

Chapter forty

The benches stood mostly empty at the Bottom of the Cup. Like the three tankards sitting in front of Geth. He waved the barmaid for another and snatched the foamy drink without a thank you when it arrived.

He should have been alongside Hadean, feasting in his great hall. And yet there was no celebrating the death of the king's closest living kin, even after his treachery. Especially when Geth had been the one to kill him.

"Had to be done," he grumbled to himself.

And by Geth's reckoning, Hadean's had plenty of enemies still. True to her kind, the witch Pythelle had vanished like smoke. More than a few scheming lords yet lingered further south, holding out on their king in his hour of need. Geth took a sip of the dark, bitter brew, looked at the tankard in his hand. No, the only thing worth celebrating was Phelan's decision to stay, a decision that had saved Geth's life, and the king's.

But even Phelan was late that night. Geth glared at passersby and downed more drinks until the door to the inn opened to admit Neary. Geth looked over the tall Umbelman's shoulders, but the door swung closed behind him. Neary hurried red-faced across the room to his table.

"Thram's balls," Geth said. "What's Phelan done now?"

"Been taken prisoner, Sergeant. By Melagus!"

"Prisoner?"

"They're holding him in Towerrock."

Geth kicked his chair back, shook his head to steady himself, and followed Neary outside and across the bridge. He didn't ask why Phelan had been taken. He already knew. Inside Towerrock's walls, he found Melagus emerging from the Lord's Hall.

"What have you done with Phelan?"

The counselor scowled, a bundle of ledgers pressed against his chest. "Did you really think he could rob the whole of Towerrock with no consequences?"

"You may suspect him, but you have no proof."

"Not yet."

Geth's expression must've betrayed bloody thoughts. The worm raised a hand.

"Careful. I'm the one person who can save you."

"Save me? From what?"

"From your past."

Geth opened his mouth, but the counselor leaned in close, one finger held to his lips, voice low.

"I offer this as a courtesy, in thanks for your service to the king."

"Offer what?"

"A man has arrived asking after the likes of you. And your friend. A man called Palladine."

Palladine. Geth felt dizzy. "Sonofabitch."

"You know him."

Geth could only curse.

"If you are wise, you'll flee."

"And leave Phelan behind for that bastard? You don't know me very well."

"You don't know me either, it seems, if you think I would hand over my prisoner before he's had a chance to return what he's stolen. Palladine won't stay long. The Ilars are coming."

"All the more reason for me to stick around. You need me. Hadean needs me."

Melagus shook his head. "You're wanted by a Hand of Justice of Pellon. Would you really put the king in a position to forsake the allegiance of the Sworn Realms?"

Geth cursed again.

But it wasn't Melagus's fault, not this. Could he really ask Hadean to ignore the demand of a fellow king? Especially now? The look on Hadean's face as his uncle died in his arms...

Gods all damn you, Palladine!

Geth shook his head, tried to think. "He'll want Phelan—"

"Your friend means nothing. If you leave, the Paellian will surely follow."

Neary had already arrived with a pair of horses. The lanky fighter reached into his belt pouch and pulled out a handful of coins. "It's all I've got but it'll get us to Umbel City."

Geth blew out a sigh. "I won't drag you down with me, Neary."

"I'm not leaving you—"

Geth climbed into the saddle. "Someone needs to stay and vouch for Phelan. There's no one else but you. Make sure he gets a fair trial."

Melagus scowled again, but Geth ignored him. Neary stepped forward to press his coin into Geth's hand. He saluted the big warrior with fist to heart.

Geth returned the gesture, spurred his mount out the gates without further goodbyes. Halfway across the bridge, he twisted for one last look at the moonlit walls of Towerrock. Pain shot through his side with the motion and his head swam, but he kicked the beast beneath him and left at a gallop.

The River Road carried Geth south and away. Ale-muddled wits tried to consider the angles. If there was any other alternative, he couldn't see it. Melagus was right. Even if it served the bony bastard's own purposes, Geth had no choice but to leave. *You're in the hands of the gods now, Phelan.*

Miles passed beneath him. The wind slid its icy fingers through the collar of Geth's cloak, and a hangover settled in to add to the ache in his ribs. He swore. Weeks and months he'd spent fighting for Hadean, fighting for Umbel. And yet with his mere presence, Palladine managed to strip it all away.

"No choice but to kill him," Geth said out loud. "Somewhere between here and Umbel City, hit the bastard on the road and have done."

With the Ilars soon to sweep down, Palladine had no choice but to ride south. The chance would come, maybe at an inn, or at some remote campsite while his men were sleeping.

The thought of making camp reminded Geth just how tired he was himself. He'd covered a dozen miles already—a good head start he reckoned. Leading his mount off into the brush, he tethered the beast and bundled up as best he could. He slept.

When he awoke, he wasn't alone. "What the—"

A man in hunter's boots crouched beside Geth's horse, watching him. The stranger said nothing but flicked a glance over the big warrior's head. Geth craned his neck to find a second man with the same lean build and pug nose crouched a few yards behind him. The pale moonlight gleamed along the length of a sword in his hand. Geth's sword.

"He's here," the first man shouted over his shoulder.

A voice echoed from somewhere near the road. "The twins have found him!"

Horse hooves crackled through the underbrush to Geth's left. He wasted no more time. Tossing his blankets overhead at the one brother, he rolled to his right and came up with a kick at the second. The man caught it on an upraised forearm but fell back with a grunt. Geth rose to meet the arriving horsemen just in time.

"There he is!"

"Bring him down!"

A Paellian sword sliced the air. Geth ducked beneath it and stepped inside to clutch an arm and drag the wielder from the saddle. A second rider had no choice but to veer aside or trample his fellow as Geth stripped the first man of his blade and flung him in the other's path. A quick thrust pierced the downed soldier's mail, but the rest kept coming. Soldiers in white tabards, dappled in moonlight, converged like a swarm of hornets.

"He's mine!" a familiar voice cried.

Geth lifted his sword to slash at the nearest rider, but something struck his back like a boulder coming down a mountainside. He stumbled to one knee. Agonizing pain shot through the injury in his ribs. Cursing lilies sprang from their mounts, piled on him from every direction, punching and grabbing.

"I said he's *mine!*"

Even from the bottom of a heap of enemies, bloodied and breathless, Palladine's voice was unmistakable. When his vision cleared, Geth saw the captain's shaved pate striding toward him, flanked by those pug-nosed twins. A limp sling hung from one of their hands. That explained the blow to Geth's back.

Two lilies dragged Geth to his feet as Palladine arrived. He tasted blood but parted his lips to bare a red smile anyway. "Just the man I was looking for."

Palladine ignored that. "In bonds at last. A small measure of justice. Better than you deserve."

"Came all the way to Umbel just for me, eh?"

"You weren't so hard to find. Follow the path of ruin and destruction. That been your life's work, hasn't it?"

"That. And disgracing puffed-up lordlings."

Palladine snorted. He drew his sword, slid it under Geth's neck. Geth met his steely blue stare with all the hatred he had.

"Do it you mother-rutting bastard."

He braced for the killing blow, but Palladine sheathed his sword. The look of triumph on his face was enough to make Geth tremble with anger.

"I think we know who the real bastard is here," the captain said. "The murderer. The *whoreson*. I know your sort better than that young king, that's for sure. I know the base clay you're molded from, the virtue-less pursuits a dog with your spots always returns to."

Those words landed on Geth like blows, especially now, in his final moments. But there was no reliving his life. He shook his head, reminded himself of all the bastards that would serve him in Vorda's halls, proud warriors bested by him and no one else.

"Send a message to King Hadean," Palladine told one of the twins. "Let him know we've found his precious friend, in spite of his lies."

His friend?

Geth called on every god. *Bless that man, Hadean. My king.* The night air never felt so clean as it filled his lungs, the cold of the mud nothing to him, honest loam of Umbel.

"Bet you thought Hadean would hand me right over, didn't you?" He said, unable to contain his smile. "Thought you'd find me in a gutter somewhere or roaming with a band of thieves. You think you know me better than King Hadean? Ha! You really are a pompous ball-scratch, you know that, Palladine?"

"I have you now, that's all that matters. And justice will be served. Your stain shall be wiped from the sworn-realms once and for all."

"Do it then. I die a hero."

Palladine took a step forward, leaned down so his face was close to Geth's. The big warrior looked him in the eyes, uttered a final prayer.

But the captain just took his chin in one hand. "Die a hero?" He snorted. "Oh no, you don't get to die. Not until you've been reduced to a gibbering fool."

A vomit-stinking bag went over Geth's head, but Palladine's voice was still there, beside his ear. "Get used to the dark, Geth the Fatherless. That's all your future holds. It's the Tower of the Moon that awaits."

A Message from the Author

Thank you for reading DOG OF WAR. If you're interested in following Geth's journey, an excerpt from the sequel HAIR OF THE DOG follows. Also, if anyone's curious about the dice game that landed Phelan in Palladine's clutches, join my newsletter at www.deankastle.com/newsletter.html to get the FREE short story THE HAND OF JUSTICE. As an added bonus, you'll also get THE WAY OUT, another free short related to the series.

Cheers!

DK

An Excerpt from HAIR OF THE DOG
Chapter One

Geth awoke in darkness. Memories of angry fists, of road dust, and an iron door tumbled through his head. It was a while before he remembered where he was, and when he did he wished he could forget.

The Tower of the Moon.

Landed yourself right up calamity's asshole this time. It took something special to book a reservation in Pellon's most infamous prison, and yet Geth had managed it. Windowless confines excluded all sunlight, but a trap door in the ceiling opened each night to expose the moon's baleful eye. The weight of it, it was said, could drive a man mad.

But Geth reckoned it was hunger that would kill him before anything else. His belly ached so bad even his teeth hurt. By the ragged breathing to either side, he knew he wasn't the only starving bastard in there either.

"Hey, you," he addressed the darkness, "when do they feed us around here?"

The darkness made no reply. If anything, it got quieter.

Geth scooted across the knotted wood floor, reigniting pain in each limb. He bit down a curse, reached a hand through the blackness until he touched an oily shoulder. "I said—"

"Ahh!"

"Easy now—"

"Ahh!"

Geth let the poor bastard slip further along the curved stone wall. *Mad as a castrated piglet, that one.* He settled back against the cold stone of his prison, stomach no better off for the exchange. *Maybe I can eat one of them.*

Or maybe an end in the tower was exactly what a gutter-born sellsword deserved. Geth croaked a mirthless laugh. He had to applaud the gods their timing, presenting the bill for a lifetime of misdeeds only *after* he'd fallen in with a righteous cause. He thought of King Hadean back in Towerrock, surrounded by the Ilar siege, trapped among questionable allies. Then there was Phelan, jailed for his own transgressions, and Neary, Kerrel, and the rest of the dead-man dozen.

"Gods all be damned!"

But anger only made Geth hungrier. He took a deep breath. *They have to feed us*, he reckoned. *To stretch out the torture if nothing else.* Eyes were useless in the utter dark, so he cocked an ear. Prison mates wheezed to either side. The sound of heavy breathing seemed to echo from somewhere beneath him as well.

A cellar? Could there be food down there? Geth frowned. He ran a hand along the timber under his rump. Feeling around the curve of the walls—over stinking, yammering madmen—his fingers found an opening in the planks where a curling stone stairway plunged along the edge of the walls into the tower's depths.

But instinct paused the big warrior where he was. For all the reeking bodies and limited space, not a prisoner lingered within yards of that stairway. Geth tapped the top step. *What are you hiding?*

There was an easy way to find out.

Feeling his way back from the edge, Geth crept through the darkness toward the wheezing of his nearest cellmate. Grabbing the shrieking bastard with both hands, he dragged him across the floor and dropped him straight through the hole.

"Ahh!" Thuds and curses sounded on the way down, followed by scrambling noises as the man hurried back up. "How dare you lay hands on Lord Wels!"

"Sorry, er, my lord." Geth thought it best to play along. "Forgive the accident."

"There will be a reckoning! Once my men have freed me, there will be a reckoning for this indignity!"

"I just—"

The one called Wels lowered his voice to a hiss. "Do you know what lies below? An *unspeakable* evil."

Now we're getting somewhere. "You wouldn't stow *me* down there, would you?"

"I just might!"

"And there's no food down there either, I reckon."

"Certainly not! When my men arrive, you'll find out for yourself."

"C'mon now, friend," Geth lowered his voice, tone conspiratorial. "Are you telling me you're planning a bust out? How will your men get past the guards? Must've been dozens of them."

A pause. "For now."

"For now?"

"Since your arrival. When no one comes for you, the number will lessen."

Geth opened his mouth, but Wels wasn't done.

"And when my followers come, they will come in swarms! They will breach the walls, storm the parapets…"

Geth's ear had turned toward the spiral stair. The lord's rants seemed to have roused whoever—*whatever*—lay below. From the opening in the floor, the scuff of leather on stone announced a footfall at the top step.

No matter how Geth strained his eyes, it was impossible to see through the darkness. But there was no mistaking the tension in the air. He sat up on the balls of his feet and listened. What sounded like two separate patterns of breath echoed through the dank prison. The prisoners stirred. Jostling for position, if Geth wasn't mistaken. Then they went still. If they had been quiet before, they went utterly silent now.

Like hunted prey.

"Where's our new friend?" a voice said.

Geth held his breath. One of the pair passed him by no more than a yard. The noise of a struggle broke out a few feet away, followed by a gasp, a shriek, and the familiar ranting of Lord Wels.

"Hands off! You'll pay!"

"This one will do," a second voice said.

Wels's indignation turned to a piteous wail. "*No!*"

By the echo off the tower's lofty rafters, Geth reckoned the fight had turned desperate. Heavy breathing became panting, followed by grunts and more terrified cries. Something tore. It wasn't until Geth recognized the slapping of flesh that he understood what Wels had meant by 'unspeakable.'

"Sick bastards."

Geth edged forward through the dark at a crouch, hand outstretched until he touched a gyrating body. Anticipating the swing of an elbow, he skipped to one side, threw a fist into where the man's exposed ribs would be. Wels squealed and scampered away as his tormentor staggered off him.

By then the second rapist had made a grab for Geth with both hands. Expecting a blow of some sort toward his midriff, Geth swatted downward with his left hand, reached out with his right to grip a ragged shirt. Something sharp sliced his left palm—the strike he'd expected—but he caught hold of a wrist and held on tight. With his right hand, he yanked his enemy in close, grabbed the back of the bastard's neck, pressed his own forehead against the man's temple in a wrestler's hold.

Even in that squalid pit—maybe especially so—there was comfort in the familiar feel of combat, the push and pull as Geth grappled. He felt half-alive again. What wasn't so familiar was the weakness in the knees that sent him backpedaling under his enemy's press.

"Damn you, Awer!"

Using the bastard's own momentum, Geth released his grip on the neck, swung his right arm under and turned to bend and throw the rapist overhead. The thud of flesh on timber, followed by a hollow grunt, told Geth his enemy had landed flat on his back, lost his wind. Geth pummeled with one fist where he thought the sonofabitch's head would be, but in the darkness missed, running splinters into his knuckles as he punched the floor. The blackness came to his aid a heartbeat later as a kick from the second man scraped past his right side, granting a warning and ample time for Geth to sweep the man's standing leg, crumpling him beside his fellow.

But that was everything Geth had. Panting, legs shaking, he edged backward until his heels touched the wall. He strained to hear over the blood pumping in his ears for the rapists' next advance. Gods be praised, the only thing he heard was the scuff of feet descending stone stairs.

Visit www.deankastle.com/books.html get your copy of HAIR OF THE DOG.

About the author

Dean Kastle is the author of the DOG OF WAR Epic, SWORD SONGS, the forthcoming LEGACY Series, and many short works. In addition to a love of 'story' in every medium, he's a rabid foodie and soccer fanatic. As far as he's concerned, Pluto is still a planet, and the oxford comma is a matter of taste. He doesn't wear a beret or write with a fountain pen, but he does own a life-size replica of the Iron Throne. From that perch, he plots his next tale. Readers can connect with Dean by joining his newsletter at www.deankastle.com/newsletter.html, on X, or on Facebook. He lives in fly-over country with his wife, three kids and (yes) a dog.

Printed in Dunstable, United Kingdom